THE
NEPENTHE
PARK
CHRONICLES

ALI KINTEH

First published in Great Britain in 2016
by Rogue Press Limited.

The Nepenthe Park Chronicles is a work of fiction.
All incidents, dialogue and characters are products of
the author's imagination. Any resemblances to persons
living or dead are entirely coincidental.

A CIP catalogue record for this book is available
from the British Library.

Paperback ISBN 978-0-9934609-0-6

Also available as an ebook
mobi ISBN 978-0-9934609-1-3
epub ISBN 978-0-9934609-2-0

Typeset in Centaur MT by
www.chandlerbookdesign.co.uk

Printed in Great Britain by
Clays Ltd, St Ives plc

ACKNOWLEDGEMENTS

I AM ETERNALLY INDEBTED to my father and mother who fomented my love of books and the written word from an early age, and to my brothers and sisters, their respective spouses and their children.

To Nyima and her delectable family. To Kaiser, my perpetual luminosity and the love of my life.

To Mr. Hill, Mr. Woodcock, Mr. Cullis, Mrs. Rhone (Barclay Primary school); Mr. Dunstone (Leytonstone School); Mrs Sheila Robertson, Mr. Thomas Kweeday, the indelible Mr. Adams and the inimitable Mr. Hooke (Norlington Boys School).

To Ousman Kinteh, who planted the initial seeds of the story many moons ago; Mariama Kinteh-Fernandes for her conceptualization of the book cover; Debz Hobbs-Wyatt, author of "No One Is Watching," who fine-tuned the manuscript meticulously. Mohsen Mastaan and Abdullah Chaudhry for their photographical vision and logistical support in making this novel possible.

A special thank you to Arslan Akhtar, Audrey Atkinson, John Chandler, Paul Jones, Adhana McCarthy, Jack Ngo, Latrell Oscar-John, Imran Patel, Kishan Ramsamy, Rebecca Souster and Marcia Wells.

My eternal gratitude to Mrs. Eileen Lesurf, a truly remarkable woman for her exceptional kindness to me when I was a boy. Wherever you are, thank you.

Author **Ali Kinteh**,
August 2015
Artwork by Jack Ngo

Dearest Tracey,
I hope you enjoy the book.
Best Wishes

Ali

*"Rejoice, O young man in thy youth;
and let thy heart cheer thee in the
days of thy youth..."*

(Ecclesiastes Chapter II Verse 9)

CONTENTS

1

ALL ABOUT ADAM...
NOTHIN ABOUT EVE!

"I FUCKIN HATE DIS PLACE," Lollipop said in the midst of an implacable conurbation called Cricklewood, with all its heft and toil. "I never asked to be born but I get given dis fucked up life!"

His eyes gamboled at the tapestry of voluptuary flesh that ambled past in mesh dresses, nude colored jeans and cropped hoodies.

"A bag of frozen peas' got more incentive than you," Stacey said. "You could get a job if you tried—"

"I *have* tried. It's a hand over fist world, fam. Dat's why I ain't got no love for dis city. It's never shown me love... Even tha girls go on cruddy..."

He had ingratiated himself in the fog of daydreams, emerging only in the pugilistic dusk to smoke skunk with his friends, enjoying their temperate solidarity at best. After a while, it became increasingly self-evident that the confines of the Nepenthe Park Estate were too narrow for his preening ego. He had observed wraiths through the whirling dervishes of skunk smoke while he lay despondent in his bedroom and they spoke to him of a gilded future. So he had ventured onto the Cricklewood Broadway, where delirious girls of vain accord tread a jaunty stroll and flicked their inky locks whenever he gestured that they approach him; where shambling boys sashayed their slender hips within their tapered jeans. The boys seemed ill at ease than the girls on the streets; their brooding figures were taut and nervous. But such were the times, these days of strife.

He was wiry and looked older than his twenty years, and his footfalls were leaden. Stacey, a cute tenderfoot, was invariably hale and had feline serene eyeballs.

"You enrollin in college in September?"

"Be real, Stacey. I'm done wiv college—"

"More like college's done wiv you, blud. Enrollin four years in a row must be a world record!"

"I only enrolled coz everyone else did. I'm jus gonna do my ting on road an hustle some peez—"

"It's harder to make peez on road these days. No one in tha endz ever has any peez. So whateva you wanna trade, everybody will wish to buy. Coz they ain't got no peez, they'll just take it from you. They'll shank you if necessary. So what are you gonna do? Seriously?"

"Fuck knows what I'll do, Stacey... I'm jes gonna bun some bud wiv the man dem till I sleep."

They crawled along the macadamized nave of the Cricklewood Broadway. The fuggy heat was uncouth and cruel. The caliginous smell of *Shawarma* from a Lebanese restaurant rose from the sautéed spit where it sibilated. Next door, the Somalian-owned internet café habituated scores of people into the inversions of Facebook and FaceTime, Instagram and Skype, pseudo-communicating patiently with those they would never meet, while declining to pay heed to their keyboard-stomping counterparts. Further up the street, Anglo-Pakistani butchers carved the bloodstained limbs of dead animals with cleavers and axes, and displayed the bloody steaks and tenderloins in the shop window to entice their sarcophagus customers. African women marauded into a hair and beauty store that sold rancid pastes that lightened skin and fraught Brazilian manes that embellished their scalps. Bulbous men wearing jagged facades watched over that hubbub, positioning themselves at the egress of each aisle like sentinels in a penitentiary. Their neighbor Mr. Salameh, owner of electrical store *Salameh and Salem*, proclaimed tantalizing bargains for the latest gizmos and gadgets in a humdrum voice:

"I've iPhones, iPods, iPads, have I!
Smartphones, dumb phones, all types of phones, oh my..."

"Look at dat poser in dat whip," Stacey said. He gestured towards the driver of a Golf convertible who seemed eager to rejoin the traffic by forcing the nose of his vehicle into the face of the moving cartage. "You see him? You see what he did?"

"What did he do?"

"He clocked dat chick by the bus stop, tha Asian-looking chick wiv tha dark jeans an' knee high boots—"

"Yeah. She'd definitely get it... What did he do wrong?"

"He parked his car an' gone to get her number. She says no, fuck off you dickhead; he gets rude, an' people at the bus stop tell him to fuck off too. Now look... the traffic warden's given him a ticket coz he's on a double yellow line... Now he's wylin at the traffic warden... What a mup!"

"You can tell he shots..." Lollipop watched the capricious oaf roar down the Broadway, while the girl, the warden and the bus stop community chortled triumphantly. "He's baited himself. Look at him; brand spankin whip, gold chains, loud music. Everyone knows he shots—"

"Don't *you* wanna be a shotta, Lollz? Don't *you* wanna ride like dat donut?"

"I wanna be a businessman. When you see a regular shotta, he's shinin. He's got his whip, music pumpin, phone to his ear – regular people clock him easy: we know you shot! A businessman rolls simple whilst he's rollin paper. Dat's the problem wiv bare man on road! They don't know how to make peez an' stay invisible—"

"If they're bruk, man roll invisible. When they're rich, they have to shine—"

"Exactly! Why do man rise an' fall so quickly? Olders dat were big five years ago are no longer about. You remember Midnight? Cut down by lethal man wiv their skengelengs; Tea Leaf, sliced on street in broad daylight; Smiley, in tha pen for life. He's no longer smilin coz he *never* made any real peez; Nukz, so-called original hustla from Wembley, tried to out-shoot the Fedz. He gets gunned down by armed Fedz wiv less than a bag in his back pocket… Mickey Kanu, bodied by some bean-head at some Pajama Party coz he had the same Omega watch as the breh who shanked his skin; look at Gregory Foster, big man from back in tha day! He's come from the pen, an' he ain't even got two pence to rub together to keep himself warm from the cold. Dat's why tha breh's dat run tings now ain't gonna be around in five years coz tha youngers will take over. They're gonna be more ruthless. But they'll make the same fuckin mistakes…"

They recalled the bewildering roll call of deceased *gangstas* and gullible saps slain by the bullet or the blade. Remembering their fallen kinsmen was a common past time. They were inculcated against such tragedies after having tales of their grisly demises revisited upon them. They were seemingly inversed against the alternative, for this was the life they knew. They even mocked the umbra apparitions that strayed back onto the streets having forfeited the life of a *hustla*, because prodding uneasily upon the path of piety meant dire poverty. The specters from the shadows had called for their return to the *grind*, and promised infamy and plenitude. In the world they roamed and lived in, neither Lollipop nor Stacey could help being complicit with scrofulous folk.

For the Nepenthe Park Estate was their home: London's most notorious housing precinct was their sole universe, a microcosm of the greater universe. They hoped to prey aplenty and die therein, whether poor or poorer, through fame and favor. Not through fortitude but foul play. They were somewhat contented with the estate's recent structural renaissance but reveled in its clichéd myths of yesteryear. Situated above the spine of the A406 highway, the grim high-rise tenements that had bedecked the skyline for decades, like giant cemetery cairns erected in the graveyard of the Titans, were torn down by the council to raise tract *überhaus* dwellings. They had lived through the decay and the regeneration; the mighty metanoia of mortar and mucilage had substantively aided Nepenthe's deliverance from its malady.

"*Where* tha girls at, maaan?" Lollipop said. "All I see is fourteen-year-olds in roughed up tracksuits an' single moms pushin prams. *Where* tha proper broads?"

"You gotta go south if you're lookin for your Rihanna types—"

"So, you're tellin me there's no gal in Cricklewood?"

"It's Thursday. They're probably at work—"

"Let's go back home an' play some PlayStation—"

"You can't ever make up your mind, can ya? You've got loads to moan bout an' always someone to blame—"

"I blame the government, Stacey—"

"I blame you, Lollz… You're jus bitter coz tha next man's got it better. Stop wylin, cuz. You've been wylin all day…"

Lollipop was no longer listening. He gazed unsparingly at a callipygian bi-racial woman perched on Kurt Geiger heels. Her eyes were shielded by Tom Ford sunglasses. Her baring tank top pressed against her pillowy breasts. She caught his appraising eye.

"Look at dat, Stacey! Waaaw! You see Bonita Applebaum right dere? Ouch! Her arse is a dream! I ain't ever gonna look at an onion the same way again! Check dat hip to waist ratio, cuz…"

Stacey masqueraded his snap glances at her. She offered a caustic smile.

"She's clocked me, Lollz! She's clocked me! What, is she watchin me? Yep, she's watchin me cuz—"

"Naaah fam! She's got her sexy eyes on me… Dat's my peng ting there… I saw her first… Now watch me get dem digits!"

As he walked into her shadow, a piddling fever bewitched him.

"Alright there babes!"

"Hello fuckster!"

"Fuckster?"

"Was there something you wanted?"

"I want you, innit—"

"How random!"

"Tell me bout it! I see you standing there… lookin good… I said to myself I've gotta have you, no matter what. So what? Can I get your number, babe?"

She listened as he repeated, almost verbatim, the same colloquial hucksterisms she had heard from other swains. He watched her amrita mouth bifurcate, beautifully.

"Dat was so lame. Haven't you ever spoken to a woman before?"

"Yea, course I have… Can I get your name?"

"No."

"OK. I'll… I'm gonna call you… Bonita Applebaum, coz you look like her!"

"Uh-huh… and I'll call you… err… Adam because you look like Everyman!"

"All bout Adam… Nothin bout Eve!"

She seemed to like that. She removed Tom Ford to appraise him. He hoped to start a conversation of reciprocal interest.

"I'll just guess… dat you work in dis salon—"

The sarcasm continued to drip from her regal lips. "I'll just guess dat you've come to rob me—"

"Yeah… And I'll guess dat you're waitin for your man to come pick you up—"

"I guess you'll do a runner when he does!"

"Who me?" He cackled softly at that supposition. "I'm from North Wezzy, born an' breast-fed. Seven inch thick arms from NW10; bare metallic energy dat makes me a hustla by day, lovemaker at night. Former lion tamer, ex-underground cage fighter, babe. You like?"

"I guess I'm still guessin, aren't I?"

"I think you need me to put a ring on your finger—"

"I think you've got a bad case of infatuation, Adam. Take a wet flannel to your groin and go lie down till it settles."

"I... I... I think we should go out for a likkle drink—"

"I don't think we're goin out for a likkle anythin, so don't waste your breath!"

"I'm no waste man. I'm just hungry. My blueprint for success includes you. You can have a starrin role. But only if you let me have you for two lifetimes!"

She was drawn to his feral *echt* and witty piffle, though her vulpine smile was his sole consolation. A blue Punto paused a yard from the pavement, initiating a sigh of relief.

"My baby's here, Adam. His poor ears must have been burnin him."

"Just go tell him dat you're endin tings wiv him an' dat you've got some next breh. I'll wait—"

"You'll be waitin a very long time. Goodbye Adam!"

She waved ta-ta like a spoilt princess as the car sped past him towards Cricklewood Lane.

"Don't tell me you fucked dat one up," Stacey said.

"There are thousands like her in dis city, cuz—"

"Jeez, Lollz. You couldn't even pull a toilet chain!"

Lollipop could still smell the perfume that had protruded from the skin of Bonita Applebaum, the lush metallic aroma of peaches and pineapples. Her dulcet timbre had dittoed like the lyre. She was already mythologized within his mindset. All this cultivated an air of tragedy.

"Did you get her digits?" Stacey said.

"Did I fuck?"

"You idiot! You tripped when there was no wire—"

"And you think you could do better coz you smoke more draws an' do the nine to five?"

"You didn't even play to win... but you still lost—"

"If you want a chick like dat, you gotta have bare peez. I bet her manz got peez. You could tell. He was shinin... Bonita's high maintenance. Her skin's flawless! I gotta roll deep... I might ave to ring Sanjay an' see if he can bring me in—"

"Sanjay ain't ever gonna help you!"

He said no more on that subject for he sincerely hoped Stacey was wrong. And he thought no more of it lest it never happen. Bonita was perhaps gone forever but he couldn't afford to have his hustling ambitions hoisted onto the sharp end of a catapult and hurled recklessly into the firmament.

"Damn! I just can't stop thinkin bout dat chick," he said. "*God, I love her mouth!*"

They retraced their steps, past the gallimaufry of Central European shops and into Mr. Salameh's store. Customers seemed ingratiated by the tawdry toasters and other nugatory kitchen appliances on sale. Others ambulated among the fanciful shelves that housed iPods and iPads. Lollipop bemoaned the nullity of his wallet.

"You got any peez you can lend me? I wanna get an iPod."

"I'm bruk—"

"You're as tight as a gnat's arse—"

"I thought you had an iPod already?"

"Yea, I did but I left it on the bus the other day—"

"Can I elp you boss?" Mr. Salameh interrupted from behind them. He was a thrifty Persian hoar who spoke through the nose, but was thornier than they supposed. "Are you looking to buy, or are you just... err... looking?"

"I'm lookin to buy, in bulk," Lollipop said.

"Oh, my!" Mr. Salameh said. "That's absolutely fantastic!"

Stacey laughed uncontrollably. He sunk to the back of the shop, clutching his jaw.

"I got a friend from Congo in the import, export business," Lollipop said. "He wants me to make contacts wiv a trader on a regular basis."

A blanched simper spreaded Mr. Salameh's bearded cheeks. "OK. I'll give you my business card. You give it to your friend?"

Beguiling thoughts ballasted Lollipop's fickle mind. The booty behind the glass partition would temper the loss of Bonita

Applebaum's booty as well as his swirling angst, periodically at least. Three or four iPods could morph into money and the thought of money chimed its metronomic discord. He could countenance the remainder of the day selling iPods on the street. And then he could shine and swagger like the richest of men.

He goose-stepped towards the back of the store where Stacey preyed upon the chaotic affections of a teenage shop assistant.

"So you a shiners den?"

"FaceTime me and you'll see!"

"F'real. I can lay the pipe on you tonight—"

Lollipop stood arrogantly between the slipshod pair. The girl was forced to slip away and Stacey was sipped a diabolical proposition. His alluring eyeballs sunk woefully into their sockets. Crystalline beads formed upon his diaphoretic brow.

"Naaah, Lollz. 'Low it… If you don't do nothin, then you do nothin wrong, do ya?"

"Fuck it! I'm tired and bored. Let's be fuckin immature!"

He approached the infatuate. She was perpetually smiling at Stacey. "Can we take a look at those iPods please?… Yes, yeh, those! Benji here wants to buy his lil sister a present for her birthday—"

He observed the stage with a furrowed gaze. A sinewy male with a weighty beard had mounted a ladder to change a fluorescent tube. A deluxe female dressed in an amorphous abaya served robotically at a busy till. And at the front of the store, a scarecrow-of-a-man rowed belligerently with Mr. Salameh.

Stacey, now servile to his avaricious longings, selected four iPods of the most expensive kind. He ignored the pubescent protestations of the infatuate. Lollipop reluctantly clung to his favorite in his prayer-perched hands and then became conscious of this needless behavior. He slipped the iPod back. Stacey watched him with bewilderment.

The veiled cashier clutched her fervid bound. She raised the alarm in a foreign tongue. Lollipop and Stacey moved on tiptoes towards the exit so that they couldn't be snared by the labyrinth aisles or the tufted assistants with rolled-up sleeves. Mr. Salameh, having disposed of the Scarecrow, crocked his fingers like a preying cat.

"Put the iPods back," he said in a trembling overture that sounded like weeping. "Then you leave my shop. We'll pretend this never happened... as long as you don't come back..."

They sprinted through the exit and onto Cricklewood Lane. They were pursued with puissance by the two tufted ones. Stacey's splendid strides and stout heart beseeched him from capture. He darted between litterbins and lampposts, parked cars and piqued pedestrians. Their pursuers half-hoped for an extemporaneous hand to intervene in their favor but people preferred to spectate rather than muddy themselves. The vespertine hours were fast approaching and nobody fancied the paltry inadvertence of becoming a wounded hero.

There was a gradual weakness in Lollipop's running, but he dared not cease his flight. He barged a woman aside who flip-flopped with her Tesco bags. He coasted past a pair of decrepit pensioners and their pet pug.

"I got a knife... I got a knife," he shouted at any potential have-a-go heroes. "Stop me an' you'll get shanked!"

A police patrol car unhinged itself from the traffic to pursue him. His canter was reduced to a high-speed walk. Fatigue had sequentially crippled his limbs. A second police car pulled abruptly before him. An officer lunged forward with an anchored claw against the nape of his neck, plunging him to the pavement.

"I ain't got nothin on me... Get the fuck of me... Gettt offf meee! Why y'all fuckin wiv meee..."

Mr. Salameh advanced earnestly from his Nissan Qashqai. His clammy T-shirt strained against his beer gut.

"He stole four iPods from my shop. Four. I followed the other thief but he got away. We're going to prosecute. I have it all on CCTV—"

"CCTV, my arse—" Lollipop said with a Medusa glare from the floor.

"Your arse indeed! You're a bloody, bone-idled fool. Taking what's not yours! What's the matter with you?"

As Mr. Salameh ranted, people crawled out of shop crevices and pub holes to gawp at the quaint theater being played out on the street. A pair of PCSOs were in attendance, inert drips with weepy eyes. Two dozen schoolgirls dressed in bogey rhubarb and custard uniforms sucked on rimy ice-poles. To them, there was nothing more deliciously gratuitous than bad boy expediency. The crows that augured ill-tidings from the rooftops looked bewildered. From the floor, shards of concrete rubble bored into Lollipop's incorrigible jowl. P.C Harvey, of yare appendages and cherub cheeks, bent his knees to speak to him.

"We're gettin you to your feet, fella... No funny business, OK?"

Lollipop nodded reluctantly. They lifted him to his heels. Concrete debris remained fused to his cheek.

"I wanna know why's man gettin harassed like dis... I'm goin bout my business an' dem donuts are accusin me of bein a tealeaf... I ain't no thief. Search me if I'm lyin—"

"Don't you wanna sit down, fella? You look like you're gonna fall down—"

"What, fall down? I've been down already—"

"Don't his eyes look glazed?" Harvey invited his minions for their opinions. They promptly nodded their unanimous accord.

"They do, don't they?" one said gleefully. "They look very hazy to me, like he's gonna pass out. It couldn't possibly be for the fact he's been smoking marijuana!"

"What's dat, officer? Is dat the new twang?"

"You smoke marijuana, don't ya?"

"Looks like *a few of you* been smokin marijuana—"

"Where are the iPods, mate?"

"I ain't got no iPods—"

"And I suppose you haven't got a knife as well?"

"If you thought I had one, I'd be handcuffed already—"

"What's your name, son?" another officer said with an Easter egg bonce. He smelt as though he had just bathed in a tub scented with lavender oil.

"Andrew Spencer—"

"You're sayin it like we're supposed to know it. You got ID?"

"Nah, I ain't."

"How can we be sure that's your real name?"

"I was christened Andrew Christopher Leighton Spencer—"

"On your mother's life?"

"What's my mother gotta do wiv it?"

Harvey's rambunctious mitts invaded Lollipop's pockets, fondling his Oyster card, rattling his loose change and keys, ruffling his collar, accreting his dolor.

"Can you go easy on my pockets please? Can you go easy on my pockets, officer—"

Harvey looked exasperated.

"See I told you, officer. No iPods. Can I go please?"

"We're not done with you yet, fella—"

"You boys just want me to make your day—"

"Absolutely, and it's gonna be as easy or as hard as you make it!"

There was to be no lull nor let-up in Harvey's hostility. He asked trenchant questions about his visit to Mr. Salameh's store, and about his accomplice who got away. P.C Lavender zapped his fingertips with a scanning tool and tarried dispassionately. Salameh snarled at him haughtily. The Two Tufts rodomontaded their heroics to the PSCOs. He evaded their eyes and stared up at the gambrel roofs and potted chimneys of the Broadway. The crows seemed reluctant to settle elsewhere. Harvey gestured a colleague forward.

"Handcuff him," he said.

The cuffs clicked around Lollipop's wrists before he could tense a muscle. "Trevor King, that's who you are!" Lavender said.

"Wowzers! Dumb Fedz know my name—"

"Aged twenty, previously arrested and cautioned for the possession of cannabis... Threatening behavior... Common assault... Convicted for driving without insurance... Driving under the influence of alcohol… Driving without a driving license… And what's this?"

"It could be worse—"

"You're sooo coming with us to the station, fella—" Harvey said, fiddling a silver cufflink.

Mr. Salameh shook a plumped fist. "If he returns my property, I won't press charges. If he doesn't, then we're going all the way with this, to the Old Bailey if necessary—"

"Old Bailey? Are you fuckin stupid? I ain't got your fuckin iPods. I'll be out in three hours max, trust me."

"What did you say?"

"I said I'll be out in three hours. I'm a Jedi Knight when it comes to these situations, ya don kno!"

Harvey waved a cautionary finger. "Hey, a little less of that language. I've bent over backwards for ya, fella—"

"Yeah, yeah, Stinky. Jes make sure when I get to the station, I get my phone call—"

"You're not getting no phone call—"

"And you're a dickhead. You remember I tol you. P.Cs like you ain't shit. Take your uniform off and you're a regular breh like me… Dat's why I ain't got no respect for P.C Plods like you—"

"And you'd know all about respect, I'm sure—"

"The real porkies work for Trident and Special Branch. The only kick you get outta your job is when the lollipop lady gets knocked over by a car an' you gotta do traffic duty—"

He was cast unceremoniously into a waiting van. As the pub boars returned to pouring beers down their gullets; as the rhubarb and custard schoolgirls ebbed into the lineaments of the town; as the crows decamped from the rooftops to wander the sky, Salameh remained on the sidewalk with the PSCOs, bemoaning police sufferance of knaves and novice fools. Supple juveniles simply mutated into hardened criminals if unchecked by unyielding deterrents, he grumbled. To Lollipop listening from inside the van, that was bullshit.

* * *

His ocular nerves pulsated and itched as if there were ticks upon his eyeballs. His belt was removed and so were other loose accoutrements. "Can you not lean on the counter please?" the custody sergeant said. "This ain't a fish and chip shop!"

"When can I get my phone call?"

"You'll get your phone call when we say so!"

From the orthoclase walls, they heard the angst keening of a prisoner, and the venting of authoritarian command. Everybody ignored the commotion. Then the jeremiad intensified. So they stole a glimpse at the corridor. A canerowed fellow was surrounded by a troika of cops.

"You ain't takin my DNA," he said. "It's against my human rights, man. You can't be stickin needles an' injections in me—"

The inspector stood over the recalcitrant prisoner, hot fists clenched by peevishness.

"Look here, Femi," he said in his Glaswegian brogue. "Don't make this shit worse than it is. There's no needles, no injections, nothin to give you nightmares—"

"When some old lady gets mugged on the street, dat's gonna give you enough reason to come an' kick my fuckin door down—"

"Don't talk rubbish. This is standard procedure—"

"I ain't been convicted of any crime—"

"You've just been cautioned, Femi—"

Femi recoiled as though he was shrinking from the halitosis of a camel. "I want some water!"

"You've already had three cup fulls—"

"Well, I want another one. And you ain't takin my DNA!"

Flinting adrenaline pertused the nubilous eyes of the inspector. One of those nubilous eyes caught Lollipop and a ursine pack of officers. He pretended not to notice them at first. Finally, he exhaled his frustration: his appropriated frugality shorn out of necessity.

"Get the gentleman another cup of water," he said.

After a short susurration between the inspector and his officers, Femi was bundled out of the corridor.

"You get all sorts in this place," the inspector said. "They moan, moan, moan. They even moan about the color of the toilet paper!"

Lollipop tapped the tips of his churched fingers against the desk while the other officers feigned laughter. He wondered whether the presence of others had saved Femi. He convinced himself it had. He asked for several cups of water. They felt obliged to give him his fill.

They led him through several umbilical corridors. They found a draughty cell and tipped him in. After ten minutes of persistent pacing, he thumped at the steel doors and protested his innocence. There was nothing with him that could relieve his ennui, no skunk or coke, no shot of poison. A turd deposited by the previous inmate floated in the toilet bowl. The globose lighting was a shade of orange, two shades too bright. The woolly blanket upon the makeshift bed-cum-settee reeked the odor of a mort man.

His ire shattered the sepulchral calm. He protested his innocence in a meager voice but no turnkey came nor cared. He turned his ire upon Stacey, who had probably flogged the iPods for much less than they were worth, using the proceeds to treat some floozy to some weed in return for fellatio. And here he was, sodden with self-pity, subject to aleatory whim. After a final ejaculation of anger, he sat upon his lean ankles. He gradually succumbed to a tortured sleep.

* * *

Nearly five hours later, Lollipop's cell door flung forward violently. A man with an anemic face and dewy eyes stomped through on sturdy heel. The door slammed promptly behind him.

"I'm Ben Brown." His voice was as shrill as a fife. "I'm your legal representative!"

Lollipop was unimpressed by his Herringbone suit and his Anello & Davide Cuban heels, but any advocate from any solicitor firm would suffice him right now. "I hope you got somethin in dat briefcase for these fools—"

"What fools?"

"Tha fools dat brought me here. I can't believe what happened to me today—"

"Neither can I—"

"Why drag me off road in handcuffs and lock me up for six hours? Ain't dat kidnapping?"

"If only life was as simplistic as that!" Ben whipped a notepad from his briefcase and began scribbling untidily. "You know why you're here, Mr. King. Needless to say, that doesn't need to be explained by me. What have you to say in your defense?"

"I'm innocent!"

"You're not the most original person in the world—"

"What's dat supposed to mean?"

"I hear the same tedious pleas of innocence from the same persuasion of men in identical circumstances. Excuse me for seemingly passing judgement since I'm merely a defense operative, but I couldn't help but pass comment."

"You're obviously not a road man. If you were, dis shit would happen to you, like every week. Coz it never happens to you, it doesn't mean dat it doesn't happen—"

"Then the solution would be not to become a road man!"

Lollipop felt too weary to fight back. He climbed into an opposing seat and folded his arms. With one hand arched around his jawbone and the other poised around a gel pen, Ben asked for his version of events. Lollipop cautiously related his rehearsed fable.

"I met dis pumped up breh outside the shop. I didn't know his name or nuttin. Can't even remember what he looks like... I just called him *my man*. We go into the shop, he's chirpsin some gal. I'm goin bout my business... All dem Asians are starin at me in the shop, like I'm gonna do somethin. One of dem came up to me and said: 'We know what you're up to. You ain't got no peez so you ain't got no business...' He left me wounded... Then *my man* comes back, jacks some iPods and tells me to jack some. I ain't no thief, ya get me… Why am I gonna jack an iPod when I've got three already? When I turn round, two guys are coming up to me, saying they're gonna move me… I get scared and run… They let *my man* get away and they come after me coz they didn't like me from the start… Don't you think dat's fuckry?"

"Like a hart in a nest of vipers, I presume—"

"The Fedz never give man a bly. They're always stoppin man on road. Man could be goin shop for his nan an' tha Fedz wanna know what's in his carrier bag… They did dat to one of my boys once, raided his bread an' milk. Dem dumb pricks must have thought that the French loaf he was carryin was an AK!"

"I'm ideologically unqualified to comment," Ben said with a cursory smile. "It's best we start the interview."

The quaint cur hummed as he scribbled some more and Lollipop was loathed even to look at him. He was obviously a parlous fellow, high on hubris and a hater of *thugz*. The adverse monotony was soon breeched by the police and their pablum.

"You've got that same red tie again, fella!" Harvey said as he shook Ben's big hand. "It never brings you luck!"

"It's maraschino cherry actually," Ben said and tucked his colubrid tie beneath his blazer.

The interview started once they had settled themselves. Lollipop was feline with his gestures, precise with his choice of words.

"So," Harvey said. "If you didn't nick the iPods, I wonder who did?"

"If *my man* told me his name, I'd be tellin—"

"His name was Benji—"

"Really? I just called him *my man*—"

"I don't think you're telling the truth—"

"How's dat?"

"We've spoken to several independent eyewitnesses. Their account differs from yours—"

"Dey saw me with the iPods???" Lollipop paused to aperçu every person in turn at the table. "Dat's tha question. Did anyone see any iPods on me??? When I left tha shop, did anyone see me leave wiv any iPods??? Yes or no?"

"Either way, we believe you knew your companion—"

"Don't you think if I knew him, I'd rather he were here instead of me? I ain't gonna get locked up for six hours for nobody. That's just fuckin stupid. If I knew him, I'm tellin!"

"Why did you run?"

"Coz I was scared. One of their shopkeepers, dis big pub guy walks over and starts threatenin me—"

"Threatening you? He said you seemed a bit lost reading the price tag—"

"And you believe dat? You're gullible, mate. I can read, yeah. I ain't dumb. I can read. I've read *Shakespeare*, *Fifty Shades Of Grey*, the *Bible*, Zadie Smith's *Yellow Teeth* an' all the Harry Potter books. Course I could read a price tag—"

"Now you're dodgin the issue—"

"You asked if I could read an' I proved I can. Obviously, the shopkeeper lied—"

He aimed to wear them down with sinuous determination. He observed them as they scribed on plain white sheets. The interview was now trite and it was late in the night. Somebody appeared to be peering through the gauze window to the side of him. Ben was silent to the left of him.

"So you're sticking to your tale about the Artful Dodger?" Lavender said. "He makes off with the iPods and you're prepared to take the can? I bet he's very grateful for friends like you—"

"If you wanna speculate, den you can but you don't get to the truth by guessin—"

"My client has told you his version of events," Ben said. "Are there any further questions?"

"We'll continue our investigation to ascertain our course of action," Harvey said. "We'll review the CCTV footage again. Then it's up to the CPS. Mr. King is free to go on the condition that he doesn't return to the *Salameh and Salem Electrical House*, and that he returns to this police station at a later date determined by us so that he may be informed of any further action. Interview terminated at 2318 hours."

"About time too," Lollipop said. "Now you guys can get back on road an' catch the real criminals!"

The abatement of the interview was a slight triumph. He followed from behind as Ben and Harvey chatted earnestly during their languid procession towards the custody suite. Ben said something about a drink-up in Northolt involving Tanquerays and Tequilas. Being a good solicitor depended on being a good drinker, he said. Harvey kept on laughing and kept calling him mate.

"How am I gonna get home from here?" Lollipop said to nobody in particular. "Can't I use your mobile Ben? You must have free calls. I can get my cousin to come pick me up—"

Harvey and Ben looked at each other.

"You can use the payphone," said a police administrator with short relaxed hair pasted upon her scalp by dollops of dried-out gel.

"I ain't got no money, an' my mobile ain't got no credit. Can't I use your mobile, Ben?"

"You can use the payphone like she says," Ben said.

Lollipop reverse-charged the call to Marius. Marius' mother refused to collect. Despondently, he slotted a £1 coin and asked Stacey to collect him. Stacey said he'd be there as soon as he could. After collecting his possessions, he sat on the steps leading to the police station. The wind throttled the trees. The sky spat water, and so did the ducts in his eyes. He cared not whether his jeans were drenched or his hair was sodden. The souse consonants rained upon him by his so-proclaimed advocate had dampened his ardor. He had stolen nothing, yet the sheet he held had him charged as having done so. He vowed that the sullied home of the duplicitous would never house his body again.

Ben tooted his horn as he spun away in his silver Passat CC. Not at him of course, but at Harvey who stood at the gate to wave him off. His iPhone vibrated with a text from Stacey: "GET 2

KILBURN PRK ST- IM DERE N MY MUM'S WHIP."

After asking for directions from pedestrians every thirty or so paces, he soon arrived, drenched by sheaves of rain. Stacey watched him approach with doleful sympathy.

"Big men are fools!" Lollipop strapped the seatbelt across his breast. "They ain't got no love for tha lil man. I've met some fools in my time, but dat idiot tops the lot. I should've faded him wiv a left hook."

"Who's dat?"

"My solicitor, innit. Dat breh's so far gone it's unreal. I ain't usin his arse again. His way of thinkin was like we weren't from the same planet. Breh was from Uranus, or one of Uranus' moons—"

"Can I ask a question, Lollz? Why did we take dem iPods?"

"Why not ask me why do I use oxygen? Why do I drink apple juice instead of orange juice? Why does my internet connection shut down every night at 10.20pm until 11.48pm? Why does the Roadrunner always outsmart the Coyote?"

"How tha fuck am I supposed to know?"

"To live, Stacey. Too live."

"What you're sayin doesn't make sense—"

"Everythin dat makes sense is bullshit. Certain man are rockin Avi jackets dat costs more than their whips. Does that make sense? It doesn't, coz nothin is what it seems. Hate's tha new love, cuz!"

Stacey started the engine with a terse smile. Lollipop had remained gladiatorial against any accusatorial voice and he felt it pointless appending his irascible mood. It would be akin to running after an out-of-service bus in his flip-flops, he thought. Instead, he felt it necessary to inform Lollipop of his father's inquisitional rage when he learnt of his arrest and repose himself thereafter.

Cricklewood, by night, was filled with gregarious and gaudy types. Lambent streetlights lit the piccalilli scene. A throng of covetous females corralled outside a rufescent club named *The Probe*. In their midst were a Motley Crue of garish males dressed in urban regalia. *Salameh and Salem* had closed, and a gaunt fellow wearing a skullcap gazed quietly through the shop window. An around-the-clock Albanian supermarket fomented their trade after midnight as shoppers purchased fresh bagels and discounted fruit. Lollipop, after watching them, reclined in his seat and thought of the translunary beauty Bonita Applebaum and how she doused him with vitriol, when all he wanted was her endearment and her equidistant cakes. He ripped his charge sheet and hurled its shreds out of the window. Stacey hummed affectingly to Stooshe's lubricious vocals from the radio. The callow kid had probably enjoyed an orgiastic moment where iPods and fellatio were traded with that fallow shop assistant.

"Where's my cut from the iPods?"

"Cut? The only cut you're gettin is your dad's uppercut—"

"You know she snitched on you. She told the Fedz dat your name was Benji—"

"Coz dat's what *you* told her. She knew my real name, fam."

"So you get the booty on both counts an' I'll get a judge dat will give me a bird for dis. You think dat's funny? You think dat's fair?"

"I'm gully, Lollz. You got caught. I'd never get caught——"

"I know I weren't on your conscience when I was locked up coz of what you did. But you were on dat chick's conscience when she gave you brain!"

"I'm tha gingerbread man, or have you forgotten? I get away in any circumstance. Even if they'd dispatched a helicopter, I'd still get away—"

After fleeing the bind of Cricklewood, they were granted a gracious wind on the North Circular Westbound. Within his territorial girders, Lollipop's inertia slowly acquiesced. Flowers seeped their scent along Hill Street as fine rain fell. As they parked beneath his bedroom window, he overheard the tomfoolery of his friends gathered in the middle of the road, their ornery voices seethed above the tenebrous din of the A406. He spent a few hours with them before plateauing homeward to face the wrath of his father.

2

PETER PAN HAS A PLAN.

LOLLIPOP PEERED THROUGH THE bathroom window at the congregation of his friends along Oscar Close. His beleaguered eyes scoured the scene. His carking shoulders sunk. His friends seemed far removed from his *hogra*. They bantered and spoke, and laughed at each other's jokes. And though he could count on the fiduciary care from one or two, he had isolated himself in his abode, taking no visitors for a day or two.

"You should go back to college," Fernando, Stacey's father, had said, scratching his accipitrine nose thoughtfully. As he offered his avuncular counsel, Lollipop watched a vein twitch high in his temple. His own father Augustus took an opposing view.

"Why not go Salvage? Buy a few hubcaps, wing mirrors and put an advert on eBay? When you've sold that, you'll double, triple your dough easy. If you wanna make money, quick money, learn about the mechanics of the car industry—"

"Fernando reckons I'm better off at college—"

"You need a trade. Guys go to college so they can fuck about with girls. College is a fucking youth center. It's a fucking joke!"

He had gone to sleep at the firstlings of daybreak, having spent the night FaceTiming females. Burdened by Cimmerian anxieties, his pastimes were an apathetic trend: Joanne, his benign but libertine companion, was a piquant delight. Smoking skunk with reckless abandon was a compulsive one. He raved whenever he could afford the luxury, and mugged the seemingly vulnerable to subsidize a night-out. In between that and everything else, he listened to grime religiously.

He walked into the brightly lit lounge cramped with unstinting endeavor like an IKEA showroom. The causeuse was Corinthian leather, emerald green. The cotton-pleated curtains were ashen-gray and organdy. A potpourri of cookery books filled the shelves. The coal fire warmed his ankles.

He gazed studiously at a picture of his deceased mother above the fireplace. She had died from pneumonia when he was three and he held no memory of her. Those that knew her venerated her. They said his father was never the same after she passed away. But Augustus never spoke of her and was moved to anger when he once dared to press him.

He so desired the Arcadian love of a mother. As a child, her loss was more lucid when events like Mothering Sunday were commemorated as school themes. And so, he had only his elder sister Kasia to rely on constantly to recall the days of their mother.

She spoke about the love his mommy had deluged them with, and the Minnie Ripperton songs she would sing to them. There were weekend trips to their grandparents in Ilford, and boat rides upon a propitious brook. Mommy treated them to picnics that consisted of orange juice, sausage rolls and tuna sandwiches. As they reclined in the riparian shade, nan enthralled them with stories of St. Lucia and Holland Park in the sixties, despite being repeatedly interrupted by Lollipop's cross-examinations. Kasia said that he was so inquisitive that mommy predicted he'd become a scientist or a solicitor when he came of age.

He had often lay in bed, scouring the faintest memory in the deepest caverns of his liminal mind. For sure, he remembered his nan's commodious apartment on Loxford Lane in Ilford, decorated to her recherché tastes, smelling of his grandfather's Henri Wintermans. He recalled the Enid Blyton-type stories.

They were repeated often enough. He even remembered the gully brook and cramp boats. But no photo or story could jump-start any physical delineation of mommy and so he had always retired, angry and dejected.

His grandparents had retired to St. Lucia after their daughter's demise, and memories of Kasia belonged to another lifetime. She had migrated to New Jersey and married a Canadian pilot. But neither he nor his father could visit because of their convictions. And she never called.

Augustus and Laverne, pausing for several intimate interludes as they came down the stairs together, interrupted his reverie. The flat was fogged by carcinogen smoke, caused by the cigarette clamped between her primrose lips. Augustus, supposedly indisposed to cigarettes, never breathed a word against her puffing, though much had been said about the prohibitive skunk he imbibed. He was also forbidden to play his psychedelic songs in stereo, but special disposition was granted her to irritate him with her obstreperous dolphin shrieks while she meditated. And he loathed her anility; her tetchy segways into his affairs was severely at odds with his recalcitrance. But since he remained flayed by the malcontent of recent weeks, he thought it prudent to be ambivalent for the time being and make a peace offering.

"Would you like some coffee, Laverne?"

"Your coffee leaves a lot to be desired, like another cup of coffee—"

"What bout you, dad?"

"I couldn't trust you to make it well—"

"So nobody wants breakfast den?"

"Breakfast at three? What time you serving lunch?"

"Lunch? Now you're getting carried away—"

"We won't be getting carried away if we started suggesting that you started putting down a likkle somethin for the rent!"

"Once I start makin dough from shottin Johnny's mixtape, I'll sponsor the rent monthly—"

"Aren't you too old for that nonsense?" Laverne said.

"What nonsense?"

"You can't be Peter Pan all your life—"

"Who wants to be Peter Pan?"

"You do, and people who think like you do—"

"Dat's nice! People tellin me how I think an' feel. Man gets kicked in the gut every day, and you wanna tell man how he should scream—"

"Once you realize that silly rap records won't make you rich, you'll scream louder!"

"So what did you wanna do a long time ago when you was young, Laverne?"

"I can tell you what I didn't do. I wasn't bone-idle. I was never in trouble with police. I never mixed with the wrong crowd. I never wasted fourteen hours a day on a flipping X-Box—"

"I suppose you never had a boyfriend—"

"I never had a criminal record—"

"And neither does dad—"

"Your dad's different. He took the rap for an old friend—"

"Yeh, yeh, yeh. I've heard dat story a million times now. He thought he was a martyr but ended up a tomato..." He laughed, though they were not amused. "... But I ain't goin down like dat. We're gonna clean up once we put out a banger... The masses will say we're good, even if you won't..."

Laverne blushed to remember the last time he hadn't begged money from his father to tend to his monocausal constitutionals. As a teenager, he'd knock on their bedroom door whilst she was unclad beneath the counterpane to ask his father for money so he could have a haircut. As a juvenile heel, he was no different. She gnashed her teeth as he spoke about the skullduggeries street hustlers employed to temper their hustlings into legitimate projects.

"I really need an intravenous drip of coffee after listening to that bollocks," she said.

"You don't believe it's possible—"

"You won't be the next Nero Sandz—"

"I'm gonna be bigger than Nero Sandz. I want dat house on tha hill too. I want what's owed to me—"

"What's owed to you?"

"Whateva I can get my hands on... And I won't get it by workin. I gotta grind—"

"You're not even grinding, Ned Kelly!" Augustus said.

"Why are you bothering, Augustus? He really isn't our problem—"

"Oh, shut up Laverne. You're boring—"

Augustus hauled himself at Lollipop and crushed him against the wall. His cumbrous hands were fettered around his throat.

"Don't you ever tell her to shut up again... She's right. You're just a dreamer who does fuck all... If you're not careful, you'll end up like that waste man Dominic—"

"If he were my son, I'd have kicked him out long time ago," Laverne said. "Honestly, if sorting out his own life is such an inconvenience to him, what chance has anybody got?"

Augustus released him at her bidding. He asked if she was OK, as if it were she that had been physically scourged. Then he expounded a magnificent speech worthy of Ben Hur, harking back to his recrudescent journey from the pesky streets of Peckham to his virtuous service with the British Army in Northern Ireland. Despite the sus laws and three million unemployed, he had created many businesses. He had also lost thousands of pounds in delinquent investments. He learnt valuable life lessons despite the setbacks, avoiding virulent folk and becoming prudent with cash. He had been a bus driver, a baker, a bouncer, a bailiff. All he desired was for his son to acquiesce into adulthood and forge a career in a viable trade.

Lollipop had learnt to tune in and out of his father's bromides. Sure, he was fascinated by the endearing parables from an age-old hustler's scrapbook. Tales of superlative courage in Belfast gave him goose bumps, and Augustus evangelized business initiatives as if he was gifted with the empiricisms of a Lord Sugar. But when the speech foghorned into a fusillade of his own grievous failings, he cast his mind to his most visceral desires like Nicki Minaj's incandescent curves or his future fame as a road baron. But he could no longer slip into that El Dorado mindset.

"Look dad! Don't wanna know how good it was in your corduroy trousers, warming yourself by a Paraffin heater while you watched the *Black And White Minstrel Show* on your black-and-white TV set wiv your funny high-top or whateva you call it. You never built anythin for me. Dat's why I gotta start from scratch!"

"And what the fuck does that mean?"

"Forget it, dad. If you don't get it, then you never will. But you watch, when I make it. Everyone will be lickin my arse."

He trudged from the room, dragging the soles of his feet. The oleander and her bitch chided his parting remark. He locked himself in the bathroom and sat upon the travertine tiles. And after wrapping a bathroom towel around his head, he wept bitterly.

* * *

Stacey leaned against the graffiti wall that bore the names of his *fam* – names that he scrawled in coloristic calligraphy several nights previously. He was *building* a spliff. He hummed a grime diapason as he rolled the rizla paper. Marius, a Grecian hirsute of a boy, sat on the wall above him. He was favored by many females because of his spruced mien and beefcaked preponderance. Johnny Freelander, mocha-colored skinned with a chiseled thorax, wore ornate designer shorts that ballooned around his waist like a parachute. Mark, a saturnine spirit with an equine face and an adolescent beard, declined to partake of the draw. Wrapped around his shoulders was a PLO scarf. Ratty's antecedents were from the Congo. His rasping verses had engineered a record deal with his collective *Network Kidz*. And finally among them was Krista and Lydia, both were staunchly emulous of each other – Krista spoke speedily and was argumentative, tawny skinned with tight buttocks; Lydia, a bookish girleen with Betty Boop eyelashes and beestung lips, had a lilting TV presenter's tone. She constantly exchanged amorous glances with Stacey. The ubiquitous heat induced a sauna sweat to every brow and bosom.

"Zahra's havin a barbeque dis evening," Lydia said. "I swear down; her mom makes the best ribs. Any of you man coming?"

"Naaah!" Ratty said. "I went to her barbie last year. It was bare armshouse. One breh pulled out a burner on dis next breh coz he checked his sister. Blaze ran out di yard screamin like a fuckin gal."

"Well, I'm goin," Lydia said. "Dem ribs are to die for!"

They were distracted by four spry teens, three of them faunlets. They led a beetle-browed moose towards a row of lime-painted garages that was tainted by crude graffiti.

"I know dat girl," Marius said. "She's been about, you know, and she's only fifteen. She's nuff messy."

"Lil Elliott's gettin his dick washed," Stacey said. He lit his joint and dragged from it, exhaling the effluvium from his nostrils. "She's a barrys, always on a lil suckey suckey. Who wants a daughter like dat, cuz? She must give her dad bare migraines wiv her nastiness!"

"What do you call boys lookin to get piece of tha same gal?" Krista said.

"Put it this way, Krista," Ratty said. "I'd do tings that would make Hugh Heffner blush, but I'd be diggity damned to speak about it in public."

"Dat's nasty!" Krista said. "They stick their junk in, one after the other, regardless of what she might be carryin or what one of dem could pass onto her. Boy, they'll be queuing outside the STD clinic come Monday morning, scratchin their dinga-lings hard."

"What you hatin for?" Johnny said. "Dem boys are young. Of course, they're gonna be curious an' go after every sket they see. It's a natural ting, Krista."

"What, is dat what you did, Johnny?"

"F'real. Dat girl gives good brain. I'm sure every man here would want her on their nut sacks!"

"Not me!" Mark shook his disagreeable head. "Human beings weren't made for such depravity—"

"Yea, not Mark," Johnny said. "He's still a virgin. He's still lookin for his first fuck. Me, I jizzed on her face last week—"

"Dat's some grimy shit," Stacey said. "You know dat chick's only fifteen. You could wing for dat, blud."

"She sure didn't look fifteen—"

"Try explainin dat to the Fedz when they come knockin—"

"Try explainin dat to poor Ashleigh," Krista said with a wry smile.

"I don't have to explain anythin to anyone," Johnny said. "It ain't like I forced her. She could've said no. Besides, every man's a bigamist whether they're single or happily married—"

"Ashleigh's graftin a nine to five as well as payin tha bills an' raisin your two kids," Krista said. "An' there's you, collectin Jobseekers an' givin out facials—"

"Yep, dat's the system for you. It makes it harder on the man dem. That's what makes girls like you talk down to man like me coz you think I'm stupid. But I ain't stupid. I ain't gonna worry bout gettin a job an' bein told what to do by some chief. I'm a hustla, an' a hustla brings home more peez than a friggin nine to five—"

The boys often harped about hustling and their reasons for it. Since they were thirteen, their meeting point had been against the graffitied wall, usually by night, under the achromatic halo of a street lamp. They discussed the vagaries of world affairs with doomed optimism, through the goggles of their self-deprecating wits. They chattered earnestly about the voluptuous lifestyles of hustlers while sharing the anodyne skunk. They spoke of the girls that they laid with and the others whom they desired to lay with. They debated each other over the casuistries of latitudinarians in high places, whose malfeasant activity tormented them with deliberate constancy.

"For a hustla, the sky's the limit," Johnny said. "He can make £900 an hour. He can even make £90 an hour. If he makes £9 an hour on road, den he ain't no real hustla. He shouldn't be on road coz he's flopped. If it don't make peez, den it don't make sense!"

"So how much have you made, Johnny?"

"I'm makin aiiight peez, Krista—"

"Err, but you're not on no £900 or £90 an hour—"

"On road, you're not paid by the hour. I'm talkin bout what you earn on average—"

"An' dat's what you're gonna teach your son, to hustle? To go out on street, no job, no education – just play hide and seek wiv the Fedz all day. As long as he's makin peez, he's blessed?"

"My... my... son can make up his own mind when he's older... coz he'll see tings different from how I see dem.... We'd be livin in different times... For me, in my time, I'd rather go hungry den to be tha tailor's dummy. People think coz they're the office manager, they're tha tailor, but in reality, they're the fuckin dummy!"

"Stop makin an arse of yourself, Johnny!" Krista said. "No decent father wants his kid hustlin. Would you like Caydee-Lee hustlin tha slums... or suckin off three man-at-a-time like dat poor girl in the garage? And if you say yes, then you're tha biggest mup that's ever walked an' breathed in Nepenthe Park."

Ratty laughed like a villainous bastard. Johnny loathed him more than he loathed Mark. He wanted to seize his shrubbery hair and triturate him into the dust. Instead, he cast his gaze towards his spindly boy Jardel, playing happily with his tousle-haired friends in the play area, and cautioned him to be careful. His children belonged to the future, and the future took care of itself. And Ashleigh was a fantastic mother, in spite of her fragmentary flaws. Should anything happen to him, she possessed the foresight to see his babies through, as his mother before him. And hers before her. His mother had raised him without the aid of the sperm donor who chanced two pumps and a squirt on a debauched whim and became a latent bogeyman thereafter.

"Can someone pass me the draw?" he demanded.

Stacey handed him the joint. He took three bitter drags before handing it back.

The three faunlets that had frolicked with the fluff exited the garage. Columbia urinated against a lamppost. Elliott Walker climbed the roof of an abandoned Corsa and posed as a human crucifix, hawing some rap song about being king of the world. Shekaidy was locked to his Galaxy, already arranging another rendezvous with another moose. The fluff took another route. They were no longer interested in her pert mouth.

"Look what the cat's draggin!" Krista said.

They turned to watch a lone figure trotting towards them; it was Lollipop, scraping his feet nosily against the caliche soil.

"Where you been, Pepper Jackson?" Johnny said. "Man ain't seen you for days—"

"I've been lyin low—"

"You got any iPods for sale?"

"iPods?"

"Don't go on like you don't know. Man heard you got shift!"

"I'm blessed. I've been court nineteen times, three minor convictions, pocket change fines. Same ting next time round—"

"I was involved in some madness," Johnny said. "I was wiv Cane and Blaze down south couple weeks back an' some breddas were on some hype ting for no reason… I was at some traffic light. These breddas came at me in an A4. Askin me what area I'm from! I'm like: 'What's it to you?' He's like: 'What, what, what blud. You want beef?' I'm like: 'You want beef coz I've stepped in your area? Fool!' The lights turn green an' den I'm gone—"

"Where were you?" Lollipop said.

"Elephant and Castle. I get lost easy down dem sides coz everythin looks tha fuckin same. As I'm goin down Old Kent Road, dem boys are followin. I'm in New Cross an' they're tailin me still. I come to some next lights. Dem lemons are three cars back. Dey come runnin wiv baseball bats. I got hit a couple of times, but you could tell they were pussies coz dey didn't even swing hard. One of the dem went for my head. I ducked an' caught man in his jaw. Cane sliced one. The Fedz were there in like ten seconds. Dey arrested me an' the mup who got sliced. Everyone breezed. Lil South London boy tol tha Fedz I sliced him whilst I never. Now I've gotta go court over dis shit, even tho dey found no prints on tha blade!"

"Jeez! I know how you feel, blud," Stacey said. "One minute, you're goin bout your business an' den some chief comes up wiv somethin stupid an' ruins your day."

"Bare madness gwanin——" Ratty said.

"Dat's what people don't understand," Lollipop said. "They think you can move from road to somethin decent at the flick of a switch. My dad an' his bitch's goin on bout how I need a job reh reh reh, like it's me dat's lookin for drama. All dat talk needs to get locked off coz peeps jus don't know."

"Did you hear dat, Krista?" Johnny said.

"You lot can make excuses," Krista said. "At the end of tha day, it's all bout choices——"

"An' it's my choice to get attacked by some prick wiv a baseball bat?" Johnny said.

"Lock off dat talk, Johnny," Lollipop said. "No point preachin to the ignorant——"

"Who you callin ignorant?"

"You maybe goin uni, but you can still be ignorant. How many politicians you see in Parliament dat's been Eton, an' they're still ignorant? You can go Oxford and Cambridge and have no common sense whatsoeva. You get common sense on road... Real life, yuh get me!"

But Krista was unrepentant if most were offended. It was not as if perpetual boys had a monopoly on bad beginnings and felt that gave them license and liberty to err plaintively as an outlaw.

"Boy, if I've touched a nerve, dat's because people are on my last nerve——" she said.

"And dat's why I'm on tha *spontaneous grind*," Lollipop said. "I'm on my last nerve too. It's long lookin for a job. Who's gonna gimme a decent job? They ain't got no decent job for man coz man don't fit. Gimme a job so I can live comfortable, innit... Dat'll get me off road; a good job wiv prospects... and decent peez!"

"Only fools and horses work," Johnny said. "An' I ain't a fool or a horse."

"Tha way I see it is dis," Marius said. "Firstly, the more you do for dis country, the less dis country does for you. Second, if you're English, den the worst place to live is England. So as long as you don't hurt no man, woman, child or living thing, I'm backin moves."

"Where will we be five years from now?" Lydia said. "Thugz eventually gotta come off road too, for better or worse—"

"In five years, I'd have a first class degree in Law and I'd be operatin on an international level," Krista said.

"I'll be an international superstar wiv nine Grammys an' eleven MOBOs, happily married to some peng celebrity wiv a fatty, an' we'll have twin girls on the way," Ratty said.

"I'll still be hustlin an' bussin caps," Lollipop said.

"In five years, I wanna give up the weed," Stacey said. "I wanna be an architect. When I smoke draws, my imagination comes alive. I draw shit beyond imagination. But I'm still givin it up though, the draw dat is."

"I just wanna tap Babestation babes all day—" Marius said.

"I just wanna worship Allaah," Mark said.

"I don't know where I'll be," Johnny said. "I ain't no dreamer. I ain't gonna front. Y'all believe in Leprechauns an' the Tooth Fairy."

"What did I say dat was unbelievable?" Lollipop said.

"You ain't never buss a cap in your life," Johnny said. "And you probably never will."

"You lot gimme joke," Krista said. "Why walk on the wild side of the cliff when you can walk peacefully on the High Road?"

An Audi R8 V10 screeched past, halting fifty yards from where they loitered. They turned to stare with reverential awe. Gregory Foster emerged from the vehicle. He saluted Johnny with a simulacrum of a Black Power fist. Johnny raised an acclaimed one back. The owner of the Audi troused Gregory with mocking invectives. The faint flicker of his scorching tones seared in the sunlight.

"Dat's Marvin fuckin Crowe," Ratty said. "Boy, Gregory's havin dat... Blimey! Man is takin him for a dickhead in his own endz... Y'all better listen out for gunshots..."

He implied that dealing with a recusant *gangsta* was akin to a Faustian pact, if not worse than that. He spoke of what they knew to be true: Procrustean folk like Marvin Crowe were the curmudgeonliest of souls. Even after shaking hands on fecundating deals, the repulsing stench of treachery perturbed the air. Myopic loyalties was shorn out of reticence. An ironclad yoke vehemently betrothed them. They treaded the treacherous fault line and kindled the deathly fire. Each was prepared to slay the other over a wrongfully deprived penny. Each considered the other the subaltern. Each considered himself the sadist. They prodded each other till they teetered to the end of their deviltry, where the felling was definitively swift, often sanguinary, and mercilessly extreme.

Ratty related to them fables of Marvin's unalloyed anger; how he assailed a bereft woman because she failed to pay her debt. He called her mobile repeatedly but she ducked his calls. Until one day, as she walked her son to school, he emerged from behind an oak tree and attacked her with an axe. From her hospital bed in intensive care, she made certain he got three times his money after hearing rumors that he planned to sneak past hospital security and shoot her dead in her hospital bed; how he mauled a university student in her halls of residence after she, too, defaulted on payment; how he snared a snitch who sourced information to the police. The father-of-four was cinched to his seat whilst his petrified partner was set upon by Marvin's acolytes. They extirpated her face with acid. They stubbed lit cigarettes upon her skin. When he finally confessed under much duress, Marvin seized a machete and removed his head from his convulsing body. Better it was for the beheaded man's mistress to seek asylum from the government of Afghanistan, said Ratty, for she was far safer on the streets of Kabul than on the streets of London.

Lydia doubted his testimony. Random cruelty frightened her.

But Ratty swore in catechetical terms that he spoke the truth. And Marius, Johnny and Lollipop seconded him. They faintly heard Marvin's bile-speckled caw and Gregory ventilating his lame excuses. Only Marius took his gaze away.

"I wouldn't trust Gregory wiv my Yaris," he said. "He'd drive back in a Nova."

"Stop hatin on Gregory." Johnny extinguished the final remainder of Stacey's joint. "He ain't no yute who started hustlin yesterday. You remember the nang big boy rides he used to own? Like he'd business wiv you're clapped-out Yaris. Gregory's gonna come back bigger than ever!"

"I hope he does," Ratty said in a tone that was anything but sincere. "I really do."

Still, they observed the street's most vicious practitioner in the smog heat, his raffish hair of dusky red, the gas blue dye of his denim shirt and Timberland shoes. He vociferated Gregory, who curled a frail gray lip at the guttersnipe dissing. And when Marvin was satisfied, he climbed into his Audi and sped towards the T-junction of the road and beyond. Gregory crawled into his babymother's abode.

"Spontaneous grind!" Lollipop said. "It worked for Marvin. It'll work for me ten times more."

"Lucky for you, you're stuck in your own lil fantasy world where your sickness won't hurt you much," Ratty said.

"And when you droppin your album, Ratty?"

"Careful the Fedz don't catch you in another state of madness—"

"Breh's been sayin he's droppin an album for the last three years. Man had to roll deep to raise funds—"

"You keep gassin bout my past, but dat made me the man you see standin before you. No regrets, rude boi!"

Lollipop changed the subject. "So, we still goin studio, Johnny?"

"Caydee-Lee's ill and I'm strung out—"

"I'll catch you man later," Lollipop said with a wave of his hand. "I'm off to smoke some draws... an' settle some scores!"

"*Spontaneous grind?*" Ratty said after Lollipop was out of earshot. "Tha only *spontaneous grind* he knows is linkin chicks on short notice. Breh's like him calculate their wealth by the chicks in their phone books, not by the chicks they're fuckin! He ain't got no chick anyway… Breh's goin to bed tonight for a night of passion wiv himself!"

*   *   *

The closing credits of *EastEnders* had scrolled down the TV screen. There was nothing else to watch, save the endless streaming of music videos on MTV Base and the tedious re-runs of comedy classics on G.O.L.D. Lollipop flicked impatiently through the multitude of channels. The Sky remote was his life synopsized; a multiple of choices but nothing sufficed. Eventually, he settled for *Channel Slam*.

Their grime videos were terminally average. Verses were doused with stupefied apathy. It was the same rudderless dross from Brockley-born rapper Drum. The angular-faced rapper, remotely attractive to the eye, patrolled his South London *favelas* proudly as he performed a self-penned composition titled *Dreams After Yesterday's Stories*, yet another querulent urban humbug. He could feel the glacial breath of the police on his nape, he proclaimed in polysyndetonic prose. He was always broke and shamelessly misunderstood. He had experienced no paternal love, little brotherly love but swarms of womanly love. His detractors were crab jar fatalists whose own insidious natures would bring about their ruin. Fortunately, he was a diamond in the dirt and a man of God and, therefore, destined to triumph in the final analysis.

Next, a disinhibited rapper named Ambrosia-Nectar. Her copacetic dance moves were kinetic. "This is what ya missin!" she said, accentuating her cleavage by cupping her rotund breasts. She boasted about "having a big butt for a white girl," and how she purposely wore her jeans low to show her butt aperture to omnivorous *thirsty boys*. Lollipop drooled over her swaggering scorn.

The next video featured IC3, three rappers contesting their drollery affections for a Natalie La Rose lookalike. They cavorted around her and revealed their chiseled adornments in the pouring rain. They extolled their Trey Songz-like encomiums about her sexual candescence and sank before her on bended knee. She seemed content in going home with them all at the end of the song.

He hurriedly phoned Johnny.

"We should be there on *Channel Slam*... Why haven't we dropped a video yet? Blud, we're slippin—"

"I'm tryin to put my lil girl to sleep cuz," Johnny said, and promptly hung up.

Local grime act Be Elze Bob's music video followed IC3. The auricomous Megan sang a balladry about a basehead she once loved, and how their relationship descended into bellendery and strife. Be Bob, a Caucasian kid with cornrow plaits and a vibrissal chin, and Elze, his puckered-faced bi-racial half-brother, had a machine-gun command of their lyrics. Dark-glassed heavies nodded their heads egotistically every time the camera homed in on them. In one shot, Lollipop and Marius posed with a Porsche 997 that wasn't theirs, though on the account of their vain posturing, you'd think it was.

After the making of that video, Be Elze Bob invited their adherents to their abode on the Tony Blair Estate. Lollipop recalled the largesse they received at the high-octane after-party on a sub-zero night; crates of Kopparberg, busty babes in bodices, journalists from *Jam*. Johnny had been intoxicated by several Jagerbombs. On the way home, he was askance at his fortune thus far. He suggested a plot that would visit ill upon Be Elze Bob. Malignity, he argued, was right in certain circumstances because it redressed the needless depredation he endured. God, Providence or the Numinous had shunted the luckless without justification and favored cunts without cause. Why must he remain the least luckless of the unlucky? Why shouldn't favor be bestowed upon him instead of the parvenus Be Elze Bob? Perhaps they were in league with Satan, hence their vituperious name. That alone explained the absurdity of their success.

Lollipop was affrighted by the sudden presence of his father, whose corpulent frame bolted out his bedroom lamp.

"How come you didn't knock?"

"I don't need to knock—"

"If you caught man strollin naked, you'd go blind!"

"You thought about what I said?"

"Yeh, I did."

"So what are you goin to do bout it? And I don't wanna hear shit about college. Only a lazy bastard would think about college at your age—"

"I got myself a removals job. Some breh said he needs a hand three times a week. He'll pay cash in hand—"

"How many times have I told you never bullshit a bullshitter?"

"I ain't bullshittin you, dad—"

Augustus wielded a thunderbolt in the form of a flimsy envelope, tossing it into his lap.

"That's the electricity bill. £245.28. I've paid every bill in this place for twenty-five years. I think I'm entitled to a break, especially when my son demands that I knock before entering his bedroom. When he demands shit like that, I'll demand that he pays this bill by this time next week otherwise he won't have a bedroom for me to come knocking on because his broke arse will be out my front door—"

"And whose idea was dat coz dat sure don't sound like you speakin?"

"Now you can divert, digress, take what I'm sayin an' tie it into a friggin bow for all I care. Pay that bill if you wanna continue living here. And there's gonna be more bills coming your way, so be prepared. If you're unwilling or unable, you can get the fuck out. I'm a bailiff and my job is kicking out careless bums that don't pay their bills. Go figure!"

Lollipop's first instinct had been to pack his bags and scarper. He'd spend the night sleeping on Stacey's bedroom floor and then he'd check into the Homeless Unit the next morning. He'd probably be made to share a squalid block with a posh-voiced, pale-faced, gaunt-jawed heroin addict named Hortensia, or a deadbeat mom named Celeste and her offspring sired from a smorgasbord of males. The solace he desired came from the loveless steamy hot cup he casually sipped from Joanne, but even she wasn't replying to his WhatsApp texts. How dare he be held to a punitive ultimatum by his father, enslaved by that caustic necromancer, especially when he was his father's son, and his father, his only parent?

He studied the electricity bill. "For fuck sake!" he said. "This is the biggest rip-off since forty acres and a mule!"

3

BRITISH LAW ENDS AT
THIS DOOR

SHAZAD MAAJID OPERATED UNDER a pseudonym Sanjay Mandylor. He preferred not to be known as a British-Pakistani Muslim among the passels of inquisitory folk. His verboten works contravened his religious obligations and puritanical ideals. He claimed that he was an Afghan Hindi from Helmand Province, Afghanistan, and that his elder brother was being hunted by the SAS in the Swat valleys of Pakistan because of his prominent involvement in the exporting of heroin. That heroin was transported to London in the sewn-up bellies of slaughtered sheep, through to his uncle's butcher shop, where it was then distributed with haste. Lollipop had long admired his sustained deceit and his warped wisdom; the way his puerile blandishments were instantly undoubted by those of his school of thought. His avowals included his entrepreneurial father, a self-made millionaire who fashioned five restaurants himself after being fastened as a cook in early life. The simple truth was that he was a lecherous rich kid, segued between his well-heeled family businesses and his own seedy cartels. With such privileges, he was drunk with solipsism. But his good fortune, sign-posted to the Emerald City, was grievously wasted upon him.

They first met in their few weeks together at Highbury College. They had loitered in disused warehouses, smoking skunk until their eyes revoked like red baubles. They pumped iron at the gym every day, and forayed every Friday night to *The Probe* in the company of obtuse footballers and spunky glamor models. Sanjay's copious generosity was his most redeeming quality. And it was this that made him the repository of all Lollipop's hopes then, and he remained so today.

They embraced like old brethren and went off for a cruise in Sanjay's scintillating motorcar.

"You were always the realest muthafucker, Lollipop—"

"And you're packin carrots like a fat rabbit—"

"You know me, fam. I just come back from Dubai. I stayed at the Burj Khalifa, where Kings and Presidents kotch. Blud, you ain't lived till you've been to Dubai."

"Yeh, I'll get to Dubai one day… Next year's holiday's destination—"

"Always tryin a ting, Lollipop, aren't ya? Always tryin a ting—"

"I've gotta push up the pace. Don't wanna be bang smack at the bottom no more."

Sanjay nodded with firm deliberation. His donut-shaped beard was spruced neatly around his ashcan mouth.

"F'real. You see dis Mercedes, yeah? Customized to my fucked up needs. James Bond meets Knight Rider. Acura ELS sound system… Porosus croc leather seats… Garmin sat-nav… Uconnect Web… Set me back by ninety bags!"

"You're whip's peak! You must pick up chung gal in dis whip—"

"Hell yeah! Last night, me and my cousin Maz boned some McDonald's chick in the car park. She had a whackin dirt-box. She couldn't keep her eye off my car… an' my Big Mac!"

Lollipop shuffled uneasily in his seat. "Hope I ain't sittin on any cum?"

"You're cool. We got *all of it* in her."

He noticed some premature gray hair on Sanjay's left sideburn but said nothing lest it pricked his vanity.

"I wanna start shottin but not on a small ting—"

"What you wanna shot?"

"Anything, cuz."

"Can you get your own punters?"

"I can get these endz locked, cuz."

"I can get you bare food, as much as you need, wheneva you need, all from a yard in Leyton Town... How much peez you got?"

"I ... I ... was hopin you can start me off on credit—"

"Credit?" Sanjay's snout twitched at the mention of the word.

"Yea, like I get a couple keys of you, move dat on, an' pay you. Tha next load you get in advance—"

"Bruv, I can't do dat. I gotta have peez upfront—"

"What, you can't grant me dis one favor?"

"Blud, dis is *business*. I'm a businessman. You're a businessman. Don't get pissed coz dis ain't personal. You want somethin from me? I've got dat somethin for you. Bring tha means of exchange an' den we 'ave a deal. C.O.D, blud. Cash on delivery. No means of exchange, no deal—"

"Yea, but a good businessman's gotta invest in the future, not just in money but in people—"

"Naaah blud. If you believe in yourself, you can't have other people investing in you. You gotta invest in yourself. It don't matter if you're piss poor. You gotta bring somethin to tha table. You bring nothin to tha table, you won't get crumbs... What, you can't conjure up two bills to start?"

"Fam, you and I... Dis partnership... has real potential—"

"Now there *is* somethin you can do for me..." Sanjay's attention was momentarily drawn to an olive-skinned female whose fetching dress was coerced by the rowdy wind.

"I'm listenin, fam!"

"Yeah, yeah... I gotta lil move for ya... but it's gotta be done proper—"

"Don't take tha piss, Sanjay. If you don't wanna hook me up, dat's cool. There's bare man who'd bring me in—"

"Go and see dem den. Why bell me? I'll tell you why you've

belled me. Coz I'm tha illest breh you'll ever see. I can help you. But nothin comes for free… These are ruthless times, blud. Taxes an' tha standard of livin are goin up. The only thing's dat's goin down is you an' me."

"So, what's tha move den?"

"Some mup I need you to fix. I need him moved violently. The problem is when he gets moved, he's involvin tha Alphabet Boys. That's why I need someone on it from outta town."

"Why do you want him done up?"

"I caught two brehs runnin a credit card scam in our restaurant. We tortured dem till they said who sent dem. Dat scam got us blacklisted. We're payin bags to suits to prove our innocence. But I want him fixed. You do it for me, an' I'll give you a key for free. In advance!"

"Dat sounds like a five grand job—"

"I could pay a crackhead a score to do dis job, Lollipop. I ain't gonna insult you by offerin a crackhead's fee so don't insult me by overchargin… I know you're tired of pissin in the wind. Doesn't mean you should try pissin against my leg. All I need is for you is to ram dem cage fighter fists of yours into dat old cunt, and I'll set you off nicely. Say yes, and you'll get your key today. You got the punters, yeh? What's stoppin you now except yourself sayin no—"

"You know I can do it. But a key? Come on, rude boi. You can do better than dat—"

"I can't. Dat's tha ting, blud. Remember the bud we use to smoke back in the day? Tha shit I've got in Leyton's better. Leyton's a half-hour drive, son. You could smoke it all if you wanna, or you could be shottin in an hour. Your profit will be infinity percent coz you never put no peez in to start wiv. All you gotta do is nail dat fuckin cunt to the floor. It'll take you ten seconds!"

There was an expatiated awkwardness inside that Mercedes-Benz. Sanjay inserted some chalky pulverulent into his nostrils. The giddy nausea that followed abounded his eyes into two globose balls of anemic white. He gurned, then wobbled his jowls earnestly.

Of the sort of drugs he used, Lollipop knew not but he cared not. He was vehemently lost in thought. His insatiable rapacity redounded his reason. He decided not to haggle further.

He had conceived a ruse. He was, after all, coldly analytical. He'd simply sub-contract the hit to some parturient young gun, and be done. They were neophytes in Nepenthe who would obey him more readily than they would their own mothers: Lil Elliott, whose churlish disinhibitions was classic comedy for the older lads. There was his doltish brother Gus who possessed a pernicious temper. His navigability to such a task would be fluid; Shekaidy, Johnny's fourteen-year-old sinewy cousin, was all ears to Lollipop's didactic squalls about the *spontaneous grind*. He was the most impressionable of the lot. And then there was Havoc, who was often hazed across the head by Marius and Johnny because of his obstinacy towards his seniors. He'd make the ideal appurtenant if he hadn't such loose lips. Any of these doofus bastards could be blackballed into becoming avenging angels, whilst his energy be mothballed and individuated for the greater good. He'd be free to undertake a thrilling metamorphosis from simpleton to *soulja*, trading in rocks and grass. His sober realism dictated that he steer clear of Sanjay's tenuous problems.

"You have a deal, fam!" he said. "Gimme the food now and you'll get your wish before the week's out. Den we never talk bout dis again coz I don't wanna bait man. You'll end up feelin sorry for the breh... Trust me, rude boi!"

* * *

"Everyone in Leyton knows me," Sanjay said as he turned onto its protracted High Road, and then through a bewildering number of inlets and arteries. He seemed intent on driving home his éclat by hooting his horn at random pavement folk.

"Where's my DVDs?" he shouted at three Chinese men standing tautly outside a factory, dressed like extras from a Bruce Lee film. "My DVDs? I got my girl, popcorn but no DVDs?"

He shouted derisively at a schlump walking her Stafford. "Oi, sexy!... No, not you... The lamppost!"

He asserted that the surrounding streets of the Leyton Green Estate were bandit country at the best of times, and this was not the best of times. Only two days previous, a gun had been fired at a youth in Fletcher's Park. The police ticker tape sealed off the area as Forensics examined the fallen shells, and the cells of the fallen boy. He ventured among the somber tenements in his superfluous Mercedes under the watchful eye of bovine falconers and potty-mouthed cullies. These cards paid no taxes nor groomed no fields, yet they policed their postcodes like medieval landlords with pitchforks. *East* was where these striplings were more territorial; where they boasted that they invented the grime underground movement; where there were fast-food chicken shops at every fifty paces on the High Street; where there were vertical heathen drinking dens on every street corner but scarcely a nightclub in each of its five boroughs. Or so Sanjay said.

Along Capworth Street, a haggard woman slogged the road like a discarded caprine. Her graying skein shriveled and spiked as though it was barbed wire.

"Check out dat green woman from Planet Greengross," Sanjay said. "I had her workin for me since I was fifteen."

"I can't believe breh's would separate from their hard-earned peez to bang dat scatty granny—" Lollipop said.

"Not all brehs get regular sex. So I provide a service for those dat don't. Sex is like currency. Without it, you'd lose your metrosexual mind. Dat's why decent-looking brehs dat aren't gettin it would fuck dat!"

He parked outside an impoverished pebble-dashed house. Lollipop looked about him earnestly in case somebody sneaked up upon them. Sanjay held his iPhone and car keys in a sloppy bind. They walked across the manicured lawn towards the front door where a notice warned rather menacingly that *British Law Ends At This Door.*

"This is my brothel," Sanjay said. "Come in, an' be visually pampered."

Lollipop looked not entirely at ease among the sleaze. The scent of cheap perfume tickled his nostrils. Dust fizzed around the red light bulbs like a cluster of flies. The lulled log fire and counterfeit tiger-skinned rug was cast like the set of an eighties porn flick.

"You see Therese dere?" Sanjay said. He gestured at the swarthy stacked woman click clacking in patent stilettos. "She's my favorite. I get to deposit my DNA in her any time I want… She could feed a Third World country with those breasts."

Therese flicked her Worzel Gummidge curls, flashed a synthetic smile. "He likes to tease me," she said in a West African-transatlantic drawl. "Take no notice of him."

"What do you mean take no notice of me? You'd better take notice, bitch. I'm your fuckin master. I fuckin pay you. You work for me so you can feed your little bastard. If I don't pay you, he starves! Where's everyone else?"

"Keeley's finished with your uncle's friend… She's in the shower… He hit her hard on her face—"

"I don't wanna know Keeley's problems. And Clit-vana and Whoria?"

"Svetlana and Gloria are upstairs with David—"

"How much shit you got?"

"Huh?"

"How. Many. Bags. Of. Draw. Have. You. Got?"

"Draw? Oh! Four."

"Cool. And. How. Much. Money. You. Bitches. Made. For. Me. Today?"

"Today? I made two hundred. Gloria made a hundred and seventy, but altogether we've got seven hundred and thirty."

"Only seven fuckin hundred? Upstairs, Therese… Show me tha dough…"

Lollipop waited in the lounge where the radiator was lined with peephole knickers. He was giddy at the mere thought of making money. The prelude to *the hustle* was akin to a baby foal taking his first steps. The hour was fast approaching where he'd become a much-vaunted chimera stirring dust devils beneath his feet, an utilitarian conjurer of riches and bitches. He heard Sanjay strafe her with a niagara of racist slurs, confabulating the perverse reasons on why she must serve him. He cozied himself on the seat and flicked through the pornographic magazines on the coffee table. From the outside, a dull stick in a dark side suit peered through the window. Perhaps he had come for a degrading assignation!

"Come round, boss," Lollipop said, and gestured him to the front door.

Dull Stick retreated upon seeing him. He vanished down the street like an apparition that had strayed into a world it had no place in. Lollipop thought of pursuing him. He was curious as to whether the man had arrived by accident or whether he was intent on perversion. Perhaps he was a vicar, a judge, an MP, professions that shone with ecclesiastical virtue. His father had a theory on such so-called honorable gentlemen: they were conservatives by day and in public; liberals at night and in dark corners, climacterically occasioned by the female participant in labor ten months later. The system stunk of fatuous hypocrites like Dull Stick. A videophone recording of a supposed respected gentleman knocking on the door of a stew could have sufficed a bribe that could have enabled his hustle. Lollipop smiled as he conceptualized that idea, but the opportunity had long passed. He pulled his headphones over his ears and listened to Nero Sandz.

Upstairs, Therese was pinned face down upon a porous mattress as Sanjay forced himself into her anus. Her short sharp hiccups morphed into elongated volcanic gasps.

* * *

Sanjay drove along the A406, westbound. Lollipop squeezed a tousled bag in his palm.

"Jeez, I'm feelin for dat chick Therese—"

"Ya like her, yeah?"

"When I think I got it bad, she's got it worse—"

"If your heart bleeds like dat, you should go work for The Institute for Destitute Prostitutes."

"We're all waifs an' strays, but you gotta have a heart for the helpless—"

"Maaan, you're a contradiction. She cries an ocean and you wanna help her skin! Maybe you should gimme the food back!"

"In my world, true victims are guilty of nothin. Dey get kicked square in the plums daily. No one should tell dem how they should scream."

"True. But if you fuck up like she did, you suffer the consequences. Standard. And if dat makes man pissed, I couldn't give a shit."

Lollipop stuffed the draw in his pocket and said nothing.

"You're think I'm a cunt, don't ya?"

"Therese would say you're a cunt—"

"But she's more of a cunt than I could ever be. She leaves Africa on someone else's passport. She leaves her son behind wiv some relative. Her husband's shottin in Germany until he gets himself banged up. She works for my cousin as a cleaner till he caught her thieving hand in the till. He says he's callin old bill. She's like: 'Fuck no! I'm an illegal immigrant. I need the money. My son's gotta eat,' an' goes on and on like the world's unluckiest female. My cousin's a bad man, and he's like: 'Free up the narni and you go free.' He fucked it and brought me in. I'm like: 'I'll have dat,' and took her passport. I bone her in ways she don't let her husband. I feel no way... Now you? You'd probably 'low it, an' dat's why you're rollin cheap, blud. Some breh will owe you peez an' you'll 'low it coz his fuckin nan died last week."

"Joker!" Lollipop said. "You done know my rep already. I'm the most merciless of men—"

"But you're different wiv females?"

"Tha world's a hard place. People are hungry. They'll cross a thousand miles of water on a dinghy in search of a better day. What if Therese was your sister?"

"My sister won't do what Therese does. They're wired differently... You're obviously new on road. After a year, you'll be wired differently—"

"Stop the car... Stop the car, blud!" Lollipop could barely perceive his senses. "Dat's tha chick I chirpsed in Cricklewood last week... Dat's me... Why's dat prick harassin her?"

Sanjay slammed a foot upon the brake, provoking a melee of horn blowing from behind. Lollipop hurried from the vehicle and leapt after the phantasmal houri, whom he thought he'd never see again. She was quarreling with her moist boyfriend. The jangling of her haughty tenor snuffed his antiphonal cry. Amused strangers pointed as she pulled his hair and punched his cheeks whilst mocking him.

"Yo Bonita!" Lollipop said. "You in any trouble?"

The opposing pair paused to face him. He, a TOWIE clone with Hollywood white teeth and milquetoast idiosyncrasies, kindly asked that he mind his business. She, a brazen vamp with an orotund tone, waved a terrifying finger.

"I'm dumping dis pansy like you predicted!" she said.

Her diabolical affectation was in complete contrast to the diabolical scorn of last week. She was no longer gelid, though her fingers were when she touched his arm. He observed her sinuous body. Her skin was the color of a Caramac Bar. Her alluring posterior caught his deviating eye where it rested momentarily, then glissaded towards her buttercupped navel. And there was that seraphic aroma of peaches and pineapples.

The Clone argued for a second chance but she censured him cruelly, and Lollipop felt inclined to laugh callously into his face. Sanjay, having docked his Mercedes on a red line, moored himself against the Clone. He hoped for a fray so he could throw a fist therein.

"I could dash you in my boot, take you to a field and bring you back in an ashtray," he said. "And your family would never know what happened to ya!"

"What tha fuck?" said the Clone. His gait alluded that he was poised to flee, and flee fast. "How did it go from me an' my girl to me versus two guys? If you want her, you'll soon see what she's like... Don't think you've won, tough guy!"

"Bounce along, dickhead. Bounce along," she said as he trailed away at helter-skelter speed. "You're lucky I'm lettin you jog on. Dis could have ended badly for you, so count yourself fuckin lucky..."

Lollipop found her exorbitant fury fascinating. For sure, he could bridle her sultry wings. He'd readily be the cuspidor to which she could spew her contrarieties.

"You see, I told you you're gonna be mine," he said.

"Who says I belong to anyone?" she said with the hauteur of a diva.

"I belong to you—"

"You say the corniest things—"

"Don't most breh's tho?"

"Yes, they do. No wonder girls get stressed in dis fucked up rigmarole."

"So what, can I get your number?"

"I think she'll want *my* number, Lollipop!" Sanjay said. He sandwiched himself between her and him. "Look at her pengness! She's waaayyy above your station..."

Lollipop cawed to the heavens in dolor. He loathed such predatory joustings; he and his brethren cognizant of a pretty girl, and then proceeding to haggle over her as if they were traders on a Stock Exchange floor.

"Sanjay, what you doin? Dat's my ting—"

"She ain't your ting. She's fair game—"

"Sanjay, she's my ting. I was on it since last week—"

"She ain't *your ting*, fam. I ain't gonna fight over a chick, but she's hawwwt... I've given you a new life an' you can't give man a bly? You're gonna need new kneecaps wiv all dat beggin you've been doin lately... So 'low it, man. I've given you favor after favor after favor... Can anybody short of Jesus do more for his friends?"

"Err, excuse me?" she said. "I ain't interested in what you're offerin—"

"What do you mean... you're not interested?"

"Don't you speak English?"

"Wow! What you bein like dat for?"

"I have to be like dat. Obviously, you can't handle dat—"

"So you'd rather roll wiv my bruk friend than take a ride in my ninety grand whip?"

"Stop gassin nonsense, and stop tryin to diss your friend—"

"You don't believe I've got a ninety grand whip?"

"You're as useful as the log lady—"

"Lollipop knows I got bare gal; black, white, Asian, blackanese... I'm an equal opportunities employer..." He pulled Lollipop towards his bosom for a contrite hug. "... Hey, I'm lettin you have dis one... Don't fuck dis up... Look at your face! Jeez, the look on your face... You owe me, cuz. Again!"

He scampered back to his car, as if nothing happened.

"What the fuck?" she said. "Your friend's an excited breh. I was wishin he'd pack his trunk and fuck off—"

"He bullshits a lot. It ain't his whip. He lives off his dad's fame... Fuck him. Let's talk bout us—"

"I didn't know there was an *us*—"

"You're waaayyy too fruity for Droopy from Guadeloupe. Don't know why you peng chicks like to underplay your cards. You got *pretty chick wiv limp dick syndrome*—"

"I tore dat limp dick up a long time ago, hun. He weren't even my boyfriend. He was spendin for my benefit. He got some pity fucks, but I'm done fuckin wiv him!"

"I know dem ones. They chase you from PM to IM, DM to Viber, email to phone, door to door. The endz are full of thirsty brehs—"

"Brehs have to swim very hard to keep up wiv me—"

"If I give you my number, will you use it?"

"Give me a reason."

"I could think of several. We'd be a breeze, you and I."

"You're sayin dat coz I'd look good on your shoulder—"

"I'm sayin it coz I wanna be your dear friend—"

"You're sayin it coz you wanna get my knickers off!"

Lollipop was surprised by her breviloquence. "You're goin on raw!"

"I… break… shit… down—"

"I'd like to break you down—"

"I'll FaceTime you and we'll see."

"Can you be tamed, Bonita?" he asked as she recorded his number.

"My name's Sophia," she said after a long attentive stare that gored right through him. "It's not Bonita. And I'd be your future ex-wifey, if you ever fuck me bout!"

It had been a while since he had a girlfriend; Monica, a Filipino minx, of salmon pink cheeks and exquisite taupe calves. He was more of an awkward calf himself then. She was a demi-vierge, and an extremely opinionated one. Sexual wordplay was like brinkmanship. Consequently, her inveigling temperament exhausted him. So he embarked on a copulatory caper with another. When his infidelity was discovered, she promptly annihilated him in the college common room. Since then, he had avoided relationships in favor of those that gave up the vagina all too easily. Girls were an aesthetic feed rather than a requisite need. Sex was mostly perfunctory but often rushed. French kissing was an intense ingredient of dribbly saliva and masticating tongues. Fellatio was the ultimate aphrodisiac, save when the *ratchet* tried to kiss him afterwards. Who cared if she came or not, so long as *he* did. But that would matter to a houri like Sophia. *Bocat moves* would become a requisite feature.

After bidding him farewell, she walked the pavement as if it were a catwalk. Even Sanjay's repeated horn blowing failed to disrupt the cadence of her stride.

"Damn," Lollipop said. "If there's such a thing as being too chung, she'd be it."

"You got dem digits by some random alignment of the sucker stars," Sanjay said.

"Blud, don't ever cock-block me again. Fam don't do shit like—"

"Blud, I ain't a cock-blocker. If I did, it'd get fierce. But I must confess. She's fierce… But I ain't gonna lie… She looks porcelain-like… I've had dem fake types, all caked in make-up an' walkin bout wiv all dat silicone. You think you've got the most chung chick on tha planet but when she wakes up in the morning in the bed beside you without the make-up, she's lookin like E.T!"

"I'm better than I thought I was—"

"You're nearly as good as you think you are, Lollipop. But I don't rate you as much as you rate yourself."

Lollipop could care less about his opinions but he vowed to demonstrate his appreciation for the drugs and his opprobrium for the malice, when both botherations were primed for culling. So he reclined in his seat and listened in silence to Sanjay's hubristic claims of trysts with amply stacked lap-dancers at a certain gentleman's club.

4

...TO LIVE AND DIE IN NEPENTHE...

"SOMEBODY'S GLUED MY LACES together, daddy," Jardel said. Johnny Freelander concentrated his vehemence upon *Assassin's Creed*, sinking his incisors into his bottom lip.

"Daddy?"

"What?"

"Somebody's glued my laces—"

"Who's glued your laces?"

"The Boogie Man of course!"

"What you on about, son?"

"Grandma says the Boogie Man likes to play tricks on little boys and girls—"

"Your grandma's talkin doo-doo! The Boogie Man don't exist. You can't be believin all dem weird stories—"

"Oh, but he does exist. I've seen him! He's a scruffy old man and he drives a dirty old van wiv a very loud bell. And he goes round people's houses and picks up old furniture—"

"Dat ain't no Boogie Man. Dat's the Rag and Bone Man."

"Same difference, daddy. Could you do my shoelaces please?"

Johnny reluctantly halted his fun and helped Jardel with his shoelaces. His boy was a blessed joy, with dimpled cheeks and cookie dough skin. The milky lotion that his mother had apportioned onto his face and limbs after bathing him had rendered him an effulgent glow. His tiny finger crept towards his nose for a chary pick.

"Are we still goin football, daddy?"

"Yea, you're gonna see me score bare goals today. Your dad's gonna be runnin rings past bare man. Your dad's tha best footballer in tha endz—"

"Mommy says Uncle Stacey's tha best footballer—"

"Your mommy's a bean-head. And so is your Uncle Stacey!"

Ashleigh, eavesdropping momentarily from the outside, turned her head around the door and handed him his mobile. "Twang's on tha phone," she said before retreating.

"What's gud, Twang?"

"Yay! What's gud, bredrin?"

"So what, fam? You listened to my tune?"

"Yea, I heard your tune—"

"Did you like it?"

"Did I like it? You know what, blud? I don't wanna disrespect man but I'm callin you out, cuz. First and foremost cuz, how can you call yourself a rapper? You're nothin but a ringtone rapper, blud. You spit like Bart Simpson. Consider yourself lucky dat you ain't got his stupid voice—"

Johnny ushered Jardel brusquely from the room. "What you on, cuz? You've got my CD mistaken wiv somebody else's. I get bare ratings from bare man. I bootlegged 2,000 copies in South London last weekend—"

"I may get stoned, but I'm not stoned stupid. I *know* South London. No one's buyin your tune. It's competitive in dem endz. Bare MCs would have you... Lil Brazen Raisin from Peckham would mop the floor wiv your afro if he were to battle you. He won't need to dip your head in no bucket. Your perspiration would suffice—"

"Fam, you know what? Fair dos if you don't like the tune, but don't disrespect man like dat. I can hear your boys laughin in the background. Dat's why you're brave."

"Actually, the whole of London Town's listenin to dis, Johnny Freelander. You're bein merked on Bling Radio, fam. We've just played your tune and we had bare callers beggin man to turn you off... You're atonal, abysmal and fooking anal. Your CDs done frisbeed itself into the bin. You're blacklisted on Bling!"

The phone clicked in Johnny's ear. Drenched with self-pity, he busied himself by packing his football accoutrements into an old Nike sports bag. He could slay Twang without equivocation...

"I'm goin Stonebridge Market next Sunday," Ashleigh said, entering the room again. She had perse eyes that were fervid, and salmon pink lips that seldom smiled. "Lindsey knows this breh who's got a stall sellin kiddie clothes. I can get a discount for the kids coz she's a regular—"

"Where's my fuckin football boots?"

"I put them in tha closet—"

"Why did you put em there? Who told you to fuckin move my boots? Why you gotta move every fuckin thing I put down? I don't fuckin move your stuff... Don't fuckin move mine!"

Ashleigh mopped her brow soberly. He became a one-man whirlwind as he burrowed through the closet.

"Am I tha only one wiv a fuckin brain round 'ere? I tell you to do somethin simple an' you always fuck up. Either you're doin it on purpose to wind me up or you must be fuckin stupid."

He seized his size-elevens from the closet before slamming it with brute force. She lofted her hands as if she was under arrest.

"Please, you're embarrassin me... Lindsey's in the kitchen... Jesus, I'm sorry, Johnny... I won't do it again—"

"Dat's what you always say, Ashy... Dat's what you always fuckin say... Dis is your last fuckin warning."

He waddled towards the front door like a diapered toddler. Lindsey watched him leave.

"What, you can't even say hello?" she said, a crude smirk whipped across her freckled countenance.

He paid her no mind and slammed the front door behind him.

Ashleigh finally bared her teeth.

"Fuckin wotless bastard! You can't flap your chops when lil boys ring your phone dissin you coz everyone knows you're a brown nose, but you'd rather run your gums at your woman coz you think it makes you more of a man! Little arse lickin bitch!"

Her eyes were a tear short of a cry. Lindsey's ones lit up like moon dogs. "Why do you let him treat you like shit?"

"Mind your business, Lindsey—"

"You ain't mindin yours! That's why Johnny's constantly linkin ratchets and hoes—"

"I don't like arguin in front of my kids. Dat kind of environment messes their brains. More parents need to consider stuff like dat."

Lindsey followed her into the kitchen. Young Jardel trailed them from behind. "I'd be more concerned dat your man can't keep his dick in his pants, Ash—"

"Whateva Lindsey! Remember when you had armshouse wiv your man last week and the Fedz came by? Basically, people were givin you the same advice you're givin me coz he was playin you. An' den when I called you last night, you tell me you can't talk coz you're too busy ridin him—"

"Sean's my *dick in a glass case*," Lindsey said with a singsong inflection. "He's *never* cheated on me. I heard rumors, and things got out of hand when I confronted him. Some nosey prick called the police just to complicate the situation. But it's sorted now."

"And I bet sexin Sean's like a religious experience," Ashleigh said. "The joke was that you forgot to hang the phone up coz you were busy screamin: Oh God! Oh God! Oh God!"

Lindsey watched her hawkishly. "Well, I don't mind blasphemin my way into heaven..."

Caring and despairing for pesky Johnny was not easy, for he was the most incorrigible of men. Malice was his right, he had stubbornly declared, though Paradise was forever in his sights. His slalom path dictated that he make nonsensical avowals of *the thug* and drone the mendacious mantras of *the grind*. He was servile to fey superstitions.

His irascible aspersions were arbitrary. Ashleigh knew of his hussies, including the fifteen-year-old dumbbell beguiled into suckling his bellend, but felt bounded. She endured his put-downs whenever he spritzed miserably in his lair. She bore the occasional throttle, and Lindsey predicted that his fist was forthcoming if she didn't up and leave with the children. Her closest friend Shakira warned that her purblind credulity was shameful and weak. Her herbivorous mother cautioned that his cussed decline would hasten her downfall and so it had. At the tender age of twenty-one, Ashleigh Liebeschuetz was already staring at the ultimate abyss of the scrap yard, thanks to Johnny Freelander and his rainbow-chasing desideratums. The belief that she was more astucious than he consoled her. And whenever he was mollified from the colossal strains that befogged him, he became the virile Fudgesicle lunk she was first enamored with. She'd forgive him once more, and fall in love with him all over again.

"You're like a Stepford wife," Lindsey said. "I swear down. You should get rid of his arse. Pronto!"

"Stepford wife? I just want an easy life… I say sorry for things I haven't done… just to keep the peace… just coz I want an easy life. It's easier for me to do what he says den to be moaned at. I'm like his fuckin mother… When he pisses on tha toilet seat, I'm tha mug who's gotta clean it up coz he can't take a piss straight. An' if you can't take a piss straight, how can you do anythin else straight?"

She went out onto the balcony and sobbed quietly. Her asperity could no longer be dissimulated. A few prudent tears brought scant relief. She returned to the kitchen and poured herself a glass of water. She mumbled between sips.

"I think to myself, I don't wanna be alone… Then I'd say, you know what? I'd rather be alone coz it's much easier. You know, I just wanna be cuddled… I just wanna be touched… You know. I miss all dat… But he's always pissed… He wants me a certain way, and I just tag along… When I look in tha mirror, I don't even recognize me no more… When we argued in the beginning, I'd go toe-to-toe wiv him… Now I'm like: OK, Johnny… I'm sorry, Johnny… I won't do it again, Johnny... Please Johnny... Fuck me up the shitter coz I like it like dat Johnny..."

Lindsey collapsed nosily on the dining table and howled with laughter, much to Jardel's bewilderment.

"And he's so fuckin gobby," Ashleigh added gamely. "Now I don't bother wiv his foolishness. He's a complete waste of calcium, protein, water and crap... How does he remember the words to his shit lyrics when he can't remember where he puts his keys in the morning? What's more important? I'm jus sick of his kneel-before-Zod attitude."

"He's lower than a snake's belly in a bottomless pit," Lindsey said. "He thinks he's gonna make it on a Jay-Z tip. Dat's his deluded view from the bunker. But dat ain't ever gonna happen—"

"Johnny would kill you if he heard you talk like dat—"

"Like he's killin you softly coz it ain't happenin for him?"

She caught Ashleigh circumducting her pretty eyes. She changed the subject.

"You do know dat Eliza's run of wiv Gregory?"

"I'm not surprised. I always knew he liked Eliza coz of tha way he looked at her, even when Nat's about."

"When a breh flirts wiv his wifey's bishes, dat means in his skank, dutty brain, he's lookin to fuck one of those bishes. I swear down, Eliza and Gregory must have been fuckin for the last three months..."

Perhaps even longer than that, Ashleigh told herself. Perchance, she had seen them together in Westfield's Stratford buying lingerie just before Christmas. Gregory had said he preferred the black laced embroidery that resembled a spider's web. Eliza said she'd buy both the black and the red. She'd model them both so that he could choose which he really liked. But when she confided her suspicions to Johnny, he told her to mind her business.

"Yesterday," Lindsey said. "Tanya came in from work and... she caught Gregory tossin her salad—"

"You're fuckin kiddin me!"

"I swear down! He was buried between Eliza's legs like a beaver—"

"I'm surprised Tanya didn't pass out!"

"Tanya done her fuckin nut. She was like: 'Get tha fuck outta my yard. I'm gonna get you merked, Gregory. You're fuckin dead!' Eliza's like: 'Yeah yeah, whateva! We were gonna tell you lot we were together anyway.' Gregory was shook. He never said a word. But Eliza was sayin dat Nat weren't looking after Gregory's needs anyways and dat's why he came to her. Tanya slapped her and Lil Elliott an' Shekaidy had to pull em apart. There was such a palaver! The Fedz came, and dey helped em leave. Tanya wanted to keep dem prisoner till Nat arrived. Dey were lucky. By the time Nat reached, they'd left. Nat's been phonin an' textin but no one's botherin to answer their phones!"

"Jeez! I've heard of daredevils but dis is ridiculous. I'm screwin for Nat. Dat's why family these days means fuck all. Your own family can fuck you up, literally as well. Do you know where they're stayin?"

"At my yard!"

"You're fuckin kiddin me!"

"They came by last night wiv bare black bags. I couldn't really say no, could I? Eliza's been a good friend from way back when. I put Bradley, Ladaiya and Simeon in one room, me and Sean in our room, and they're squeezed in the boys' room—"

"Boy, I wouldn't wanna be queuing for tha toilet in your yard. Waiting time for a piss must be forty minutes!"

"I'm screwin for Tanya though! Imagine her comin home findin her daughter's man fiddlin her next daughter? Dat's not a good look!"

Ashleigh narrowed her eyes thoughtfully. "I'm screwin for Nat! Girl must feel like shit. That's fuckin nasty! Why take someone else's man? Your sister's man, of all people? I don't blame Gregory. He's a fucking man, and a man would fuck a mannequin if it had a hole an' double D tits! But like I said, peeps these days ain't got no morals. Sometimes, I think people like tha piss taken out of dem coz they jus sit there and take it!"

"You're sayin dat bout Natalie," Lindsey said. "But you could so easily be sayin dat bout yourself."

She reclined comfortably in her seat, soothing every corpuscle, flexing every sinew. Why spare the meek malingerer from the truth?

"Anyway, what do I know?" she added. "I've never had dat experience. I'm a queen. I don't know what it's like to be cheated on. Guess if you're happy wiv dat kinda treatment, it's all gravy!"

Ashleigh was not heedless on how insidious Lindsey could be. Such mind-shackled musings were commonplace in the cerebral cortex of her female coterie. Males made better company.

* * *

For most of the young denizens on the Nepenthe Park Estate, Miracles FC and El-Ninio was the biggest soccer game of the summer. Miracles, managed by Stacey's father Fernando, were subscribed to by the natives. El-Ninio, a team of ASBO laden delinquents, was run by local bookshop owner Tafari, a Nyabinghi Rastafarian of delicate build with graying locks, a monocled eye and a Taliban beard. Every day he assumed the same sedentary position by the entrance of his bookshop. Lollipop tried sneaking past him after discreetly selling skunk to a couple of pre-teens in an adjacent alley. Nevertheless, Tafari's owlish oculars spotted him emerging from his foxhole.

"Maarnin Trevor!"

"What's poppin, king? You and your boys aren't gonna be ready dis time! You're due a good hidin from tha last time you beat us—"

Tafari harrumphed as he shook his old head. "Mi waan mek yuh know sum'ting? Why yuh waan chat too much bout how brilliant yuh is, an' den all mi see yuh do pon di football field is slide an' huff an' puff coz yuh can't catch di football?"

Lollipop vividly recalled hanging onto the coattails of an El-Ninio winger appropriately nicknamed Ronaldo, who left him for dead with every deft touch. Tafari had said he had *nuh meat an' potatoes* then.

The football game, in truth, was of minor importance to him. Scrawny pound notes from happy punters brought salient rewards.

He lived and earned by the callings of his mobile. Punters were forever poised with their illicit orders. He was forever on-call to deliver, wherever that may be.

To the suburban roads of West Drayton he would carry his toxins, scampering across the busy lanes of the A40 at the behest of Brenda, a Panglossian lone parent who sorely needed heavy doses to soothe her surly strife. Or to Fitzroy, a recovering smack head who had relapsed, and was heading speedily on a dual carriageway to Tartarus.

By night, he frequented the pathways of Camden. Hoveled by narrow street markets, opaque fortune-telling houses and satiated wine-bars, he mingled among vagrant dealers and peddled the killing produce. Plain-clothed police officers, like crocodiles hiding in still reeds, blended among their anemic prey. Things occasionally went full circle in these parts. More often than not, the trader apprehended the day before was back on the streets selling the day after.

Bushey was another secret haunt for the vexed, enterprising youth. Four hard-wired customers purchased and puffed anonymously within its country walls. The first, a scrofulous stockbroker headhunted by the city's finest, acquired cocaine resin in abundance whenever he hosted vulgarian parties for his vajazzled floozies and horndogged homies. The next two were a pair of Middle Englanders, painfully liberal folk, who happily smoked reefer as if they were inhaling the aroma from a cup of Earl Grey. They spoke to him of their opposition to all wars and their hope for the unanimity of all races. From him, they purchased three long finger-thick lumps of cannabis wrapped in cling film every week for their personal consumption. The final other was an achromatized hip-hop zealot who imitated the life and times of Eminem as his *Sunnah*.

"Your draw's top shelf," was his frequent exclamation whenever Lollipop delivered his super strength skunk, its seeds and leaves kneaded and apportioned to his acerbic tastes. He'd pound his fist against his chest repeatedly like a wannabe Tarzan, his martyr's glare apparent. "Time I get my Jobseekers, I'm bellin your mobs to get my food, blud... You gotta watch out for all tha haterz in dis concrete Babylon!"

To the west of the Brent River lay the metropolitan quarter of Ealing, its terse taverns and decorative duplexes, one of which was the abode of the bloviating dexterous belle Tayo. She spoke with a deluxe gabble that had tinctures of Lagos but spindrifts of Manhattan. Her pooterish manner fellated him. She couldn't fathom the desultory beast that was her incandescent self, and recognized only the worst in humankind. She hosted regular soirees for her ungelded cohorts of sensuous boys and precocious girls; all nebulous social climbers, all from whom she sought favor.

"I'm seeing someone who plays for Arsenal," she told him on his last courier run. A glass of Cristal Methuselah spilled churlishly in her grip. "But I'm not telling you who he is, in case you tip the media!"

He was careful not to prick her nebulous bubble as she nestled in her eyrie, wearing a black halter neck dress and gladiator boots. With six hundred pounds worth of Indo-European excrescence binded to her own inky strands, she had money to burn. So he continued trading those specious commodities he could purposefully justify, into quarters of opprobrium, whether affluent or deprived. His prestige among his peers was quantitatively enhanced. No longer was he greeted with golem sneers. He shied away from magniloquent posturing, so as not to incite dubiosity. Occasionally, he received ogles of envy from the hustler-shy refuseniks killing time, but that came with the territory.

He headed for Stacey's home, to meander his mind. Stacey's room was decked with pictures of hip-hop bunnies bequeathed with copious charms. DVDs of ruminative classics like *The Elephant Man* and *Donnie Darko* were stacked shoulder high. The Unicorn Dartboard of old, on which they once did battle, remained pegged against a wardrobe. They hadn't played darts together since Year 10.

"I bring wiv me an offerin of sinsemilla," Lollipop said. "You got some rizla, old chap?"

"I don't normally smoke tha highest before a game," Stacey said. "But I'll make an exception today."

Lollipop mumbled with schoolboy relish as he prepared the resin. Upon completing the joint, he lit it. He sucked two asperous pulls from it, reveled in its tang, and presented it to Stacey.

"It's dis shit what fucks you up!" Stacey said. "You can have it in moderation but you can't be excessive like Ratty otherwise you'll 'ave red eyes like him. What's happened wiv your case?"

"Got found guilty innit; £800 fine, 120 hour community service. I had to write a letter sayin sorry to dat salami bean-head. I done paid the fine already. You should've seen their faces when I said: 'Fuck the installments. Dere's your peez. Now fuck off—"

"Johnny managed to buss case over his South London beef wiv a shank involved and you can't wriggle out of some minor ting—"

"Johnny hyped his involvement. Dat's why dey ain't pressin charges. If it happened as he said it happened, he'd be on remand till his trial date."

He plucked the joint from Stacey's paw. He pursed his empurpled lips to take a drag.

"Where's my cut from those iPods you flogged?"

"I ain't got no peez for you, blud—"

"Blud! You sold all dem iPods, an' you ain't bringin me in?"

"Who tol' you I sold em?"

"I know you gave one to Shakira coz I've seen her wiv one. Where are tha other three?"

"Nevermind, Lollz—"

"The world's smallest violin gets played for tha hustla. Skeen! Dat's how man stay!!! Iiiight den! I bring man in on some draw an' he's goin all craven wiv his iPods... You keep dem iPods... You wanna know how much peez I'm makin? I don't think you really wanna know otherwise you'd be killin it yourself!"

"I never worry bout peez on a Sunday. Ballers like me need to get their game face on... By the way, my dad ain't ready to hear your late excuses anymore. He reckons you'd be late for your own funeral. You'd better make sure you're on time otherwise he'll kick your ras out of tha team—"

"Is that how Fernando Brookes is goin on? I've been playin in his team since I was twelve an' he wants to kick me out coz I missed three games. Unless he's signed Messi, den dat decision doesn't make sense."

"He doesn't need to sign Messi to make a point on you—"

"Well, look at his team den! You got Gregory on the wing who couldn't cross a lottery ticket. You got Mark who never tracks back. Two-twos yea, you got skills, but you're greedy. Marius ain't got no pace. Johnny wants the No. 9 shirt but never scores. An' then you got Ratty goin on like Corporal Jones—"

"And what bout you and all dat *release me* shit? *Hit the baby* and *mind the gap?* You crack me up f'real—"

"Dat's what you call passion... You need to learn bout passion. It's like Michael Jackson and *Heehee*. He brings out *Heehee* and *Shamone* without realizin coz he's got passion for music. A baller likes me needs release. You gimme the ball, I'm spiritually released..."

Stacey's gaze became loaded as he listened to Lollipop's preamble. The hairs on his arm crawled as if they were black ants trotting eerily over his flesh. Such was the tyrannical melancholy of the joint; its venial infliction was an ode to the alleviation of the moment. He rubbed his arm to stem the tickly sensation.

"Dat's some good skunk you got there," he said.

"I should have charged you for the pleasure—"

"You're not tha only postman who delivers on a Sunday, Lollz. Damn you delivered, but when will you bring man in on your riches?"

"You'd be like a goldfish in a tank of piranhas. I'll bring you in, even tho you won't put a coin in my meter... See, I don't carry no grudge. If you get tha grind on ruthlessly an' focus on gettin dat paper, you'll be all right dis summer. It ain't bad but circumstances are, so you gotta get tha grind on dis year. I'm serious, cuz!"

* * *

Stacey was still considering Lollipop's offer long after their conversation. Working London's West End as a bartender was a mere subsidiary towards his lifestyle. Mom's purse and dad's wallet previously topped the cost of a pair of trainers, but they loathed to give him money whilst he loafed around. They expected him to go to university, but he had swarmed with the college IT-crowd and loitered the common room. The barman at the strepitous *Grimy Bar* saw more of him than his lecturer. He played pool, drank beer and embarked on all the hormone shanghaies of youth. He pursued pert-bottomed girls with synthetic frowns. He raced mopeds on the grassy plains of Fryent Country Park. Assignments were left to snatched moments before bedtime, a night or two before deadline day.

His final grades reflected his lackluster efforts. His parents admonished the failings of his anti-pedagogical college. They claimed it cultivated a hedonistic lifestyle for laggards and stragglers in its common rooms and classrooms. They bemoaned him spending vapid hours in his bedroom listening to Soulja Boy and *Turn My Swag On*, Bruno Mars and *The Lazy Song*. They feared he might be drawn to a life of mediocrity, and act as a varlet for cullions like Lollipop and Johnny, if he was not doing so already. Stacey insisted that he would stay clear of Lollipop's bezonian ways and that he was not unmindful of Johnny's scabrous schemes. His exam results were discommodious but not irremediably so. He promised to work harder. His father was satisfied with that answer. In his youth, he had been afflicted with senioritis, preferring to partake in weekend shindigs and kept company with improvident fools. However, his mother was far from appeased. She did not raise a *waste man*, she told him bluntly, flapping her arms like a pelican.

So he became a bartender to cease her wailings. But the bathos of work was like mothballed purgatory. He believed that a temporary diversion onto some maniacal street hustle would keep him up to speed with the pincer movements of Blaze and Lollipop. This hectic temptation was borne out of the sickly relativism that decreed that the base commerce of the street was more honorable than the unhatched offerings of a nine to five. He felt his lack of ambition was costing him dear. His futility lay pared for all to see. The morning dew had subsided. And so had his options.

He cantered across the pitch to retrieve a football. Ashleigh slipped over to his shoulder. She spoke with a breathy purr.

"So I hear you're wiv Lydia now?"

"Boy, news travels fast—"

"You could do so much better, bubz. Truss me; tha girl ain't your type."

"We'll see how it goes, innit."

"You know how far back you and I go? Back in the day, we were tight. I'd like to think we're still tight."

Her luscious face was encumbered by a stymied frown. She pricked the wet soil with her heel repeatedly. She wished to expand her prejudices further, though thankfully for Stacey, divine intercession came through a decrepit van juddering painfully across the park lawn towards them. Its brakes screeched like a swooping raptor. She raised her eyebrows towards heaven.

"Who tha fuck is dat?"

"El-Ninio!"

"East London boys, innit. They've gotta be, coming across town in a van like dat—"

Her palpable bottom strained against her hip-hugger jeans. He stole a glimpse. She almost caught his gaze.

"Does... does Johnny still have beer in his cornflakes?"

"You know Johnny. He loves his music and kids!"

"And he loves you too, right?"

"More than Lydia will ever love you, bubz. She's onto you coz she's new. It's a status thing for her to say dat she's wiv you, particularly when everyone loves you and she just loves herself."

Stacey nodded tentatively. Ashleigh Liebeschuetz, that redoubtable expert on ectopic love!

El-Ninio's infantry emerged on the grass in exultant mode. Leading them was a paunch teenager wearing a *Security* baseball cap and a stout woman with cerulean painted fingernails. They threw truculent glances at Stacey and Ashleigh.

"W-what's gud, Stacey?" said the youth with the cap. His voice jittered like a scratched CD. "Y-y-you've got a f-f-f-full team dis time?"

"Yea, man. We're ready for you!" Stacey said.

The team's laughter ensembled like the adjacent thunder.

"No sad stories dis time bout you ain't got enuff players!" hollered somebody from among them.

"El-Ninio's gonna get merked today," Stacey said. "So boy, say your last words!"

In the changing rooms, his father Fernando Brookes stared down at his ever-shrinking list of names.

"Anyone knows where Ross is?" he said to nobody in particular.

"He got shift last night, drivin wiv no tax an' insurance," Marius said.

"And where did you hear that?"

"I checked for him dis morning. His lil brother told me."

"And Gregory?"

"Gregory got a lil domestic goin on," said Blaze, his glaucous eyes beaming.

"Wifey's got a contract out for him, wanted dead or alive," Marius said.

"I heard he climbed into the wrong bed in the middle of the night," Ratty said. "When he tasted what was in dat bed, he found it difficult to climb back into baby mama's bed—"

The door slapped opened. Everyone raised their fickle heads to watch Gregory Foster. He shuffled in with the gait of a bowlegged duck.

"What was in my baby mama's bed, rat features?"

"I know you're no longer in it—"

"You're always inner inner man business. It's my family business—"

"No one cares about your dysfunctional family business—"

"*My* dysfunctional family? I don't wanna fuck you up, Ratty. Not today of all days—"

"Hey, you guys – cool your boots!" Lollipop said. "Seckle... Continue dis ting after the game—"

"Fuck me up?" Ratty said. "Dat's what Tanya's lookin to do to you, rude boi—"

"That's enough!" Fernando said. "If you want to talk about your troubles in private, I'm all ears. But right now, I need a team that's focused on winning the game."

"I don't think Gregory's focused for tha game—"

"Why's dis rat-eyed prick watchin me? Why's dis eediat lookin to start wiv me today?"

"Anymore of this and neither you or Ratty will feature," Fernando said. "I don't care if it leaves us short on numbers. I ain't gonna have two grown men arguing over stupidness..."

Gregory snucked to a corner in the changing room. Ratty plunked his bony backside on the bench.

"... The team basically picks itself," Fernando said. "We've only got eleven players and five absentees. I can't say I'm surprised... You can tell those five persistent absentees not to bother turning up again. The ref wants all subs before the game..." Cue groans of disapproval all round. "... Everyone makes sure you've got your five squid. No subs means you don't play!"

Johnny turned to Lollipop with the taciturnity of a coy fellow. "You got a fiver to lend me?"

"You're always askin for money, maaan!"

"You got it or not?"

"Yea, I got it. But Johnny, if you ain't ever got no peez, how do you feed your kids?"

"Did you hear Twang on Bling Radio today?"

"No. Why?"

"Nevermind."

He took the coins from Lollipop's outstretched palm and slipped away towards Fernando.

"I've got sooo much hate for dat dickhead Ratty," Gregory said. He took Johnny's place next to Lollipop, ravissant and vex. "I could shank dat breh an' feel no way—"

Lollipop raised a quizzical eyebrow. "You heard Fernando! 'Low the arms house. Focus on the game—"

"Fuck the game! Dis ain't gonna get me trials wiv Chelsea. Ratty don't wanna see my anger!"

"Anger's good, cuz. When peeps see anger... real anger, they step out of your way coz no one wants to get hurt. Anger gives you tha edge. You gotta use dat anger Gregory, or dat anger will use you."

* * *

The referee was a mousy fellow with square hands and a Borat moustache. He was haltingly polite, smiling at every player who neared him from ten paces. Tafari stood by the touchline, stroking his great beard like an ancient philosopher contemplating the cosmos. Fernando shook his hand warmly and they wished each other good luck. Substitutes beside him stretched their limbs to their physical apex. Gregory held two thumbs-up at Eliza who spectated near the touchline with Ashleigh, Lindsey and Shakira. Young Jardel bounced on his neatly laced trainers and cheered on his father.

Finally, the referee blew his whistle. Stacey, head down and shoulders hunched, raced for the ball. The ball fell to El-Ninio's Corey Knight, a human obelisk with colossal thighs. He punted the ball up field without hindrance. Tafari applauded his decision.

"Lick tha barl 'ard when it drop to yuh so! Nuh hesitation..."

From the goal kick, the game resumed. Stacey charged down the wing, glided past the full back and looped the ball into the penalty area. Marius hitched a ride on the defender's back and nodded his effort over the stanchion.

"Reeeef!" said the aggrieved defender from under Marius.

The referee smiled bashfully and signaled a goal kick.

"Dat was a blatant penalty!" Lindsey said. "Dat breh should be playin rugby!"

"I like the way Marius plays rough," Shakira said. "But when he picks up the player from the floor after foulin him, he's goes on innocent!"

"I didn't see no penalty," Eliza said.

"Of course, you didn't," Lindsey said. "You got your eyes on Gregory on the wing!"

Eliza guffawed like a duck. "Yea... Everyone's gonna be runnin joke bout me an' Gregory. I don't mind tha celebrity status tho. We really appreciate you puttin us up, Lindsey—"

"You guys can stay for as long as you like—"

"Thanks, but we gotta keep movin. We gotta view some dope flat in Brixton later. I'll leave Nepenthe in a handcart wiv my glad rags, but I'll be back in a Balboni wearin Loubs, believe me!"

"What bout Ealing?" Ashleigh said. "Cosmopolitan. Big arse houses, big arse gardens—"

"Anywhere, except here. I don't want to live and die in Nepenthe an' end up like my mom, freein her narni to every man dat walks. Ever since I was swimming in my daddy's scrotum, I knew I was gonna be big in dis lifetime. My mom ain't worth a sack of manure—"

"You're among friends, girl," Shakira said. "Just say what you really feel bout your mother!"

"If you had a mom like mine, you'd be embarrassed—"

"I know what you're sayin," Ashleigh said. "Don't wanna be rude but I'd shudder if Tanya was my mom. You're nothin like your mom—"

"Natalie takes after my mom," Eliza said. "I take after tha milkman!"

"*Release me...*" shouted Lollipop from the pitch. He improvised a buccaneering run through the opposition's defensive lines. "*... Release me*, Johnny... *Release...*"

Johnny complimented his sprint by spinning the ball towards him. However, Big Corey interjected with a spirited tackle.

Lydia, standing alone by the touchline, became prey to the cursory chuntering from Eliza's girls.

"Lydia's goes on stoosh," Ashleigh said. "I don't think she even frees up for Stacey!"

"Stacey's keepin her quiet—" Shakira said.

"Can you blame him?" Eliza said. "If I was goin out wiv dat, I'd keep it quiet too! When she gets her degree, she won't be takin his plums in her mouth anyway... I wanna know who Lollipop's fuckin."

"Lollipop's never had a wifey," Ashleigh said. "He pipes skets like Joanne on a regular—"

"She's had a lot of cock, dat one," Lindsey said. "No breh would wifey dat with her CV. Maybe a Save-a-ho would. Bare man have drilled dat to the point of no return!"

"Does Sean ever go around her yard?" Shakira said.

"He checks for his nephew," Lindsey said.

"So he's not getting a piece den?"

"Sean ain't gonna fuck his dead brother's woman—"

"An erect penis has no conscience, Lindsey. Breh's gonna peck an' nut on a plate—"

"You think Lollipop's buff den?" Eliza inquired to sundry.

"He's an idiot," Ashleigh said. "He's always got somethin to say bout nothin. He's always lecturin Johnny bout getting rich—"

"And he can't play football," Shakira said. "Look at him! He's only deadly when he's offside... And I do know what offside is before anyone starts!"

Eliza fiddled playfully with her chandelier-shaped earrings. "I fucked Lollipop once when we were in Year 11. We had tha same maths lesson so we'd bunked off together. We bought some bud from Ratty. Then we went to my bedroom and smoked till we were blazed. Then we tried to out-fuck each other. When he buss, there was bare gooey shit everywhere. I swear down: all dat baby batter an' no babies... Wowzers, boy! We smoked more dinkie dow an' fell asleep. My mom walked in on us, starkus bollockus in bed. She was screwin dat we fucked. She wouldn't speak to me for weeks. But dat was a bom feelin, truss!"

"You're lucky he didn't blow you up!" Ashleigh said.

"I was late dat month. I remember bein shit scared but I danced when I was on the rag. He keeps askin for a grind. I keep tellin him to fuck off!"

"Girl, you've got a thing for thugz!" Shakira said.

"Which girl hasn't?" Eliza said.

Loud cheers reverberated from the pitch. El-Ninio had scored. The corking Ronaldo had boogied around several outstretched shins and rolled the ball past the diving Sean.

"Dat was supposed to be your man," Ratty said to Gregory as he jogged past him. "You see, you're not focused... You're not wiv it today, brah! Your mind's elsewhere—"

"I'm real close to bussin your lil head open," Gregory seethed from under his breath. "Carry on pushin me, you dumb fuck! Carry on!!!"

Miracles restarted the game purposefully. Several quick passes resulted with Marius blasting the ball from twenty yards, thirty yards over the stanchion.

Stacey's hands were upon his scalp in despair. "I was on. You could've passed it over, fam!"

Marius brushed his protestations with an apologetic hand. He jogged to the halfway line breathing heavily.

"Ratty ain't yet mastered the telescopic reach of his legs," Shakira said. "He controls the ball like a baby giraffe—"

Ashleigh pouted her lips suggestively "You know what, yeah? I don't know tha first thing bout football. I know all tha buff players tho. When Johnny's watchin *Match of The Day* an' tells me to come an' watch Arsenal, I'm watchin their arses an' thinkin: hmmm. I wouldn't mind followin dem into the showers afterwards to scrub a few backs!"

"*Release me Stacey...*" Lollipop said. Stacey contemned his cry and rolled the ball to the over-lapping Marius. Marius squared a pass to Gregory.

"Hit the baby!" Lollipop said, jousting for space with a willful center back.

Gregory looked up with his beady eyes. He swung his boot towards the ball, but caught the crisp Harlesden air. The ball treacled harmlessly over the line for a goal kick to El-Ninio.

Ratty grumbled like a wild boar with a tummy ache. "Nobody pass the ball to dat mup…. Dat breh ain't wiv it today… Nobody pass to him… He's done…"

Eliza frowned at his impertinence. "He should be careful Gregory doesn't buss his arse—"

"He would've done it already, don't ya think?" Ashleigh said.

"Gregory doesn't wile out," Eliza said. "He's calculated. Dat's what makes him dangerous—"

"*Release me*," Lollipop insisted. Stacey aimed a pass before Corey impeded him to the ground. The ball sailed over Lollipop's head and was collected into the grateful arms of the opposing goalkeeper.

"What the fuck was dat?" Lollipop said. "I couldn't have got dat even if I was on a motorbike!"

Ratty applauded him. "Keep makin dem runs, Lollipop. More of tha same, son. More of the same…"

Ronaldo was the fount of El-Ninio's alchemy. The earth folded beneath him, and Miracles' defenders were recumbent before his swashbuckling skills and John Travolta turns. Ratty extended his tripod-like leg and plucked the ball from him. The ball was retrieved by Corey. After much incremental confluences, Ronaldo was once again the recipient of the ball. When he tried one-step-over too many, Blaze unceremoniously scythed him into the dust. Penalty!

"Leaky defense, Fernandooo!" Tafari said without a hint of reproach. "Yuh 'ave to close dat drippin tap before di flood set in!"

Gregory charged towards the referee, uttering acid expletives. The referee held his poise like a ballerina and red-carded Blaze for his infraction. Gregory was cautioned yellow for his foul mouth. Ronaldo dispatched from the penalty spot. 2–0! There was near sexual hysteria from the lady of the cerulean fingernails. Ratty chided Sean over his paltry Superman dive.

Fernando, masticating tiresomely by the touchline, exhorted encouragement. Johnny careened forward fancifully. Three El-Ninio players chastened him back. He needlessly conceded a corner. From the resulting kick, Big Corey soared over four defenders and steered the ball with his forehead into the net. 3–0.

"Dis game's done," Shakira said. "Miracles must feel like its Kick in the Nuts Day today. They're so fuckin useless. We may as well go Burger King an' get some food. I'm not goin to stand here wiv my *Miracles play good stuff* goggles on. We'd be gone till November an' they still wouldn't have scored."

5

THE FALL AND DOWNFALL
OF GREGORY FOSTER

T HE RADIO PLAYED YET another sad love song for the surly
mourners huddled around the kitchen table. Natalie Walker
tucked her chin into her billowing bosom. Her kohl-eyed lashes
blinked with unappeasable sorrow. Her mother Tanya, dressed in
a no-frills tracksuit, flickered about like a sparkler but exhibited
a cold caprice. Her graveling clamor had been coarsened by her
over-indulgence for John Player Specials.

"In a parallel Solar System, fookin Gregory would have been
cooked and eaten by us bishes," she said.

She almost collided with the flu-ridden Lil Elliott who clutched
his muggy brow.

"Oh for fuck's sake, Elliott—"

"My head's bout to explode, mom—"

"I wish it fookin would!"

Lil Elliott sniffed pitifully. The gathered assemblage quietly prayed
that he vanish elsewhere so that Tanya could return to the annals of
the unchaste. Ladelle Yates, surgically enhanced on top and adorned
in a paisley dress, cracked her fingers with glee. She had already
fueled the toxic air by recommending phlegm-filled discursives as
sufficient punishment for the comely wench and her pond life lecher.
Rebecca Lares was indecorous and giggly in a bottom skimming skirt.

Her coiled tresses were bedraggled into an untidy chignon. They were both fictive kins of the Walkers, and they belted a monolithic medley of unfettered violence that further confounded Natalie.

"Dat's why you can't do *nothin good* for people," Tanya said. "Coz they always turn around an' do shit when you least expect it. I should've dealt with her there and then when I found her sticking her nasty tongue down his filthy gob!"

Natalie cast an imploring gaze at everyone in turn. Her shameless self-pity impressed no one, lest of all her mother. The scene was primed for bloody retribution, yet she showed little enthusiasm for slaughter. At first, she had sobbed bitterly for hours. Then she had phoned Gregory and begged him to extirpate his desire for Eliza otherwise she'd change their daughter's surname from his to hers. When that proved redundant, she reproached herself for being ugly and cried some more. To the assembled Amazons, such slobbering incontinence was intolerable.

Tanya marched towards the kettle and switched it to boil. "Chin up, lass. Unfortunately, shit happens. I just hope they get crabs."

The kettle seethed in the corner.

"Can you stop talkin like dat please?" Natalie said.

"Don't tell me you're defending him? All he does is sit on his bollocks all day——"

"No mom! You're takin tha piss right now. You really need to shut your gob——"

"It's not me you should be pissed with. I'm on your side, Nat——"

"She's right, Nat," Ladelle said. "Are we expected to kiss Gregory's arse till the end of time?"

Rebecca's molybdenum body clopped towards a seat like a decrepit parkhorse. "Fair dos yea," she said in a husky timbre. "Eliza was safe way back when. But she's turned into a proper waste gash dat's got a serious craving for cock. The bitch needs to seriously close her stankin legs before it's too late!"

"If my man cheated on me for dat ugly sket, believe, they'd be arms house," Ladelle said. "I'd fuck her up and slay the bastard in a second. I've told my boyfriend already: he ain't got no reason to speak to dat two bob tramp on road. Anyways, tha next time I see her, she's gonna get banged up coz boi, she's out of order!"

In the far corner of the room, a near-dead varmint bestirred. "What, what? Bang Gregory up? Are you mad? D'you know who Gregory is? Jokers!"

"Gregory's over the hill," Tanya said. "He's not on the paper chase no more coz he's been caught slippin so many times—"

"Aiiight den. Go on den, an' think you're Wonder Women—"

"So if some bad man shagged your girlfriend, it's all gravy, yeah? You think if Gus was sittin in your seat, he'd be talkin like you? You're such a clown—"

"Gregory would fuck yous up in a second. Y'all wylin like you're gonna do him somethin—"

"Shut up you dickhead! Eliza's a sket, end of. Natalie needs to kill tha shady bitch, never mind sending her nasty WhatsApp texts. And I doubt if Gregory could fuck anyone up!"

"It's all very well cussin Gregory, but he ain't sayin no to free narni," Rebecca said. "And lastly, whose side are you on, Elliott?"

"Who me?" Lil Elliott said. "I'm neutral."

Natalie watched Tanya serve tea to those present, save the vitiating traitor. "Nobody has to not like them just because I don't," she insisted.

"Yea, but he's your brother," Tanya said. "The least he could do is to give you moral support."

"Moral support ain't gonna change nuttin!" Lil Elliott said. "Yeah, Eliza maybe a ho, but she likes sex just like everybody else. But Gregory's a badass G. He's been tappin dat arse under everyone's noses and no one suspected nuttin. Dat's nuts!"

Natalie wept again. Rebecca and Ladelle winced at her keening.

"We're the unluckiest family ever!" Tanya said. "All these things happenin without rhyme or reason... I've got to go court tomorrow for Gus' mystery. Who knows what possessed Gus to go all the way to Walthamstow at four in the mornin to beat up someone he's never met? He won't say… And I don't know why Natalie can't go and find Eliza and—"

"Look mom! I've told ya. I'll deal wiv her—"

"We shouldn't have to be dealin wiv freak goings-on like this—"

"Maybe there's a lil bit of voodoo in our family—" Lil Elliott said.

"The only stinkin bit of voodoo dat's fucked everythin is Gregory," Rebecca said.

Tanya looked monotonously angry. "I've got that mandrake plant for voodoo. So it's not dat… We're just unlucky…. Gus is going down for sure. Elliott will be in jail soon. Terrell doesn't wanna fuckin know, conveniently for him of course… I'll give Gregory his due though. He's always well turned out. He'd even brush his teeth after munching a biscuit. But he's from Planet Terrell, and on that planet, they'll make out wiv just about any woman. Nothing's sacred… I caught him watchin my breasts on the sly nuff times! It was only a matter of time before he'd hit on me! I swear, if he had put a grubby hand on me, I would've laid him out."

"You're sayin he was gonna hit on you too?" Natalie said.

"He literally wanted to fuck dis family—" Rebecca said.

"Even a color-blind llama on Prozac could see that!" Ladelle said. "Why can't you, Nat?"

"That's why dis family should be *fuckin him up*," Tanya said.

"You lot gimme joke!" Lil Elliott said.

As they delineated Eliza's level of tawdriness, a superlative scowl cinched onto Natalie's countenance, as if she were possessed by an *ifrit*.

"You know what?" she said. Lil Elliott's tepid head rose like a cobra's. Ladelle's face was puce with anticipation. Rebecca's was flinty. "I ain't gonna sit here, twiddlin my twat. I'm gonna find dat bitch an' punch her in her fucking mouth!"

Tanya took several refreshing sips from her teacup. "You sound like you're starting to think," she said with a faint smile.

* * *

Gregory Foster was a brooding roué with fruity cheekbones. His plush scowl and bronzed abdomen confected almost every woman he touched. He kept a consociate of devout fuck buddies in spite of his bilious infidelities. He never forgot a slight nor forwent an opportunity to reward a right. Hubristic hater aggravators loathed him. Females with cathartic portrayals suppressed their cordite lust for him and he was willfully adroit at secreting that lust.

Five years ago, his eyes trampolined every curvature of Natalie as he cruised Neasden's streets languorously. He almost swooned from his sapphire-colored Cherokee and onto the road.

"You see dat light-skin ting?" he said to his companion. "Dat's how I like my chicks, brown an' round. She's got the curvilinear curves, fam... She's got the curvilinear curves... Jeeez!!! Look at her tits, fam! Dem tings are like a full course meal!"

He honked his horn. She arched her neck. He licked his LL Cool J lips at the promontory of those heaving fruits, rising and falling, rising and then falling. "Yi! Yi! Yi!... I'm lost, babe. I'm lost... But I've found you... What ya sayin, sweetness? You're peng! ... What, can I get dat number, mami?"

She obliged him, but not before several rounds of deliberate horseplay. After a protracted game of text message tennis, he asked her to his flat in Willesden Green. His home was an Aladdin's Cave of HD TVs, turquoise tropical fish tanks and fulgent lamps. They smoked skunk, talked and cavorted. They watched *Life And Lyrics* starring Ashley Walters. Halfway through the film, he depucelated her on his shag.

"He's a dish, isn't he?" Tanya said after she was introduced to him. "You can tell he's worth a few bob. I'd hold on to that mast if I were you."

Natalie did, and devotedly so through frigid weather. Lil Elliott and Gus also affirmed their taut allegiances. "My sister's man runs North Wezzy," they told folk whenever they felt slightly threatened.

"All we gotta do is bell him, an' he'll bring half of London down to fuck you up!"

They became his messenger boys and protected his flagitious metals, bristling at anybody who neared the garden shed. Such adherence was rewarded, for Gregory saw to it that they were kitted with designer robes and that they buzzed around on scooters. Tanya, her life blighted by beggary and bankruptcy, caroused in the generosity of her *son-in-law*. For her 40th birthday, he arranged that she be chauffeur-driven in a Hummer Convertible to *The Emperor*, a Chinese restaurant in Stanmore frequented by opulent gastronomes. There she guzzled Petite Sirah and englutted Crispy Duck as if it were her only meal in Shangri-La, before hobbling back to her vale of tears.

"My biggest mistake was falling into bed with the wrong men," she told Natalie in a moment of self-disparagement. "That's why I'm the brow-beaten bitch that you see. Men just come, chip away at me, bodge me up an' den scarper to some next bitch. An' the next one comes along and does the same shit, and it just wears me down. I wish I had your luck!"

Eliza, observing from afar with morbid curiosity, hadn't subscribed to her mother's savage world-view of males. She had hoped for a Cinderella-type deliverance from the weighted steel that asphyxiated her discordant family, but the salmagundi of males she had encountered were inadequate. Gregory and Natalie flaunted their affection *ad nauseam*, and that irked and hurt.

Her ex foppish beau was a poor replica of the real thing. He declined to hustle for the most part of the day. At night, he prowled the streets like a giant crab, on the lookout for a dangling handbag or an idle iPhone. As soon as he dispossessed someone else's property, he hared down the street and never looked back. The ponderous one, however, made a series of bungled robberies, culminating in several have-a-go heroes pinning him against Oxford Street's concrete floor until the police arrived. And he was fully confounded when Eliza dumped him after he phoned her from the police station to inform her of his predicament, and whether she could arrange bail.

Her next boyfriend seemed the authentic type. Hailing from the eiderdown of Egham, he boasted of brazen misdeeds; of firing a pistol at a pursuing police car until it crashed into an oncoming bus; of leading a Spartacus revolt against the screws of Strangeways Prison that almost succeeded had it not been for a turncoat within his ranks; and then stabbing a rival repeatedly in the face with a screwdriver for winking at his then girlfriend. But while they shopped in Ridley Road Market, his Spartan valor imploded. A few paces behind, a hooded man with scintillated eyes and a sculpted mouth seemingly followed, incessantly so for the last ten minutes. He seized Eliza's arm and fled, hoping that he might escape the Harryhausen anthropophagite in pursuit.

She was peeved by his trepidation. "What tha fuck's tha matter?"

"I- I can't be around these sides, Eliza… Too many pagans wanna start on me for no reason… Man in Hackney just want beef wiv man from different postcodes—"

"I thought you said you had bare cousins dat controlled Hackney— "

"Did I say dat?"

"Yeh, you did. I remember everythin you say. You said you had three cousins from London Fields an' dat they had fifty boys in their Crew, an' dat Crew ran Hackney—"

He breathed a sigh of abated joy as his hooded *pursuer* stooped to embrace an elderly shopper and assist her with her shopping.

"You thought dat breh waz bout to eat you, didn't you?" she said, nodding in the direction of the helpful hoodie. "You should stop believing everythin you read in tha papers—"

"Hehehe! Hehehe… It's just my street-type spidey sense—"

"I can't be goin to certain endz wiv you an' all of a sudden, you're gettin nervous. Don't think I never clocked him coz I did, way before you did. I can't believe it. You're more of a fuckin girl than I am!"

His attempts at resurrecting his machismo were shattered

thereafter. She soon discovered a much softer side. He dithered whenever she ceded the vantage point. He sobbed after they first had sex. His love for saccharine R&B ballads made her nauseous. She preferred Bossa Nova Jazz. He felt inclined to ring her every two hours.

"Whose wiv you babe? I can hear a man's voice in the background—"

"It's the TV!"

"Sorry, boo! Lovin you makes me paranoid… I wanna wifey you off coz you're wifey material… I'd never have kids so you'd keep dat body coz you're body's off the fuckin chain! We'd have to adopt, unless YOU wanted kids—"

She loathed such weakness. Only a neutered male would be so insecure as to propose marriage to a woman he barely knew. Only an emasculating male would encapsulate his *I love yous* in a creepy, self-pitying visage.

"You're my future!" he said, waking her at three in the morning when she had to be up for work at six. "I wanna lick you in tha strangest of places an' give you multiple orgasms… I'd marry your skin tomorrow. We could go halves on a baby and put peez down on a mortgage—"

"You've been wiv me for two months, and you wanna marry me? You don't even fuckin know me! I don't ever wanna get married anyway—"

"OK, we'll have a civil partnership ting den. Give up your day job, and I'll pay your bills—"

"You know what, leotard? This is the fuckin end. Don't ever call me again, you dizzy prick!"

He begged forgiveness through a slew of texts. She complained to Gregory, who miniaturized him further by depleting him with death threats. He vanished thereafter.

Then she socialized with the affluent wide boys from work, with their cathedral-sized wallets and daemon-like plans. Such obstreperous cats dolled themselves with clinquant rings and

Breitling watches. A ruddy mulish lawyer named Ben Brown importuned her to date him. He was ten years older than she but hot-wired with cash. He brought her gifts from her Amazon wish list and took her to exquisite restaurants. He was part of a group of salacious solicitors that nicknamed themselves *Thee Renegades*. After work on Fridays, she accompanied *Thee Renegades* along the backwater of the Embankment, to an unvarnished tavern on Tudor Street. She was soon put off by their nauseating craving for beer. As their relationship intensified, Ben insisted that they be discreet.

They had catharsis sex in hotels rooms, waking up to Beluga on toast and Pinot Noir for breakfast. The supplementary frisson of being caught by the Epping Forest Rangers was an intemperate thrill they both shared as they romped indivisibly in car parks. But Ben was a bounder with morose thrills. He reported manufactured discrepancies about her work to her line manager. He recorded their intimacies on his mobile for the regalement of *Thee Renegades*.

Ben Brown, though not unlike a *gangsta*, was no Gregory Foster, and she became devitalized with him. He was getting more out of their trysts then she, and she loathed being sidelined by him.

"Why is it you can't look me in the eye at work?" she said, staring stubbornly into his. "Is it coz of a guilty conscience?"

"I don't do guilty consciences—"

"Neither do I. To tell you the truth, I don't care if we're exposed—"

"You'd better. I'll be a partner in this firm one day. The firm's got a strict policy on shenanigans—"

"Shenanigans? Is that some crude euphemism for bonin the receptionist?"

He redoubled his lewd laughter. "I haven't got time to give you an emotional top-up at work, Eliza. You know the score. You'll get all the attention you need after work."

She stood him up upon their next arranged booty-call, leaving him to pine priapismic in the hotel lobby. He blitzed her with texts and calls, but she ignored them. He saw her the next day at work, flirting outrageously with a DHL delivery agent. And the water cooler engineer. And the maintenance man. And the post room boy. He could remain dispassionate no longer.

"You're now formerly of our parish. I'm the gateway to your better future, if you co-operate. I could pull strings and get you promoted—"

"Why don't you just fuck off, Ben—"

"Fuck off? It'd have been easier for you to fuck me—"

"Go home, and fuck Mrs. Brown—"

"Quit your selective amnesia. Why don't we nip in the toilets so that you can err... recant your... err... tomfoolery?"

"Sorry, Benjamin. I don't speak geek... and you're fuckin rude—"

"You like it when I'm rude—"

"I'm not joking, you bastard!"

"By opting for a pejorative verb, you've carelessly blighted your future. We'll see how you fare with your gangsta man on the street where you're just another fuck piece or drug mule."

A quiet interregnum passed between the pair. Each left the other to their individuation until Eliza received a restive call on her mobile.

"Are you fucking my husband?"

"And who the fuck is dis?"

"I'm Ben's wife... We've got three children, Kingsley, six, Ambrose, four, and Delilah, two. You should be ashamed of yourself... I've read your emails to my husband and I know you were with him at the Royston Hotel last month... Are you sleeping with my husband?"

"I am, actually... I'm getting dicked down... As I'm sure you're well aware, he's not dat good anyway. But he says I'm his best fuck—"

"Don't flatter yourself. It's only sex and you know it—"

"You could say dat. He's a kinky bastard. He loves it when I belt him and call him Toby. But I prefer my men homegrown and gangsta anyways so you can have him back without the receipt. No hard feelings, babe!"

The next day, Ben flew towards her as she smoked peacefully under the vestibule.

"What did you tell my wife?"

"What you *didn't* tell your wife—"

"You've made an enemy out of me, Eliza. If you wanna fuck up my life, I'll fuck yours up. A thousand percent!"

She was shunned thereafter. *Thee Renegades* filed complaints that she stole longer lunch breaks and stationery. Work, saved on her PC the night before, disappeared from her hard-drive the morning after. The IT bod, designated to solve the mystery, claimed her work was irretrievable because there had been no work to retrieve. Her game face slipped when she rowed with a frump over a jammed printer. The frump called her a slut and Eliza promptly assailed him. She was summoned unto the auspices of senior management and, in spite of her counter allegations, she was summarily dismissed. She returned the following day, armed with Gregory, who made ballistic threats at Ben. They dispersed just before Harvey and his colleagues arrived. She took the firm to a tribunal. They blinked before Judgement Day. They paid her thirty thousand pounds in an out-of-court settlement.

She sought refuge once again in the cantonment of the hood. Cornballs were given no quarter. Authentic *gangstas* were a scarce breed. At home, she was forced to endure her overwrought sister highfalutin her adorations for Gregory as if she was the only woman on earth who had tasted love. She observed studiously the cleaves that bounded the mercurial symbiosis of their bond. She delighted in the pettifogging that culminated into high-decibel rows and object throwing. Gregory confided in her, complaining of Natalie's abject monotony as she battled her weight and other self-esteem issues.

"I've tried to do what's right, each and every time," he said. "But why's she fuckin trippin? Why can't she be wifey an' deal wiv whateva's troubling her and let me go out and bake the dough?"

"You wanna hear some real talk?" Eliza said. "Nat ain't on my level of womanhood. She's not enough for you. I know you're fuckin other girls but I don't blame you. I hear things, but I won't tell a soul—"

"What you heard?"

"Things!"

He grabbed her delectable arm playfully. She hung herself in his cinch. He tacitly stared as she threw her head back and laughed churlishly. Corporeal components of her bodily ensemble seared his fervid loins. Her breasts propounded themselves behind her muslin blouse. She crossed her elegant legs. His gaze settled upon her denim skirt.

"What things, Eliza?"

"Things... bout you, Gregory—"

"What THINGS, Eliza?"

She kept clicking her teeth. "Bout you... fuckin around.... bout you seein Shirine who works at Samuel's hairdressers... and dat you're bonin Melissa, Curtis' ex... and I know you're on a regular linkage wiv Andrea who lives on Hills Street. Dat's where you were last Thursday or were you not?"

"You're a hot ting sellin mad dreams—"

"Don't I know it? I'm the realest woman out there, and you're just a naughty boy. But, like I said, I don't blame you. If I had a tenth-rate man, I'd do the same."

Gregory licked his nectarous lips and pondered the deliciously absurd. There had been a passive-aggressive feud between both siblings from which sprung a mutual mislike. Eliza was an izmel, Natalie a glaive. Could he disport on their night and day difference? This concupiscent fiend, with her teeming spheres, had more thrift and thrill than his distended glaive. "... *I'm the realest woman out there, and you're just a naughty boy...*"

He leapt to his feet and stumbled awkwardly into the night for some Harlesden o2. He could hear her siren call to philander her kitty kat. As he kindled a cigarette, he killed his desire for her. He hurried to the abode of a juvenescent filly and fucked her instead. When he returned home a week later, he tried to make nice with

Natalie but she ventilated her anger before sundering him and his chattels from her abode. Eliza helped him pack with vitiated joy.

In her absurdity, Natalie cocooned herself within her room. She drank liquor by night with tireless application. Her alarming tears cohered in her glass with the vodka. Gregory visited her at weekends for *Sky Sports*, sex and *Southern Comfort*. When she became pregnant, she conveyed to him her good news.

"My dad weren't never there for me," he said as he felt the flutter beneath her belly. "But I'm gonna be there for my kid... I swear down, I'm gonna change. I'm gonna jump off road and hold down a proper job..."

By the time his daughter Tiana was born, he was a lobotomized version of his former self. The inner-city streets were sanguinary without precedent. Kids were killed for frivolous cause. Drug dealers were apt for the hunted. Rival dealers turned viciously upon each other. Calloused drug addicts were used to snare the nemesis of another. Up-and-coming delinquents ventriloquized the regressive knavery that went before them and set out to earn their spurs. Chains were torn from necks, rings plucked from fingers, guns clucked in faces. Gregory's finances were disgorged by an opposing firm. They kidnapped him from his flat and beat him till his face was sallow and several orifices bled. He was only released after he helped set up an associate, who was set alight by a blowtorch. Gregory feared reprisals for his part in the betrayal.

"They took my fuckin money," he confessed to a confederate. "All the peez I earned in five years went in ten minutes flat. Those cunts jacked me in my yard an' there's fuck all I can do bout it... coz no one's lookin to back man. I need to get some peez quick!"

"I've got an insider at a bank in Welwyn Garden City," said the confederate. "She knows what time the security van comes round with the dough. Time they begin unloadin, we'll simply get paid. No long ting. You'd be a fool to miss out on this one, fam."

And Gregory was no fool. Armed with rebores and V For

Vendetta masks, he and three others sped along the M25 to collect the spoils. He remained in the car as the getaway driver. The others stormed the van, held their guns aloft and seized whatever they could. They made off with £13,000.

Gregory thought nothing more of the robbery until he watched the reconstruction on *Crimewatch UK*.

"I'm a film star," he told his heathen gathering. "I'm Scotland Yard's most wanted... Look who's playin me? Some beat-up prick..."

"The bank has promised a reward of £20,000 for vital information that leads to the conviction of these dangerous criminals," a boil-faced detective told the nation. "If you've any information, no matter how insignificant you think it is, please get in touch now on 0203 007..."

Variegated blowhards, with their dicks hard for the reward, were already on the phone to Crimewatch detectives. A few days later, he was arrested while being spruced in a barbershop. The police laughed with ostentatious mockery as they led him away with his hair half cut.

"Guilty," declared the forewoman of the jury triumphantly after less than two hours deliberating the evidence, for and against him. Gregory and his myrmidons had been contaminated with SmartWater from the robbery. The dye was still upon them, five months after their infamy.

He spent three years in Wandsworth Prison, flirting with Islam and other comparative faiths. And when the system returned his liberty and he returned to his *endz*, it was as if he had returned to a different land. His former acolytes were mostly dead or jailed. The remainder sought an honest life. He wished to pick up from whence he left but the roads were no longer Eldorado, where rich pickings could be made from selling rocks and grass. He was unable to preserve his lofty pretensions. A cousin had wrote off his beloved Jeep in an accident whilst he was in prison, and was unable to compensate him — since that cousin was murdered in his bedroom by unknown miscreants. The police had confiscated his jewels and invested it in their war chest in their fight against his kind. Former hirelings occupied his former territory and they were the heirs of *the grind*. He had been the iconic heavyweight they had idolized. Now his *youngers* were cueing eagerly to knock him out.

"Is dat Gregory Foster, dat scatty waste breh from North Wezzy?" whispered a gap-toothed schoolboy to his friends. His chelonian eyes followed Gregory and Natalie as they shopped through the aisles of Asda. Sadly for Gregory's withered ego, he was within earshot of every word.

"He ain't all dat," said another, baldhead glistening like a malteser. "He looks like he's fallen on hard times. I reckon I could have him tho. If I spark him in a fist-fight, my name would go up in lights!"

Young Malteser was tickled pink at the prospect of felling a Titan. His companions dared his temerity.

"What if he's strapped tho?" cautioned a third.

That lingering thought was enough for them to back off. But to Gregory, such ignominy was disheartening. He hadn't been awarded the status of *elder*, who'd been there and done it all. Past feats were forgotten, palpable fears erased. So every time he left home, he stowed a gun in his jacket. It was the most capping of deterrents.

"What you gonna do bout money?" Natalie said. "I can't keep givin you money for your bud when you should be gettin dat yourself. An illegal immigrant comes straight off the banana boat and finds himself a job whereas you can't. Something's seriously wrong there!"

Gregory had never worked an honest day. DBS checks were an indigent fork in the road. Tussled and biffed by persistent rejection, he arrived at a recruitment agency on Acton Lane, which promised work of an unspecified nature.

"What? Is it warehouse work?" he said hopefully.

The office operative, a milky-skinned Rosa Klebb with a baritone voice that had a soupçon of Moscow, frowned ruefully. "Come tomorrow morning. Four in the morning. Work comes, but no guarantees... Some days, you get work. Some days, no..."

At such a beleaguered hour, he congregated outside the recruitment agency alongside ten starch-faced Latvians, a couple of soaked Kurds, half-a-dozen misty Brazilians and several hardy Angolans. Lips were charred and chalk-white. Hyperborean squalls rustled their awnings. Nobody knew what the work entailed; whether it be tipping baked tarmac onto a dual carriageway with cars zipping at sixty miles an hour around them or risking their fingers feeding apes in the monkey's enclosure at London Zoo. Each knew that they needed the money more desperately than the next man. And that the work should be made exclusive to them, and then their respective kinsmen. After an hour of waiting, a foreman pulled up beside them in a red mini-bus.

"I need eight," he said, holding up the same number of fingers for the benefit of those that couldn't understand English well. Ejaculated cries of "Me! Me! Pick me!" followed. Gregory snorted and saw no reason to beg. The foreman selected his packhorses and ushered them into his vehicle. Gregory was left on the sidewalk without as much as an acknowledgement. The throng of rejected bodies dispersed into the dawn. A car swooshed through a puddle, covering several in rainwater.

"Fuck off back to your country," said the driver, raising a two-fingered salute. "This is fucking England. This ain't fucking Muslim land. We don't want no fuckin Bozzos or Kozzos 'ere…"

The salutation was returned. "You fucking racist English! Get out of tha fuckin car and say that, you fucking English bastard! We fuckin run you over with your own car…"

As Gregory strode his malevolent boots upon every concatenated pavestone, he couldn't countenance poverty nor the disapprobation of the cards that were dealt him. He could countenance the impropriety of death or a jail sentence. The finality of those things were more sentient. He sauntered past the shops on Harlesden High Street. They stood like forsaken sepulchers. A whistling drunkard urinated as a dog would, hoisting one leg in the wind as he pole-vaulted his pee against a tree. Gregory ignored this asocial proclivity. So did the roustabouts. After the drunk had zipped himself up, he begged them for change so that he could buy breakfast. Gregory said no flatly. So did the roustabouts. As he stumbled away, Gregory wondered for what purpose he existed, except for the surplus of drink he had inflicted upon himself. The drunk was like his pilgarlic father, who was no more washed up then the Special Brew he downed.

As he walked through the winding alleyways that led to home, the Nepenthe Park Estate stirred beneath the alabaster clouds. Autumn leaves wrestled with the alarum winds. Laverne watched him through the window, her vacillating veneer veiled by the curtain. Augustus stood behind her in his nightwear, cradling her broad waist. By her front gate, Natalie watched Gregory imperiously as he approached. The cold air ebbed into her flesh.

"I thought you're supposed to be at work?"

"The agency ain't got no work. They made me leave my bed to catch pneumonia in the freezing cold…"

She had anticipated some sort of cop-out from his deceptive crevice. Of course, he was fearful of that laborious ogre called Work with its banausic bawl and its plodding rank-and-file subjection.

"So, I suppose you're goin back to bed?"

"May as well!" He tried to sound merry, pulling it off quite well in fact. "Then I'll be on the grind later. No one's puttin my swagger on check—"

"Well, you'd better have dat lie-down before you implode," she said with a snarl, her teeth showing.

"You got some peez I can borrow, just to credit my phone an' get some draw? Call it an investment, babe!"

She shuddered at that utter excrement of a plea. He shuddered too, at having to ask, and because of the cold.

"No, I haven't," she said. "And fuck you for asking!"

His immediate thought had been to bloody her mouth since it had needlessly disrespected him. Her tartuffery was staggering since it was he that maintained her until he went to prison. He watched her walk down the path from which he came.

He decided against returning home for some much needed kip for he couldn't bear to face the miserable sow that was Tanya. She had once subscribed to his lugubrious troubles and had sympathized with his contumelious treatment by the authorities. Only yesterday, he overheard her assertion that he was a deadbeat. He had challenged her with an impassioned requiem of his hardships since prison and threatened to move out. Questioning his capability as a father was the mother of all disrespects. Tanya's opalescent face had darkened ominously as she listened to his soliloquy. After he finished, she was remorseful. She apologized and called herself stupid. Tiana was blessed to have the best father in the world and Natalie was lucky to have him. She said he could stay for as long as he wanted and that he was no different to her than her own sons. He tactfully accepted her apology but doubted her sincerity. And as he shivered by the gate, he miserably accepted that their respect for him had defaulted because of his unhorsed fortune. In spite of his scuffled weariness, he stomped off to Johnny's flat, with whom he could release his resentment of those he apportioned as the cause of his diabolical conundrum.

"Dat's life for you, innit," Johnny said after listening to his diabolical whine. "Dat's why when I get a hundred grand, I ain't breakin bread wiv fuckin *nobody*. Everyone wants a share when you got somethin but time when you're low on funds, how many people came good for you? Even your own mom will say no when you needed £10. But when all is goin well, she's sayin to the world: *"Dat's my son right dere!"* That's *after* you made it… Even she showed you no love when you were a day late and a nugget short…"

Gregory listened as he smoked his weed with a stern moue. Gratitude was an execration long forgotten in the minds of Tanya, Natalie and the rest of mankind. Johnny advised that he be merciless upon his second coming, and succor nobody.

"Check it, Gregory. Who backed you when you were in the raw pennz? No one invited you on their floor when you were on the express elevator to hell, goin down. Man weren't feelin you den. Man was goin on cruddy…"

Gregory enjoyed his time with Johnny, not least because they were on the same page. They played on Wiis, smoked skunk and drank Cîroc. They debated Kafkaesque and Orwellian conspiracies of the day but neglected tangible realisms of their day. They spoke of Kemet and eschatology, and how Jesus was really Horus and Father Christmas was a demiurge of the ungulated Satan. They writhed with malice at the psychedelic lifestyles of celebrities; yet agreed that it was necessary to engage in the unconscionable and live like those they envied. Johnny ridiculed the maleficence of Britain's foreign affairs and the cabbalistic cults that orchestrated proxy wars and pestilence. "At the end of the day, the UK's a skank," he said windily, completely medicated by the nepenthe puffs of a Maduro cigar. "It would screw anybody. Dat's why you should bang it bare-back!"

It was here that Gregory became more familiar with the younger lads on the estate. They were precociously mammon like he, except for Mark, an erudite vessel, who took no part in sloth smoking or talk of girl poking. Mark preferred preaching like an Old Testament Prophet and telling apocryphal tales. By dawn, he lucubrated verses from the Holy Koran in near word perfect Arabic, sometimes breaking into sobs as he pondered hermeneutic Hadiths detailing the wrath of Allaah, Most Merciful. Lollipop wasn't interested in linear discussions about the Bohemian Grove and millionaire rappers selling their souls to Baphomet in return for infamy.

"I don't believe all dat hocus pocus bullshit," he said as they shared a spliff in Johnny's kitchen. "I'm only focused on goin hard an' cleanin up these endz."

"Where do you get your food from, blud?" Gregory said.

"You wouldn't know tha breh—"

"Truss me, I know *all* the guv'nors—"

"Naaah, not this one—"

"There ain't no more peez to be made on road, blud. Dem days are done—"

Lollipop donned the rictus smile of an offended man. "For you, maybe. You want man to give up coz you have. You see these pinkies in my pocket?" He produced a pelf forth in a bundle and shuffled it nosily. "Dat's only four hours work, an' there's much more peez due for collection—"

"Breh's makin peez all day long but no bring in for his fam—"

"When I've made the kind of peez you once made but didn't bring me in, I'll gladly bring you in, fam—"

And then his phone rang. Unlike the others who bellowed into theirs as if it were a tannoy, he talked into his like a horse whisperer. Then he bade farewell without stating his destination. Gregory never uttered a bad word against him, but felt profuse envy because his own strife seemed perpetual.

He was grateful that, despite his putrefied fortune, he was still a bravura in bed. Females were satiated by his pulchritude. And he couldn't resist coalescing with smoldering teases, whether swarthy or red-boned *wifelets*. The tarty and the classy, the sassy and the nasty offered themselves as an unhallowed catholicon to his chronic satyriasis. Some *swallowed his kids*, as it was colloquially put. Others allowed him to abuse their cleavages and navels as a dumping spot for the alveolated money shot. He always wore a condom lest they breed offspring he didn't want or he caught an STD from an infected cunt. And two or three inured themselves into kowtowing debasements, of which he recorded on his HTC for his personal amusement.

He'd come and go at crepuscular hours. Whenever he returned home, there were pawky rows with Natalie about money and milk, nappies and of that ilk. Afterwards, they succumbed to a seething but soporific session of make-up sex. Her labored body would deliquesce as he bestrode a torrential percussion. Her prurient groans were mellisonant. His gaboon mahogany skin, made moist by her dripping perspiration, looked magnificent. He careened inside her with resolute thrusts. Every taste of his embouchement felt right. She squeezed his pulpy bottom tight with her white tipped fingernails.

"Who's your fuckin daddy?" he said.

She impaled herself upon him and undulated like a majestic serpent. Her limbs were limp. Her vagina was a frenzy of lush water.

"Who's your daddy, bitch?"

She tried to defy him by saying nothing, but his grueling durability soon subverted her. She finally collapsed onto his sweat-glistened chest after reaching a sixth orgasm.

"You are! You ARE my daddy... I so fuckin... hate you hun... Oooh... Oh Gregory! I... fuckin... hate... you..."

Her yin in the outside world mattered not in the yang of the bedroom. He reigned upon the jangled waves of sheets and quilts. If she displeased him, he would deprive her and she loathed being deprived, for she thoroughly enjoyed her sex. And every morning, Eliza coaxed him suggestively at breakfast with her dishabille frocks and her lascivious caprice. And she palpated his griping contentions by luring him into her pink perineum pot whenever backs were turned.

"You're not one of those who hustles a nine to five," she said, after bringing him to completion moments before. "You're a road man, pure an' simple. I can't see you pushin paper or stackin boxes. You're tellin me a swan should be proud to be a duck?"

He stormed from the bed in a huff. His quarter-erect penis drooled its viscid matter as it bounced between his muscled sandy stems. "Don't I know it? For the life of me, I've been tellin her what you already know. But does Nat listen? Does she fuck?"

"Darling, you don't push dat point far enough. Watchin you is like watching a Tarantino movie coz I've got to watch one scene from four angles to understand you properly—"

"Dis ain't no grimy Tarantino flick. Dis is real life. Can't get a job coz everyone's askin for a DBS. Nat's wylin bout peez even tho she makes her own. Tanya's goin on ya di da di daa in her ear bout men bein no good reh reh reh—"

"Boy, if I were you, I'd go back to doin what I do best—"

"How am I gonna raise peez if Nat doesn't want me shottin?"

"So, you're not shottin coz Nat doesn't want you shottin?"

"I wanna do right by Tiana. I can't be feedin her belly wiv drug money—"

"In dat case, get a job at McDonald's. At least Tiana gets a free Happy Meal every time you finish your shift—"

"Are you mad? I can't work at McDonald's. Not when you get to my status!"

"You better think of somethin. You owe Nat five bills and my mom was sayin she should be on you till you pay—"

"I go to dat fuckin agency every fuckin day, an' there's nothin substantive, yuh get me. Everyone's Eastern European in dat place, an' they look after their own. What else can I do?"

"I think I'm gonna cough out a lung!" Eliza said with a fiendish chuckle. "Why do you let dem bust your balls?"

"No one's bustin my balls—"

"You said it yourself. They're boyed you off to McDonald's and you didn't say shit back. Believe me; they'll *make* you pay back tha five hundred—"

"Listen. I ain't payin shit. I spent thirty grand on her, and she's on bout five hundred squid. If I wanted to, I could kick off. I've done it before—"

"Like fuck you have. And my mom, she just wants you for herself—"

"How do you know dat?"

"She's wayyy jealous of you both. She's hatin your situation… You should just go back to shottin on road. They don't even need to know. As long as you're bringin peez home an' supportin Tiana, they can't say shit to you. You're a fuckin grown arse man, Gregory. Don't let anyone take you for an idiot—"

"I ain't lettin no one take me for an idiot—"

"They're takin you for *an idiot*. My mom ain't gotta clue bout men coz she's only ever been wiv first-grade shit-bags, and I never knew what you saw in Natalie beyond her big tits an' light-skin. She's four cheeseburgers away from being fat… Tiana's done sucked tha juice out of those breasts anyway."

He slipped his balls beneath his shorts and sighed. "Cool... I'll jump back on road... I'll hook up wiv my boy Marvin. He keeps askin me to come out and grind five bills a day—"

"When did dis Marvin make dis offer?"

"Bout six weeks ago—"

"And you're still *thinkin bout it?*"

"I thought bout it—"

"Do you know how much peez you've lost *thinkin bout it?*"

"If I do dis, you'd better not say nuttin to nobody. I'll look after you, truss me, but you've gotta keep it zipped, yeah?"

"I'm a different animal from Nat. I don't need your peez or your bud. I couldn't care less what you do wiv your life coz I don't business. I won't be in livin in these endz for much longer. You better believe dat, bredrin!"

Eliza's words plucked an infelicitous chord. A swan and a duck were not equal. Neither was a hustler and a tarmac layer. The *gangsta's* lot was more winsome. Whimsical indeed, for he was found wanting on the legitimate plain.

"Men are one of three sorts," she said. "They're either stallions, mules or maimed goats. You're a maimed goat right now. OK, you fuck good but you gotta do a lot more before I start spellin your name backwards... I'm a kind of woman you're not used to, Gregory. Just pray you don't lose your balls in tha bedroom coz you lost your balls on road..."

After slipping his crucifix around his neck, he strode onto the balcony for a cigarette. The Harlesden skyline was ensanguined by the terracotta sunset. In his mind, he elicited a montage of great days gone by before shaking his head at current ills. He could hear Eliza's deriding fangs cussing without censure despite the Everest windows. Despite the incessant sucking of his cigarette, he felt no soothing. Natalie and Lydia were engaged in plaintive chatter on the green beneath him. He knew his name was being defamed in the undulating breeze. All because he couldn't be the reconstituted man that Natalie yearned for. Yet the banal drug dealer that Eliza willed him to be was ineluctably enticing. He plucked his mobile from his back pocket and phoned Marvin Crowe.

He was summoned to a housing estate in Acton to iron out terms and conditions. Upon his arrival, he was made to stand in the hallway and converse while the drug king defecated into a toilet bowl.

"Blud," he said in a Baron Greenback drone, between the breathy grunts and the occasional brisk roar. "I've got bare foot souljas on road shottin, bringin me twenty, thirty bags a week… I don't need another shotta… I need a gunrunner, a delivery bwoy. Each delivery guarantees commission… Don't worry; you're not workin for me. You're just a man from the outside comin in… If you get caught, you keep yo mouth shut an' I'll get some peez to your family… And fam, if you do anythin stupid, I'll send you to hell on a blast of a strap!"

Gregory was politely non-committal and quietly galloped away. What followed were the most moribund of days. Rosa Klebb had no work for him. His enemies remained exorbitantly less than serene in their quests against him. He remained a sequestered creature to Natalie, and a whore to the squaw Eliza. Both treated him with borderline cruelty. And Lollipop pendulumed his depositories before his friable face. Other bugbears kept him awake at night.

A fortnight later, he returned to the scatological Marvin who welcomed him with galvanic zeal, like some prodigal bairn of his. Two hours later, he delivered two guns to an eerily delectable mother of four in North Kensington. He had made £800. He felt like a man again.

6

SISTERS AREN'T DOING IT FOR THEMSELVES

THE AFTERNOON SHADOWS WERE lengthened by the malleability of the white sun. Natalie was formidably grouchy. A cluster of rustic peacocks were with her, smiting their cohering knuckles against their corresponding palms.

"You seen Eliza?" they asked Lydia.

Lydia pointed to a bosky portion of the field, where Eliza and her companions exalted in the breeze. Ribald diarrhea seeped from the mouths of those rustic peacocks.

"Look at that uncultivated vagina!" Rebecca said. "She's flaunting your man already. She's watchin him play football like she's wifey—"

"Blouse fuckin beat!" Ladelle said. "You'd think she ain't got a care in the world! You've gotta seriously end what she started."

Natalie pulled her cropped jeans towards her waist and wiggled her hips back into them. Tanya projected her voice, like a Muezzin in a minaret.

"OIII... ELIZA! YEAH, YOU! YOU SKET! LOOK WHOSE COME TO BUST YOUR FANNY!"

The entire soccer field stood to attention like trainee officers on a platoon field. At the far corner of the pitch, a silhouette figure hurdled away like a rabbit scampering towards his warren at the blast of a hunter's rifle.

"You call yourself a big man?" Ratty said. "Look at you, blud! Dat's you for the rest of your life, always runnin away—"

"Go... and fuck a duck, you cunt!" Gregory screamed back.

The referee sounded the final whistle. El-Ninio had triumphed emphatically, though most had forgotten the score. The lady of the cerulean fingernails leapt in the air and screamed "Yesssssss!!!" in near Meg Ryan counterfeit. Tafari beckoned El-Ninio to the changing rooms, and away from the scourging that was bound to follow.

Eliza careered down a fallow pathway. She sucked a cigarette arduously before casting it towards the sylvan half-spent. The preponderant mob galloped after her, heckling the drum beats of a war-like jamboree. Members of the Miracles football team hastened to join them. Lil Elliott appeared more salubrious as he slalomed beside Eliza with his tongue hanging out. Tanya's misbegotten joy was heartened by the enthusiastic noises.

"Why you walkin away, Eliza?"

"Coz I don't wanna talk to you—"

Natalie puffed like an aging steamboat. "Well, I wanna talk to you..."

Eliza chucked some inaudible verbiage her way.

"What did you say?"

Eliza finally halted, her countenance hideously loaded.

"I ain't got nothin to say to none of yous. Coz I know two-twos, you've made up your mind already so I ain't gonna bother explainin myself—"

"So you CAN explain why you're fucking my man?"

"Gregory's NOT your man. And we've nothin to discuss—"

"We've nothin to discuss?"

"Unless you have!"

"The situation's simple. I don't want you anywhere near my man... I don't want you anywhere near my daughter—"

"Is dat it?"

"Just make sure you stay the fuck away from Gregory—"

"You tell him to stay the fuck away from me—"

"No, you tell him tha next time you see him—"

"I'll try, but what if he can't keep his hands to himself?"

"You really are far gone, ain't ya?"

"He's in love wiv me, Nat."

"What did you say?"

"I know you ain't deaf, darling—"

Tanya sensed a dithering Natalie could misfire the moment. "The shame's too much to face, ain't it? Your sister's boyfriend! How low can you get?"

"I've done nothin to be ashamed of—"

"Of course, you haven't! I saw how excited you'd get every time Gregory walked into the room while you're wearing your slutty skirt, bending over so low that everyone could see what you had for breakfast..."

Squeals of laughter came from immature elements of the mob. Horrified shakes of the head came from the levelheaded.

"... You're one nasty ho, Eliza... I'm your mother... I ought to fuckin know—"

"Dat's right! I'm a ho from a long line of hoes—"

"You need to get a life," Natalie said. "Cos true say, everyone knows dat you're a sket an' dat's no joke, sneakin round just to get your lil bit of dick. Gregory's nothin but a waste man anyway, poncing money coz he never has none... I hear bare stories bout you, bout how you can never keep your legs closed—"

Eliza rolled her eyes earnestly. "Say what you wanna say. You got your bodyguards wiv you. If it were just me and you, you wouldn't say sh..."

She reeled instantaneously as a howitzer smacked her cheek. She swung a punch back like a discus thrower but oppugnant fists rained upon her with sheer constancy. Tanya and Ladelle had also weighed into the adversarial heap.

The cajoling scent of *schadenfreude* discolored the air. Rebecca and Shekaidy held aloft their video phones and filmed the fray.

Ratty grumbled about the unfairness of the scrap. Lollipop and Marius bemoaned the preposterous decline of family values. Stacey wormed his way through the maladroit crowd. Lil Elliott attempted to stop him. He was circumvented with ease. He jettisoned over Eliza amidst the catapult of blows.

"'Low it, people—"

"What the fuck are you doin?" Ladelle said. "Get out of the fuckin way—"

"You lot ARE family! Try settling dis behind closed doors instead of hangin your dirty laundry in public—"

"What's it to you anyway?" Natalie said. "This is between me an' dat nasty skank… If you wanna back THE bitch, you'll get taken down wiv THE bitch!"

An erubescent flush to Stacey's face dissolved several sadists into hysterics. With a weary intake of breath, he sunk into the crowing mob. Natalie turned to her gratified public.

"Where's dat fuckin no good tosser Gregory?"

"Gregory's a prick from the year dot," Ratty said. "You don't need dat waste man in your life!"

"Where's he gone?"

"The moment you came, I see him runnin off wiv his tail between his legs—"

"Tell him he can fuckin run, but he can't fuckin hide. And tell him I want my money… I don't care if he has to sell his arse on tha street to pay me!"

Eliza sucked a swollen lip in abject silence. Rebecca stepped forward, camera phone still rolling.

"One more thing, biaaatch!!! Don't beg friend wiv people jus to get their man coz you're butterz an' can't get your own man… Gregory's only messin wiv you for sex, you waste bitch… I don't ever wanna know your skin. You disgust me. I don't want you comin a hundred yards from my yard, coz knowin you're nasty red-eyed self, you might be after my man…. Skank fuckin dog—"

"Once a fuckin dog, always a fuckin dog; an' dats what you've always been, way back when!" Natalie said. "You've always been jealous of me, haven't you?"

Eliza simply shimmered to the scene. Presented with a neither nor argument, she felt obliged to say nothing.

"I hate you..." Natalie said with a faintly spooked grimace. "... for fucking up my Sunday!"

Lil Elliott adjudged this the ending and led her away gently. The main sway of the satanic herd subsided. Only Tanya occupied the same ground, snarling at Eliza.

"She went fuckin Rambo on your arse!" she said, before stomping off to join her clan.

Eliza was calcified that no molten tears burnt her cheeks. Her derelict friends constellated around her, exhibiting their concern.

"I'm fine," she insisted about thirty times, each time less convincing than the last.

"You've lost an earring," Ashleigh said.

Eliza touched both her ears before fidgeting with the naked earlobe. Stacey and Shakira searched the long grass. Lollipop grimaced like a constipated mule.

"Boy, you wouldn't ave thought Tanya was your mom—"

"Dat's families for you!" Eliza said tersely. She ignited a cigarette, pushed it between her wroth lips.

Ashleigh fanned her neck melodramatically with a magazine. "I could never put my hands on my daughter an' shame her in public—"

"You know what, yeah?" Eliza said; her mouth sagged to the left the more she spoke. "You know what, yeah? I'm gonna let it slide. Y'all know dat if I lost my temper, I could've started a war... Believe me, I was hardly scared. She called me a skank ho coz I fuckin look good."

"You've won anyway," Ashleigh said. "You still got Gregory. What did they get?"

"My family needs blastin to the fuckin moon," Eliza said. "They do no fuckin good on this planet!"

Gregory joined them belatedly. The seams of his draws showed as he high-fived his blanch-faced lads. And then he delivered a priggish homily on how simple formation changes to Miracles would have induced the right result.

"We lost coz we treated the ball like a grenade wiv the pin out... I ain't playin for Miracles again... No fire, no desire, no nuttin... If Fernando had three of me, he won't need five of you..."

The lads laughed respectfully. He cracked more jokes like a game show host. He pointed at a small airplane making a zipping farting sound as it glided through heaven.

"Yea, dat's funny dat. Hehehe..." Then he broke into an impromptu rap.

> "We're goin thru some serious times,
> Coz dis ain't no gold mine,
> An' me don wanna 'ave to break your spine..."

Eliza paced pensively back and forth along the grass, her hands half-clasped. "Don't worry bout tha earring. Gregory will get me a new pair..."

He engorged her gob with an obscene snog. "You all right, Shortz? My, you taste sooo fuckin good. I didn't play well coz my mind was on you—"

"Really?" She sounded unconvinced.

"You gotta lot of tension in your shoulders... Papi's gonna take you home and we're gonna fix dat... My legs are killin me, sta'. Anybody got any Deep Heat... Or Deep Freeze? You lot are lame... I could murder a stone cold Ginger Beer right now. Dat's some sik beverage. Once dat drink goes into you, it puts your thirst to sleep... You got any peez, Eliza?"

"Shame you didn't stick bout to see Natalie an'Tanya—" Lindsey said.

"What did they want?"

"Dey wanted to kick your arse, blud!" Lollipop said.

"You know what, yea? Fuck the whole clan! They ain't got nuttin to say. What can they tell me? I done told Tanya already, ya nerr mean! I'm wiv Eliza now… Natalie's gotta accept dat. It's simple tings really. Me an' Natalie are done. There ain't no point her sendin me text messages beggin man to take her back, coz me an' her are done, finito… kaput… Bout they're gonna kick my arse—"

"She wants you to sell your arse on road an' pay back her money—"

"Stop bein a cunt, Lollipop. You're better than dat, yeah—"

"Blud, I'm jus sayin what she said—"

"Don't mind what she said. She's pissed. She'll say any shit. Dat's what girls do. Yuh don know dat already. So why are you bein a cunt? After the dust's settled, I'm calling Natalie an' squashin dis. We still gotta lil girl together—"

"At least you're still thinkin bout your daughter—"

"I think bout my daughter every minute, fam!"

He put an arm around Eliza and kissed her again. Their companions trundled away and left them alone.

"Where did you fuck off to?"

"What, you wanted me to be part of dat? I don't do other people's problems nicely—"

"Other people's problems? If I put a tail on you, they'd call you a weasel—"

"If I stayed, it'll be more fucked up than it already is—"

"Dat's convenient, so you left me to deal wiv it—"

"It's YOUR fam, Eliza. Like you ain't never had a fight wiv Nat in your life coz you rowed bout make-up? Or your mom's never tanned your hide coz she didn't like what you did? It's your family. I ain't getting involved… My mom and Jacqui belled me earlier, talkin shit bout why I dogged Nat. Dey wanted to speak to you. I'm like: Naaah. You talk to me. I'm *your* business. Ya neer mean—"

Her eyes rolled like fruit machine dials. She cast another spent cigarette into the bush.

"You're tha chick they love to hate…" He leaned in for an intense pet. "But I don't hate you… You make me wanna nut in my pants—"

"Nooo…" She pushed him away and took a lone route that led to a discreet side exit.

"Fuck you if you wanna be like dat," he said. "I ain't into your pipe dreams… It's tunnel vision from now on…"

Lollipop tapped a cheeky paw upon his shoulder. "Blud, don't ya mean its *Chucklevision* from now on?"

Johnny joined them also, having strayed from the bile and vitriol others had enjoined and enjoyed. "What you been on, cuz? No one's had dis much heat since Osama!"

"I've fuckin won, you get me," Gregory said. "Dat's why everyone's screwin bout now. I'm gully, tha illest. I'm tha truth!"

"Man, I see shit today dat I thought I'd never see," Lollipop said. "If you run into Tanya an' Natalie anytime soon, they'll cut your fuckin legs off."

"Dem sisters ain't doin it for themselves!" Gregory said. "And their mother behaves worse—"

"F'real, dey need to be straightened out in a strait-jacket!" Johnny said.

"Tanya knows I got love for cougars!" Gregory said.

"So Tanya could get it?" Lollipop said.

"Give your fuckin head a shake, Lollipop," Gregory said. "I've pecked dat nuff times!"

Their mouths gaped in the benign breeze. He looked around him in case somebody eavesdropped on his scuzzy revelation. A swath of moths winnowed in their near space.

"Raaah!" Lollipop said. "I've known Tanya all my life. She's like an auntie, fam. She gave me lifts to school back in the day and bought me ice-creams when the summers were hot—"

"Why would I lie? Real talk. I buss bare fat loads on her and in her till I went jail. After I come from jail, she said she made a big mistake and to forget what we did."

"She's thrown a curve ball to make you look bad," Johnny said. "She's slime. You should da exposed dat shit, rags—"

"Don't forget she's Tiana's nan. I ain't proud of dat shit anyway.

They'd say it only happened in my head, even though I know for a fact WE happened, yer neer mean!"

"Believe, it hasn't been a good day," Johnny said. Out of the three of them, he looked the most woeful. "I should have stayed in bed. Or just sat at home writin positive barz, puffin dat la la la!"

Lollipop elicited a rictus grin that didn't crack. "Dere's three rules on road dat I live by! Rule number one, when you link someone business or pleasure, make sure you're met by a face you can vouch for. It reduces the risk of a set-up. Two, never agree to carry out somebody else's plan exactly. If the plan's to go north, den you say let's go northeast and don't compromise. And finally, never sleep wiv a girl who's got more problems than you. Now dat one's always worked for me!"

7

MONEY MAKES THE
WORLD GO ROUND...
BUT LOVE MAKES IT SPIN.

"So, WHEN'S THA LAUNCH PARTY for your single, fam?" Twang said in his musty studio overlooking the River Brent. Reticulated rain drummed the corrugated roof above.

"October 25," Ratty said. "Hormones Nightclub hostin the illest... Tickets £20. Doors open from ten... Place is gonna be ram. Party's gonna be mad, so come and support dis movement. Top MCs are gonna be dere: Moody Boy, Lil Brazen Raisin, Tora Bora, Ambrosia-Nectar, Tock-Sick, DJ Swine, DJ Spiderman, and Yours Truly spittin barz like no other, coz you know diz is usss—"

Twang held the CD with reverence, as if it were a divine relic. "Really an' truly, your tune's a banger, fam. Before we wrap up, you wanna holler at anyone out dere?"

"Jeez, I'm flippin dis coin... First, I wanna say boo tha haterz. Haterz help me do better an' I get stronger each an' every time... You give me tha inspiration to spit barz. I produce beats dat gets me a half a mill deal dat sets me up for life, all on tha back of your hate. So thank you! Thank you for your hatred. And secondly..." Twang anxiously gesticulated that he calm the fuck down. "... Dis is to the sperm donor who weren't around: Mom raised me an' Solomon, grindin two jobs. Solomon's at Oxford studyin medicine and I'm killin dis set. So I got dis message for you, big man. If you were seedless, you'd be pointless. We don't need yo' brak self. You never worried bout us, but that's OK coz I made it. So fuck you! An' fuck all the sperm donors out dere, settin family franchises everywhere but aren't caterin for their kids…"

Two miles away, Gregory could enjoy his Crabbie's beer no longer. His palate curdled to the bombast on the radio.

"How can man go on live radio and chat shit? No wonder they call dat breh Twang coz he obviously gets twanged easy."

Johnny shook his grievous head. "Ratty kisses clart to feather his nest. I know why he's sayin what he's sayin. He wants bare gash jumpin on his shit CD. Breh's won't buy. They'll just copy his shit, but the gash, who loves to gas, spend their peez easily. Dat's why dat fuckin mangina's hollerin at single moms—"

"You read bout breh's like dat in comic books. Man dem don't hate Ratty coz they're haterz—"

"He was sayin tha other day dat he gets more girls than you, an' dat you only get girls coz you're light-skin—"

"Does he even *get* girls, Johnny? What gal has he drawn dat's made you look twice? And don't say Joanne, coz I've fucked Joanne…"

Ashleigh froze as she listened to their kinetic chat. She liked Ratty. He had always been courteous to her. Sure, he was conceited but nobody deserved such rudimentary ire.

"I got these ideas in my mind right now," Johnny said. "I don't even wanna say dem out loud—"

"Say it cuz. He deserves madness—"

"Twang's tellin lies dat he pranked me on his radio show. I ought to slice tha bastard—"

"Shank him and you'll suffer. He probably fucks wiv Fedz—"

"How many people you reckon listen to his show tho?"

"You lot are paranoid," Ashleigh said plaintively. "Even *I* can see he weren't talkin bout you—"

"Why am I paranoid, Ashy?"

"You're tellin me Ratty was talkin bout Gregory when he was goin on bout sperm donors? Come on; is dat what you're honestly sayin?"

"So you know him better?"

"I didn't say I know him better, Johnny. One man's yuck is another man's yum. You can hate tha dude but you can wish him well—"

"So you'd go out and buy his CD?"

"Support tha movement, like he said—"

"Support tha movement, like he said—"

Gregory burst into hoots of laughter. "Dis is too funny… Jesus, dis is super funny—"

"You're a fuckin embarrassment, Ashy! One man's yuck is another man's yum? What tha fuck? You are so fuckin naïve. Dat's why if some random breh wants to fuck you, you'd be there thinkin he only wants to be your friend. You know dem ones? He checks for you an' pulls out his cock. An' you'd be offerin to sew his pants coz you're thinkin his zip's broken!"

"Seriously, Johnny? When you were in tha pen, did I ever cheat on you?"

"How am I supposed to know—"

"If I did, you'd know bout it coz tha breh who fucked me would tell you—"

"And what's your point exactly?"

"I wasn't makin a point, Johnny. All I'm sayin—"

"Yea, I thought not. You're not street. Time you settled wiv me, you switched off and got comfortable—"

"Yea, I ain't street. I switched off and got comfortable. What do I know?"

Gregory cheered at the philippic exchange. He turned his mollusk-like glare from Ashleigh to Johnny, and then back again.

"You see what I gotta put up wiv?" Johnny said. "If I do Twang somethin, all the Fedz need do is speak to her and she'll fuck up my alibi in five minutes—"

"I ain't got dat kinda worries," Gregory said. "Eliza's street. Wifey's proper clued up. Classic ride an' die chick. She holds it up on road, better than most man… Eliza an' I are telepathic. We mentally transmit shit to each other!"

"I'm goin around Lindsey's," Ashleigh said. "I gotta return her Avon book… and I need some air—"

She gathered her papers and walked straight through the door.

"Fuck off Ashy!" was Johnny's parting remark.

A block away, Stacey recoiled at the harangue emanating from the radio. He drenched strawberry jam upon his heavily buttered toast. His mother Sondra stared at him.

"What's the matter with that silly boy? That was so uncalled for. And why are we listening to that wretched radio station?"

Fernando folded one leg over the other as he read *The Guardian* on his iPad. "Ratty needs help from Knee Jerkers Anonymous," he said without looking up.

Stacey was distracted by the clatter of footsteps from the outside. He looked through the blinds. Ashleigh was subject to the caterwauling winds. She walked past the wisteria of the opposing block, holding aloft a wet white umbrella.

"There goes the girl that got away," Fernando said mischievously. "I bet that still burns you, doesn't it?"

"You're bout five years late, dad. I'm wiv Lydia now, or haven't you heard?"

"I've heard, but I see how you look at Ashleigh. And if I can see it, who else can?"

"As usual, don't know what you're talkin bout, dad. Lydia's tha one. Ashleigh loves her thugz—"

"And that's why she's barefoot and constantly pregnant," said Sondra with a taut expression. "What's wrong with these smart women who make stupid decisions when it comes to non-productive males? I've always told the children to seek relationships that help them develop as people. It ain't about their swag. Come on, really? I'm proud that Stacey's got himself a lovely African girl. He's made a productive choice. She's worth investing in. Who's won? Him or Ashleigh? Be serious!"

"God's got a cold," Stacey told himself.

He loved pluvial days accessorized by brontides and lightning. They impressed him as much as they depressed everyone else.

Who could forebode the culmination of the constant rains of autumn? And who could predict the wily precipitations of a desiderated chalice, especially when she gnawed into becoming positively vicious? Not his pugnacious mother, though a casual genius of a woman. Nor his sage father. And these were the foremost two whom he looked up to.

"Marius reckons relationships are long," he said. "He reckons it's an expense breh's don't need nowadays—"

"Marius is a little filth pot," Sondra said. "I'd rather you didn't listen to him. I know men who are forty-plus, who still act the same way when their hormones were raging at fifteen. No thrift, no development, no growth, no planning because they're still dealing with age-old issues. Your father, thank God, was different. He was sensible but shy, but he's a very productive man. I spent months waiting for him to ask me out. Yes, I liked him but there weren't no way on earth I was going to approach him. And when he finally decides to do something about me, he sends me an anonymous Valentine's Card."

"Did he now?" Stacey said.

"Aren't Valentine Cards supposed to be anonymous?" Fernando said.

Sondra playfully ignored him. "He wrote this poem in the card; it said something about brown sugar and wild horses! It began with: *'Girl, your hair is smooth and rich like silk. Come sit with me on the park bench, and tell me what you think.'* I'll never forget that corny line—"

"But it served its purpose!"

"How did you find out it was him, Momzy?"

"My friends and I had him as our number one suspect. But when I asked him, he denied it."

"It wasn't quite like that," Fernando said, tapping her softly on her bottom. "You and five of your nosy friends ganged up on me in the common room. I had no choice but to say no—"

"You continued to deny it after you walked me home that same day. I have to say, Mr. Fernando Brookes, I was very disappointed.

I told my mom and she was like, what a chicken?"

"How did you get together in the end?" Stacey said.

"He got word that a predatory character was interested in me. If he didn't make his move, he may have lost me. Forever."

Stacey concentrated his glare through the window again. Chalices and chickens. The vagaries of love. *If he didn't make his move, he would've lost me. Forever.*

* * *

Stacey had loved and lost Ashleigh Liebeschuetz forever when she was a middle-class prelapsarian raised on an Enid Blyton-like cul-de-sac in North Wembley. They had been friends from fifteen. She was the first female to elicit amatory causations from within, of which distilled plenty of unheralded addlings. Up to the age of fifteen, she had been home-schooled and was as malleable and docile as they came. She introduced him to her tenebrous mother and her mother adored him. But the likes of Lollipop had grown envious of their friendship.

"You should've bagged dat bunny by now," he said. "Thirsty breh's are gonna be on dat, trust me. If you won't ask her to become wifey, someone will."

And he was right. For on a visit to the Nepenthe Park Estate, the cormorant Johnny was enchanted by Ashleigh's halva exoticisms. He engineered his quantitative caprice the moment Stacey's back was turned. They exchanged mobile numbers, and soon enough, bodily fluids. And Johnny confirmed the relationship to him in his normative crude fashion.

"You see your buff friend Ashleigh," he sneered disdainfully as he roped an arm around Stacey's shoulders. "She came round my yard yesterday, and I fucked her silly in my bedroom... I put her to sleeep, fam! When it comes to chicks like dat, I'm blastin it raw... Maaan, you shouldn't be lettin dat slide thru your fingers, but thanks, rude boi!"

Lollipop was delirious when told of the outcome. "Johnny dogged you on Ashleigh and you still call him fam! Fuck me, blud! If the jackboot was on the other foot, and believe me the jackboot *lives* on the other foot, he'd be spittin blood to dis very day."

Nothing was more gratuitous to Johnny than having his new girlfriend being best friends with a red-blooded mammalian. He told them plainly that they could no longer be friends. They were embarrassed by his volitional prejudice but he succeeded in seguing them apart. Ten months later, she was made pregnant by Johnny. She abandoned her salubrious home with Mother and moved into his flat.

* * *

The rain relented gradually. And when it finally halted, a rainbow revealed its fluted beauty. Most of the children at All Saints School stood in awe of it. And they were also in awe of the two strangers who had come to visit Lil Elliott.

"Ratty's extraaa!" Marius said, kicking the pile of crispy autumn leaves with his Reeboks. "Instead of goin on radio and plug his tune like every MC, he disses bare dads. What a mup!"

Lollipop turned on Lil Elliott. "Your dad might finally seckle after years of tha hit an' run games wiv your mom after hearin what Ratty's sayin bout people like him—"

"I see my dad on a regular—"

"When?" Marius and Lollipop said in unison.

"I spent half-term at his yard, innit... We saw Gus in the pen together. We're tight—"

"So what, he don't come to your yard?" Lollipop said.

"He doesn't come coz of my mom. He don't want her smokin but she doesn't listen. He says it's bad for her womb. She gave him too much backchat. He walked out an' said he weren't never comin back—"

"What the fuck?" Marius said. "He can't tell her what to do in her own home. They're not even together—"

"Really and truly, she should listen coz he gave her four kids. My nan's got cancer coz she was on like fifty-a-day... Everythin fucked up after he left—"

"What's dat supposed to mean?" Lollipop said.

"Gus started goin crazy. Nat's a dyke. You done know Eliza's story already. Family life just went pear-shaped. Dat's why dis country's fucked..."

Marius plucked the delicate jonquils beneath the hedges, tearing them from their stems. "... Maaan! Most people aren't fucked in dis country, even if they don't have much peez. They still find time to get pissed, smoke draws and have crap sex... Come to think of it, I should hang out round Elliott's yard more often. See if I could get all three, but not the crap sex of course! Your mom's one of dem MILFs I'd love to peck. Her cougar arse would definitely get it—"

"Fuck off, man!" Lil Elliott's spleen was self-evident. They supposed that he might cry but he didn't. "Dat's my mom. She may not be the ticket but you don't talk bout bangin your breh's mom."

"You hurt him, Marius," Lollipop said. "You should apologize—"

"I ain't apologizin. Not my fault his mom's a cock monkey swingin from cock to cock. If she lets me, I'll nut it rags! You can't beat a bit of ole skool!"

Lollipop spied four sinewy six-formers watching him intently. One of them ignited his loins with her preternatural bloom. He beckoned her towards him.

"Yeah, you light-skinned ting... Yeah, you... Come 'ere!"

He had an acquired relish for butter-creamed bi-racial females with sable hair, peachy rumps and augmented breasts. Bi-racial females were the mesclun of the earth, the marrow fount of the human well. Her saffron-dyed hair was French-braided. Her eyebrows was synched and she had a brimful mouth. She seemed keen but her stiff-necked friends led her away.

An aghast man emerged on their path, having spied the trespassers from a classroom window. He was alarmed when the rake contrived his earthy overtures towards his students.

"I take it from your appearance that you're not pupils from this school," he said.

"My *appearance*?" Lollipop chuckled dryly and turned to Lil Elliott. "Who's dis chief?"

The man replied before Lil Elliott could. "Elliott Walker, lunch is over. Shouldn't you be in science?"

"Gimme five minutes, Mr. Placide—"

"Your science class began minutes ago, Elliott. You need to get to your lesson now and…" Mr. Placide gestured Lollipop and Marius towards the main exit. "… Can you please leave the school premises? Otherwise I'll call the police—"

Marius spat a mouth full of phlegm on the floor. "Call the pussy ole police! Like you think we run from dem slices of bacon. Dey run from we, ya don know!"

The teacher scratched his canerowed bean and hurried away on nervy heels. Marius was poised to pelt him with a pebble but Lollipop stopped him. He had already devised a plan against the tetchy *Obergruppenführer*.

"Who was dat mup, Elliott?"

"Mr. Placide? He's the Deputy Head—"

"What car does he drive?"

"He's got a Polo—"

"Battered or in spanking condition?"

"It's ain't nothin special. He bought it a couple of months back coz he passed his test. All dat peez and he buys dat shit whip—"

Lollipop cased his eyes upon Mr. Placide who had shrunk into the distant ken. "Go back to your lesson as he says. Don't make a fuss. Don't do nothin stupid an' attract attention for bout a month. Then bout two months from now, get yourself a baseball bat and a balaclava, and smash his whip to fuck. Make sure nobody sees you. I want more dents in it than the fuckin moon."

"I could do dat wiv my eyes closed—"

"No, you couldn't. If you fuck dis up, you'll have boi dem on you. Tha doing is easy. The hard bit's not havin it come back to ya.

Dat's tha discipline."

"I hear what you're sayin. I can handle it—"

"You're lil brother said tha same shit when I sent him on a mission. And look where he is now—"

"Yeh, swing a big fat one on the windscreen for me, blud—" Marius said.

"And get me dat light-skin ting's number," Lollipop said. "What's her name? Mia? She's fleeky... Yeh. Get me dem digits... I got plans for her punani!"

* * *

Though Lollipop was hardly a fan of Ratty's music, he was keen to learn from him the machinations of the music industry. Ratty had his doubts initially, but Lollipop's marauding reputation as a burgeoning hustler put to bed his prejudice. He invited Lollipop to his 48-track studio in Wembley. He played *Congo's Risen Orphan* through his leviathan speakers. When he rhymed about himself, his enunciation was lazy. When he preambled about his mother's sacrifices, his projection became maudlin. The coda was a garrulous diatribe against the sperm donor and the world; an asymmetrical crescendo of clanking drums and syncopated strings brought the song to an industrious end.

"We shot the video last week at a warehouse in Plumstead," Ratty said with a hubristic sigh.

"Tune's sik," Lollipop said. Throughout the song, he had tapped an uneasy foot while Ratty's staves had jigged their delight. "If you cut me a percentage of your label, I'll sponsor bare expenses."

"What percentage we talkin?"

"49%."

"49%? You tryin to rob me? If anythin goes wrong, you lean on me for 2% an' den *you* control the label. Free dat, blud... I got better terms from Sanjay—"

"Sanjay?"

"Yeah, Sanjay. I bumped into him the other day. He offered 40% for a tidy sum—"

"How much was dis tidy sum?"

"Dat's classified info brah!"

"What else did Sanjay say?"

"Bout you? Ha ha. He said he could expose you, blud. He said he could go deep on you. Real deep!"

Lollipop disliked the impudence in Ratty's tone, but Sanjay's duplicity bore his greater contempt.

"You get moist easily, Ratty," he said. "You're a bean-head, but it's what you boys do best. No wonder the world's buyin Africa… for the third time!"

Already, he sought to countermine Ratty by forming a rival label and making Johnny Freelander his first signing. Johnny was a charismatic rapper with more melisma. His symphonics exhibited organic offscourings that plagued working class heroes, unlike Ratty's didactic screeds that talked down to folks. As for Ratty and Sanjay's genial alliance, he was positively sure it would end badly due to their majestic narcissisms. So he left Ratty to his mulish ways and exited the studio with a droll grin.

Sanjay conveniently became Ratty's cater-cousin. Fame, he proclaimed, was an opiate to be downed in substantive doses, to edentate the masses and empower the ego. Ratty took a correlative view.

"I want tha whole world talkin bout me," he said. "They could talk bout what I'm reppin or who I'm fuckin, so long as they're talkin!"

Together, they visited radio stations in Willesden and Wembley, Tottenham and Tooting to promote his launch event. As they sat for hours in the mundane traffic, Ratty spoke vividly about himself.

"I ain't just doin dis for my mom. I'm doin this for my cousins and uncles murdered in Zaire… We're asylum seekers in Peterborough… I'm nine in a foreign land… My dad left us coz he was a coward. He hid behind booze and whores… I could have done street crime coz I was vex but I didn't want my mom goin court, hangin her head in shame…"

He recalled how his mother worked ninety hours a week as a dinner-lady and a domestic, to make certain her sons had opportunities denied to her, having been raised in a bucolic home amidst a protracted civil war. Recently, he had lightened her burden by purchasing a brand new Peugeot as well as settling her long-term debts.

Sanjay rubbed his solar plexus as he listened. "I hear you fam. Your mom's story's like my dad's when he first landed in London. But he's a self-made millionaire now. You and I are like brothers… from different mothers…"

Ratty introduced him to his manager Foe-X, whose thrasonical chatter consisted of alleged late-night business calls with America's leading rapper Nero Sandz. Accompanying him was a figent muliebrous named Muna who served as his PA. Sanjay liked the way she spoke in an ersatz street monotone. Whenever her mouth pouted, he thought of fellatio; his sudorific hands grabbling her stramineous cropped hair while feeding her with his starchy penis. There were others in Ratty's camp, well versed in phony blandishments, but he wasn't warranted with such bagatelles. Wishful falderals were for saplings like Foe-X to contend with. He hired an accountant, his cousin Khalid, to take stock of the label's numismatics, whilst anointing himself the bellwether. Muna's low slung ice-blue denims and vertiginous heels hadn't escaped his pubertal gaze either, and he soon made her his.

Ambrosia-Nectar, the biggest R&B act in the realm, was propitiated to perform at Ratty's launch party. She displayed her conceitedness during the negotiations, much to Sanjay's chagrin.

"Is your tune charted in the top 40?"

"If I sell 10,000 CDs an' I get 10,000 downloads, I'll make top 20 easy—"

"You didn't answer my question—"

"My manager's dealin wiv all dat… I'm just dealin—"

"No... Wait... Wait a second... Shut up for a second... I'm lookin out for ME, OK? I get bare pagans ringin my line daily, chattin bout they're the next big thing reh reh reh when they just want me on their CD to shot more sales coz really and truly, nobody knows dem... I google their name and they're on nobody's search engine. So I look out for me, OK? I'm expensive. Time I was fourteen, I was on my own. I don't have a manager. I'm managin! OK?"

Ratty promised her the premier VIP lounge in the gods. They would perform a doggerel medley on stage together. Grey Goose and Jameson would be on tap all night. A goodie bag containing designer toiletries and M&S vouchers would be gifted her. But her mule-headedness remained.

"You don't give bees honey," Stacey grumbled distastefully after she waddled out of the door with her nine-person entourage. "Realism's a bitch and you should da told dat skank to fuck off..."

"... AND I want a slot for my brother, Robin Cruz," she insisted in a phone call two hours later. "He's got devilry and dash. He'll blow it up—"

Sanjay seized the mobile from Ratty's hand. "You say you're lookin out for yourself. Why ain't ya?"

"Why... Why you on my line? Put Ratty back on."

"I'm the manager. I have the authorization. You want your brother on, you talk to me—"

"If my brother ain't comin on, I'm pullin out—"

"You can do dat if you want, but here's tha situation. I got media links in Indo-China. Ratty's launch party's gonna be live on cable in Indo-China. Dat's a potential audience of three billion. Dat's nearly half the world! If 5% of the population's watchin, dat's 150 million people. Dat's Elvis, Mick Jagger territory. How many CDs can you shift in dem places? If 5% of 150 million buy Ratty's CD, dat's 7.5 million album sales. Compare dat to Nero Sandz who sold 6 million units worldwide. Ratty's already out-sold him in Indo-China. We're not even gone onto concerts in the Bird's Nest in Beijing. We ain't touched UK, Japan, Europe or American markets yet...

Like you care bout dat shit anyway coz you're thinkin small. You're just negotiatin for more friends on VIP lists, more champagne, more spotlights, more legroom, more cushions. Where's your vision?"

Ambrosia-Nectar felt compelled to row her boat back, but not before Sanjay delivered a bumptious rebuke.

"Personally, I'd rather you stayed at home and watched it on your Sky box so you know what you lost. Then the next time I offer you a deal, you'd bite my fuckin hand off!"

"When I see you, I'm gonna bite your fuckin nose off!" Ambrosia-Nectar said.

Ratty's private felicitations eventually cooled her berserk fury.

Twang agreed to be the main DJ with miniature fuss. Sanjay applauded his visionary zeal. Comedian Joey Kafuffle, the night's compere, galled at the seemingly lack of organization.

"It's like dis is some joke ting dawg an' I ain't clownin," he whinged in a languid drawl. "I specifically said all peez needs to be paid in full, twenty-eight days before the show. Only a week to go an' you ain't paid me, blud."

"Forget what was said before," Sanjay said. "Times are hard wiv the economy these days. Everyone's gotta cut back, even tha government. I got a new pay-related performance deal for ya. You get paid in full after tha show, and it all depends on how many laughs you get—"

"Listen. I ain't no amateur. I've been doin dis ting for twenty years—"

"And you ain't a household name yet! So who's the joke ting? This shit dat I bring has never been tried. Simon Cowell would love to dream dis up. A new artist's havin his debut live on cable and the internet and you're goin on like you're doin us a favor! You either tag or blow—"

Joey slammed the phone down. He dialed Ratty and whinged some more. Ratty referred the veteran amateur back to Sanjay.

"So you taggin or blowin, dawg? I've gotta lot of figurative types ready to step in if you're ready to step off—"

"I'm gonna do it... as a favor to Ratty, yuh get me——"

"Whateva, fam. I may have long pockets but I've got short hands. I'm skilled in the sabermetrics of the game. I smell bullshit like you smell pussy. And I know you're pissed so don't front. Wheneva you deal wiv me, it's all bout pay-related performances. Realism's a bitch. Dat's what you should have learnt in dem twenty years!"

*   *   *

In spite of the juggernaut of rain that poured from heaven, Ratty's launch party had brought an effervescent mood to the gloaming streets of Mill Hill. Muna orchestrated matters from her trusty iPad. While Foe-X gallivanted his infantilism before the females, it was she who designated the dressing rooms for each act, who signed off deliveries of props, who dictated the chroma of the stage lights, who had the final word.

"You look fuckin sexy!" Sanjay said. He wrapped her Chanel scarf around her pink neck. She smelt of *Alien*.

"You look better," she cooed.

"Nah. You look better." He glanced intently at the record of attendees ascribed to the gatekeepers. "Jeez! I could hear cash registers ringin in my head. Money makes the world go round——"

"But love makes it spin," she said and kissed his philtrum.

Ratty was embellished in a billowing Moorish sartorial but his resolution was less than confident. He complained of some unfettered contrivance by Lollipop and Johnny that may ruin his day. Sanjay tried to allay his suspicions in spite of his discomposed drinking.

"For fuck sake, where's your game face?"

"Why's Muna let dem in? Ain't she in charge of security?"

"Maaan! You need to loosen up..."

He led Ratty down a stone staircase and into a pervasive cellar loaded with old chattel and a stained mattress. From his pocket, he produced a bag of yayo and a pair of fifty-pound notes. Whilst he prepared the devourings, Ratty, chilled by some sibilant draught, watched his spindly shadow.

"Tha snowman couldn't melt in here—" he said.

"The snow's bout too, son. Take it in, fam..."

Ratty did as he was bidden. Sanjay watched him with an invariable grin. After a plethora of sniffs, he made way for Sanjay who absorbed voraciously.

"Bet-taaah!" they neighed together.

Sanjay's phone rang. It was Muna. Lollipop was demanding that his girlfriend get in for free. Johnny's splenetic spiels were a worry. Ambrosia-Nectar was erupting. Several males had been turned away for not being suitably attired. She was close to breaking point.

"Get Foe-X to help you," Sanjay said. "He should deal wiv any trouble head-on. It ain't right he's abandoned you... I'm in a meeting, hun... Be wiv you in fifteen!"

He turned to Ratty, eliciting a boorish chuckle. "Know dis, yeh... Lollipop tried to get me to pull out y'know, not be your partner... I invested in dat hater and he wants to keep me out of investin... investin in our label!"

"Waaah!" Ratty's cheeks irradiated upon that revelation. "And Lollipop's goin on like he's a self-made hustla!"

"Self-made hustla, my arse! He practically begged me to help his skin. Gave me a sob story bout his hard life. Like listenin to an Oxfam appeal. He cried a fuckin ocean. I wouldn't be human if I couldn't push a few keys his way to get him started!"

"Cried a fuckin ocean? I shoulda been there, fam—"

"Tell me somethin, Ratty. What's the point of Foe-X?"

"He's been my manager for two years—"

"But he ain't done shit today. He's left Muna to do all the work—"

"He's my tight bredrin, still. Man made me believe in myself when people doubted me—"

"No one's doubtin you now, Ratty. You can stop believin in him. I stopped believin in the Tooth Fairy when I realized it was my mom puttin tha shrapnel under my pillow—"

"Blud, I can't jus drop my boy. At least let's see how things are six months from now—"

"We ain't got six months. We may not have six weeks if dat crawler's checkin gal when he's supposed to be workin. You may as well let Muna be your manager. She's presentable, posh and she'll take you places—"

"Muna works for him—"

"She works for me now. She'll do what I say. Either he's out. Or I'm out. I don't fuck wiv crawlers!"

As they made their way back to the main hall, they noticed Johnny sitting in the lounge with his thighs pushed together, one hand on each kneecap, spewing hubristic sludges into Lydia's eardrum.

"You watch, yeah. Six months from now, it's my turn! I'm in the studio every day. Ashy hardly sees me. My kids cry, where's daddy? But I'm forever makin bangerz like a tsunami and tha Seven Nation Army, all in one!"

"Did you hear bout my radio interview?" Ratty said.

"Naaah. I don't listen to *Bling*, rude boi!"

"How'd you know it was on *Bling*?"

"I didn't say I knew it was on *Bling*. I said I don't listen to *Bling*. But I'd presumed you'd be on there since Twang pays rappers to go on his spot!"

"He didn't pay me, cuz!"

"You're not a rapper!"

Ratty cast a leathery gaze upon him. "Foxes have holes, birds make nests. Lions build dens, but sperm donors smoke ses. Is dat right, fam?" – Johnny stared wonderlessly into the spatial air – "I'm controversial all day long. I speak my mind and don't business who I offend—"

"Tha dawg's gotta lead the blind," Sanjay said. "Dem muthafucker's been plottin against Ratty since 7/7 an' he had shit to do wiv it."

Muna, from nowhere, imposed herself on the scene. She asked Sanjay to have a word with the club owner who had grave reservations about the use of pyrotechnics on stage. Then she took Ratty by the arm.

"*Jam* is ready for your interview. You ready?"

Ratty nodded and allowed himself to be led by her.

On the podium, Twang stood as if he were the Pope before a Xmas mass. He embraced the babel discord by raising his arms. Two scantily clad females wearing Union Jack colors gyrated him while he ambled towards his decks.

Blaze prowled the dance floor. Females danced in phalanges, croodling to the lyrics, ears fine-tuned to every strand of rhythm as they contortioned and twerked to Twang's records. Blaze dared to request a shimmy from a wheatish maiden in denim hotpants. He was found wanting. A second girl wearing Diamante platform heels spurned him with a brusque gesture. Then he spied Sophia alone, sipping a Sambuca by the bar, and was bewitched. She looked magnificent in a hectoring décolletage.

"Is it true you're Lollipop's girl?"

"Who's askin?"

"Blaze, innit."

"I'm a pyromaniac too. You and I will get along fine."

He took a seat beside her. "Can I get you a drink?"

"St. Ides please!"

She accepted the drink. Not a word of thanks.

"Dat breh's gotta 'ave somethin big, an' I mean somethin big, to have a chick like you."

"Believe me, he has!"

"Last year, he could never bag a bunny like you!"

She observed him with a wry smile: an importunate munter with pitted skin. Whose sincerest affections could he possibly secure, she thought. Not even the plainest Jane!

"Do you smoke?" she said.

"Nah!"

"You would if I set you alight!"

"Is dat meant to be some joke?"

"Jokes are subjective, bredrin—"

"I used to go school wiv Lollipop: me, Stacey, Marius. All us boys use to roll together every day of the week. We know each other's secrets—"

"Tell me a secret, fuckster!"

"I gave him his road name. Breh used to have a big head and a skinny neck, like a lollipop. I gave dat breh his road name. I gave him his manhood. Ask him now, an' he'll lie an' say some different shit."

"It's a bitch eat dog world!"

"Have you fucked him?"

"Many, many times. Why do you ask?"

"I just wanna know. Do you fuck people dat aren't your man?"

"If I like 'em, then yeah—"

"Breh's like Lollipop would fuck chicks dat aren't his to fuck. An' if you believe dat he would never do dat to you, den you're dumb."

"Never is a very long time, baby—"

"Here's my number." He gave her his business card. He watched her read it. "You call me, if you need anythin: CDs, DVDs, garms, jewelry, computer games, anythin you can think of... And when big man disappoints, bell me still. I'll take you shoppin. I'll fill you in!"

"I bet you would!" she said, as she downed St. Ides.

*　*　*

To Ratty's heartened relief, the club was filled with scented glamazons. Leggiadros and Apollonias, dressed in diaphanous drapes and hipster jeans, paved the dance floor beneath the fluorescent lights. There were Barbarellas and Betty Boos, Jahreen the Dreams and Jessica Rabbits, pert delightfuls reified in their decorative essentials. By the bar, bacchanalian drinking went unabated. Jamocha-skinned boys sipped firework cocktails with milky brunettes in clinquant skirts. Variegated males were embellished by D&G jeans and Haruache trainers. VIP bloggers downed the free booze and tweeted their oleaginous extolments from their smartphones. Ratty and his band became bartenders for half an hour, serving drinks whilst giving impromptu interviews.

Ratty's mother paraded a multi-hued batik decorated in West African-styled swirls and motifs. His aunt wore a configuration of flamboyant yellow and traffic-coned amber. They were drunk with joy. Their small speeches invoked the loudest cheer. Ratty joined them for photographs. The cacophony of genial applause tarried the club. He performed florid verses in their honor. Mom and Auntie B quietly departed thereafter. The bellicosity of the dance floor was a little too racy for their Baptist dispositions.

Ambrosia-Nectar, wearing a white whalebone corset, climbed onto the stage and performed with a septet of metrosexual dancers known as *Boy Cheer*. They were marvelous to behold. Then MC Hashtag strewed his lyrical verbiage onto a delightful melody, and even the mournful Johnny nodded his accord and approved quietly. Ratty took to the stage with his contingent. He stared over the sea of his heads and performed *Congo's Risen Orphan* and other compositions from his album of rhymes. Afterwards, Robin Cruz bounced around the stage on his Yeezy Boost 350s, synergized by his own rapture. He remained on stage over his allotted time, proceeding to freestyle a lode of lyrics even after Muna ordered the DJ to halt his record-scratching. Sanjay then cut his mic.

"Foe-X said dat I could drop my newest release on stage," Robin Cruz said.

"Foe-X ain't got no authority here," Sanjay said. "I'm tha supreme authority—"

"Don't get it twisted," Foe-X said. "You're only the money—"

"Subtract dat money an' tonight was never happenin—"

"What do you know bout music, bruh? Who do you know in music? Fuckin nobody, dat's who. Ratty, I tol' you shouldn't bring in dis prick—"

"Well, Ratty's got something to say to you. After you've heard it, you'd kill yourself, bruh. Tell him his current status, Ratty!"

All eyes were on Ratty, who couldn't bring himself to look at his chief enabler.

"I need you to fall back on dis one, fam. I appreciate what you done yeah, but I ain't got a role for you right now since Muna is now managin' an' Sanjay is—"

"So dat's how you goin on? I've been backin man since nobody knew man, an' man is goin on cruddy on tha launch of his first single? Dis is what I tellin you, let's put dis ting down on paper but you're goin on like your word is your bond... Your word ain't worth shit, cuz. You wanna drop me like a lead balloon? Dat's OK... What goes around comes around. Come eighteen months, you'll be packin baked bean tins in Lidl's. Remember, I'm tellin you dis—"

"You've finally shown your true colors," Sanjay said. "You're supposed to pray for those who despisefully use you. But don't worry! We bless those dat curse us!"

"No hard feelings," Ratty said hopefully.

"Fuck your feelings," Foe-X said.

He swung for Ratty, who was agile enough to duck. Plenty caught hold of his propelling arms before they reached its target. Ratty swore at him and accused him of being dilatory and infantile.

"You got your yard dogs an' yes men wiv you but I'm tha only one who tells you THE TRUTH!" Foe-X said.

"Get outta 'ere before you leave dis club in a hearse!" Sanjay said.

Muna took the woeful man away and suggested that he go home and unwind with a spliff and a beer. She would intercede for him later. But Foe-X's hubris had been wounded and he wanted no future part in this charade. He snatched his Brunello Cucinelli overcoat and made hay in his Pajero under the early morning sky, to a destination unknown.

Joanne calibrated inextricably to the lecherous desires of the Cercopes' by the bar. Sanjay desired her for his cesspit needs. He viewed her goodies with favor.

"Damn!" he said, glaring lecherously at the profundity of her buttocks. "She's ass-tronomical, fam. I bet she's never eaten a salad, just cassava and yams for her!"

"I thought Muna was wifey—" Ratty said.

"I'd shed tears of joy if I get to poke dat. I swear down. Why don't we get her to milk us together—"

"Together? Are you mad? Tha risk of crossin swords is always high—"

"We could do a porn flick wiv her—"

"Why don't you find yourself an Asian gal, blud?"

Sanjay was mithered at such a suggestion. "Why you bein so fuckin racist for?"

"Calm down, booty juice breath! I'm just sayin if she's gonna get beast fucked on camera, it should at least be with a black breh, preferably a dark skinned brotha like myself, who can fully appreciate a Mount Everest arse like hers. And yes, she's already degraded herself wiv me before but dat's cool coz I'm a future rock star. Now if I ever catch her wiv you totally arsed out by your boys, I'd be totally offended."

Sanjay's expression changed markedly. "I didn't even know the bitch was black till you mentioned it. It doesn't matter what color a bitch is coated in anyway. It isn't like she's wholesome, cuz. Or is dis a case of each to their own, you racist muthafucker!"

He ushered Joanne towards him with an extravagant sweep of the arm. She accentuated her large keister in a gridded mini-dress, tossing her artificial mane that spun like a horse's tail. She did this repeatedly between her shoulder blades as Sanjay charmed her and made her chuckle. He bought her a glass of Alsatian wine. His clammy paw soon clasped that prized keister.

* * *

As the revelers cavorted to the acoustics beneath the foudroyant lights, Sophia took Lollipop on a befuddled walk, to the mossy promontories of the River Brent. The surge of dark waves crept tediously towards the strand, retreating its charge before repeating its cycle. Four bipedal silhouettes huddled around a bonfire, and a slender youth among them plucked elegantly at the strings of a Takamine. Sophia took him further along until the strumming and crackling bonfire hummed cordially in the breeze. They halted in the zephyr.

"I want us to fuck here," she said.

He rubbed her hirtellous arms as they smooched. He slurped her areola gratefully with his mouth. They swooned awkwardly to the muddy floor. They hurriedly undressed themselves. She rolled him on his back. The earth was moist but the air was grody and the bellows from the trees caused his spine to shiver. Earthworms and snails wriggled contrariwise near him, rain bathing in the fine drizzle. A toad croaked ominously by the waterfront.

"Someone might see us," he said.

"I want them too," she said.

He couldn't extrapolate on what excited her so. He preyed upon her multifarious blessings to keep himself from failing her. She watched Blaze sitting on a log in the near distance. He had already exposed himself and was foaming with ebullition. The ornery of her votaries procured her pleasure. She sucked her thumb and hastened her intensity. He chugged beneath her, strewing all he could from his kernels. Then she climbed from him and lay in the grass unabashed. He tried to kiss her but she moved her mouth away.

"Was it good for you?"

"Dat was fuckin fantastic, babes!"

"Did you cum?"

"Yeaaah hun… I came loads. You must have known… Didn't you… like cum?"

"No."

"Oh! I thought… What? You never?"

She gathered her stray tassels and began to dress. "What tha fuck does it matter? … Let me get my clothes on… in case I get done for somethin… dat wasn't worth it…"

He watched in near horror as she belted her Escada jeans.

"Dat's somethin a man should never ask," she said, half-speaking to herself. "Did you cum? Have you cum yet? If I came, you'd fuckin know. And if I didn't cum, you ain't up to tha fuckin job!"

"Come; let me finish you off den—"

"I don't need finishin off. I need a drink!"

She bounded away in her Guiseppe Zanotti stilettos, leaving him crushed on the wet grass. Who was to blame for this carnal calamity? His prowess had never been a problem, even while stoned or drunk. Right now, he was neither and he wished he were. He was at his tardiest after fucking, and fucking up.

The River Brent inveigled into torrents as the rain fell faster. He slipped on his clothes and buttoned his coat and hurried towards the club. The strange youths had gone. Their fire had yet to be extinquished by the rain. Stacey canoodled with Lydia beneath a bus shelter. Their incremental passions filled him with envy. He pushed his hoodie over his bean so he wouldn't be seen. Marius and Johnny conversed with three apricot-tanned females from out of town, trying to segue a way into their vajazzling vaginas. He strode furtively past them and onto the insuperable dance floor. He scurried into the bar where she sat among a dojo of fog demons, imbibing a Campari. He languished before her, dripping wet.

"What happened?"

"Did somethin happen?"

"Don't fuck bout Sophia. How do you expect me to concentrate in the fuckin rain?"

"My ex and I managed it in the fuckin snow."

"Who was he, the Ice Man?"

She downed her Campari and asked the bartender for another. He sat beside her and placed his mitts upon hers.

"Jesus, you're wet!" She pulled her hands away. "But at least dat's more than I'll ever be."

Still, he moored himself against her. "You remember what we did after Carnival? Your Range Rover, Beachy Head, full moon, midsummer's night? You said it was your best ever—"

"I lied—"

"Sophia, you're fuckin nuts—"

"And you have none!"

"Fuck you, yeah! Just coz you're buff, dat doesn't make you special."

He plied across the dance floor and into the night. The rain had petered out already. He lit a joint under the colonnade, and tried to smoke his anxieties away.

Pretty girls like Sophia St. Clair were a problem. Catatonic cornballs on Twitter was the cause. They aggrandized her onto a celestial plain. He had read some of their fatuous tweets from her 166,000 followers. Most were batshit crazy. They had fawned and re-tweeted her unlettered sentences as if it were divine writ. She had accused him of insecurity when he bemoaned the drooling creeps who explicitly propositioned her on social media. He replied that he was less than bothered. What man, in his utmost confidence, would be even slightly perturbed by the patently absurd? They could not keep her for a minute, let alone possess her in their dreams. He was more concerned with what this servile bullshit was doing to her petted brain. Henceforth, he would be painfully uninterested in mercurial love. Was this the reason why she had prevaricated endlessly out of her elliptical mouth? Had she not thought that her ceramic charm would hoodwink him into not doubting her sooth? She had lied about having a *gangsta* stepbrother, whom she refused to name. She paltered about her own *gangsta* credentials being far superior than his.

"Is dat the best you could do?" she said after he had narrated the story of his arrest in Cricklewood. "When I was thirteen, I'd go into hair and beauty shops and have a field day. I shoplifted bout fifty times. Never got caught once!"

The zoot had worked its magic. He decided it was time to leave. Blaze straggled towards him, accompanied by a nauseating peal. He was bamboozled by the beer.

"You lucky bastard! You've been tellin bare lies to bag a chick like dat. Enjoy her while it lasts—"

"I ain't you, blud. Dat's what you do. Now fuck off."

Blaze danced in the featureless puddles amidst the broth of dog crap.

"Sweet Moses! She's gawwjus, blud. She's got a teardrop arse... I'd love to rain on dat ho..."

Lollipop cast his zoot aside, and cast the deplorable cunt against a heap of rubbish bins. He thundered several kicks into the whelp's body until he pleaded mercy. By the time Marius and Johnny sprinted over to step in, he was satisfied.

"Blaze, I'll set you on fire if you ever disrespect me again," he said.

Sophia had watched him fight from under the colonnade. She followed him to the car park. There was an awkwardness in her bearing.

"Sweet Moses! You certainly banged him up—"

"I should've banged you up—"

"You'll get a second chance to—"

"You and I are done, Sophia. Remember I dumped you. Not the other way round—"

"You're dumpin me? For what reason?"

"Coz you're overrated!"

She laid her forehead against his shoulder blade and put an arm around his side. His timorous rage slowly evaporated.

"Shit, you intimidate the hell out of me," she said.

"What do you mean?"

"Mean by what?"

"You said I intimidate the hell out of you—"

"Well, you do—"

"So what was your performance all bout den?"

"I was just bein a bitch. I'm sorry, Chicken."

He lifted her head from his shoulder blade. He looked into her unearthly eyes.

"Where I'm from, there's nuff peng gal. They're poppin out on road like a factory. One born every minute. I like you bad, real talk yeah, but I ain't no thirsty breh. Ask Stacey or Johnny or any breh who knows me from way back when. I weren't forkin out for no gal. Even if we went McDonald's, she's gotta pay for her own nuggets wiv her own shrapnel. You changed dat. I'd even treat you to horse-riding lessons coz you're my girl."

"So I changed you den?"

"I can change back to the monster I was before—"

"You should be careful when you mention girl and horse in the same sentence—"

He neighed nosily over her jibber. "Kiss me and apologize—"

"So it's you that gets to do the forgiving—"

"I said, kiss me and apologize."

Slowly, she sucked the air from his mouth with her concolorous dahlia lips. He cooed gratefully and closed his eyes.

"You make me feel safe," she said.

That revelation convalesced his anxiety. *She made him feel safe.* He cosseted her in his arms, daring not to let her go. His anomalous Lorelei was the cause and cure to his neurosis. She was his worth in his worthless state. He would love her into obscurity. He would love her perversity. He would willfully endure her, for she could not be broken. If only she were docile and simplistic and constant. If only she would follow him into Empyrean above, Abaddon below. If only.

8

DOVES ON THA
CADILLAC...

JOHNNY KEPT COURT BY the graffitied wall. His grievances
were plenty but nothing grieved him as having to wait for Lil
Elliott who was in possession of his skunk. Gregory showed him
candaulisms on his mobile and boasted that he was blessed by
female benevolence, and that he was unlike any fellow on the estate.
Marius pelted a conker at a wandering fox and old man Dominic
stirred in acute silence. Finally, Lil Elliott emerged sheepishly
from his front door and Johnny's voice boomed towards him like
a foghorn.

"What tha fuck, yellow bwoy? You can't have man wait an hour
for his food. I ought to phone Lollipop and tell him to sack you
coz you're too fuckin slow!"

Lil Elliott's touched everybody's fists. "My mom wouldn't let
me outta my yard. I had to sneak out."

"What did you do?" Johnny said.

"I got suspended from school, innit. Somebody mashed up Mr.
Placide's whip. Some prick reckoned he saw me do it. You know
what? *I did it!*" A draught of bravado cataracted his spine. "I'm
gonna bitch-slap dat snitch once it's over!"

"Is that how you're goin on?" Johnny said.

"If you were me, you'd do the same!"

Gregory embraced him warmly. "Good answer. Good answer. Go wan, younger. You're peak. So what did you do when the Fedz came for you?"

"Dey asked me bare stupid questions. Mr. Placide called my mom down, innit. I gotta big her up. She backed man. She's wylin like: 'Nah, it ain't him. My son ain't no angel, but he ain't no devil either. Why's my son gonna smash up your whip? Where's your proof?' Reh reh reh. She weren't havin it!"

"Once they think it's you, you're guilty," Marius said. "Why be surprised when the enemy acts like tha enemy—"

"Anyway, enough of dat shit," Johnny said, holding out an acquisitive mitt. "Where's my food?"

Lil Elliott revealed a small cling film ball squashed in his cute palm. Johnny grabbed it greedily.

"So you're coming back to my place to bun it down?" Dominic said hopefully.

He claimed to have lived a vilipend lifestyle in accordance to the stoicism of the streets. Nowadays, he paced the pavements in a droll trance. Cocaine and Ketamine were the poisons he siphoned in his pitiful abode. The escapades of the *youngers* excited him. He related to them hyped war stories from the iniquitous nineties. Unbeknown to him, he was ridiculed for his exiguous meeds from the *grind* and recognized for what he was – an addled aging homunculus with rotten teeth, knocking on forty but without attaining middle-age certitude.

"Lollipop does tha best food now," he said. "Charmer was my boy, and I was ridin dat Colombian airline for six years. But since Lollipop started shottin food, I deleted Charmer's number—"

"I'm goin to my bed—" Johnny said.

"You can't do dat," Dominic said. "You wanna lose man an' bun it down without yours truly. I know your plan!"

Everyone laughed raucously. For that, indeed, was the plan.

The susurrus wind flogged their coats and coerced the leaves around their feet. The vignettes they recalled from memory induced cheer, away from the intractable tides they dog-paddled in.

"I wish the world could go back to when we were kids," Gregory said. "We lived coz we didn't know. Now we know, we can't live. I remember listenin to some of dem artist's dere, tha flava of tha old skool, Beverly Knight an' ting—"

"You should da been bout in 1992," Dominic said. "Dat's when street life was street life like Randy Crawford said. No CCTV, no internet, no Twitter timelines. No Fedz tracking you from Outer Space. Harlesden was like Harlem in dem times. I had a wiked music collection in dem days. Maaan, I'd be up Vibe City every weekend, buyin my vinyl. But Vibe City's closed down. All coz of the fuckin internet!"

"You've jumped off tha internet?" Marius said.

"I don't even *use* the internet, blud. It's the biggest scam of all time. The government wants everyone online so they can monitor y'all and peeps are fallin for it like lambs to tha slaughter. You're wanna take a dump, you put it on Facebook. Then some sad fuck re-tweets it and the whole world's gassin bout your dump like it's their business! Truss, whenever MI5's lookin for you, all they need do is Facebook your arses coz you're easy to find!"

Lil Elliott blew his nose into the wind. "You could Facebook me but how many Elliott Walker's would you find? Millions..."

Two aliens were quiescent in the bushes, contiguous as they peeped through the shrubs. They edged towards Johnny and his assemblage; slowly, stilly, hoping to remain unseen.

"I've got some rare imports of Burning Spear tracks," Dominic said. "You can't get dem nowhere, blud! Nowhere!"

"Burning Spear?" Johnny said. "You're more Britney Spears than Burning Spear, blud. Why you so prang? Man like you *can* use the internet. Government ain't gonna fuck wiv you coz you're no threat!"

"I'm a threat," Dominic said. "I got a strap and it'll blow man to fuck—"

"What you got?"

"An ArmaLite AR-24!"

"Ya lie—"

"Tell him I ain't lyin, Gregory. You seen it."

"I seen it, Johnny. He ain't bullshittin—"

"I might need dat sometime," Johnny said.

"Anytime, cuz," Dominic said.

He raved on indiscreetly about pridian times, and his embarkation onto the street grind at the age of nine, and how the ArmaLite fell into his ownership after its owner Midnight was gruesomely slain. He was boring his comrades, chuntering on about his desire to become a chrononaut so he could put his past wrongs right.

"Maaan! You should da seen me back in the day… Everyone was scared of me… police, soldier, bad man… I was down wiv O.P.P—"

"More like you were down wiv P.O.L.I.C.E," Marius said.

"Cuz, I was *never* down wiv no police. You can't be makin jokes like dat coz it only takes a careless word to ruin a man's rep and on road, dat's all a man's got—"

"Seckle your skin, Dominic!" Johnny said. "Dis ain't 1992. Eeeka-Mouse ain't on *Top Of The Pops*. N.W.A's gone solo. Normski ain't doin his ting on BBC2 no more. We ain't tha Musical Youth happy-go-lucky generation. Fuck 1992, fuck tha beat box and fuck electric boogaloo—"

"And fuck tha internet!" Dominic said. "You got Wikipedia but how many youngers can show me Ghana on a map?"

"Who gives a fuck where Ghana is on the map?" Marius said. "Knowin where Ghana is ain't gonna get man paid."

"Why you think nowadays the yutes are shottin their own mixtapes?" Johnny said. "No one relaxes their hair like your lot did coz your label said so. So support tha yutes an' not no jerry curl sellouts. Learn from us. If you had bigger bollocks in the eighties and nineties, we won't be in dis shit-hole today!"

"Whose dem people over dere?" Lil Elliott said.

The first alien had unruly eyebrows that jigged every time he chuckled. The second wore a baseball cap. Her porcine lineaments were smudged by the penumbra of the street lamps. Both wore matching lengthy leather jackets. Gregory tried to tune in to their pitter-patter voices against the elements but to no avail.

"Boy dem!" he said.

Whatever guise they took, their idiosyncrasies were the same – uniform or without.

"You sure, Gregz?" Marius said. "You're not bein paranoid."

"In the slums, you gotta be paranoid!"

Dominic sniffed the windy air incessantly, as if they carried a peculiar scent.

"Welcome to our endz, boys in blue!" he said. "We know you're police. You watch us. We watch you—"

"Dey comin over," Johnny said. "You should've just kept your big mouth shut—"

"I've blown their cover. They're comin over to chat shit!"

The portly woman stared kindly into their faces. "Do you lads know where I can get an iPhone from?... I know it's a strange question coz it's nearly one in the morning and I'm freezing my tits off out here... I need an iPhone, the newest model... You... You lads know where I can get one from? I'll pay good money for one—"

"Do we look like the Carphone Warehouse?" Johnny said.

"Do you live on this estate?"

"What's it to you? We done know you're Fedz. So bounce. You've gotta be tha worst undercover Fedz in the Met police—"

The man with the unruly eyebrows laughed like a bear. "That's a first! Actually, we're journalists from *The Daily Dazzle*. We're doing a story about the availability of stolen smartphones in your bits—"

"In my bits?" Marius said. "Fuck dat shit! Look, we ain't no gang, but you'll find what you're lookin for... You're in our faces and we ain't jacked you. You're lucky you've come here on a good day otherwise I'd punch you in your face..."

* * *

From Krista's bedroom window, Lydia spectated the drama below.

"Fedz are out in force tonight!" she said.

"Why am I not surprised?" Krista said. "Those waste men have been out there all bloody evening. Thirty years from now, you'll see their balding heads out there, drinking Guinness and smoking bud. I hope your boyfriend doesn't end up like that."

"Stacey's not even out there…"

Krista joined her by the window. Flashing blue lights placarded the Close. Johnny protested against the fucking lunacy of police exuberance with a vitriolic mouth. An officer warned him to mind his gob. Krista sighed and returned to her desk.

"What do you think they did?"

"Does the police need a reason for coming at them?"

"I've *never* been stopped by police. But if I was police, I'd harass those thugz every day. A thugz on permanent PMT. He switches every hour coz he's got issues wiv the world and his wife and most of all, with himself."

"Oh God! Another one that's drank the kool-aid—"

"Stop being a bleeding heart, Lydia. Too many fools love to promote the stereotype. It's those fools you gotta avoid, no matter how cute they look… And then you've got scumbag girls tryin to go on bad, tryin to out-smoke and out-fuck the fools. When they grow up, they'll be permanently on benefits and they'll never, ever amount to anything remotely close to success in their entire lives, even if they lived for two thousand years…"

Lydia returned to her seat, slightly discombobulated. For the duration of their study together, Krista had cussed the lowborn with a viperous tone, blaming them for their own maladies. The five thousand-word screed she composed was immured with that belief.

"…Those dickheads have their beliefs and I have mine. Avoid thugz, souljas or whateva they call themselves at all cost, no matter how cute or charismatic. They will lead to your serious downfall. Two: Never go out wiv a man who has a babymother. Because when they go around and see their kids, they're still fucking their babymothers... Three: Never, ever, ever, ever become their mother. They think it's cool to call their girlfriend *Mami* but I'd be offended, insulted, displeased, annoyed, repulsed, angered... and pissed the fuck off if my man called me that!" Without warning, she aimed a broadside. "I was disappointed when you said yes to Stacey. I know he's light-skinned but seriously—"

"I didn't go out wiv him coz his light-skinned..."

"Ashleigh used to go on about how buff Johnny was. She doesn't say dat shit anymore. She's stuck wiv the wotless git. Now she treats him like an invalid and gives him unlimited blowjobs—"

"Well, at least Stacey doesn't wanna be a rapper like everybody else—"

"What does the road geek wanna do? Or does he even know?"

"You can't help who you fall in love with, Krista—"

"That's what crazy arse women say when they fall in love with Death Row inmates—"

"Why do you look down on peeps like you're from a different class?"

"I AM a different class. I don't speak and think like they do. It's a fucking shame that when the world sees me, they think of them. That's the albatross around my fucking neck—"

"The world's to blame for that, and not them. You said it yourself. Why's the world's so discriminatory? Why's everyone on constant survival mode? Why can't you see that? Who's mindfucked here?"

"The world ought to be *more* discriminatory, Lydia. That's how we get *less* prejudice. Puppy love leads to a dog's life. Or a dawg's life, as Stacey would say. Think of all those jail visits, court trials and then the inevitable Clear Blue when he blows you up. You're so mindfucked you suspend judgement. Good luck and enjoy the race to the bottom!"

Lydia watched as she cackled maniacally. She was, after all, free to accrue her snobbery to whomsoever she pleased. No doubt, she believed her blue-eyed *übermensch* of middle-class stock, some formulaic physician whom she hoped to marry, would arbalest her into the stratosphere above the hoi polloi and away from shocking wastrels like err... Stacey. Lydia could no longer study and so she bade her goodnight.

These chastening days were aplenty and they almost drove her crazy. The street reeked of the skunk that Johnny and the rest had smoked earlier. Stacey's bedroom light was out. Usually, she would throw a pebble against his window to wake him but she chose not to disturb him, tonight.

His gentility was a tableau of everything she had envisaged in a man. Yet everyone seemed jealous of her germinal gain, none more so than Ashleigh. She had been conspicuously cold. Still, Lydia propitiated her one-time friend one final time via WhatsApp as to the cause of her *froideur* but Ashleigh replied with lofty disdain:

"Sorry hun – rumors ain't my thing. You believe dem rumors. I'm onto what's important like my kids, Johnny and me, so bless you..."

Perhaps her neutered maladies had been intensified by Johnny's morbid melodies! And it couldn't help her cause having that termagant Lindsey in her stride...

Lindsey, twenty-seven years going on seventeen, was one of the world's great tattlers. She had produced three babes from three men. The father of her youngest was Sean, a trainee electrician, and he raised her other children as if they were his own. Nevertheless, his sober equanimity bored her no end. He worked long hours but he never took her anywhere. She became a Facebook junkie, exchanging libertine messages with an American soldier serving in Kuwait, and other cosherers who expected to be kept. Much of her time was spent watching raffish television. And Lydia despaired of her attention to detail on the lives of celebrities she read about on TMZ, and how she chittered earnestly about *Real Housewives* and the Kardashians, as if she knew those celebs personally.

Natalie Walker was the last sane Mammalian on Planet Nepenthe, and Lydia admired her forbearance. She could have simply despised all men after the Judas breachings of her sister.

But the ritual burning of all things Gregory and the deed poll changing of Tiana's surname from his to hers were the only reprisals enacted. Six months on and those somnambulant days had passed. There was no need for man-sized Kleenex tissues, bitter prates of retribution or listening to male-bashing anthems. Gregory became a mere popinjay; Natalie revealing how he enjoyed feasting upon her lactating breasts and being fingered anally during congress. How Tanya wept at her indiscretions!

Hormones Nightclub was where the decadent raved, where the olive-skinned flagrantly dry-humped the honey-glazed. It was where Lydia, Natalie, Ladelle and Rebecca arrived on most Saturdays. And it was here that Natalie first found comfort in the arms of the inverted but ambisextrous Eugenie, a Sapphic Ukrainian with polar ice-cap teeth and mauve lipstick. When they first met, they osculated on the dance floor, before the buttinsky and the gapeseed. Thereafter, they were inseparable, and no one dared demur over their relationship. Even the loquacious Tanya kept her infamous gob firmly shut.

Eugenie's refined tastes induced Natalie into a world of the vernissage and horse-racing, and Natalie encouraged her to get her tongue pierced and give her regular cunninglingus with it. Behind closed bedroom doors, there were many sybaritic deeds that involved boot black dildos, Mephistophelean red horns, votive candles and other bedroom candies. Lydia often found them reclining, opalescent shanks wrapped around each other; Eugenie's rubious head resting upon Natalie's mighty bosom as though she had been suckled. And Eugenie loved wearing partially unclad kaftans that revealed her pert posterior, which Natalie, at her pleasure, sought a grope or a smite.

Lydia often sought their company whenever she returned from campus. Their bohemian revelries were contrary to her orthodox rearing where excursions of that nature had been long extinguished by her puritan mother. Liqor flowed with constancy at the Walkers and so did the music. She made way to their home after lunch, after Stacey said she'd find him there.

"You look buff in dem jeans," said a dreadlocked fellow, taking a breather from painting Natalie's front door. "How about if I take you out one evening for a likkle glass of wine?"

"How about if I tell my boyfriend?"

"Well, you can't blame me. My missus left me years ago an' I'm a desperate man—"

"Well, you're a DIY man. Go an' drill yourself a hole in tha wall!"

In the living room, Natalie served Bailey's Irish Cream to Stacey and talked up the benefits of getting hammered. What was so wrong with being Dionysian and merry while lush melodies serenaded her, and her companions teased each other gently and reveled upon each other's loving gaze? In the end, they were inclined to agree that weed was only as rustic as the male who smoked it, and alcohol no less credulous than the female who necked it. Lydia told them about the dreadlocked handyman, and of Krista's barbs on Stacey. It still bothered her, but her botherations were wittingly calmed by Eugenie and Natalie.

"Krista's a washed out one," Natalie said. "She'd be pheasant shooting, eating swan sandwiches, as well as voting UKIP. You know those ones? They hate migrants, forgettin dat their grandparents were migrants…"

Gregory slammed the door open with a rugged cry. Natalie leapt to her feet, her bosom heaving with anxiety. He stumbled towards her like a Friday night drunk.

"So what? You're sittin here wiv your friends drinkin MY Bailey's and nobody asks me? Skeen den! No one's gonna offer man a drink? Man gotta help himself den, innit!"

He took a strident swig from the phial, draining it off its contents. Much of it spilled down his shirt.

"So you've finally shown up?" Natalie said. "You ain't checked on Tiana in six months? Don't bother explainin yourself otherwise we'd be here all week—"

"I'm Tiana's dad, yuh get me. Coz we're finished, it doesn't mean dat me and her are done. She's my blood, yuh get me. She can only have one dad. But really an' truly, you're too fuckin stupid to work dat out—"

"Tiana don't even ask bout you no more—"

"Coz you've turned her head. She's my daughter—"

"Yeah, an' dat makes her so proud—"

"Of course she's proud. I had bare shit goin on. Dat's why I ain't been seen. But I've got a criss new flat, and I've done painted her bedroom pink. She can come an' live with me an' her Auntie Eliza—"

"Auntie Eliza??? Eliza's only her daddy's fuck buddy. And if you think I'm lettin my daughter anywhere near your skank fuck ting, you're seriously mistaken."

"What? You think you've got a monopoly on her coz you're her fucking mother? What bout tha things you do? You ain't no Catholic nun—"

"And I suppose Eliza is?"

"Don't think I don't know you're out on the corner, sellin it—"

"Sorry love, but dat's what your cum bucket does—"

"Eliza's a million times better than you. Why do you think I left you for her?"

"I couldn't care less about your reasons. Eliza will get rid of you soon enough and you'll be a right laughing stock then—"

"When I first met you, Nat, I only wanted to fuck you. But dat's OK coz you wanted to do me too. But you got fat; you let yourself go…" He sniggered like a pantomime baddie. "… You couldn't leave dem cupcakes alone. Dat's why when I was fuckin you recreationally, I was thinkin of Eliza to get more mileage…"

Natalie curled herself slowly into a seat and stared at the space between her sandals.

"… I wounded you wiv dat one, didn't I? I got lots more where dat came from… I want Tiana washed and dressed. I want her clothes and toys packed in a suitcase. You got ten minutes or I'll leave you in a state."

"Yo fam! 'Low it—" Stacey said.

"You ain't got kids so you can't feel me, fam. Not my fault you've backed tha wrong horse—"

"Tiana ain't even here—" Lydia said.

"What do you mean *she ain't here*? I'll go get her myself!"

He strode upstairs to seek her out. They listened to his clamoring and cursing.

"Where's Tiana? What, you're hidin Tiana? Boy, if she ain't ready in ten minutes, I swear down, yeah... I'm gonna put someone in a hospital bed—"

"She's at a birthday party—" Eugenie said.

"Whose birthday party?"

"That's none of your business—"

"Dat ain't up to you, gorgeous. You're not fam, so fuck off!"

"You go AWOL for six months and now you want your daughter—"

"Sorry? Who tha fuck are you?"

"I'm Natalie's partner—"

"Natalie's partner? As in... Natalie's girlfriend? Boyfriend? Are you shittin me?—"

"You should be shittin yourself!"

"Stacey, is this f'real?"

Stacey nodded solemnly.

"Since when, Nat? So you like girls now? What, you don't like man no more? What fuckry is dis?"

"You're tha fuckry. You've always had a problem wiv reality... This is as real as it gets—"

"Real as it gets? Dis is sick. Dat's even more of an incentive for Tiana to come and live wiv me. What, she gets up in the maarnin and sees you in bed, goin on like man and wife... Tiana's gotta live wiv your sick experiment? Naaah... Naaah... Naaah... You think you're bi-sexual but you're just sick in the fuckin head—"

"She's gay," Eugenie said. "And you're the one that's sick in the head—"

"Nat, tell your bully boyfriend to watch her mouth. Coz I'll 'arms her up like a man if necessary—"

"Listen to you! Arms me up? Like I'm supposed to be scared—"

"I couldn't give a monkey's whether it scares you or not. Look at you! Natalie's new man—"

"Fuckin leave or we'll call the police—"

"You're not a man, bitch, but I might have to arms you up like one—"

"You put your hands on me, bitch, and you'll lose all your moldy teeth in a second—"

He grabbed a gun from an undergarment and pointed it at Eugenie.

"Say another word and I'll drop you—"

"Put the fuckin gun away..." Natalie said.

He seized Natalie from where she stood and pressed the weapon hard against her vertex. His gaze fell against her statuesque teeth. He kissed her dainty mouth.

"You still love me, don't ya..." he said.

She pulled her mouth away. Eugenie controverted him with crude nouns. Lydia scrambled from the room to dial 999. Stacey could hear himself panting against the discordance. Gregory redounded his eerie laughter.

"Blud, put dat ting down before it goes off—" Stacey said.

"I tol ya I weren't playin—"

"Think how dis is gonna look when Tiana hears bout dis—"

"You gonna tell her?"

"I ain't tellin her shit, I swear down... But you don't want her walkin bout wiv her head down—"

"I jus miss my baby... I ain't doin dis to embarrass her... I jus wanna spend time wiv her... an' jus hold her and tell her dat daddy loves her... an' dat he's sorry for bein a selfish prick... You make sure dis doesn't get out, Stacey! I'm lookin to you to see dat it don't... I'm comin for her next week, yeah... Dis ain't over!"

Natalie pursued him after he fled. Eugenie and Stacey followed her onto the front porch.

"Just let him go, maaan," they pleaded.

Natalie was bewildered by a direful foreboding but fearful of his violent streak to call him back. Stacey and Lydia ushered her into the house and bolted the door.

"It ain't safe for him out there—" she said.

"Leave him go," Lydia said. "The police are on their way—"

"You called tha Fedz?" Stacey said.

"You got any better ideas?" Lydia said.

There was a frightful knock on the front door once they returned to the living room.

"Who is it?" Stacey said.

"Work men!" said an implacable voice.

Where was that factotum who worked on the front door, Stacey asked himself. He had probably taken flight once Gregory waddled in with his weapon. He marched down the hallway and prepared a dressing down rehearsal in his head. As the front door yawned, he was cast onto the pit of his stomach. Several authoritative noises snapped at him like barking coyotes.

"… DON'T MOVE… DON'T MOVE…"

"… STAY DOWN… DOWN… ON THE FLOOR…"

"… STAY COMPLETELY STILL…"

"… HANDS OUTSTRETCHED ON THE FLOOR… STAY DOWN… DOWN, I SAID…"

"… WHERE'S THE GUN?... WHERE IS IT?"

Natalie and Lydia remonstrated with the police to turn their guns from him but they searched him thoroughly. He lay inert and listened to the protestations of the women. Only when they were satisfied he was unarmed did they haul him up. A policeman with an insipid voice suggested that the women take him to a merry-hell of a pub afterwards, and that he be potted with pints for his troubles. Stacey was chafed by their ambivalence. Oft-told tales of deaths by cursory fingers belonging to ashen-faced marksmen chimed his indignation. He went out onto the porch for an anomalous cigarette.

* * *

"So? What happened?" Eliza asked the moment Gregory returned.

His posture contrived the tumescence of a triumphant man. He was rain swept. He dusted the raindrops from his jacket.

"Tiana's at a sleepover party, but Nat said she can live with us from next week—"

"And you fuckin believed dat?"

He shrunk into the kitchen and seized a Becks from the fridge. She clasped her forehead with an angry paw.

"Jesus fucking Christ! You're so fucking gullible. You ain't gonna have her next fucking week… They fucking lied to you, and you just fucking had it! I knew it, I fucking knew it—"

"Nobody's takin my child away from me, Eliza. Nat knows me better than anyone. When it comes to my child, I ain't fuckin playin—"

"When I saw you coming my way, I should've crossed the fucking street. If you were a fucking horse, you'd be fucking glue by now—"

She slammed cupboard doors and spewed his egregious failings. He feigned a need to use the bathroom. She said nothing. He sat on the toilet seat, smoking cigarettes in quick succession. Fetal ideas corralled in his head about running away from his countervailing strife. He sat among the smoke plumes, anathematizing himself until he wept.

After years of sequential mutiny, there was little consequential bounty. An onerous life had plunged him into a well of ennui. After months of selling guns, his wages had been usurped by the odious crackpot, Marvin Crowe. After favoring Eliza above all things, he was nothing but a poltroon in her eyes. He was a poltroon in everybody else's eyes. He hoped people's emetic suppositions about him would cease if he left for a while. They'd naturally levitate towards other matters. And when he returned, he'd be better equipped to repair fractured relations and repay dismal debts.

When he emerged from the bathroom, Eliza was pettifogging on her Vertu. He cleared his throat and slobbered some meek sentences. She ignored him, clod that he was. After a while, the sadist in her portended that she'd be better enthralled by his theater. She hung up, waiting for him to speak.

"I gotta get to Bristol."

"Of course you do!"

"I've gotta few moves planned... Once I'm sorted, I'll come back, peez in my pocket, and we'll take Tiana.... We can move south like we planned... Babes, you listenin?"

"I heard you, darling. You're fucking off to Bristol."

He lifted her to her feet, constricting her arms with his hands. "What's your fuckin problem, Eliza? Do you wanna smack in your jaw?"

She laughed deliriously. "By tha fucking way, you're flappin your gums at tha wrong bitch..." His grip loosened. "...So don't bother or I'll ignore you like the animal dat you are. Chat all you want to. I'm just gonna laugh in your face... What, you're gonna beat me? You couldn't even beat your dick!"

Gregory was flatlined by that put-down. He looked lax, lazy and less. He tried to embrace her.

"I'm sorry, babe—"

"Go, fuck yourself!"

Her petrous heart fermented its fury. She let him embrace her after much ado. She was as soft as swansdown. He was as rigid as a tombstone. He kept kissing her mouth, smudging her blue cherry lipstick, tasting with relish the hybrid malodor of skunk on her breath.

"You know I'd never lay a finger on you—"

"Then why the fuck did you say you would?"

"I dunno. I say stupid things when I'm vex—"

"Did I get you vex?"

"No—"

"Exactly. Next time you get vex, count to ten in your fucking head. If Nat pushed your buttons, why didn't you fuck her up?"

Gregory promised he'd never be cruel again. Her kohl-eyed lids locked onto her Vertu again. Her acrylic nails chuntered nimbly as she typed.

"You better not be textin some breh?"

"I am, actually—"

"What?"

"I've told him I've a boyfriend, but he won't take no for an answer. He wants to take me out to dinner. Such persistence!"

"Don't make me ave to bang him up, y'know—"

"Don't be stupid, Gregory. He's my boss. He pays me so I can pay your bills. You fucked up my last job, remember? You want me to go through dat shit again? I'll just have to think of a way of keepin him happy."

"Keep him happy? How?"

"Look. Dat isn't your problem. Your problem's Nat not lettin you see your daughter. Deal wiv dat—"

"But... Yea... But... You know Nat seein some next girl now—"

"Nat could be makin out wiv a unicorn for all I care. You didn't do what you were supposed to do. All dat bravado from before was basically bollocks—"

"Nat got dealt wiv already. I swear down, yeah... I said to her: 'Go get Tiana. I ain't playin.' She was shook... She was like: 'Tiana's gone to some sleepover'—"

"Did you ask her where?"

"She gave me the name of some donut endz... Dagenham—"

"What, Tamara? My half-sister? She lives up dem sides... Carry on."

"She started runnin her mouth like some psycho so I just buss some shots at tha ceiling—"

She broke off from her texting. "No way—"

He showed off his Sig Sauer P229, and reveled at its residual strength. "Dat's why I gotta lie low in Bristol—"

"Are you serious? Was my mom there? What did Nat do? Shame... I should've been there to see—"

"Yeh, I gotta get to Bristol an' go undercover till dis blows over—"

"I bet they were shook. They must have been brickin it. Oh shame... Shame... Shame.... I've gotta text Lindsey an' get her to check what's happenin."

She sent messages to Lindsey from her Vertu. She threatened macro vengeance upon Natalie and her child.

"You're gonna take her daughter away, Gregory. There's nuttin she can do about dat... I'll make Tiana call me mommy. What can Nat do bout dat? Fucking nothing, dat's what... By the time you're finished wiv her, Nat'll be in a psychiatric ward, singin my name all day long... Eliza... Eliza... Eliza... And as for dat old dragon, dat cap should've gone off inside her bottom—"

"Eliza, stop it. You're cold, man. I ain't doin dat... I ain't doin dat... Why don't you duss out of my business—"

"And why don't you pack your stuff and get your scabby, scatty broke arse out of my flat?"

She held her glare in his face without blinking. He bounced his head knowingly. She bounced hers back.

"Aiiight den! You want closure? K den... I'll come back for my stuff later—"

"Later? If you don't take your stuff now, I'll put it on the street—"

"No, you won't! My mom's comin for my stuff, and it'd better be here—"

"Oh! It's your mommy again. She's forever goin on bout how much money she's got. You know what, Gregory? You've got the longest umbilical cord known to man! Boys an' their mom's! No wonder mom's get jealous of their son's girlfriends. It's coz they can't compete—"

"Like I said, my mom will come for my stuff later. You don't touch nuttin!"

"I won't touch you or anything you own wiv a barge-pole!"

He slipped his coat on and slipped out, dragging his tardy trainers beneath him. He didn't say goodbye. She watched him disappear into the lineaments of the town. His troubles were ubiquitous, perhaps contagious as well. His masochistic veneer was a sham. He was a good idea once, but now she was bored.

* * *

Pedestrians bequeathed Gregory with spry gazes. The driver of a black Mercedes Vito cast an appraising eye upon him and changed gear. Sprigs at the bus stop pointed him out deliberately. Even a kindly Affenpinscher attempted to gnaw at his ankles. Such precarious birrs coerced him into a taxi shack.

"Have you got an FI driver dat can get me to All Souls Avenue?" he asked, half-joking.

"All our drivers are Formula One drivers with Formula One wheels," said the controller, not joking.

Gregory's cabbie looked nothing of the sort; diminutive, portly, buzzardly. The car was an old-something-or-another, made in the early noughties. Once they neared his mother's street, he scampered from the car with fabulous strides. The cab driver cursed after him but he didn't care. Mohammad had *bin had!* After a few minutes of stern running, he stumbled into a phone booth and dialed Natalie with the last of his coins. His call went unanswered. He left a windy message.

"Nat, the strap weren't loaded… You think I'd hurt you? I'd never hurt you, Nat… Don't press charges, Nat… You want me in tha pen? What you gonna tell Tiana? You put her father away for five years an' tha strap weren't loaded—"

The coin box stomached his pounds. He stormed from the phone booth. A black Mercedes Vito swayed crudely before him. Four men wearing balaclavas sprung forth. Their leader made no attempt to hide his face.

"Get in the fucking van," he said.

The tentacular mob overcame him after a terse scuffle. His cries were of no avail to the public. The van doors were duly bolted once they had impounded him within. Somebody turned on an electric drill. It whizzed in the darkness.

"You're playin out an-aged old cliché, cuz!" Marvin said. "Cliché's as old as dirt, as old as time… Man owes breh peez.

Man tries to check breh's baby mother and adds insult to injury. Man tries to hide. Breh finds man. Man comes out wiv excuses as to why peez is not forthcoming. So naturally, breh has to pop man—"

"Dis is sooo fucked up, Marvin… Why come after man in a fuckin van?"

"You're lucky I did, cuz. I was bout to go to your babymother's yard and run thru a hostage situation—"

"I ain't wiv my babymother no more. She's engaged to a Fed—"

"You fuckin liar. You tell lies all day long—"

"I swear down. On my mother's life—"

"So clearly I ain't gonna get my peez. K den. What bout Nicole? You checked for Nicole?"

"Who, me? Naaah, fam. What you take me for?"

"She's showed me tha pic you sent her… You sent her a picture of your dick—"

"It weren't me, blud—"

"How bout if I just write off your debt… and I write you off too—"

"'Low it, fam. Don't do dis… I'm meant to see my daughter next week… I'll get tha dough from my mom—"

He was surprised by a sibylline voice whose lambent mutterings came to the fore. She was made chimerical by the darkness. She looked upon him as a supplicant and foe, and without the tenderest regard.

"Fuck your mom!" she said. "Fuck you and your fuckin mother! I don't know why you're wastin time wiv him, Marvin. He's fucked your peez and he tried to fuck your wifey. Why should you take fuckry from a nobody? Drill his kneecaps…. Behead the cunt… Merk him… Dat's the forfeit… Standard!"

The horde hectored him as they held down his quaking limbs. Marvin rotated the drill bit from a rotary hammer into his beautiful flesh, piercing his kneecaps. His cries of anguish were met with wails of laughter. Then he was thrown onto the dual carriageway before the precipitant cartage. He struck a series of bonnets and windscreens raging through the drizzle before he was finally tossed to the roadside. By the time the Emergency Services tended to him in a fetid tarn of blood, the elixir of life had long departed his body.

*   *   *

On the day of the wake, Stacey visited the Foster family to pay his respects. Congregating upon the front porch were friends of the late Gregory Foster offering their tributaries. Lollipop carried a wreath decked with lilies and presented it to the family. Ratty delivered an impelling oratorical before a local cub reporter about his sorrow on the death of his *one-time brotha.*

"Yea, we sometime didn't see eye to eye," he said. "But we cry when we 'ave ta tell a brotha goodbye—"

In the living room, Tanya locked arms with Natalie and sobbed exorbitantly whenever somebody sobbed. Gregory's eldest sibling caterwauled in his bedroom. Mrs. Foster was a simile of abounding fortitude. Gregory's elder sister Jacqui spoke with Johnny, Stacey, Ratty and Marius about the exequies. She advised that they co-operate with the police enquiry rather than seek vengeance.

"If I hear anythin on road, I'm goin straight to the Fedz," Ratty said. "An' I don't business if man label me a snitch—"

Johnny's cavernous glare almost perforated Ratty's face. "You get to hear bout certain things dat happen, ya feel mi. Boy, I'm tellin you if I find out who's done this to my bredrin—"

"You'll go to the police," Jacqui said.

A bibulous fellow clutched a Special Brew can as he loitered by the front gate. He shook his head tentatively at each mourner who neared him. "I'm Gregory's father Leon," he told Stacey in a lispy sibilant. "I know y'all heard mean things about me. He was only a baby when I broke up with his mother… She told me he weren't mine. What was I supposed to do? I left it because if she said he wasn't mine, he wasn't mine… But you can see him in me, can't you?

When he was ten, I asked the question: 'Bernice, is he mine or isn't he?' And she said: 'He's yours...' I tried reaching out to him, but he told me he didn't need a dad... My son's death didn't even make the national news. These things happen so regular nobody cares... Made page eight of the *Nepenthe Park Chronicles*. They had something about a tenth-rate celebrity courting a local girl on the front page. They thought that was more important... Your kids will break your fucking heart. But that's the point of loving them..."

The front pouch was a makeshift shrine for Gregory Foster. Family and friends convened with brimful eyes. Shoulders shook with stifled weeping. Bottom lips were bit. White candles were lit. Chelsea football shirts were laid. The local pastor closed his eyes and prayed. Mrs. Foster read some of the messages of condolences while Tanya's body acquiesced around her tender frame. Natalie sobbed without restraint. Tiana listened as Johnny eulogized her father. Ashleigh said nothing. Above them, the Harlesden skyline burnt red...

"Gregory's lookin down on us," Johnny said. "You see dat cloud in tha sky? That's him... Check out the face on the cloud... That's my boy, Gregory... Lookin down..."

Bud talk was nonsense talk, Ashleigh told herself. As she lent an ear to their mourning chat, she wondered why those who uttered exalted praise for Gregory had been so contemptuous of him whilst he was alive. More importantly, she couldn't envisage the unquantifiable demarcation of breath and death. Where was he now that his body lay in his mother's house? Was he being judged by a Strangelovian Committee? Was he in a stygian subterranean netherworld, precipitated by the Devil's pitchfork into the gauzy fires of Tartarus, his conflagrated soul incinerated in the rancid pits of Malebolge? Would his soul be received by divine seraphs with Tinker Bell wings, and saddled on the back of Sleipnir to a Watership Downesque terrain of marshmallows that looked like mushrooms from afar, paved with rivers of Cadbury's milk chocolate and fountains of honeycombed syrup? Or was he residing in *Thug Mansion*, the afterlife that Tupac spoke of, living the life of a boulevardier along with the other *thugz* that had passed away before him? Or perhaps there was no afterlife; just an ineffable Erebus that went on eternal until the timeless endless end. Her mother had said only the wicked truly died; the Uber-Galactical Glorious Being extinguished their souls forever and that was the ultimate sequestration, for every human soul had a dread of permanent death; but the good folk lived on, through the tremendous maw of an accelerating universe, becoming suns and stars. Light upon light. Surely, there was no Gehenna beyond the grave for Gregory, for how unjust would that be.

"Breh was a true soulja in life," Lil Elliott said. He stood to the right of her. "Remember what happened, a day before he died when the Fedz harassed us? If it weren't for him, we'd be wingin. He calmed the situation—"

"F'real! He's the last of his generation," Lollipop said. "I ain't ever gonna forget dat breh!"

Dominic spoke of days gone when there was no fear of gunmen, when the only drama was a scuffle in school or a ruckus on road. Now children carried small-caliber, sound-suppressed pistols. Girls walked with flick-knives. Sluggards had a lust for notoriety. The pressure valve was on red, rendering many striplings dead. He called for a return to the generic days of his youth.

Johnny agreed. "Every time I leave my yard, I wonder if I'm gonna make it home to my kids or if I'm spendin the night in jail. Or if I'm comin home in a body bag…"

Ashleigh felt a jitter. That pithy opine was no joke. Her children fatherless because he pranced the streets as a footstool for fools like Lollipop? Such impatience for death. She needed a cigarette. She pootled along the road to smoke one in private. Lindsey tapped her from behind and joined her. She hadn't subscribed to the reverent mourning. Her giddy disposition would not allow it.

"You can polish a turd wiv varnish but it's still a turd—" she said.

"You're thinkin the same as me den!"

"I'm only here coz he was Sean's friend—"

"I don't know why tha fuck I'm here!"

"Did you see his body in the box?"

"I refused to go—"

"I did. His head's like a shriveled raisin… Looked nothin like him—"

"Coz it *isn't* him. Dat's his shell upstairs."

"I clocked him waaay before Natalie did, Ashy. If he offered it, I would've taken it and not thought twice about Sean. My only regret's dat I never got to fuck him before he died—"

"You aren't supposed to fantasize bout fuckin the dead!"

"It's terrible, dis… But dat's all it is, terrible—"

"What's terrible is me havin to Sky-Plus *Mob Wives!*"

"Have you noticed you-know-who hasn't showed up?"

"I don't think anybody cares coz nothing's been said—"

"Just goes to show she never loved him in the first place."

"Maybe coz it's embarrassing—"

"Embarrassing? Fuck dat shit. Her man's dead! I phoned her an' gave her my opinion but she's like: 'My hotness will burn you bitch! You low life gyal. It ain't easy bein moi!' I'm like: 'Listen to you bitch! I had you in my flat for a month rent-free an' dat's how you speak to me.' I'm like: 'Shit, I just realized, maybe you *are* being serious??? Nah, you can't possibly be, but cheers again for the laugh.' And I just put the phone down on her arse."

Ashleigh laughed. "If she did come, she'd be wasted on sight!"

"This ain't no time for jokes," Sean reprimanded from behind.

"If you think you're the boss, you've got it backwards, babe!" Lindsey said.

Ashleigh smiled apologetically at Sean. He looked deliciously ambiguous with a well-lubricated face. His cuspidate hair suffused like cauliflower leaves. She often mused that there was *something about Mary* about his hair. The song-sheet ritual mourning continued well after midnight.

* * *

Sophia arrived before midnight. She climbed from her Ford S-MAX Titanium in a snake print bodycon dress and acrylic heels. She bounded past everybody in slow motion. Blaze shrink-wrapped himself into a corner. Lindsey muttered bilious words into Sean's ear. Ashleigh groused that her arse was too big. Rebecca and Ladelle asserted that she was a pesky strumpet from Lewdshire who had probably been one of Gregory's numerous bedfellows. Stacey put them right. Marius greeted her warily and galloped to fetch Lollipop.

"How come you're here?" Lollipop said after they embraced.

"I had to be here. Your mobile was off and so I rang your dad. He said you were at Gregory's wake... He gave me dis address and here I am. Is there anythin I can do to help?"

"No, there isn't," Leon interrupted from behind. "I'm Gregory's father. I sure loved my son... I'm sure gonna miss my boy—"

"Of course you will, hun—"

"Who does Bernice think she is? She's arranged everythin without consulting me... Who does that bloody woman think she is? As if she brought Gregory into the world by herself—"

"Just chill, Leon—" Marius said.

"How can I chill?" He kicked an empty Budweiser bottle as it rolled towards him. "Mi nah sleep till my son funeral, ya feel me? Me nah eat nah drink till den—"

"I'm sorry for your loss," Sophia said. "When I first heard, I knew I had to be here—"

"Was he a friend of yours too?" Leon said.

"I didn't have the pleasure of really meeting him but my boyfriend thought really highly of him. And so did everyone. Again, please accept my condolences."

Lollipop was pleased she came, and on how well she articulated her condolement to a friend she never knew. She was prim and appropriate. It was positive proof that she cared.

"I'd like to personally pay my respects to him, if I may," she said. "Say a prayer, if dat's OK—"

"Of course it is, my love," Leon said. "Just follow me."

Elegiac bodies huddled on the doorstep. Leon pushed past them deliriously. Sophia stayed swiftly on his brogues. Tiana neighed loudly in the hallway. Natalie tried to mollify her. Tafari spoke to a sober congregation in the lounge. His speech induced laughter and weeping in quick succession. Standing beside him were Ms. Foster and Tanya, Fernando and Sondra. Leon led Sophia up the stairs, onto the sinuous upper floor.

"She never let me speak... People treat me as if I weren't his father. They'd say I had no right to take you to see him... I have every right... I'm his father... Let them try and stop me... Wankers!"

He pushed upon a creaking door. She followed him. White ephemeral candles lit the room. A sanitizing fragrance expurgated the heady air. The aggregate remains of Gregory's cadaver lay in a coffin upon the catafalque, blue suited in blue shoes. His eyeballs had retracted into their sockets. His marl countenance looked glacial. A large portion of his scalp had been sutured. Death's pallor had kissed those succulent lips. His argillaceous skin were sallow.

The coffin fell upon her searing gaze. She mumbled a conjuration of words. Leon closed his eyes and said amen. With one eye trained on him, she reached into a handbag. She took hold of her Samsung and snapped a photograph...

*   *   *

She caught up with Lollipop outside. Stacey and Lydia were with him.

"You know what Sophia?" He laid a strong arm around her sultry waist. "Stacey's my boy! I'd back tha Glock to back him in ANY grimy situation. It'd be skull and cross bones time, bare lootin and shootin once I hear he's bodied!"

"Let's hope it doesn't come to dat!" Stacey said.

"I got dis theory," Sophia said. "I call it the 3am theory, bout what makes a good friend. Flick through the names in your mobile. Study the names on dat list. Can you visualize calling dat name at 3am coz you're stuck in a jam dat can't wait? If you can't, get rid. There's no point knowin dem. Not in dis lifetime, not in dis city."

"I don't know how anyone, in their right mind, who'd be quick to back the Glock——" Lydia said.

"You obviously haven't lost a loved one——" Sophia said.

"I have, actually. My dad was killed by a stray slug when I was three. And he wasn't in no gang——"

"Naturally, I'm sorry to hear dat but if dat had been my dad, my family would have tracked his murderer and beheaded the cunt."

Lydia looked astonied. Yet another addlebrained bint, who had fallen for an unscrupulous scoundrel! Nasty bones made up her body. Discerning folk would do well to avoid her kind.

"You wanna ride wiv us?" Lollipop said. "We're gonna go kotch at Johnny's and smoke some draws——"

"We'll ride home wiv Stacey's parents," Lydia said.

"Stacey's whipped f'real," Lollipop said. "Wifey's tha boss now. Dat's cool. We'll link at church tomorrow, fam."

"So *that* was Sophia?" Lydia said, after Sophia and Lollipop had departed. "What. A. Cow! Who the hell does she think she is?"

"'Low it, Lidz——"

"If dis weren't what it was, I'd have torn her flippin head off. And Lollipop? He's an excited breh. How can he say he's quick to back armshouse, on today of all days?"

"Lollipop's cool. He gasses too much sometimes but you gotta forgive him, you know——"

"No, he's not cool. He's an ignoramus. When he said dat, a chill went down my spine."

Stacey tried to rub the chill away with the palm of his hand. The nimbus clouds above meanwhile exhibited driving rain, forcing the condolers to retreat into the Foster family residence.

9

THE BOOK OF JOLEON

A SHLEIGH LIEBESCHUETZ AWOKE AT six-thirty, awash with gaiety and ado. After bathing herself with Balenciaga Paris, she herded her whippets into the bathroom. She washed them thoroughly and victualed them with Shredded Wheat. Lindsey turned up at eight-thirty with her own noisy offspring. The debouchment of the internet was her deliverance from the staid Sean.

"I've got a Skype date wiv Clifford Miles III, United States Marines," she said. "He's hench. Sean's workin in Reading till late, and I've got tha whole yard to myself—"

She had long invited Ashleigh to partake in the confectionary of American servicemen stationed in the ruddy sands of Arabia.

"I got a nice one for ya," she said, tapping her tablet and revealing a catalog of Facebook friends. "He's Latino... Corporal in the Marines.... Raul Estrada... Twenty-two... Boy's shit hot... Imagine straddlin Estrada! You'd definitely like him, Ash—"

Ashleigh had always refrained from frisson linkages on the internet. In spite of her recommendation, Raul Estrada could may as well been a superlative brute. She kissed her whippets and waved them good day. Then she made herself ready for work.

Johnny remained asleep in bed but she dared not wake him. Throughout the night, he had buried his head before scraps of A4 paper in the living room, composing sophomoric songs. Substances that befogged his mind aided the cataract of his expression until he became somnolent. Then he crawled sluggishly into bed and curled himself against her, though sometimes he loathed to touch her. Then sleep would overtake him until the noonday brightness shone across his jowls.

She worked in the administrative wing of Harlesden Brook Hospital, where her colleagues satiated themselves with yucky teas and pointless crowing. Work was the ideal haven against Uroboric Man, who preferred to impugn her every action.

"You're getting lousy peez as their shit shoveler," he said after studying her pay slip. "I could earn your monthly income hustlin on road in a day—"

"Well, why don't you?"

"Coz I'm concentratin on my music, you speng!"

"I wanna dance professionally, but you said I can't—"

"I ain't havin you rubbin yourself up against some next man. My gal as somebody's hip-hop honey? Naaah!!! Fuck dat for a laugh!!!" By default, he always tempered his base grouses with words of emaciated benevolence. "When I'm ready wiv my videos in bout six months, you can choreograph my dancers. I'll pay you. You'll have dat on your CV, and dat'll be decent—"

She absolutely loathed his songs. And as far as he was concerned, her employers consisted of cocksuckers, responsibility duckers and outright muthafuckers, whereas he was the boy drummer, the conniving plucker, accompanied by a cunning cadre of like-minded others.

"If he's rubbish, tell him he's rubbish," said Shakira, misty-eyed at her tight-lipped endurance. She worked in Accounts at an adjoining office. "If my boyfriend ever came to me with some lyric dat I weren't feelin, I'd give him the Simon Cowell treatment!"

They always met at lunchtime to chat about the insanitary tales of others, luxuriating themselves around a table in the courtyard, where they nibbled on salads and sipped on smoothies. Their conversations had recently centered upon the new porter named Joleon. He was a sultry tarse. They had perved him during their lunching hour as he whisked the wounded and pregnant on wheelchairs.

"What a lovely piece of fuckberry pie!" Shakira said.

Ashleigh marveled over her quasi-lust, how it kinetically migrated from one man to the next in the nictitate of an hour. Three days ago, she had drooled over the UPS deliveryman who resembled Ludacris. Three days from now, she would seek some T.I or Wiz Khalifa lookalike, and her desire for Joleon would abate.

"Would you stay faithful to Johnny if Joleon came along?" Shakira said.

"If Johnny saw how fine he was, he'd *have* to 'low it—"

"And what would happen if he didn't 'low it?"

"I'd still let Joleon put his whole penis in me, but dat's between us and the devil of course! What bout you?"

Shakira pondered the question and then said, "I'd audition him with his tongue. If he can work it well, I might give him sight of my nunu."

"You're a child of the sun, baby!"

"I'm not the only one. Plenty of girls here have already mindfucked him to the point of no return—"

"I'm mindfucking him as we speak!"

Joleon seemed light years ahead of the caviling Johnny. He was pert and cocksure. He had the oculus of a fallow deer but the disposition of a Bandersnatch. His shaven head suggested commination of a kind. His broken-faced bucolic looks had the scars of many wars. From his mélange features alone, she couldn't tell from which bailiwick of the earth his antecedents first crawled, whether he was Persian or Pashtun, Arabian or Ecuadorian, Gypsy or Jew.

It seemed she was invisible to him at first, sliding past her in their first instances unaware. Then she wore seamless tops and Brazilian-cut jeans, and within three days, he called her out.

"Goodness! You new here?"

"No, but I know you are!"

Her eyes slipped to the supple schism of his bosom, upwards at the contours of his frolicsome lips, downwards to the area between his legs. He took her paw, stroking it with a cursory rub.

"You're the kind of girl dat could get any man—"

"Rubbish!"

"You're not often appreciated?"

"We're all underappreciated—"

"Tha right kind of man would appreciate you. Then you'd be walkin around wiv a big smile on your face coz you've got his back and he's got yours. But the wrong type makes nuttin happen and if it happens, it's on his terms. Then you walk round screwin, coz whilst you've got his back, he's busy buggering yours."

She wondered if he was nothing more than a perceptive poseur who rubbed the fur of every other pussycat in the place. But his words stroked several chords. Soon they regularly convened outside the loading bay, smoking cigarettes and talking about each other's lives.

"You got a man den?"

"He's a child in a man's body—"

"What team does he support?"

"He's a Gooner—"

"He's emotional den?"

"About Arsenal, yes. When football's on, he ain't bothered bout anythin else. I'd be like: 'Johnny, what about me?' He's like: 'Ashy, it's Arsenal. Don't interrupt!' It could be Outer Mongolia versus the Deepest Darkest Village in Peru and he'd be gawping at the tele—"

"Modern times! People wanna live their lives through others. I bet when Arsenal loses, he feels his life ain't worth livin."

"I keep a razor in my drawer. Sometimes, I don't know whether to cut his throat or slit my wrists—"

"My ex-girl had razors in her drawer too. Good job she doesn't think like you do—"

"So, how does your new girlfriend think?"

"I'm happily single—"

"You're lyin."

"You think I need to impress you?"

"No. Of course not. Why did you split up?"

"Relationships are never fluid. They run their course but I keep things civil for the sake of my son."

"How old is your son?"

"He's six. I love him to bits... I must be borin you talkin bout me all the time—"

"We can talk bout you till you're tapped out—"

She imagined his oft-returning propensity to love and hate immeasurably. His ex might have been a laggard in love, segmenting his hot-bloodedness with her womanish posits. She abhorred what they had fructified together: an exultant son. But he claimed he loved her no longer, and she was glad of their evanescence.

"I dance too, you know." He gesticulated a few contrived steps. She was somewhat impressed. "I've done the Brits, MOBOs, BET, Urban... Last time I done some work was for Ambrosia-Nectar at Hormones—"

"Hormones is on my doorstep—"

"Well, next time I'm in your endz, I'll swing by for a cuppa!"

"I don't think so."

"Your old man would object?"

"He doesn't want me havin male friends—"

"While he has friends wiv benefits? Sounds like a cunt."

His acuity radiated without hysteria as he asked about herself, and the neighborhood she was raised in, and how she came to work at Harlesden Brook. He asked about her parents and children, and what she hoped for in her days ahead.

"I don't believe you," she said.

"What don't you believe?"

"Dat you're happily single? It's a bit of an oxymoron—"

"A what moron?"

"Can you be single *and* happy?"

"Dat should be your startin point, don't you think?"

"You're probably right—"

"I *am* right. You're the opposite, aren't ya? Spoken for and unhappy?"

"What makes you think I'm unhappy?"

"When you care bout someone, you know their mood swings. I watch you in different ways."

She asked about his tattoos. He removed his shirt to show her. Her cud chewing jaw froze at his gouged body laced with curlicue designs and knife wounds.

"Dat's my son Lukas on my breast there… Dis one on my arm's in Latin: *'Defend The Children Of The Poor, And Punish The Wrongdoer!'* – I saw dat at the Old Bailey – Dis is my granddad Merlin, top bloke… My son, *'Ti Adoro Bambino'* – Dis one's a naked female wiv wings, my soul mate, wherever she is… Dis one's a falcon… I got wings on my shoulders—"

"Devil or angel wings?"

"Tha Devil don't exist." He changed the subject when she asked about his knife scars. "What does Johnny Freeloader look like?"

"Here he is!" She logged her phone onto her Facebook. "There he is… posin like Achilles… wiv all dat money dat ain't even his—"

"Too many people live in Cloud fuckin Cuckoo Land—"

"Don't you wanna be somethin? Or you happy pushin wheelchairs around all your life?"

Joleon laughed at her question and slung his shirt over his mesomorphic shoulders. He didn't believe in living vicariously, he said, and he completely rejected idiolatry. He lived off-line, and in the real world. He wasn't prone to magical thinking and hence never suffered the maladies subscribed from wishful thought. He lived within his means and without credit. He never wore socks nor underwear. He masturbated to lurid vamps at night on sex chatlines, and indulged in animated porn on his tablet. His BMW, X-Box One and Bose Sound System were his other pleasures. Ashleigh wondered if there was another man better fine-tuned to her needs than he.

That evening, she snuggled against Johnny. Her ardor, having coagulated for so long, roared kinetically. She spooned him ferally in a manner that he liked.

"I ain't in the mood right now for dat, Ashy—"

"Oh hun... I wanna fuck the shit out of you—"

"Get off my nuts, bitch!" He shunted her away. "How can you want dis when I'm feelin this way?"

"Feelin what way?"

"I feel... I ain't my own man no more. I'm gonna end up wiv boils on my head... Stress ain't the fuckin word!"

"B-but Johnny... how can you be stressed when you've been home all day?"

"I was down in fucking Wembley doin my M.O fucking T! What, coz you're at work, you've got needs? Fuck your needs... If you can't handle it, quit your dumb arse job!"

Of course, *his* needs had been heeded to by Category Five skets. She watched him go out onto the balcony and phone Lollipop, gossiping with torrential fury about Twang. In her turmoil, she phoned her mother for empathy. Mother embarked on a dithyrambus about men. Males were adulterine by nature, foresworn into misogyny by nurture. Many insisted that their Penelopes and Ruths remain sanitized and steadfast, in spite of their innate proclivities towards the Helen of Troys and Bathshebas. And it was no wonder that lorn handmaidens like Ashleigh sought refuge from larrikins like Johnny, who craved his own delectation, who relegated her as a passive depository of his desire. What of her own residual passions? Mother had raised her contrary to parochial, patriarchal, priapic prejudice.

"Do as thy menfolk do," was her holy injunction.

Mother could not fail to forget how Johnny perversely made Ashleigh perfidious: Nero Sandz, a New York bounder, was the most nihilistic *gangsta* artist of recent times. In spite of being disesteemed by the media who wrote mythopoeic page-fillers about his beefs with rival performers, the pachydermatous rapper was at the pinnacle of his game. Ashleigh had been hired through a dance agency to perform an evening set with him in Stratford, having mastered the complex choreography in an hour. After the gig, Nero's management invited his dancers to his five-star colonnaded hotel for a drink-up.

Nero was atingled by her coquettish badinage. They talked about Harlem and Harlesden while drinking Zinfandel. He was not handsome, and though he was considerably churlish to his enablers, he was kind to her. Her erogenous sensibilities turned him on, and his eyes and hands never left her alone. She was promptly ravished by his licentious operatics, and she opted to satiate herself with luxuria. The tchotchke frottaged Nero before the folks, the dancing despicable to the civil eye. Forests of men watched with peccant eyes and felt the corybantic fires scorching their pudendas. She siphoned his pith while they gaped on until his briny fetch trickled down her esophagus. Four satyrs took her into an adjoining room afterwards. In spite of her carbed obedience and eyes-wide-shut coercion, they circumnavigated her. They removed their raiments while their quills oscillated and then ossified. They stripped her boyshort panties and formed an untidy scrum. She wanked their laden garnishes while they groaned and tasted their parched mouths with her tongue. They groped her with their tentacles before gorging their turgid suppositories into her every portal. The musky room was stenched by the funked comminglings of a pyramid of bodies. They sputtered at each other whenever their limbs collided unintended, and she feared that they might hurt her as they jostled for her attention and hoped to morph into geysers. One spritzed his comrade with a blast of flying semen from his lateral organ. Such was their random chaos of their stramash.

Nero drank Crystal Head Vodka in a large gaming chair and watched the loveless carnality before him. When Ashleigh, smeared by the detritus of many men, showered in his suite, he joined her behind the frosted glass. They renewed their consolidated couchings therein. She chugged for air with every *fabelhaft*, febrile thrust. The teeming rascal tore off his condom, pissed against her solei and ejaculated in her vagina.

He gifted her a Pandora bracelet, which she had worn since. He wanted to see her again. She had no wish to, and gave him a dud number. They parted with a slushy overcooked kiss.

Johnny had raged petulantly as she climbed into bed next to him, ailing and so very weary.

"Your dancing career is so fuckin over," he said. "You were supposed to be home by two, and you walk in five hours later—"

"Johnny, I was ill. My battery died an' I couldn't find a cash point—"

"You'll never dance a next gig, Ashy. You've got more chance of unscrambling an egg—"

She fell asleep so soon after, and relegated Nero Sandz and his cadre of enablers as a consummated fantasy, until the evening she sat on her toilet seat with a positive reading from a pregnancy test and realized that she was very pregnant with somebody's child.

* * *

Joleon offered to drive her home after work. Or within a thousand yards of her home, so that she might not be seen by Johnny or his boys. She accepted. They didn't talk much. His hand often brushed against her when he reached for the gear stick. She knew it was no accident. He parked his vehicle on a quiet road. Nepenthe Park Road lay ahead at the T-junction. He drew her close and hemmed her against his pecks. She pushed her hands forward to cup a feel.

"You've got a body like the Holy Grail," she said.

Their mouths interlocked and their tongues clicked. His breath was tinged by the cashew nuts he had been eating earlier. She tried to stop him as the petting intensified.

"Why don't we get to know each other better?" he said as he continued to climb all over her. "How bout you take me out for a drink dis Friday?"

"Are you mad?"

"I keep wonderin what you'd be really like if you had some balls!"

"I'd fuck you wiv it, you cheeky bastard—"

"Ping me and let me know. I done know you're a daisy anyway!"

She would not be hogtied by Johnny into not going. And she was not as pliable as Joleon supposed. She walked the eight hundred yards home with a refulgent smile.

Her flat was occupied by the golems of Nepenthe. Lollipop was taking a dump in her toilet. Stacey and Marius lay couchant upon her divan, playing *Grand Theft Auto* with infinite zeal. Jardel charged towards her and hugged her thighs. Johnny changed Caydee-Lee's nappy with an unlit Camacho in his mouth.

"Johnny… I'm goin out Friday. Someone at work's leavin an' we're goin to some bar for her drink-up in Holborn."

"You can't go… You got tings to do—"

"Like what?"

"Like… lookin after tha kids—"

"But you can do dat—"

"I ain't their fuckin mother—"

"But you're their father!"

"Yea, an' the answer is no!"

"I'm going, Johnny. Whether you like it or not… This ain't tha fuckin Kremlin."

"How you gonna go if I say no?"

"You go out wheneva you like. I don't go out often—"

"Nah, you didn't say *dat*. You said you're goin *whether I like it or not*. What, you in charge now?"

"'Low it, Johnny…" Marius said.

"You gotta keep em on a short leash—"

"She ain't a dog—"

"She ain't your gal so buss out."

Ashleigh indubitably hated him at that moment.

"I'm frazzled, Ashy. You seriously think you can leave dis flat without my say so? You know what? How bout if I say you can't work no more? What den? You still think you can?"

"Now you're goin on dark, Johnny—" Stacey began.

"Guess what, fam? Dis is Johnny's house. Whose house? Johnny's house. My yard, yeah! I can do what the fuck dat I want in it. If you don't like it, fuck off somewhere else—"

He sniped angrily to himself about the importance of respect and deference, and left for the kitchen. Marius and Stacey crepitated among themselves. Ashleigh curled into a solitary seat. Lollipop, having re-entered the room, pulled puerile faces at her from behind. Johnny returned with a kettle in hand. He doused its cool water over her plucky head.

"Fuck!" Lollipop said.

His action prompted her tears.

"… So… you were sayin Ashy… Dis ain't the fuckin Kremlin, yeh. Dis is worse than dat… Dis is Castle fuckin Grayskull… and your arse ain't goin anywhere!"

She fled, weeping into the bathroom.

"Johnny, dat was fucked up," Marius said. "If you wanna do dat shit on your own, fine. But not in front of me coz den you're forcin man to act—"

"What do you mean, *force man to act?* How *is* man gonna act?"

"Man ain't gonna sit and let you do dat shit… You're forcin me to react, fool… How can you do what you did wiv your son watchin? In front of your bredrins? Dat's fuckry, Johnny. Really an' truly, you've fucked up—"

"Hey, seckle Marius," Lollipop said. "You forgettin somethin? Dat's his gal. Dat's nobody's business—"

Stacey flung his joypad to the floor. "Peace, I'm out. Marius' right. Dat *was* fuckry. Kiss the kids for me, yeah. But their dad needs an almighty slap."

Marius followed him through the front door. Johnny repudiated them both. He couldn't care less how Stacey treated Lydia. And Marius was an inutile merchant, whose moist cock had pervaded many a pudenda without qualm or conscience. He used oft-cited references about the importance of fealty, backing your boys against all else. The streets were being lost to their adversaries and it was because of useful idiots like Stacey and Marius. Lollipop listened with a tacit grin.

After Lollipop had left and the children were in bed, he knocked on the bathroom door. She let in his mulish hide. Their talk therein lasted an hour. She apologized for underscoring his regnancy before his friends and the shards of shame it might have induced. He ingraciously accepted her apology and granted her a night-out without condition.

* * *

She was outside Camden Town station at the appointed time, adorned in an iridescent vampish dress and matching handbag. An anatine herd honked raffish noises at her before moving on like tumbleweed in a stricken hinterland. She texted Joleon to say she'd arrived. Then she observed the distillation of Camden Town, its hemmed boutiques of goth ware and heavy-metal trinkets. Quotidian pylons pointed out kindled landmarks. There was rapt activity in the World's End pub. Effusive types had gathered to see some indie band perform at the Underworld. Mother had once smuggled her therein to savor KT Tunstall's sphygmic weaves on her Gretsch guitar. *Black Horse And The Cherry Tree...* She could never forget the unalloyed synergy of that moment. She crossed the street and stood beneath the awnings. She peeped through its adumbrated windows. *Suddenly I See...* Minnehaha stared back at her and that's when she wished she had worn a different outfit.

Joleon tooted his horn from behind, and beckoned her into his cabin.

"If you were here ten minutes earlier, you'd have seen me gettin harassed—"

"You wouldn't get harassed if you weren't dressed like an Opal Fruit!"

"You cheeky bastard. You can't even say sorry for comin late!"

"I had some beef wiv my mechanic and his pagans. Fuckin charged me for a problem he never fixed. Refused to give me my keys coz he's sayin I owe three bills. I said I weren't playin but dey went on cruddy. So I laid dem out. One breh came at me wiv a wetter and I ended up slicin him wiv it... See my eye? One of dem got me clean, but I banged him up wiv his own tools..."

His ample hands were bitten by bruises. Bistered smoke caked his enthralling cheeks and his right eye was abbreviated and blackened. She touched his face attentively, eliciting a rippling comber to his swinish cheeks. She was pedantic about the boy.

"You need to go to A&E!"

His parched laughter rattled like the engine of an old combine. "You should have come dressed as a nurse so we can make pretend—"

"I'm serious, Joleon—"

"So am I."

"Let's stop at a chemist. I don't want anyone seein me hangin out wiv a Cyclops."

He stopped at the first apothecary she saw. She purchased various unguents and cordials and patched him up neatly. He surveyed himself in the rear view mirror.

"Noiiice!"

"You've gone from Cyclops to Long John Silver—"

"You'd prefer my Long John—"

"Behave! So what happens now if your car packs up halfway?"

"You'd have to get out and push, babe!"

They segued along York Way to a constricted siding, the backwaters of St. Pancras International. Scrap metal merchants from the tundra touted their latticed wares on the porch of a factory. A stripling offered them cheap cigarettes for sale. Ashleigh stared at his immiserated face and cobwebbed bristles. Joleon advised her to lower her gaze.

"Is dat how North Wezzy girls bait themselves?"

"I don't know where you're takin me. I can't rely on you to have my back!"

He put his hand on her rump and squeezed it. "Whateva happens Ash, I've always got your buns..."

He led her into a plethoric pub named *The Drunken Stupor*. Upon its skillion roof spun a weathervane, the chassis of a gargoyle. Inside, ambiversive folk fermented with bitters in their palms. Several hoary types slapped Joleon's granite back. Ashleigh noticed a troika of lithe barmaids, their hairs bunned like Nereids, acutely aware of her princeling companion. Their blue quarries watched her too as she crossed the floor.

He led her to a table ensconced at the furthest corner of the cabin, near a spiral staircase. The den was benumbingly cold in spite of the magmatic glow of lanterns hung against the bricked walls. She was taken aback by the simulacrum of medieval catacombs adjacent to where she sat. *No Snobs Allowed. Seditionists Are Welcome* was sign-posted at that juncture. He was greeted by a gnomic sot with flocculent hair, who queried after his eye, and then treated them to a round of free drinks. His politesse bordered on the servile. Later, he returned for their order. She opted for the vichyssoise and a glass of Bergerac wine. He chose a salmagundi from the menu and a Fuller's beer.

He pettered her mouth, tasting the balsamic vinegar that marinated her breath. He fondled her filigreed earrings, fed her morsels of mushrooms, leaks and veal. She enjoyed her meal, and the choc fudge that followed. Their concerted affections exhibited a cheer from a kinetic crone who had just finished crooning.

"Dat's my mom!" he said. "You can meet her in tha morning at breakfast—"

"Woooh! You wanna take me to your bed already?"

"Now you're puttin tha cart *behind* the horse... as it should be!"

He watched a melancholic veil descend slowly upon her comely face as they watched another indie band take the stage. She yielded a sad chuckle.

"I do like you, Joleon. I really do hun... but we can't happen... I thought bout it, but Johnny would never let me leave him...

He'd have to find another girl an' *leave me*. He's like an Old Testament curse... It's probably best we stay friends—"

"I've got enough friends. I don't want another friend—"

"I know Johnny's a bastard... but I still have feelings for him—"

Joleon pushed aside his plate, folded his arms. "Dat's the problem wiv your type; brainy birds attracted to cunts. I see peng girls like you every day, eyes squarely locked into the distance coz the bogey in the bedroom's keepin em down. You see dem shakin their heads and flickin the weave coz potentially, dey could be getting things right in their lives. But some game-faced dick wiv no game managed to become the significant other while he ain't packin nothin significant. Believe me, it's a common theme in this day and age. You're not tha only one tied to a cunt—"

"I think it's better to live in a nunnery wiv a reliable fuck buddy wiv no strings attached. Once you're in a relationship, you ain't got no choice but to deal wiv dat shit—"

"There's choices an' there's degrees of choices, Ash. Havin a wife's a lesser evil than a girlfriend, a girlfriend's a lesser evil than, say a fuck buddy. Choice is a lesser evil than no choice."

"Relationships are never fluid, Joleon. You said dat yourself—"

"Your ego landed you in dis shit. You looked at him like he needed an upgrade. WOMAN 2.0. You thought your clunge's got a cure for stray dogs. Once you fucked him, he'd see heaven and common sense. To him, you're just a fuck and a sponge."

"I'm mother of his children—"

"He doesn't wear dat badge wiv pride—"

"Why you behavin like some wank boy?"

"I'm givin it to you straight from The Book of Joleon—"

"I'm *not* going to leave Johnny for you!"

"Venus will have to realign from Mars to Jupiter before dat could happen. You may as well run back to Johnny and play Happy Families—"

"Happy Families? Are you like dis when you don't get your way?"

"I'm consistent, babe. Dat's somethin you're not. One minute you're like: Poor me! Johnny controls my life. I can't leave him coz he's fuckin god. And the next, he's a scatty bubblegum rapper who bangs one out over Arsenal and fucks jezzies every day... Which one is he? And who are you?"

She gulped the last drop of Bergerac. "I'm gonna phone a cab. This has been a waste of my fuckin time—"

He raised his beer in salutation. "You'd know all bout wastin your fuckin time. It's what you're good at..."

The rain poured mercilessly as she flounced from *The Drunken Stupor*. Her trainers were made messy by the slob pools on the pavement. She looked back hoping that Joleon would pursue her. Her view was obscured by the obsidian fog. She checked her watch. Five past two. She checked her mobile. No signal.

She found herself lost among absurd streets that began and ended with roundabouts. Naked wet trees garlanded the pavements like wyverns on guard duty. Under the cantaloupe tubes that lit them, a man with stinking aftershave shouted invidiously at his lithe colleen. Alas, the chicken-hearted. Why don't they ever fight back? She bounded past a set of traffic lights that changed from sherry red to viridian green, and then back again one hundred seconds later. Roustabouts, in groaning factories gated by frescoed walls, labored beneath the noir monochrome of the moonlight. The skirt chasers among them hollered bawdry noises after her. She hoped for his expiatory call but her mobile still had no signal.

She walked past a block of rectangular tenements where the screechings of an overwrought cat palpitated her no end. An offal odor lingered. The rain almost ceased. The traffic moved with robust fury. By the time she found a licensed taxi, her technicolor dress was mercilessly drenched.

"Been anywhere nice?" the driver said.

"I've just come from a place called hell—"

The driver raised his clumpy eyebrows. "I finish work in an hour. Perhaps I can show you heaven—"

"Don't you fuckin start!"

When she was a mile from home, Joleon sent a sparse text: *OK, I'm sorry bey but u didnt hav 2 leave like dat.*

She sent a hauteur rejoinder: *I won't make that mistake again, u hemorrhoid!!!*

She found Johnny passed out in the living room. She read his disjunctive screeds that lay on the coffee table, more hyperbolic couplets about his raging virility. She went upstairs and undressed, showered before climbing into bed. Upon her pillow lay threads of hair that belonged to neither her nor Johnny. She plucked it with her fingers and marched downstairs.

"You've fucked some sket in our bed... How fuckin dare you?"

Johnny rubbed his serpentine eyes. "What now?"

"Who did you have in our bedroom?"

"Lollipop came round wiv Sophia. She was ill. I said she could have a lie down... What's your fuckin problem? You don't believe me? Fuckin phone him." He handed her his Galaxy. "Phone him—"

"Well, he would back you up—"

"I don't need him backin me up. If I fucked a sket upstairs, I'd tell you rags. I swear down, on our kids' lives—"

"But you have done, haven't you?"

"Lawwwd! What's dis? You've been out wiv your girly friends and they've put ideas in your head. I suppose they're all relationship experts, yeah. Do me a favor, yeah! Don't bring your wylin bullshit to my door. Otherwise you can kiss goodbye to nights like these."

Ashleigh felt terrible as she watched him go upstairs. She surmised he was telling the truth. She followed him into the bedroom and shoehorned him into a fuck. Her catatonic disposition yielded to him. He was never tender but that's how she liked it. She closed her eyes and imagined he was Joleon.

* * *

She hated him in the morning. For good reason. He was in the kitchen, engaged in bawd talk with some strumpet on his mobile.

She slam-dunked the dishes into the sink. He disguised his duplicity with a feint fable about his fucked up car, and an egregious joke about Ratty, Sanjay and Joanne. Then he gave her a piddling peck and said goodbye. He had had his *central heating* — porridge - He was off to the mechanic. Or so he said. She was left to feel as if she were ordure, and that he was overdue a sample of his own manure.

She reasserted herself by Monday. Her mind was still in earnest contrivance as Shakira cooed over the intelligence and wit of her new boyfriend, self-righteous attributes Ashleigh cared little for. The scholarly lacked temerity. Wit was subjective. She was sick of false dawns and she was highly-strung. Joleon, in spite of being a habitual hemorrhoid, was the anthracite that kept her bonfire burning, and she was in a misliked mood.

She sent him a text. *Linen room in 5 mins.*

He was there within three. She almost choked him with her intensity.

"Are you drunk, Ash?"

She traced his lips with her fingertips. "You obviously don't know the taste of wine, but I know the taste of pork!"

Her iPhone trilled furiously while she was in the throes of him. He grabbled her skirt, tore her crotchless church white panties into shreds of satin. His fingers fumbled at her blouse. He tore a button unintended.

His quadriceps were like the trunk of trees and his succulent morsel dangled before her like the trunk of a baby albino elephant. Abnormally cold but conveniently sectile. Like provolone. Johnny's, in comparison, was like the snout of an elephant shrew. She kneaded the tortoise-like rind of his scrotum with her pliant fingers. She flooded her conscience with venial thoughts.

Minadex, she thought. *For Caydee-Lee. From the chemist... No, that was so wrong... Thinking of the children at a time like this...*

Her obliging thighs were wrapped around him. Her pagan hands clasped his arse pit. She sucked on his marshmallowy tongue. His turgid balls slapped against her laevulose walls with indefatigable thrift...

Graeme... Overseas Patient Manager. Wants a trace. Nineteen suspected health tourists. Costings to the taxpayer, three hundred thousand pounds...

His eyes rolled into balls of white. He wrestled her to the tessellated floor while his mouth was lodged in hers. She was astirred by his intensity and his stertor chimes of profane lust. She sluiced alee twice, and she bit the flesh of his shoulder blade to stifle her mewing. He ploughed till he emanated his viscous content.

His axle body was moist and he was panting heavily. He kept kissing her mouth, as though he was trying to intract his love into her heart. Her legs were still lolled around him.

"I'm still pissed wiv you," she said. "Us fucking doesn't change anything—"

"It changes everythin—"

"The last thing I want right now is for you to fall in love wiv me. It'd complicate everythin—"

"Who says anythin bout fallin in love wiv you?"

"When you were inside me, you called my name bout fifty times. You called me baby bout twenty times. Either you're fallin in love or you've got Tourette's!"

"If dat's tha way you want it, Ash. I'm cool—"

"There's a good lad!"

He remained treacherously lodged inside her, leaking lumpy droplets of agglutinant goo towards her womb.

"So what happens now?"

"I've got dat data analyst comin from Kaikin Systems dis afternoon. I've gotta be on-point... I need a few minutes to sort out my hair and make-up... Shit! You owe me a pair of knickers, you animal... I can't wear dat now—"

"Can't we link after work?"

"I gotta help my son wiv his homework—"

"Lunch time again tomorrow?"

"You're just like any other bloke. You talk shit post-cum."

She rolled herself from under him. He was wholly naked, except for the Air Max 95s that kept his feet warm. She watched him dress, her ungelded aberration.

"Why you goin on like nothin's happened?"

"We definitely happened," she said with a dislocating smile. "But like I said, it changes nothin. I think you're the sexiest man ever... plus you're packin a magnum... but I'm not fallin for you coz I don't wanna be fucked emotionally... I'd fuck you physically, no problem... I don't want you fallin for me coz I don't need dis mess. It's for the best, darling."

* * *

"... I had him balls deep!" she told Shakira on the train ride home. "I ruined him in the linen room—"

"Oh my days! On Johnny's birthday of all days—"

"I don't know how dat boy functions wiv all dat blood in his cock! Dat's some birth defect, Shakira—"

A fine-spun female dressed in a tweed skirt bent slightly towards them to eavesdrop, though her eyes were fixed on *The Daily Mail.*

"Where did you fuck him?"

"I told you. In the linen room. I'm surprised you never heard the slappin noises, whereva you were—"

"You're lucky your insides weren't on tha floor. Big dicks scare me. You sure it was real?"

"I swear down! If his mom had one hand, all she had to do when he was a baby was to lift him out of the bathtub wiv it!"

"You're paintin a canvas and it's a fuckin nightmare—"

"It'd never get dat bad unless I get taken in. I know where I stand wiv Johnny. And Joleon's just another breh selling manure until he ups his game considerably. Having a big willy doesn't mean he's got the full package..."

A city lad with a bucked mouth loosened his windsor knot. His eyes bounced around the train once Shakira caught him staring.

"I'll have to get a birthday cake for Johnny on the way home... an' a birthday card from my babies... I won't be fuckin him tonight tho. I'll sleep in Jardel's bed if I have to—"

"You can't escape him if he wants it."

"I'll just have to wank him off in ways he likes. But I want it three times a week from Joleon!"

"I know you're a meat hound, but Joleon ain't no misunderstood genius. He can do a lot worse wiv a lot more... I don't know how you could choopz him, because dat's too personal. You only choopz a breh when you're in love. Don't wanna come across like you're into him. He's a link, not your hubby. You meet him, bang, bang, bang, and you're done. Unless you're in love wiv him?"

"It'd take me bout a year to fall in love wiv him—"

"Can you believe it? Everyone's listenin in to us!"

Phalanges of piteous folk, standing and sitting, turned their vacuous countenances back into their phones and tablets, but not before Ashleigh poured an acute invective into their ears.

"Dat's coz they think they're perfect people! They judge you on things that they wish they could do themselves, if only they had the fuckin guts! Otherwise, why would they be interested, especially when it ain't their business in the first place?"

10

ANY FOOL CAN KILL A
MAN CRUEL...

JOHNNY GLARED AT HIS Galaxy. "Why ain't Ashy answerin her bloody phone? Dis could be an emergency... Dis could be bout Jardel—"

"She's at work, you speng!" Lollipop said. "'You know how dem people at work stay."

"I tried her work number but they said she's gone lunch—"

"Maybe her phone's on silent... Maybe she doesn't wanna talk to you right now... Maybe she's gone to lunch but hasn't really... Maybe she's busy sexin some next breh—"

"Maybe I ought to break your neck, Pepper Jackson—"

"You ought to seckle, birthday bwoy. When she sees your missed calls, she'll get back to you!"

They kept watch over the semi-detached house with the ivied décor and the green door. Nobody stirred within. Self-perpetuating songs played on the radio; macabre stuff on how to handle one's enemies by Nero Sandz. They snacked on jam donuts and downed Sprite. An hour passed. Johnny was still wounded by his mind-shackled musings.

"I'm gonna stop her workin—"

"You must be a nightmare to live wiv. You'd be proper on Caydee-Lee when she starts secondary school, lookin into her classroom wiv your high-powered binoculars—"

"When you have a good ting, there's always someone who wants to take it away. Truss me. You think someone's not onto Sophia?"

"Of course they are. She's nang!"

"And you just sit there and watch?"

"Of course—"

"Dat's why you'll lose her—"

"I should do what you did? You blew up Ashleigh, just to keep her. Twice."

"Your girl's over the internet wiv her modellin. Breh's all over her Instagram an' Twitter, beggin a link and you're not worried?"

"Err... no!"

Johnny shook his head woefully. "You don't trust broads like Ashy. I know when she's on street, bare man are on dat. They like her choong figure, her tats, her hair, her bumper, dem kissable lips. Dat could give man a helluva worries. I don't trust man round her either, and if you think Sophia's head doesn't get turned by some shit she reads bout her online, den you got sugar in your eyes, son!"

"Sophia's a walkin wet dream but I ain't up her tail twenty-four seven. We got our own shit to do. We text regular, chat when we need to, meet when we have to, fuck when we want to, go out when we care to. We roll like dat coz we're strong. Whereas you, you're obsessed!"

"Obsessed? I'm passionate—"

"You're obsessed!"

"Nah, passionate. Whereas you ain't passionate bout nothin. Breh owes you dough and all you do is watch his front door. Why don't we break into his yard and see what we could get?"

"I don't want the family silver. I just want my five bills."

"He ain't got your five bills. Dat's why he's hidin—"

"He ain't no hide and seek champion."

"Knock on the door and speak to his parents—"

"And tell dem what?"

"Dat their fuckin son owes you peez and you've come to collect—"

Lollipop howled like a lobo. "And get baited?"

"Your pops would roll different, if he was in your situation—"

"My pops rolls political. He'd get a Court Order, knock on your door politely and begs for the debt. I'd just kick your door down, standard."

"Erm... But you ain't kickin the door down. You let a man walk off wiv five bills. Business taken a hit—"

"Five bills ain't gonna stop me from grindin—"

"We've spent the afternoon waitin for Steppy and you're sayin business ain't taken a hit—"

"I got bare punters, fam. I got two punters up city. I holler at dem on their mobiles an' link dem on a side street like some boy delivering pizza. My girl Tayo linked me wiv some stockbroker. I rinse two bags of him daily. He told me the rules at his firm: *You can't go on Facebook and you can't do Coke. But you can fuck your PA!* And then he's introduced a friend, some celebrity breh. Breh's on your TV entertainin your kids wiv *London Bridge is falling down* an' I'm shottin him three keys of the finest powder every day. So no: business never sleeps."

He started the engine and drove away. Scaramouche would be surely found... Scaramouche will surely pay...

Teenage boys in school uniform played hooky on the High Street. An exhibitionist in a cream peplum dress walked hand-in-hand with her bewhiskered scruff of a boyfriend. Mothers with buggies coiled into Primark. Refuse collectors lobbed an assortment of rubbish into waste lorries. Johnny laughed at a rambling text from Ashleigh about her colleagues' notional comparisons between his music and Drake's. They must be bluffing her, he texted back. He was more Nas.

"When am I gonna meet dis Tayo?"

"You're not her type, Johnny."

"Why? She's into white boys?"

"She's into rich boys—"

"Have you tried it?"

"She won't free up—"

"You're pussy-whipped; dat's your problem... Steppy's got your peez and Sophia's got your balls. If I were you, I'd have fucked up Steppy already. And I'd be poking Tayo on a regular. Jeez, you're not hungry or angry enough, are ya?"

Lollipop said nothing. His bloodlust was unkindled. For three weeks, he had sought Steppy, that scatter-brained shitbag, as zealously as Steppy had sought him from the outset...

* * *

Steppy had been an accordant boy from a near inscrutable home until he desired the grievous cluster of the gang life. He became bored with science, maths and english. He became congruent with the storied prosaisms of money, pussy and weed. His gynecologist father and civil engineering mother were sticklers in so far as academic achievement were concerned.

"B- is a no no in this house," they said after reviewing his exam reports. "How are you going to get to Oxbridge if you're coming home with Bs and Cs? Amma's top of her class. In every subject. In every year. And you're always in the bottom middle."

Going to Oxbridge was not regnant in his mind. Throughout the summer holiday, he loitered the streets with Lil Elliott, Shekaidy and other lads. He became emboldened to smoke weed in other people's housing blocks as his heart seethed its discontent. The histrionics he employed were at odds with his nurture. He terrorized the kiosk traders who sold international calling cards because they looked like drips and spoke funny English. After midnight, he'd trudge homeward to quibble with his despairing parents who were at pains to know what would become of their gosling.

He had witnessed Mr. Placide being affronted by Lollipop and Marius when they trespassed school territory for a sojourn with Lil Elliott several months back. He thought it classic comedy. During a subsequent school assembly, Mr. Placide grumbled at being accosted by nefarious types who were recruiting schoolchildren into gangs on school ground, and that his vehicle had been trashed as a result. Steppy noted how pensive Mr. Placide became thereafter, and how his encounter with those unscrupulous demi-gods from the street had ailed him. He hoped to befriend Lollipop and wondered why they hadn't yet been acquainted.

His bug-eyed observance fell upon Lil Elliott's footwear as they cued in the canteen.

"Raaah! Pierre Hardy trainers!!!"

"Yesirrr!"

"How much dey set you back?"

"All in a day's work, blud!"

"What, so you shot Lollipop's food?"

"What's wiv tha questions, cuz?"

"What you goin on like dat for? Didn't I bring you in on Farrah?"

"We ain't talkin jezzie's tho, are we? We're talkin bout Lollipop and he don't like man talkin bout him—"

"Farrah don't like man knowin she's a jezzie but you still got a shiner. I beg you, fam… Let me tag next time Lollipop comes round—"

"Naaah blud." Lil Elliott was indignant. "You wanna bait man by askin man stupid questions? Naaah, free dat! Man won't even entertain you. He'll laugh at you and tell you to get tha fuck out!"

"So it's like dat, huh?"

"Hell, yeah. I ain't sayin shit. Case. Fuckin. Closed."

Mia Christensen, a cognate of Steppy's, was the most lascivious of nymphets at All Saints Sixth Form. She had been scooped by Lollipop for putrid reasons. Steppy felt obliged to ask her.

"Tell your bossman bout me, innit. Tell him I move DVDs and bud… Tell him I'm open for business—"

"He'll probably laugh when I tell him dat. You can't offer him nothin—"

"It depends how you tell it. If you sell man well, he'll take you serious. Man like dat needs to take you serious. Come on, Mia. You owe me!"

A few days later, after Lollipop had sexed his Harlesden homegrown in a grotesque garage on a pungent mattress surrounded by drab walls, she told him about Steppy but forewarned he was a liability.

"They call him Steppy coz you've gotta give him step by step instructions," she said.

But Lollipop looked upon him propitiously. He was gauche and without guile, but he sure as hell was a pliable disciple. His reedy drone was monotonous. He had a big forehead. But he wanted to hustle.

He cut adrift silently like a peripatetic fox as soon as the school bells knelled the kids into their classroom, skunk interlarded with specks of crack in his pockets. He sold to Shaheen in her impoverished flat where she fed her offspring with flummery for breakfast, chicken burgers and chips for afternoon tea. She was very kind to him in spite of the calamity she suffered, her chronic ailments and cumbersome debts. He was reluctantly attracted to the vulnerable floweret. Regular clients included a quartet of Belgian students studying Sarte who purchased some blow, and middle-class girls from a private college who wanted to know. Every evening, he met Lollipop at a prearranged bolthole to pay his dues and pick up more drugs, and he was inordinately satisfied with his gains. And the next day, he'd miss lessons he hated like maths and science, to navigate his undertakings in comparative streets.

But the streets were more capricious than he envisaged. A pregnant punter named Lucy had an ill-conditioned will. She ordered cocaine from him and when he arrived with the produce, she recoiled from him as if he were a leper.

"… I'm not buying dat rubbish! I could take that and end up dead…"

As he was about to exit her flat, he was intercepted by fiendish marionettes who lay waiting in an adjoining room. They dangled him from an eighth floor balcony and took his drugs and money. They pushed a knife against his jugular vein.

"Don't you EVER come back here, you gutless git..." Lucy's kinks in her hair were serpent-like. "... See schoolboy, I've got your library card. It's got your address on, and we'll put an axe through your front door if I see you within ten blocks of this place!"

He resigned from the ophidian streets and sought refuge from Shaheen. His timorous disposal caused him to shun Lollipop, who sought his money from the drugs lost to Lucy. His school called his parents to say he was constantly truant. He told his parents he was ill. He begged to stay at his grandmother's home to aid his convalescence. His parents, concerned by his dolor, were empathetic. Sick certificates from his GP were emailed to his teacher.

"Lollipop said you'd better show up wiv his peez," Lil Elliot said in a phone call. "He said you'd better find him before he finds you. He said if he catches you before den, you will wish you were dead!"

Steppy found that message so bothersome that he carried a blade. He divided his time between Shaheen and his grandmother's, returning home at obscure hours in a taxi.

The dorsal of his street overlooked the Brent reservoir. Most nights, the favonian winds bounced off its subdued surface and around the pallescent houses of Panama Road, Neasden. Tonight, those winds were eerily calm in spite of the serein weather. The coercive tang of skunk nested the clammy air. The quarry would roost soon. No. 20 watched the loitering pixies while transferring their onerous shopping from their Focus boot to their American Fridge Freezer. They spied their road through their casement windows ten minutes later. The pixies had moved on. The limousine liberals at No. 14 were holding a soiree for their fellow cosmopolites in their four-bedroomed comfort. The Nyame's, their neighbors at No. 12, departed shortly before eight for a dinner date they had planned for months. Mrs. Nyame told the young woman on the doorstep that Asamoah would be home imminently.

At nine-thirty, a Volvo crept onto the spot where the Nyame's had parked their Alexis. A hooded youth emerged from one of the back passenger seats, paid its driver and hurried towards the green door of No. 12. Scaramouche? Scaramouche!

"Yo! Steppy!" Lollipop said.

Steppy's craw exhibited a feeble roar.

"Don't even think bout running, Steppy. You take five paces and I'll burn bare slugs in your back. Then I'll stand over you and finish you... So don't fuckin run. Whatever you decide in your brain, running ain't an option—"

"Aight... Aight... I gotta perfectly reasonable explanation—"

"I don't wanna hear perfectly reasonable explanations. You should've kept things nice an' simple, son. You've stepped down, Steppy... You've stepped down. I ain't gonna harm your skin tho. But if you irritate me, you're gone. Believe me—"

Steppy was uncertain whether to draw his blade or no. Conceited bodies emerged from the darkness. Some were poised for tomfoolery, others for violence.

"Where's my peez, fam?"

"I ain't got... I ain't got—"

"I don't want tha fuckin money. Stop actin like a shivering wreck. You can't be jumpy among your fam. I hate to see you surrounded by enemies. You'd probably have seizures an' shit. So where you comin from?"

"F-fffrom my aunt's yard!"

"Is dat where you've been?"

"I wanna jump off, Lollipop—"

"Nobody jumps off road, fam... Who's in your yard now?"

"My mom, dad, sister an' my dogs—"

"What you lyin for, blud? You ain't got no dogs—"

"Yeh," Johnny said. "And we saw your mom and dad leave in an Alexis. Registration no: MX14GHA. As if you didn't know—"

"You bring a tear to my glass eye," Lollipop said. "It don't matter. You're gonna let us into your yard. We're your fam too—"

"You're my fam too..." Steppy said.

He opened the front door. Faces masked with red bandanas made segway into different rooms. Somebody in the kitchen was cooking a saporous dish. She called out *Asamoah! Asamoah!* once she heard the sally. Shekaidy and Johnny descended the stairs to meet her. There was a loud exertion and a sharp scream. Lollipop's cryptic barbs on letting his boys *loose on his sister* caused him to calibrate Faustian proposals in his mushy brain. Lil Elliott got his teenage kicks by putting his left foot through every electrical device in the lounge. Yopz opened the fridge and helped himself to whatever he could find. Kevin tucked a portable Blu-ray player under his arm. Nutz searched Mr. and Mrs. Nyame's bedroom. In Steppy's bedroom, Columbia confiscated a Nexus One and a Wii U. Marius sat in the lounge and rolled a spliff.

Johnny recoiled at the family photos: the unctuous father holding aloft a trophy next to his porcine cunt of a boss; Mrs. Nyame wearing a ferny wig as she posed with her daughter. The Nyame's looked saccharine and ridiculous, a tribe of establishment boot-lickers. Johnny impugned that it was time to insert some ill fortune.

"Man up Steppy," Lollipop said. "You think you're gully coz you got red colors? You give gangstas a bad name. Why did you get into the grind? You ain't gully. You're no gangsta. You're jus gas. Look at you! You're decent… You could've had a decent life, but you lost me peez. I got so much hate for you right now… You should have jus seckled in tha library instead of holdin out your chest like some bad muthafucker. Your fam would've been proud… I'm gonna make an example of you. Wannabe thugz are gonna read your story in the newspapers an' they gonna learn what happens when they come across a grimy cat like me…"

Steppy begged for a second chance to retrieve the five hundred. Amma was hurled into the corner, blindfolded but still hollering. Marius warned her to shut up.

"You see dis white bag, cuz?" Lollipop said. "Dat's what I sent you out to go and sell for me. You ate the peez an' didn't give a shit. Now I'm gonna watch you swallow dis an' not give a shit. If you yam it all, consider yourself forgiven. If you don't, I'll shank your sis in tha gut!"

"What a choice, man. What a choice!" Johnny said. "What it's gonna be, Steppy? Pur-leeez tell me!"

"If I eat all dat, I'm gonna die—"

"You're a growing lad, Steppy. You could make it. But big sis definitely won't—"

"You're not getting away wiv dis," Amma said. "You may think you're big coz you're here in numbers… Don't watch that… God sees everything—"

"Faith squares the circle every time," Johnny said. "Always callin on God before you die but while you're alive, you lived like animals—"

Lollipop concentrated his bale on Steppy, who nibbled at the septic grains of white like a chastened mouse.

"Swallow all, you cunt!" he said.

Johnny's right boot stomped Amma till she became unconscious.

"Leave her alone… I'm eatin…" Steppy said. He swallowed a powdered mouthful. And another. And another.

"Eat! Eat! Eat!" Lollipop said, hazing him and his sister.

Steppy keeled over slowly. The niveous powder he engorged had thawed into miasmal milk in his gullet, and he retched and choked on its foul yoke. Lollipop sat close to him and watched him writhe. Only after he had digested his penalty, would he be forgiven and set free.

* * *

By the littoral of the Regent's Canal beneath the full moon, tenderfoots recalled the degradation of Steppy. A friend texted Lil Elliott the latest news.

"Shiiit!" he said. "Steppy's dead, maaan! Oh, maaan! He got banged up in more ways than one… But why give up?"

Hoots of fluting hysteria followed. A tootsie said he saw Steppy's limp body loaded onto a stretcher by paramedics. Shekaidy wept.

Lollipop heard the news moments later as he sat with Sophia in his Audi TT. She asked what was wrong.

"Some breh od'd on some very bad Charlie!"

"Oh shit! Was he a friend of yours?"

"He was an idiot who took risks. Bare stress must have got to him... He'll be a chicken in his next life!"

"People you know are droppin like flies—"

"You ain't told me what you want for your birthday?"

"Hmmm... I'd like a Shitz Tzu please!"

"A Shitz Tzu?"

"You know what dat is?"

"Sure I know what it is! It's what my baby's gonna get!"

He kissed her goodnight. He watched her disappear, down her pathway and into her apartment.

He phoned Lil Elliott back. "...You're takin over my business line. It's worth three bags a day so you gotta keep tings movin. If business slides, you're responsible. Snitches will get moved. You tell em youngers to keep their mouths well and truly shut otherwise I'm comin after everyone in the place, families included. And do me a favor, Google Man! Find out what a Shitz Tzu is, where I can get one from and how much they cost. Make sure it's brand new too!"

He drove to Stacey's home immediately, seeking lee. Stacey was in his Spiderman pajamas holding a frothy mug of mocha.

"What's wrong Lollz? It's two in tha morning—"

"Where were you last night?"

"I was wiv Lydia comin back from Westbourne Park. Her sister had a boy—"

"The Fedz gonna be sniffin round these sides askin questions bout me, askin where I was bout ten, eleven o'clock. I'm peak right now. Don't need dis... Could I say I was wiv you?"

"You gonna tell me what's happenin, cuz?"

"I just need you to say I was wiv you. And Lydia too—"

"Lydia ain't gonna say dat—"

"Why not?"

"Coz... coz you weren't—"

"You're gonna ave to make her. If you don't, I'm lookin twenty years—"

"Twenty years? What did you do?"

"It's bout what *you're* gonna do dat's relevant. Blud, I tol you once I'd body any breh for you. I swear down. I meant what I said. Now I gotta know whether you'd do tha same—"

"But you ain't told me what's goin on—"

"Fuckin hell, man. I ain't got time for stories. I'm stuck. I need to know if you can talk your girl round—"

"I got a bad feelin bout dis… Maaan, let me sit dis one out, Lollz—"

"You know what, Stacey Brookes, go fuck yourself. You're *dead* to me, you selfish bastard. Known you fifteen years and you end it like *dis*. Cool. Life's lesson learnt. After I dealt wiv dis situation, I'm gonna deal wiv you like I don't know you. So you better pray I get *dem* twenty years!"

The farcical headwind made hay into night, careened out of sight. Stacey scratched his ditsy head.

"What just happened?" Sondra said.

"Lollipop wanted me to cover for him. Won't say why. So I said I couldn't. Dunno if I done the right thing—"

"Are you seriously doubting your judgement, Stacey?"

"But if it were me, he'd have my back." He smacked her forehead with an open palm. "Maaan, sometimes I don't think—"

"You *did* think. Know your own mind, son… How dare he come to my house at three in the morning with that kind of bullshit? How fucking dare he?"

Stacey gulped his mocha readily and wondered whether he had imagined the last five minutes.

* * *

The requisition for a pernicious yarn remained. And so was the hunt for a credible alibi wherewithal he could sell to the police.

But his companions were fumbling gimps. None among them was so doughty who could seep no doubt. They were quick to give each other up once the flagrant whip scolded their backs. The bright-eyed Stacey was the best he could do, but the police would eventually carve him piecemeal and devour his fable. But Stacey was the best he could do.

Kidology was futile against the Metropolitan Police Force. They and their forensic teams were the best of their kind on God's unjust earth. He had to pit his wits against them. They would surely pit their resources against him, one mortal versus a myriad supplemented with a titanium will. They had the names of Quick Draw McGraw cretins and Abdul Jabbar knife wielders marked in rubric print. Surely, their bug-eyed detectives would come-a-crawling. It would only take a faint hair to fall from his butt cheek at the crime scene to incarcerate his arse.

Tayo texted for some bud on his personal line. He drove out to meet her in the vain hope that he could clear his head. As she raved on about her impending appearance on a reality TV show, an idea chimed within his skull.

"Tayo, I need a favor."

"Don't tell me! You want me to stash your shots under my floorboard coz tings are hot for you right now?"

"You're a joker!"

"I'm right, aren't I? Yesss! I'm always right—"

"Tayo, I need an alibi... I went out wiv a couple of my boys... an' they just done some shit I ain't down wiv... If they go down, they'll take me down. I can't afford dat—"

"What did they do?"

"Some yute was goin on super feisty. He didn't know when to shut up. Dey decided to teach him a lesson... Tha lesson got outta hand... He's in hospital wiv a serious injury... Fedz are spreadin rumors he's dead when, in fact, he ain't... His cousin went to hospital to see him and they played X-Box together, and so I know he ain't dead—"

"Come on, baby. If the police say he's dead, you'd have to take their word for it over the cousin's—"

"Why's his cousin gonna lie?"

"I don't know... unless he was playin X-Box with a ghost! Your story's got me spooked!"

"Just say I was at the cocktail party you just had... behind the bar, servin drinks, and like... I was here the whole time... Can you do dat? You may never have to but you never know. Just in case. You get me?"

Tayo stared out of her window overlooking the A406. She swayed to the music of Miguel. She poured herself a gulpy glass of Amarone.

"So you were my sommelier last night, right? You spent the whole evening behind the bar fillin glasses. I had you dressed in a dickey bow-tie and tight black trousers—"

"Not too tight trousers—"

"You arrived about nine. You played some Kwabs, FKA twigs, Rizzle Kicks, Rita Ora... You were behind the bar at eleven. There was a hundred people by midnight... Respectable, important peeps... The party finished at 3.30... You helped me clean up. You left before five... I went to my bedroom and had mind-blowing sex with my boo."

"Sounds good to me... Breh's I've known my whole life have let me down. I ask you straight away, and you say yes—"

"I haven't said yes—"

"So what was dat bout me behind the bar, playin Rizzle Kicks?"

She sipped some Amarone. "I'm a hypothetical barmaid, right? If you're a nice person and I give you a free drink, it's coz you're a nice person. If you're a nutter and I still give you a free drink, it's coz I'm scared of you—"

"And I'm dat hypothetical punter dat you like, coz you know I'll leave a big tip!"

She swayed to the bedlam in his brain, gliding across the room on her Carvela sandals.

"Come and dance with me, baby!" she sang in an euphonious voice. She pulled him of the sofa. She floated around the room like a ballroom dancer. He tried to keep afloat.

"So what you're sayin, Tayo? I'll make it worth your while if you say yes!"

"Hmmm… Darling… I'm just uncomfortable with the police. I got scared when I got stopped the other day for speeding. They knew everything about me. Date of birth. Address. Insurance. Everything. They were proper gentlemen though. They kept calling me Madam… I'd be uncomfortable if I was in your situation… Hmmm… I'll do it for you though, if you do me a teeny weeny favor…"

Lollipop didn't feel like dancing. But he kept up the pretense.

"… My parents were supposed to send me money for my birthday. But my dad's best friend died in Chicago and he wants to use *my* birthday money to fly his body back to Nigeria. It's kinda fucked things up for me… unless you could sponsor me—"

"You want me to sponsor you?"

"Loan me five grand until my parents come good for me—"

"Dat money comes easy for your Arsenal boyfriend—"

"He's got other things on his plate. He was meant to move to Barcelona for 40 million euros but the deal fell through. He's got an injury, a groin strain. He didn't get that playing football, if you know what I mean… I kinda feel guilty… bein responsible—"

"Five grand, Tayo? Dat's a lotta dough—"

"Not if it keeps *you* out of prison. Think about it: I *did* have a party last night, and I could place *you* at the center of it!"

At the end of the evening, Lollipop thanked her wholeheartedly. He wrestled with the matter all night but he finally deduced that a well-articulated testimony was better than none. He returned the next day with the five thousand. But he added that the rumor was true, for Steppy was indeed dead. She didn't seem to mind after he extended an extra three thousand.

* * *

Augustus and Laverne had gone to Jamaica for a fortnight. He smoked excessive bud in his cloistered room till he was fagged. Wheedled opiates provided small comfort. Polyphonic murmurings chided him in many tongues and his ravelment remained. When he slept, he dreamt that his brain lay abandoned in a desolate alley till it was discovered by an unfamiliar boy of twelve. His blood was spilled. Three syringes lay stilled. The whereabouts of his cadaver was unknown and his brain was already a hive to a colony of maggots. When he woke, he proffered a barren prayer to the hooded revenant that affrighted him in his mind's eye. He wished Steppy Heaven and all its trimmings. A caveat in his prayer was that he be excused from capture. Breakfast was French toast and orange juice. He vomited its detritus bits into the toilet bowl. Then he walked along the veranda to visit Johnny.

"Where you been man?" Johnny said. "How come you ain't answerin your phone?"

"My battery died—"

"When man leaves messages on your phone, you should get back to man—"

"Somethin wrong, Johnny?"

"Nuttin's wrong. You sleep last night?"

"Like a baby. What bout you?"

"I've been bunnin non-stop… Fam, I shouldn't have hit dat girl like dat—"

"You lil pussy!"

"What tha fuck you talkin about? I ain't no—"

"Look, I ain't got time to argue…" Lollipop paused after hearing shrieks of laughter from the living room. "… Who've you got with you?"

"Cane… Marius… Blaze… Columbia… Shekaidy…"

"So you're gassin to every man bout what you did?"

"You're so fuckin paranoid—"

"Oh am I now?" Lollipop's eyebrows writhed with fury. "You're the one who was up all night smokin crack."

He surfed into the living room.

"What's up, Cane? You still dognappin?"

Cane was willowy pink with a fain eye. "Every day! Got Retrievers, Staffs, Beagles, Dobermans. Even got a Pekingese. I heard you wanted somethin for your gal—"

"Yeh, I sorted it tho—"

"You mean Elliott sorted it. He came to me, innit. Askin bout a Shih Tzu—"

"If you knew I was after a Shih Tzu, you should've looked after me when I look after you when you get your food—"

"Blame Lil Elliott, fam. He didn't wanna say who it was for, even though I named you twice. Manz goin on like he workin for MI5. I made him pay full whack." He rolled a sly joint with his mercurial fingers. "Next time you wanna see a man bout a dog, come and see the man himself!"

As Cane cackled, Lollipop greeted the other ashcan goons godfather-like, except for Blaze, and listened to their brain farts. They talked about Shekaidy's problems having recently become a father, and how he was denied by his ex-girlfriend's father from fathering his daughter. They thawed into infantile laughter when Johnny related the story of Ratty and Sanjay, and how they had fought over Joanne.

"You man love runnin in on dat ho," Cane said. "Man might ave coodies an' don't know. Animals, maaan!"

"Ratty's borrowin peez from Sanjay and Sanjay's been usin dat to take up percentages of his label," Blaze said. "Now Sanjay's been signin his own boys and Ratty's pissed coz he's forced to sack his manager. Now Foe-X is just his foe and wants to sue his arse for breach of contract."

"Dat boy ain't never droppin dat album," Marius said. "He'll be creepin before long. Gassin bout riches when he ain't got none. Ratty saw Joanne out wiv Sanjay an' told her to go home. Sanjay started exposin his arse. It was so funny. Ask Rebecca and Ladelle.

Dey filmed it on their phones…"

By chance, Lollipop met Rebecca and Ladelle that afternoon on the block. He tried to elicit conversation about the infamous clip. They dissembled its existence in a hurry. They reciprocated his query with one of their own.

"Did you hear bout dat school boy who was forced to eat blow?"

"I sort of heard… How did you hear?"

Ladelle licked her tamarisk lips. "I know his cousin. He was a really good kid until he went off the rails wiv street scum. Won't be long before those slices of bacon start makin arrests."

"I'd like to know what Lil Elliott knows—" Rebecca said.

"You know Elliott?" Ladelle said. "Says he knows but he doesn't know—"

"What *does* Lil Elliott know?" Lollipop said.

"He reckons Steppy got ambushed in his own bedroom, and dat someone gave dat poor mite a perfect roundhouse a la Jet Li. But dat's Lil Elliott for you: A pathological bullshitter!"

"He might have to go to the Fedz if he knows what went on dat night," Lollipop said.

"Dat's what I said," Ladelle said. "But den he's sayin the Fedz spoke to most of the kids in his school, but they don't think much of the information he's given dem."

"Can't understand the police," Rebecca said. "One time, they arrested some gal for beatin up some next gal for fuckin her boyfriend, an' round tha corner some boy was literally getting stamped on by twenty man. He got sliced in a bad way but the old Bill ain't pulled the boys, coz nobody wanted to name names. Priorities, priorities. The law's brass anyway!"

Lollipop stopped by the Walker household, to lambaste Lil Elliott for his vaunted indiscretion. He was glad to find him there.

"Anybody in?" Lollipop asked.

"I'm on my jack jones—" Lil Elliott said.

Lollipop smashed a fist into his face without warning. "What did I tell you bout keepin your fuckin mouth shut?… You wanna see me lifed off?... If I do, you fuckin go down... to your fuckin grave... you lil fuck-faced purple prick—"

"I ain't said nothin... to no one... I swear on my mom's life—"

Lollipop dragged him into the living room. He trampled over Tanya's petunias and pressed him against the coastline floor.

"How come Ladelle dropped your name? And Rebecca?"

"I dunno... I swear down, fam... I dunno—"

"If the Fedz ever ask bout me, you say I'm a role model who does good deeds. If you say anythin dat leads dem to me, I'll break into your bedroom at night wiv a blade, shank you while you sleep, and go back to my bed and your sister will be in it. Am I clear, you dopey cunt?"

＊　＊　＊

Later that week, Lollipop toured the composite shelves of Tafari's bookstore. Some book titles aroused his interest: *The Socratic Texts*, *The Ordinance Of World Religions*, *Ascriptions To Africa's Intractable Angst*, *The History Of Indo-European Languages*, *The Coagulated Self-Defence Laws of England And Wales*...

Tafari mused him with an incredulous eye. "How can yuh murda dat boy and show yuh face?"

The book leapt into the air, crash-landed on the floor. "Sorry. What was dat?"

"Mi seh. Yuh murda in dat jacket... Yuh av nuh taste!"

"It ain't mine. Belongs to a friend. I ain't got no choice in dis weather—"

"Yuh cause a lotta strife an trouble—"

"Trouble?"

"I say, meh tink Liverpool will strike the Double!"

"Yeh, yeh. Liverpool. Li-vaa-pooool. We merked Villa last week. We'll take out Spurs in the semi-final come Sunday—"

"Merked? Take out? Indeed!"

Oh, the casuistries of these doggone ears! Surely, Tafari could not pertain that he was the cause of Steppy's death. He was more than a fastidious man laden with admonitory watchwords and would do more than play mind games. After flicking through the book titled *The Coagulated Self-Defence Laws of England And Wales*, he arrived at the counter, and purchased it. Tafari inserted his change and receipt firmly in his palm.

"You av sum botheration?"

Lollipop paused, just to make sure he heard right. "Who me? I'm never better. Dad's on holiday wiv Laverne and I'm gonna ave the whole yard—"

"You'll wing for life!"

"What?"

"I say, mi see yuh wife. Sophia. Yuh gal!"

"Sophia? Where? When?"

"Yesterday. She passed by in a cyar. Stacey tell mi she's yuh lady. Yuh wifey, him say. Good feh yuh, I say!"

Good for him that she was a desiderable choice or a miserable one? Tafari gestured that he step aside. A customer behind required service. He made for the exit.

"Hotstepper!" Tafari said.

Oh, the casuistries of his diminishing senses! Lollipop held the door ajar, his naked despair tangible. Tafari looked up once he'd finished with his customer.

"See yuh later," he said without a smile.

At night, Lollipop read till his eyes were sore. He re-read paragraphs comprehensively, recording them verbatim in his cerebrum. He careened to the conviction that he could hamstring a rhadamanthine and exculpate himself. All he need do was bridle the events that were sure to follow. He played out the following supposition: He'd exhibit courtesy to the Bob Cryer's and Adam Okaro's when they arrest him. He'd confer and pay heed to his advocate. He'd embrace being on remand with forbearance. He'd respect the staid cavils of the courtroom. And he'd offer evidence indivisible from the truth.

Johnny was puzzled as to how Lollipop could be so supremely self-absorbed with reading.

"Don't know why you're readin dat book. If the Fedz *are* comin, den the Fedz *are* coming—"

"Court ain't worried bout who's tellin the truth. Court's only concerned if there's enough evidence to convict."

"Is dat what dat fuckin book says?"

"You got an alibi, Johnny?"

"Yeah, I was wiv Ashy, Lindsey and Sean, twenty miles from the scene in Marlow wiv our kids. Brap! Brap! Who was you wiv?"

"Nevermind—"

"You ain't got one. Don't tell em you were wiv me. I don't wanna come tumblin down when you do!"

"Only a dickhead would drag his babymother into his bullshit and think he's gully—"

"Yeah! We'll see how far 'I was on my own in my bedroom watchin *Game Of Thrones'* gets you. Dat'll get destroyed in five minutes—"

"It'll get me a lot further than when Sean's wylin like a bitch after two minutes of interrogation. He's as thick as shit. He maybe Midnight's brother but he should've been his sister. And as for Lindsey, how can you get a mouthy chav like dat to back your story? You trust her, yeh? Once those slices of bacon offer her a reward to snitch on your ashy black arse, it'll be Hail Mary Time for her!"

He left Johnny grinding his molars.

It was seven-fifty. He had no place to go. Sophia was in Manchester at a Hair and Beauty Convention, and he felt no compulsion to kill time with his friends. He thought of Joanne and the skills she had mastered with her ample mouth. As he pulled outside her front door, he noticed a simulacrum of a male figure rooted in her living room. He dialed her number, withholding his own.

"Joanne?"

"Whose dis?"

"You know who dis is. Why haven't you phoned me?"

"No reason—"

"No reason? Is it coz of your new man?"

"What new man?"

"The man dat's walkin bout butt naked in your living room—"

"I hear you gotta girlfriend, so you can't talk—"

"You can't believe everythin you hear—"

"I believe everythin I see—"

"I wanna see you. After you see me, you'll start believin in me again."

She laughed.

"Tell dat breh to do one—"

"I can't… I'll link you tomorrow at your place. He's got a key to my yard and he comes when he likes—"

"It's gotta be tonight, Jo. Tell him your aunt's ill and you'll be gone for an hour. I'm roastin—"

"He ain't gonna let me come out—"

"You do what he says, yeh? You love him, yeh?"

"Nooo—"

"You love me, yeah?"

"Yeh—"

"I'm the one you love but you never check for me. And I hear you're fucking Sanjay on the down low—"

"Dat's lies—"

"Well, dat's what he's tellin everybody!"

"He takes me out to dinner and treats me good. If I give him somethin back, it's coz he's earned it—"

"Who you talkin to?" asked a miffed voice in the background.

"It's only a friend…"

The phone was grappled from her grasp.

"Who's dis ringin my gal's phone?" asked the hyperventilating kobold.

"Why, who's this?"

"Listen, sta'. Your time done. My time now. Don't bother ring back again, skeen. She's my gal, yannerstan?"

"I'm her cousin, fam… It ain't what you think… She's needed

at the hospital. Her uncle's sick…"

The kobold would not be pacified.

"Get into the bath before mi box yuh backside," he told Joanne before turning on Lollipop again.

"Your raaas…" The phone clicked off.

Where could he get good head at this time of night, in this town? Why pay a prostitute when certain girls offered such vicarious services for free? Like Mia…

"… I'm on my period, Lollipop!" she said with a lopsided frown.

"Still, you could gimme a lil suckey suckey… Think of all dat Vitamin C you'd be gettin."

He took her arm and led her into the bush. After she alleviated him, he exhaled happily.

"Now you can fuck off," she said.

He wept with laughter. "Dat's how man dem chat to you after you've given dem brain?"

"No man talks to me like dat. I'd spark man if they ever disrespected me…"

They headed to an off-license. Lollipop bought a packet of Silk Cut Purple and some rizla. He bought Mia a Cherry Coke and a Mars bar. Then he drove her towards her hostel. Her iPhone pinged incessantly.

"Whose WhatsApping you?"

"Some breh from college—"

"Text him back and tell him your man don't want no breh textin you—"

"But he's a friend—"

"Boys and girls can't be friends."

"I heard you gotta wifey somewhere—"

"Who tol you dat? Elliott?"

"No."

"Who den?"

"My friend saw you wiv her in Nando's last Thursday. She said your girl's very pretty—"

"Your friend's sick in the brain. She wants to spoil what you got. The world and his brother wanna break us up—"

"Do you know who bodied Steppy?"

"How am I gonna know dat?"

"He tol me he owed you peez and he was prang dat you would do him somethin—"

"Steppy owed a lotta people peez. He rolled too deep in the end. I was pissed wiv him. I would've slapped him bout, but not bodied him... Don't go droppin my name to no Fed—"

"I didn't even mention you to no Fed. I swear down—"

"Why you askin silly questions den?"

"The police came round our class askin if anyone knew anythin!"

"And?"

"No one knows anythin. But I thought you might—"

"Well, I don't so don't be thinkin otherwise."

"His sister gave descriptions of the boys who came for Steppy. The Fedz showed me the drawings—"

"Look like anybody you know?"

"Not really... She said they wore balaclavas... They had me in coz I'd known Steppy all my life... His sister said they made him eat coke coz they threatened to shank her... I've never seen a big man cry like his dad. It was awful. I had to get out of there—"

"Parents don't know their youngers. They're focused on the paper chase to even care. Steppy's one of the top shottas on road and they didn't know? He kills himself and I'm supposed to care?"

"He didn't kill himself. The truth will come out. Dis thing ain't goin away..."

Dis thing ain't goin away? A ghost of an idea came to him. He'd drive the pea-brained mignon north along the M1 and take an exit turn onto some bucolic road with a spinney and a lacustrine backdrop. Then he'd wrap a cable around her fruity neck till she died. He would tie a rock to her tattooed ankles and cast her piddling remains into the water and pray that the pond life will leave very little of her so as to riddle her identity. But she had no discretion.

She would have told someone she was with him tonight. And then he would have two deaths to contend with, and not one. Her big mouth potentially saved her.

"So, you'd snitch if you knew?"

"Dunno—"

"Best you say nothin. Dis thing's way bigger than you. You can't bring him back. If you get involved, you'll end up joinin him! I promise you—"

"I'm fallin in love wiv you—"

"What?"

"If you dump your girlfriend, I swear down I'd love you off. I mean dat—"

"You talk a lot of shit, Mia!" Lollipop said after a moment's thought. "I'm gonna take you back to yours, for my sake as well as yours!"

He drove to her hostel and let her out. His choler bottomed out after he parked outside his own front gate. His entire home space was his own. He had Sky-boxed his favorite films. His cookies and cream *Haagen Dazs* nested in the freezer. He was jaunty of heel after embarking from his car. He showboated with a Pepsi can that clattered along the pavement. He kicked it under a car. An unmarked police car.

Vehicle doors opened on cue. The guttural war cry of cops inversed from makeshift anterooms on the avenue. He had scarcely time to flinch.

"Trevor King, you're under arrest for the suspected murder of Asamoah Nyame. You have the right to remain silent—"

Foreign hands clogged him against a garden fence. His brain turned to jelly. Surging voices clanged at once. Someone repeated the name, Asamoah Nyame. Asamoah. Nyame.

"Mate, I've never heard of the fella—" he said.

"Oh, I know you have…" interrupted what looked to be the most senior officer among the pack. Her ice-blue chinks was fleeringly hostile. "… And you'd *better* be telling the truth!"

He talked his face off. She told him to shut up. They fastened his wrists with cuffs. They stormed through his flat, aided by a lopsided hound with lofty nostrils. Tanya remonstrated with them in a currish manner.

"Mom, just leave it," Natalie said. "If they arrest you as well, then you'd deserve it."

Several residents of the estate buzzed forth from their apiary. Shekaidy looked flaccid in the wind. Dominic elicited words of encouragement for Lollipop. Ashleigh observed from her living room window. Fernando exchanged succinct words with an officer. Young *gangsta* groupies watched ruefully, taunting the police for their perceived heavy-handedness.

"How come you got six bully vans for one man? Ain't dat a lil OTT?"

"Same old boi dem. Always fuckin wiv us…"

"Skeen! Fedz playin cat and mouse wiv tha Fuck-It Generation…"

The foray was over in less than an hour. They removed an iPad, a Blackberry, a notepad, three bags of skunk, items of clothing and bundles of cash. The convoy of police vehicles then dispatched themselves with vim once they'd rousted Lollipop within. Beholders to the arrest were anxious as to the cause of his arrest. After they bolted their doors, they baked theories in their kitchens and surmised their judgements in their lounges. And the Nepenthe Park Estate returned to its usual nonchalance.

11

YOUR ENEMY'S ENEMY
IS YOUR FRIEND

T ANYA SHOUTED DOWN THE demurring idiot with her iPhone pressed against her eardrum. She was as acerbic as the red onions she raucously chopped with a chilling knife.

"... Whaaat?... No fuckin way... How do you know it was him?... What?... Naaah. Dat's a serious offense, sir.... You've gotta have more than dat before you start comin up wiv those tricky allegations, sir... Naaah... You searched him?... Naaah... Naaah... Can't be right... My boy's a good boy... Well, I can't come down... I'm busy... Dat's none of your business... I don't have to answer to you, sir... Don't get pissy wiv me. I'm sick of people like you tryin to run my life...."

Lone parenthood was a discrepant business, she told the demurring idiot, of which she evoked little help or handout. Why Elliott Walker was a continual procurer of mischief in the classroom, she would never know. Why not, therefore, speak to her quondam partner? He so wanted to become the fulcrum of the Walker family. Here was his chance. Like it or not, here was his number...

Once her gibberings were complete, she chanted his name as if it were some rune to a wanion.

"Elli-ott... Elli-ott... Elli-fuckin-idiott..."

Natalie chomped on a bunch of seedless grapes by the dining table. She saw the pathos in her mother's eyes.

"Oh! What's he done now?"

"He was caught selling drugs in class. Mr. Placide's called the Pigs and had him arrested."

"What a stupid move!"

"Dat's what I told Silly Nuts on the phone—"

"I'm talkin bout dat little bellend. He shouldn't have been shottin in the first place—"

"I'm aware of that, Nat. I ain't stupid. But calling the Pigs? What if they found him with a gun? What would they have done then? Called in the fucking army? Placide's got it in for Elliott. I should march down to that bloody school and push my stiletto up his arse—"

"Good idea, mom! Get yourself arrested, why don't you?"

"Every time, Elliott picks his nose or scratches his arse, he phones me. I think he fancies me—"

"Oh mom! For fuck's sake—"

"I'm gonna ask him the next time he calls. Real talk—"

"Mr. Placide is gay. And he's a good teacher. Let's face it, mom. We're one fucked up family—"

"And why are we fucked up?" Tanya waved her knife around like a conductor's baton. "Coz the fucked up Establishment are tellin the likes of you and me how we should live, how we should think, how we should feel... If Gus beats up some old fucker in fuckin Walthamstow, they wanna take my flat away an' give it to some illegal immigrant... You know what? Sometimes I really think the Germans won the fucking war—"

"But mom, you do look the other way—"

"Meaning?"

"When you found dat gun under Elliott's mattress, what did you do?"

"I got rid of it!"

"How?"

"I threw it in the river."

"Dat's where you went wrong. You should've gone straight to the police wiv his gun in one hand, and his ear in the other—"

"And have both my sons in jail?"

"Elliott's goin jail sooner or later. He'll get another gun and trust me, he'll use it. And he'll get a longer stretch than he would have got if you just handed him in yourself and did the rest of society a favor!"

Tanya was betwixted by Natalie. She plucked a John Player Specials cigarette from her bag and lit it, sucking it for condolement.

"Father's penis scatters, mother's womb gathers, as they say. You get no thanks for being a mom—"

"Yeh well, mom. Welcome to the supermom's club—"

"I gave em his dad's number. Terrell can fuckin deal with this one. He wants to be the big fuckin daddy! Well, here's his fuckin chance!"

* * *

Terrell was far from pleased when he took a call from Mr. Placide asking him to his office but he disguised it well. He lived twenty-five miles away in Maidenhead and felt Lil Elliott would be better served if Tanya had attended instead. Nevertheless, he clambered into his Vauxhall Insignia and sped along the M4 thoroughfare, to the gates of the All Saints, where the warbled jabberings of the playground clanged in his ears. The hot weather chimed with the heliolatry of the natives. He swashbuckled into the school reception wearing an impudent T-shirt. Several of the older lads swooned at his Lacoste shoes.

He shook hands warmly with Mr. Placide of the clipped vowels and canerowed design. He was offered tea or coffee. Tea, he said, of the Tetley variety. Four sugars. Very milky. Preferably Carnation. He sat cross-legged and sipped his cuppa. Lil Elliott was led into the room by a copper, who introduced himself as P.C Harvey. Lil Elliott rubbed his rounded lobes. Mr. Placide asked him to tuck in his shirt. He only obliged after Terrell intervened.

Harvey dropped six balls of skunk wrapped in cling film on the desk.

"Elliott, can you tell us where these drugs came from?"

"They ain't mine."

"Who do they belong to?"

"Some next breh!"

"What's his name?"

"Can't say."

"What you tell us will go no further than this room—"

"Course it will. It'll come back and bite me in the arse."

"Would you like us to leave for a moment so you can tell your father and then he in turn could tell us? You won't be snitchin then."

"I ain't sayin nothin, brah."

"You're prepared to take whatever comes, Elliott!"

"Do your worst, sir!"

Mr. Placide studied the dichotomous aspect of father and son. He wrote considerable notes in his pad.

"Why did you sell weed to Uchenna, Ahmed and Wesley during ICT?"

"I didn't sell nuttin to no one."

"You do know you risk suspension from school and you may be prosecuted?"

"Yeh!"

"Do you have any comment, Mr. Walker?"

Terrell unwrapped his elastic legs and smiled waggishly. "I see it from both angles... He doesn't wanna grass. I can understand dat coz where we come from, we don't grass... On the other hand, you lot are sayin no to drugs on school grounds. Again, dat's true. Coz kids dem need to be involved in their Humanities and readin bout Churchill and Einstein and all dem man dem... So it's tricky... But if my boy's sayin the drugs ain't his, I've gotta take his word for it... I'm sorry... Coz one thing I can say bout him is dat he ain't no liar!"

"Glad to hear it," Mr. Placide said. "I'm glad you see things from our perspective... Elliott, you've a responsibility to your classmates. You've totally disregarded that. Selling drugs on school grounds is a very, very serious offense... I'm sure you'd agree, Mr. Walker, and it is for this reason, we've decided to suspend Elliott from school for a week. The penalty could have been much sterner. He's very much in the last chance saloon."

"Don't you think dat's a bit harsh?" Terrell said. "Nothing's been proven—"

"The drugs were confiscated from his person, Mr. Walker. That's a direct violation of the school rules—"

" And we'll be issuing him with a caution, Mr. Walker," Harvey said. "We feel that would be appropriate given the circumstances."

"Damn!" Terrell said. "Caution and suspension. Bad luck comes in threes. You gonna brand him too?"

"Maybe Elliott might want to add anything he feels might have been left out," Mr. Placide said. "Don't you have anythin to say, Elliott?"

"What's the point?"

"What do you mean by that?"

"You've already suspended me, innit?"

"Do you know why?"

"Does it matter?"

"Of course it matters. You've been suspended for bringing and selling drugs in school… That's an act of gross misconduct—"

"Dat's what you say!"

"So what do you say, Elliott?"

"Can't be arsed!"

"He's upset, innit," Terrell said. "Punished twice for the same mistake. You go hard on tha yutes… Don't blame him if he hates police and school wiv a vengeance after today!"

*   *   *

Lil Elliott was in no mood for vengeance. Relieved he was to be free from the coterminous walls of the classroom. Terrell took him for lunch at McDonald's where he ate two fillet-o-fishes, twelve chicken nuggets, a portion of chips as well as downing a large banana milkshake.

As he chomped hungrily, Terrell asked impertinent questions about his mother: who was her current squeeze? He was elated to learn she hadn't one. Did she talk about him favorably? No, Lil Elliott said. She claimed he was the most prevaricating man ever to draw breath, and the turpitudes of the Walker family emanated from his rectum. And what of that caddish cunt Augustus? Was he still turning up at nocturnal times, guising his disingenuous contrivances as chivalrous deeds? He never visited since Laverne moved in with him, Lil Elliott said after much studious thought, but he always asked after Gus.

After lunch, Terrell wended through Wembley's Harrow Road and its interlocking connexions, playing So Solid songs from his thousand pound sound system. Lil Elliott's balled fists rested upon each knee as his old man thrummed contingent boons from the old days. These were the streets he had frolicked in three decades ago, hanging out with his gang, playing *knock down ginger* and pinging marbles against garden fences. He pointed out the old youth center *Gordon's*, where he had communed in the evenings, safe from the bugbears that cast their dragnets discriminately and ingurgitated their jaundiced provender upon his generation.

"It's all butter down here now," he said. "They've criminalized gangs when lil Baby Nelsons are runnin riot. People forget they were children once... I used to read the Gumby gang books as a kid. So what, if the Gumby gang were on street, the police would harass dem too? It's class bullshit, believe... If you, Gus and Shekaidy trash a restaurant, you won't get a job in the city. If the Bullingdon's Club trash a restaurant, they're *guaranteed* jobs in the city!"

He drove past Vale Farm Sports Ground where he played four seasons as a left-back for A.C Antelope FC. He told Lil Elliott of his juggernaut runs down the left of the pitch and then whipping the ball invitingly into the penalty area for any *weisswurst* center-forward to thunder into the onion bag with his forehead. Injury and coquetry finally forced him of the pitch.

"I could have been a professional baller if I was serious," he said. "I'd have given Nigel Winterburn a run for his money..."

He pointed to a senescent tenement where his first baby mother Angie still lived in West Kilburn. Its tawny bricks and fringed pipes were as they were three decades ago. And so were the arboreal florids that lined the street. In those days, they held barbecues on their balcony for their friends. Hips sidewinded to the tunes of Maxi Priest, Carroll Thompson, Don-E, Soul II Soul, Aswad, Terence Trent D'Arby, Omar, Janet Kay and Mica Paris. Fried rice and jerk chicken made them glutton without complaint. Beers were guzzled without refrain, laughter was very much the main. In spite of the malignant whoresons who pillaged their pockets for the poll tax and caused stoic brows to fret, family and community weathered the tempests of the late eighties.

"How come you broke up wiv Angie if it's all gravy?" Lil Elliott said.

She wanted him to commit but he was a freewheeler. He had no time for reductives like love and marriage, in spite of the two children she afforded him.

"Then, why marry mom?"

"I've asked myself that same question every day for twenty-five years, son!"

At the age of twenty, he had gone into construction. He worked fifty hours a week for three hundred pounds, which was serious money back then. He basked in the malice of his friends who didn't earn as much. On most nights, he and those friends caroused at the *Atlas* pub on Kilburn High Street. They quaffed Usquebaugh and Drambuie, Guinness and Chartreuse in its old taproom. They shimmered to Aztec Camera and Simple Minds, Sinead O'Connor and U2. He told Lil Elliott many a tawdry tale in that pub, of how he sold counterfeit designer clothes for the obtuse landlord whilst bedding his sheen-faced landlady.

Lil Elliott knew of the *Atlas*, though it had closed a decade ago. Its latticed windows were now boarded by sheets of wood. Its garden walls were recumbent and lorn. Only its quiffed hedges received dutiful care from the council. It was here that Terrell

Walker was introduced to Tanya Kiernan. She resembled Donna Ewin, his favorite glamor model. He espied her prehensile arse and fishnet tights before catching sight of her selenian face and Persian green eyes and decided she was copacetic. He listened to whatever she spouted from her uvula, hopeful he'd be inside her vulva in a few hours.

Eight winters they shared together till he finally realized there was no Zen in that hen. His blowsabella was unable to ratiocinate. She deluged her pals with bonhomous affection, leaving him bereft of attention. So he made himself scarce frequently. Sometimes, he'd be gone for weeks at a time, leaving her brooding with a bottle of Bacardi, causing her mind to meander discursively. She became pedantic to the point of neurotic. Whenever he returned home, she sniffed his penis for the faintest notion of infidelity. Anecdotes of his ingannations were alleged by loose lips. She attacked him with profanity and clanging pans. The police were called on more than one occasion.

"Some of the rumors *were* true," he said. "But you can't expect a man to have cornflakes for breakfast every day."

"I normally skip breakfast myself," Lil Elliott said.

As Terrell cantered along the Nepenthe Park Road, he glared at Augustus' front door. A curtain in the lounge flickered. The viperid was home, moulting his troglodyte hide into human form. He was not cowered into moving onwards, however, till the moment of his own choosing. And when he did, he slowly parked his motor on Tanya's porch and took gallant strides towards her doorstep, as though he was still king of her manor.

* * *

He bought earrings and a matching necklace for Natalie, Disney toys and T-shirts for Tiana. He bought nothing for the sourpuss.

"How's Augustus Caesar these days?" He peered at the home of his execrable foe through Tanya's gauzy curtains. "And what's he doin wiv dat Audi?"

"It's Trevor's," Natalie said. "He's on remand."

"For what? Murder?"

"Somethin like dat."

"He was always a fuckin wrong un—"

"Well, Augustus reckons it ain't him—"

"He would say dat. I can't stand the cunt. After God took his missus, he wanted to take mine... Your mom feels sorry for him, so she names my youngest after him and asks him to be godfather, just to spite me!"

He had been subjected to Tanya's overweening glare since he reclined on the futon sofa. John Player, her irreverent handmaiden, lay kindled between her fingers.

"Elliott's got a lil man crush on Trevor," she said. "Dat's his role model—"

"Rubbish—"

"It's true. He's been sulking ever since Trevor got banged up... Where's dat lil tosspot anyway?"

"Who?"

"Elliott. You lost him on the way here?"

"I dropped him off at a studio in Harlesden—"

"He gets suspended from school and you take him to a recording studio? Least you could have given him an ear-bashing."

"So I've gotta give him an ear-bashing on the school's say so? Say it isn't so!"

"Everyone's got it wrong den, is dat it?"

"If it's MY son against the world, then I'm in my son's corner. Elliott's many things but he ain't a liar—"

"How was Thailand, dad?" Natalie intervened. She served him a cup of tea and a fresh creamed donut.

"Faarkin lovely!" He kicked off his shoes and whirred with glee. "Two weeks weren't enough. Everything out there's cheap. And Phuket was the bollocks... Phuket's basically a snob's way of sayin *fuck it!* And Stella? She couldn't stop nagging about the food. How can you go to a restaurant in Thailand and ask for fish and chips?"

"That's small mindedness, dad. If you go to any country, you respect the culture. You can't go to bloody Thailand and expect to live like you're in bloody England—"

"Well, try tellin that to the immigrants next door," Tanya said. "They don't speak a word of English. They walk around with *Visa Expired* stamped on their foreheads and the government does nothin. They get housing priority in London. Every other fucker gets sent to Stoke—"

Terrell licked his lips after devouring the donut. "No part of the world belongs to anybody. English people lived like English people all over the globe for centuries. They imposed their language on every muthafucker. That's why everyone else speaks it. They never integrated, except when they wanted to fuck the natives literally or fuck the chiefs figuratively. So when immigrants come here doin their ting, why's the Establishment pissed?"

"Well, fuck me! This ain't Speaker's Corner, Terrell. Conversation's bout your son. He ain't copin... I can't cope... Maybe's it's time he lived wiv you—"

"I can't take him in—"

"Stella won't let you, you mean?"

"Nothin to do wiv Stella. We're livin in a studio flat—"

"And dat flat hasn't a couch?"

"Look, Tanya. I can't take him in. I ain't got a full-time job and I'm livin in temporary housing—"

"You're fuckin useless, you are—"

"Mom! Stop it," Natalie said. "Let's not argue, yeah. Elliott's a disaster waitin to happen and if we don't bang our heads together and try and come up wiv solutions, he'll be like Gus on steroids—"

"Elliott's worse than Gus already. Elliott does shit instinctively and gets away wiv it. Gus was set-up."

"Gus knew what he was doing—"

"It was a *set-up*, Terrell. Gus is a child. As Peggy Bundy says: If you give a gun to a monkey and the monkey shoots someone, you don't blame the monkey!"

"Who the fuck is Peggy Bundy?" Natalie said.

"She was before your time, darling!"

"Elliott needs guidance," Terrell said. "If Trevor and other olders are having a negative influence on him, then dat has to stop. They're using the lil yutes to hide their shit. They throw the stones and hide their hands."

"Well, you're obviously thinkin of Elliott, and not poor Gus who wants to know—"

"I care bout dem both. I care bout all my children. I don't have favorites—"

"And you're implyin I do?"

"It's bloody obvious, Tanya—"

"I raised all our children, Terrell. All by my fucking self, yea. You was a weekend dad – easiest fucking thing in the world. You don't know em close an' personal. You just turn up on a given Sunday, swing em over your head an' sniff around me just to get your dick wet—"

"Do you really have to talk like dat, woman—"

"I changed dirty nappies. I ironed clothes. I dealt wiv runny noses. I went parent evenings. I done the school run. I was up all night in A&E. I had them twenty-four seven, and you accuse me of playin fucking favorites. Sure, I'm hard on dem but it's necessary... Eliza betrayed her blood in the worst way possible by taking her sister's man to bed. That's why we went Charlie's Angels on her arse! I'm hard on Elliott in case he becomes another statistic... Gus got set-up. Someone screwed wiv my baby's head. He doesn't wanna talk coz he's scared. All I've got is Nat. Without her, I'd probably be in mental fucking health... So don't fucking come in here, castin aspersions, bout I've got fucking favorites. This is YOUR family. Have some fucking respect for who they are!"

Terrell's teacup hovered by his lips but he didn't drink. "Tanya, Tanya, Tanya. There you go again, same old riverdance... I'm not dissin your parental credentials. You're a great mom. Lousy wife definitely, but great mom... Somethin bout dat school ain't right tho. Bare funny teachers there... When Nat and Eliza went there, they had a kiddie fiddler teachin there—"

"What kiddie fiddler?"

"Tell her, Nat!"

"Yea, dat was... Mr. Wheatley. All the boys liked Mr. Wheatley. He'd come out and play football wiv the lads. Then they found some kiddie porn on his computer. They sent an army of social workers, eight police cars, five police vans, three ambulances and a fire engine to come take him away."

"A fire engine?" Terell scoffed.

"When shit happens dat could get some media exposure, all the king's horses and all the king's men and all the queen's social services and all the queen's special interests groups try and get in on the party wiv one thing foremost in their minds: the F-word, funding!"

Terell rose to his feet, applauding merrily. "You see! Nat gets it. Why can't you Tanya? Why blame the victims?"

"I'm callin it as I see it. If Silly Nuts wants to make somethin out of his life, he has to work hard at school and not piss-fart along the Lollipop Road in search of that dirty cash. You'd think the stories of dead rude boys like Gregory would act as a deterrent. In my day, you learnt lessons fast... And what you should be doing, Terell Elliott Francisco Walker, father and fountainhead of the Walker family, rather than posturing as the fucking man, is to force that tosser to get an education—"

"I can't force an education on the boy. You can't make 'em read books... He might wanna be an actor. Does he need GCSEs for dat? He might wanna play football. He ain't getting dat off the blackboard. What if he wants to be an electrician? Mr. Placide don't know nothin bout cabling. So when peeps say, everyone needs an education, dat's bullshit. You may think something's true but is it true in Chinese?"

"Jesus fuckin wept! On your logic, I train my boys to use a potty and you come along and say it's OK for them to shit their nappies coz potties aren't for everyone... Basically, Elliott and Gus are goosed an' there's no way back—"

"I didn't say dat. Let me put dis another way. Why, in this family of four, you've got the daughters doing OK but the boys are supposedly fucking up?"

"Simple. Coz there's no constant MALE influence in their lives!"

"And who saw to dat then?"

"You weren't doin shit when you were here anyway, Terrell. You don't teach dem how to be a man in today's world. Just stupid shit about girls, football and WWF. No wonder they're struggling with pent-up rages. Lydia slept over once and walked about in a bottom skimming nightie with an arse like Table Mountain! Poor Gus and Elliott were strugglin with their little hard-ons under the breakfast table. They gave a whole new meaning to *House of the Rising Sons!*"

"Yea, and what kind of influence have you had on your daughters? One's a dyke and the other you've cut off—"

"I'm a proud dyke, dad. Don't go on like it had somethin to do wiv mom—"

"Now he's startin on you, Nat—"

"He isn't, mom. If he did, I'd tell him his fortune!"

Terrell checked the time on his wrist. "I better go. Don't wanna get caught in the rush hour—"

"Your curfew up?"

"I ain't happy wiv the way you treated Eliza. But dat's for another day!"

"What bout Elliott?"

"I've got two options an' I'll feel no way in either one you take. I can beg everyone to look at dis in its proper context so that they won't be stressed, or I can sit back, appreciate the good times from back in the day and thank God that I was born a Catholic with good skin, smoking draws and lovin Arsenal!"

Natalie had finally tired of the anile, and the anal. "You're the ultimate mindfuck, dad. You suck, straight up and down. And mom, you seriously need some meat!"

* * *

Johnny could swear by the synergetic stanza and its astral highs. Flex, the sotted studio engineer, laid the nuanced orderlies upon his tumult track. The hectoring drumbeat aided his caustic lyrics. A tottering piano piece played at the chorus.

"You wanna spit again or you happy?" Flex said. His beard was voluminous and unkempt, like the fleece of a flocculent rug.

"I'll do it one more time!" Johnny said.

He gleaned Marius, Lil Elliott, Columbia and Stacey from behind the looking glass while he stridently bounced his head in the vocal booth. After a terse overture, he exerted his doggerel flow...

> *"I want peez in large amounts,*
> *Ma garage's full of dogs dat pounce,*
> *Movin my life in major ways so every second counts.*
> *Some y'all are jealous; some 'er y'all punks*
> *Just runnin your gums an' getting lean on skunk*
> *I was itchin to kill ya. Yuh was ready to die.*
> *Time I out my shank, you're getting no bly*
> *I'll dash you in my boot like a spare tyre —*
> *I done it before; I ain't no muthafuckin liar*
> *I moved in an' out of foreign places*
> *Heistin up the Law an' never leavin traces.*
> *They see my face an' they think I'm buried*
> *My enemies will die in a hurry —*
> *Still, I ride an' I'm never worried."*

> *"Say goodbye,*
> *Cuz, I'm comin at cha — Your days on road are gone.*
> *It's my time,*
> *To get tha broads and tha money. Whateva I do, I shine!"*

> *"Bad mouth me, you can go suck my nut sack*
> *Ain't worried bout no snakes. I'm ma rat in a wolf pack.*

I'll put my gun in yo mom's mouth an' tell her to suck dat —
I'll build a zoot, then fuck my enemies' wife on tha doormat
I don't care who wants beef. Man gotta eat.
I'll jus buss my leng an' leave bare man on concrete.
Man wearin vests don't feel secure,
Coz I'm aimin for faces.
Two holes in your head. You'll be pushin up daisies.
I bring stress to my enemies. Smokin crack coz they fear me.
Tossin an' turnin in their beds. They cry like lil babies.
Go snitch to the Fedz, I'll leave you inna ditch —
Dashed in a river coz you're bound to get lynched.
I'm ridin low-key in my crepz and Mercedes;
Fruit-cake ladies wanna have my cupcake babies."

"Say goodbye,
Cuz, I'm comin at cha — Your days on road are gone.
It's my time,
To get tha broads and tha money. Whateva I do, I shine!"

As the diminuendo of the song set in, the audience squalled their delight.

"... Brap! Brap! Brap... Jeeez... Lyrics are fuckin sik... Tuuune... Nang beat... Jeeez!... Freelander, Freelander..."

Johnny smiled deferentially. He touched fists and embraced bodies. He dispatched Columbia, Lil Elliott and Shekaidy to the off-license, to fetch beer and snacks on a caper. They returned with five Strongbows, and ten Monster Munch crisps.

"I could have sponsored dat," Marius said. He revealed a foison of cash in an A4 envelope.

"Well, why didn't ya, you tight bastard?" Johnny said.

"How did you get all dat cheese?" Stacey said.

"I put an ad online, sellin my whip for two bills. Some chick rang and said: Yeah. She's on it, but she's got one eight. I said: yeah. One eight's good. So she comes down, dis red-necked Rastamouse chick givin it *wicked* and *safe* all the time. I let her try out the whip. She was proper on it. Next thing she knows, I put her on the pavement and took the peez—"

"Fuckry!" Stacey said.

He declined a Monster Munch bag. Johnny watched him intently.

"Stacey's pissed wiv you, Marius. Look at his face—"

"Stacey's always pissed. So was Rastamouse. She fought back, blud. Rastamouse tried to put me in a headlock..." Everyone was doused with hysterics, except Stacey, as Marius comically reenacted the scene – "... She could fight tho, I give her dat. Now she's cussin in Cockney... All dat Ali G talk was a front. I pushed her into some stingin nettles and buss out wiv tha peez AND the whip!"

"You don't think I've got the same toothache as you do?"

"Maybe you forgotten bout dem iPods you jacked, Stacey. I ain't forgotten. An' I ain't gonna let you forget—"

"It's different, though. You steal from a shop, it's covered by insurance. She ain't covered by insurance—"

"She's covered by experience. I educated the woman. She was fake as shit wiv her wha gwan blud bollocks. Next time, she operates on road, she'll be careful."

Marius ululated more witty misdeeds, which kept most laughing. Johnny kept a continent eye on Stacey.

"By the way, Stacey. Ashy says to tell you hello!"

"Sorry?"

"Nah, I was just sayin... Ashy was sayin if I see you, I should say hi from her—"

"Did she?"

"Yeh, man... Don't know why man is textin Ashy at funny hours—"

"I ain't been textin Ashleigh—"

"Well, she was in the toilet for half an hour yesterday. I asked what she was doin and she said you was textin her!"

"I haven't texted Ashleigh in yonks—"

"Maybe Ashy's been textin herself!"

Stacey had been mindful of his eye all afternoon. He only opted to come to the studio with these kindlings because he was bored. His mother's demand that he should swot relentlessly had induced tensions at home. Now he wished he had chosen to loiter elsewhere. And why Columbia, the nebbish youth with the glib mouth and wisteria locks, was present, he had no idea. The credulous Columbia had been sent on *missions* that Johnny himself would not do. Gratuitous tripe had been pumped into his gullible head all day. He was explicably told that he was a vassal today, but he would vanquish tomorrow if he learnt and followed and obeyed his mentor. Stacey despaired of his servility and could not bear to look at him.

Marius said that a Jane Doe in a burqa had walked into several internet cafes in South London and set up social media accounts posting pictures of Gregory in his coffin.

"Who would do somethin as evil as dat?" Stacey said.

"I'd move dat evil bitch," Johnny said. "It's obviously a breh disguised as a Muslim female—"

"So what are the police sayin?" Lil Elliott said.

"Dunno," Marius said. "Gregory's sister's pissed. Obviously, it was when the wake happened. People were allowed up to see him but nobody took pictures. What are we gonna do, Johnny?"

"His fam should be takin care of dis—"

"We're his fam—"

"Go and put Marvin in a box den if you feel so strongly bout it. Go find the mystery breh in a burqa. Don't wait on me. Do it, yeah, and see how quickly you get banged up. Like Lollipop—"

"Lollipop's one breh who don't hesitate to back his breh's, at any cost—"

"And dat's why he's bench-pressin, twenty-three hours a day—"

"You got your music and you don't care—"

"I care an' dat's why I ain't wingin. Lollipop's guilty of a hatrick of fuck-ups. He was sayin my alibi's fucked. Well, look where he is now... Dickhead!"

"We're ready to body whoeva drop-kicked Gregory along the M25," Lil Elliott said. "And we were gonna get away wiv it, the same way they got away wiv it. Remember?"

"Boy dem's got us clocked, yeah," Johnny said. "Every road breh in every borough's clocked, labeled an shelved like we're in a supermarket. They know who we roll wiv, where we kotch. They know all our street names, brah. We're marked men. If you're not in a gang, they'll put you in one on account of where you live. They radio your name to HQ to see what tribe you belong. What's your name, son? Marius Christakos... Yeah, we know you... You're from the Bait Crew on tha Nepenthe Park Estate... Dat's where Gregory Foster lived... Yeah, Marvin Crowe got boxed the other day, and we know you did it coz we know he bodied your boy Gregory... We did nothin coz we knew you would. Predictable! Now we got you, your boys, his boys, tha lot... Lifed off, mission accomplished!"

"Maybe we ought to ring Crimestoppers," Lil Elliott said. "If we tip the Fedz, Marvin will get a thirty year stretch for murder an' we won't ave to do nuttin—"

"Crimestoppers?" Marius said. "You smurf! Dat's exactly the answer I'd expect from a boy raised by many women."

They laughed long and hard. No one laughed with more despisal than Marius. The percussion of his hideous fracture rankled Lil Elliott. Such were the vagaries of his elders. A joke at his expense had put them ALL at ease. He hung his cowled head and remained silent for the rest of the session.

That evening, beneath the plangent bells of St. Peter's Clock Tower that had tolled to commemorate his baptism, a freckled maiden in a spangled dress was made to pay with her handbag.

12

IF YOU LIE DOWN WITH DOGS, YOU GET UP WITH FLEAS

WHEN LOLLIPOP RETURNED HOME from prison, he found his belongings packed in several cardboard boxes in the foyer. The stout sasquatch stirred in the dim light, snorting like a piqued bison. The *bruha* was nowhere to be seen. Neither was her broomstick.

"Hey dad! What we havin for dinner?"

"Dinner? You take your shit and get out of my house this second."

"Skeen! I'm supposed to be your son and you do dis? I get found not guilty and you put me out on the street—"

"You *belong* on the street. You've obviously fooled judge and jury but you can't fool me. I was at Court 8 every day. Everyone was scared to drop you in it, but fucking you had no loyalties. Even that silly girl who said you were at her party was lying. You walked the cat back well but I knew you're fucking guilty... It's a fucking disgrace what you did to that boy. I should fucking break you in two but I've washed my hands off you. You live with that. But not in my house..."

Lollipop wished he'd stop prevaricating and admit he was doing this for the love of Laverne. He carried his belongings, one after the other, and left them on the front lawn. He phoned Marius and cadged him to come to his aid. Watching him was Stacey, loitering on the baize of grass by the graffitied wall. He looked bereft. Blaze stood on a segway board beside him.

"You need any help, Lollz?"

"I needed your help nine months ago—"

"You never gimme a chance to say yes or no. You was goin on cruddy, like—"

"How come you never come to see man in jail?"

"I wrote to you askin if I could—"

"You wrote to me askin if you could?"

"D-d-d-did you not get my letter?"

"I didn't get no fuckin letter. Since when do you need to write man askin man if you can come visit? Marius came an' saw me. Sophia came an' saw me... Even fuckin Ratty an' Sanjay came to check man... Nevermind! If you were prepared to stick up for your boy, I might not have lost nine months!"

Marius arrived in his Cabriolet. They filled his boot and back seat with Lollipop's chattels. They whisked away thereafter along the street, leaving Stacey dead-legged in the teeth of abjection.

"Is he still wiv dat Sophia chick?" Blaze said.

"What do you care?"

"I bet she gobbles good—"

"She ain't no head chick, Blaze. She wouldn't fuck you for all your money in your bank account."

Blaze still couldn't digest how a monosyllabic coxcomb like Lollipop had harnessed such an irreverent siren. What indicative charm had he contrived that enabled him to bluff his way to her heart? Maybe it was because she was a clodpate who desired the dogged alpha male that Lollipop had woefully mimicked.

"If the world was to end tomorrow, there's three things I would do," he said. "I'd find Sophia. Then I'd fuck her. Then I'd fuck her again!"

*   *   *

Marius sped his Cabriolet along the A1 at fifty miles an hour. Lollipop remained quiescent in his seat. The futility of prison still wearied him. He tried to sleep. He succeeded for a moment. When he woke, he felt worse. He wiped the cobwebs from his eyelids. He listened to his chattels rattling in the boot. Marius kept glancing at him, like an analyst checking a Geiger reading.

"You sure you wanna stay at Sanjay's?"

"Where else can I stay?"

"I'd rather sleep in my whip than stay wiv dat prick—"

"Why? What's wrong wiv him?"

"You'll soon see!"

"He's tha only one who's offered to take me in and at dis moment, I ain't got no choice—"

"Boy, if I could put you up, I will. But my momzy sometimes goes on funny—"

"No need to explain, fam. I know Sanjay's an arse, but at least he sent me peez while I was inside!"

"Why did he do dat? Sanjay never does anythin for a reason—"

"Just like everybody else in the world today. You got a cigarette?"

Marius obliged him with one. "When you linkin wifey?"

"When she comes from holiday—"

"You and her goin strong?"

"Dat one's under lock and key."

"Do you know her family?"

"I met her mom—"

"But like, you met anyone else?"

"What's wiv tha questions, fam?"

"We're just havin conversation—"

"You wanna ave a conversation wiv me bout my gal? My gal?"

"We can't chat bout your gal, rude boi?"

"So what, you heard she's been cheatin?"

"Cuz—"

"I don't ask bout your gal coz dat's got nuttin to do wiv man. If you got relationship issues, den say so an' I'll see if I could drop man some advice. But don't go and ask man bout his gal!"

"Cuz, I just asked wanna know if you know her family—"

"She got lots of fine sisters if dat's what you wanna know!"

Marius rubbed his lugubrious brow. "Don't know what's happenin to man nowadays... I was speakin to Johnny bout putting some work into Marvin but he's so into his music right now dat—

"Johnny couldn't work nobody—"

"Well, we could!"

"Are you serious? I've been in Chelmsford for nine months, rude boi. Every day's a fuckin Sunday in dat joint. I've sat four weeks at the Old Bailey. I buss case, and you're tellin me I should body some prick dat ain't really my nemesis so I can go back to fuckin jail. Road's gone fuckin mad—"

"OK, we'll leave it den. Johnny's into his music and you're prang—"

"I ain't prang. Gregory weren't never my breh. He moved wiv Mickey Kanu, Charmer and Cane. Then he started rollin wiv Johnny. Marvin's Johnny's problem."

"You got a point there, blud," Marius said with a bated smile. "Not much you can do when it's family!"

Lollipop paid no mind to his upended jibe. If false knights like Marius had the succor to scour the streets to avenge fallen knights, then that was their prerogative. Beefs were a divergence that led to ruin. The errantry of Lil Elliott had made him enough money to stage a renaissance. Collecting that money was his first concern.

"I know man ain't pleased to see me," he said, ignoring Marius' complaint about the witless driving of the driver in front. "They better not be coz I'm takin back what's mine. I'm comin back harder and I'm cleanin up. These nine months set me back in a big, big way. If I weren't banged up, I'd be ready to jump off road right now, but dat's just the way it goes... Believe, I know man ain't pleased to see me. Krista pretended she didn't see me. Stupid bitch goes on like she shits vanilla ice-cream... I saw Havoc screwin... I see Blaze screwin... I see Stacey screwin—"

"Stacey? You sure?"

"Stacey ain't no friend of mine. I asked for help but he's got his tongue up Lydia's dirt-box. He couldn't find his voice to back a breh he'd known all his life! It's dat R&B he listens to. Too much R&B makes a man soft!"

They arrived at Sanjay's security gate. An ursine security guard directed them where to park.

"If my mom was alive, my life would be so different," Lollipop said.

*   *   *

Sanjay was an ingratiating host at the dinner table but Lollipop could not help but notice his aciculated arms. He told a story of how he finagled a toffee-nosed oaf into buying the contents of a PG tip teabag for £20 after making him believe it was hashish. He proceeded to vilipend Ratty's mountebank mates, accusing them of being irreconcilably stupid. Muna couldn't stop laughing. She wiped the tears of her tarantula eyelashes. Lollipop preferred eating to talking. The potted salmon and other victuals were delicious.

"… I was gonna tell ya before… I'll tell ya now…" Sanjay poured another glass of mango lassi for Lollipop. "Muna and I are engaged… We got engaged when we was in LA!"

"Congratulations!" Lollipop said. "Don't forget my invite to the wedding—"

"You're the Best Man!"

"Are you nuts?"

"Muna's like: Why's Lollipop the Best Man? I'm like: Duh! Why does the fat man love Diet Coke?"

"I thought you might wanna get your cousin to do the honors—"

"No chance. My parents met Muna. Dey weren't on it coz they think Muna's a short-term ting, even tho I'm spendin peez on wifey. Michael Coles watch. Tiffany necklaces. Exagona Loubs. Toe to head in Pigalle. When I told dem I'm marrying her, they kicked a fuss. My dad's like, he don't want no bastard blood in his family—"

"Dat's naughty. If two people are in love, den dat should be it as far as everyone's concerned!"

"I'm not parent friendly anyway," Muna said. "They're the most opinionated people in the world. My dad reckons I'm makin a big mistake but I told him he's not King Zog of Albania and it's my life!"

After dinner, she went into her study to work on her blog. Sanjay and Lollipop opened a cellophane bag filled with some smooth pulverulent on the balcony and indulged themselves.

"You see how clever she is!" Sanjay said. "Who's King Zog of Nigeria? Fam, she talks bout stuff you don't find in books. When I first saw her, I just wanted to tap it, ya feel mi… She's a proper camera phone cutie and so I thought, you know what: I'll wife it off coz she's supa nang an' supa smart. A gal like dat is as rare as rockin horse shit… She's the first gal I've held hands wiv in public… I wanna put a baby in her!"

Lollipop said nothing to this uxorious tripe. He listened to the wailing sirens emanating below in pursuit of its lupine prey. London was tirelessly skittish at the best of times; this elongated city-state of ten million abbreviated brethren. The skyscraping mammon cleaved the pellucid horizon. The diaphanous night-sky was untainted by neither cloud nor orb in its supreme solitude.

"No place like London, f'real," he said as he cleaned his nose of the dust. "It's tha realest place to live, wiv the realest clubs and the realest girls—"

"Dat's what you call the ultimate mindfuck, Lollipop. Goin on bout London all day when London ain't done shit for you. London ain't for people like us. Our kids won't live here in thirty years. You see all dat peez flowin from Docklands? Dat's peez made *in spite of you*. Dat's why I laugh when I hear man biggin up their endz, beefin over postcodes, goin all territorial. How's your endz helpin you?"

"True when you put it like dat—"

"Do you need anythin, like? Peez to spend, place to stay, chick to fuck. Anythin you want bruv, I'll provide—"

"It's OK, cuz. I got everythin I need—"

"Sure? You was in the slammer. You're gonna be bruk—"

"I ain't bruk. My line was on—"

"You got a line? Who's supplyin you?"

"Some breh named Pepper Jackson—"

"So how much you made from your line?"

"Enough to kick off from last time—"

"I need to buy from you, maaan. Every man round me's flopped. You owe me, fam—"

"I'll look after you—"

"Why don't you come into business wiv me? I'm startin a limousine company. Proper legit—"

"Dunno if I got dat kind of peez—"

"Shottin ain't gonna last forever. Time soon come for you to jump off… All my peez is turnin into powder… I got Muna to think off… You've got Sophia… Let me know when you got fifty bags—"

"I'm a long way from fifty bags, cuz."

Lollipop felt like shit. The drugs had only pullulated his angst and produced no highs. He blinked his somber eyelids and wondered what he was taking, and why was he taking it.

"You know, I fell out wiv Ratty over Joanne. He's racist… He believes everyone should stick to their own. He's like; he can't fuck her now coz I've been there!"

"Why don't you leave dat alone? You got Muna now. You're gonna get married—"

"Dat's the same shit Ratty said coz he wants her for himself. He even changed her number for her. So you know what I did? I canceled his contract! I got my boys in to bolt the recording studio. Breh brought his own boys down. Dey outnumbered us but we held our own. Dat cunt owes me thirty-seven grand."

"Can't believe you man are beefin over a ratchet—"

"I'm beefin over peez. I've got someone lined up for Ratty. Dat breh will cut him in half… He'll do a better a job than you did. Dat breh you were supposed to fuck up made a full recovery… I forgive you tho… You and me, we're like brothers from different mothers.

When it comes to peez, you're tha only muthafucker I can trust—"

"There ain't many muthafuckers you *can* trust—"

"To tell you truth, I didn't think you'd buss case. I thought you'd wing for eight, ten years—"

"If it weren't for some spontaneous thinkin, I'd be probably lookin at twenty years. Prosecution tried to rattle me. Dey had me in the box for a week, tryin to trip me up. I just batted away dem questions. Foreman of the jury stands up; Not guilty. Bam! DC hangs her head and I walk…"

An innominate noise from the living room caused them to freeze. They soon settled once they realized it was Muna's pussy.

Sanjay, fifty pound note clasped in a nostril, inhaled more talc. His lips looked desiccated and his eyes were wan. He painted a scuzzy image of his captive Therese. He offered her up for despoilment.

"I don't need your slave maiden, Sanjay," Lollipop said. "I'm savin myself for Sophia. She'll be back from her modellin in New York in a couple days. Just BBM your Gamer ID for FIFA so dat when I move into my new yard, I'll be kickin your arse every night!"

He stayed for a night and a day in Sanjay's sty. Marius fetched him the next evening. They left Sanjay decumbent on the sofa.

"I'm gonna rinse of dat breh," Lollipop said. "The only business we're doin together is me sellin him what he really, really wants daily. Can't ever forgive how he dissed me in front of Sophia!"

They drove to the boondocks of Bovingdon to view a dormitory. Mohammed, the citrine landlord, showed him around a large studio flat that had recently been decorated with bice and cream paint. He readily accepted the rent and the rates.

"Remember the rules!" Mohammed said. "No drugs, no parties, no loud music… Rent MUST be paid, ON TIME!"

Mohammed would mosey around the tenement from time to time, primarily to chase down a peculiar tenant for non-payment of rent. He was pyretic on all things Islamic. A week later, after they talked extensively about religion, he handed Lollipop DVDs featuring lectures by esteemed Muslim scholars, hopeful he'd convert. Lollipop took the discs but they remained unwatched. He had little time for God and His peasant Prophets. Submission did not make sense but neither did soteriology.

He focused on self-discipline. He ate only what was alimentary; fish, fruit, figs and fat-free milk. Large portions of salad, salmon, spinach and steak were consumed as well. He took no snacks nor ate no sweets nor smoked no skunk. He ate meals at set times. Calisthenics were conducted in the morning. He jogged during the afternoon but at infrequent times and on infrequent paths lest someone followed. And there were long periods of meditation that unbefogged the mind...

*   *   *

He met Sophia at Heathrow's Terminal Five almost a week later. She greeted him with considerable élan. He buried himself in her embrace, inhaling the mellifluous aroma of mangoes and kiwis. She ordered a Szechuan shrimp and a chilled glass of Vouvray at a diner. He followed suit. She asked about his arid months in prison, and that she had to make do with the toys of lonesome joys. He protested his innocence, and that he had been glad to be found not guilty.

"I would've come to the trial if you let me. I felt so fuckin useless not being around. Dunno why I listen to you sometimes."

"You would've been uncomfortable, hun. All his family was dere, lookin stoosh like royalty. His mom was wylin for maximum effect. Even my dad thinks I'm guilty—"

"Trevor, I was your alibi. You was wiv me when you heard tha news—"

"I buss case so it don't matter... Let's go on holiday. Pick a place where you ain't never been an' I'll sponsor dat next summer..."

A voluptas in plain livery asked politely if they required further service.

"You're really pretty," Sophia said. "You've got lovely hands."

The waitress seemed addled by the compliment. She thanked her regardless before walking away.

"Would you fuck her, Trevor?"

"No fuckin way, babe!"

"I saw how you looked at her—"

"I'm as good as married. I swear down—"

"I was like her, the proverbial waitress. I experienced tha times when the month lasted longer than the money. You come to work just to earn peez an' you get brehs eyein you up, like you're somethin on the menu... They promised me a first class lifestyle if I'd become their girlfriend—"

"Are you like... referring to me?"

"I saw how you looked at her. As if to say, I can own you coz I'm tha fuckin man. My stepbrothers look at girls the same way—"

"How come I ain't met your stepbrothers?"

"My parents had babies wiv each other, and wiv other people. I've got so many brothers and sisters. I don't know dem all. You've seen my mom already an' she don't do conversation. My stepbrothers are animals. If I were you, I'd be like: Fuck them!"

"But if we had a fight, they'd beef wiv me, right?"

"No." She laughed for the first time. "I'd deal with you myself."

After dinner, he drove her to his flat. He played some erotic descant on his Blu-ray player. He opened a bottle of Merlot Reserva. She took her glass into the bathtub and soaked herself in near scorching water. Afterwards, she slipped into an ethereal Daphne nightgown. She shook her money-maker to Beyoncé's perspicuity on the stereo. He sat on the bed, sleeveless arms folded sternly.

"Come here."

Her eyes sizzled with mock umbrage. "I bet you're roastin—"

"I hope you are too!"

"I bet you were fappin every night in the pen—"

"Come here, babe!"

She continued her burlesque spectacle, revealing her lusty shanks and swaying her supernal ensemble.

"Trevor, did you say sorry after you suffered?"

"Suffered?"

"You've suffered all your life, haven't you?"

"Should I be sorry for dat?"

"It's somethin you should be *very* sorry for—"

"Come here."

She shimmered herself from her gown and slipped beneath the sheets beside him. He kissed her cerise mouth, and she climbed on top of him, and he massaged her bosomy lumps.

"I need an after-fuck-fag," she said afterwards, lolling her head against the pillow. She reached for her box of Purple Kings. "They ought to 'low girls to get sexed by their man in jail, like three times a week. It ain't her fault dat her man's in jail—"

"Indeed, it isn't. Why should she suffer?"

"You and I, we think the same. We even breath the same. I breathe out when you breath in, as the song goes—"

"Dunno if I should keep doin what I'm doin or just get the fuck off road—"

"Do whateva your mind tells you, Trevor. And if you enjoy it, keep doin it."

The night passed slowly after their exigent efforts. Their incarnadine bodies rose and receded as they spooned, rose and receded in tandem. The whorls on her splendid head blanketed his felted pillow. Her skin was as glossy as the sands of the Sahara, save for the tramp-stamped dragon on her dorsal and a screech owl tattoo on her left thigh. He felt the wind whispers of her breath against his face. She looked amazing as she slept. It was no wonder the likes of Marius speculated over her backstory; envy's futile attempt to despoil true beauty. He admired the adamantine will of his dame. She, his lubricious cupcake was his adroit calf-love, his creamy ecdysiast. She'd be the co-procreator of his babies whose peachy breasts they would suckle: this percolated muse of accelerated returns, this begetter of boners, this sucker for ophidian charm, this regal slut. No longer fallow, he wrapped her in a cinch and slipped into a peaceful repose. In his hypnopompic slumber, she seemed to vanish.

When he woke up, she had been to the bakery and back. He listened to the soporific hissing of pancakes being fried. He found her naked in the kitchen.

"Stunnin cakes, babe!"

"Thank you, Trevor."

His mobile pinged incessantly over breakfast. He barely gave it a glance.

"Everyone wants to know what I'm on. All these ghouls wanna take what I've got. Why can't they leave me alone?"

"I started attractin ghouls from thirteen. Grown men were ready to sacrifice their wives and kids for a moment wiv me... I knew I had it then, but I never hugged tha limelight... I'd rather be notorious than famous. Any dickhead can be famous by accident. I wanna be in the shadows pullin strings—"

"You're some serious bawse bish for real. Peng into the bargain. You and I could be like Bonnie an' Clyde, holdin up banks an' post offices—"

"I'd rather we were Mickey an' Mallory—"

"I need to come off road regardless, babe. When you think you're winnin, you're actually losin. When you lose, you could even lose your life. Is dis shit worth it?"

"Are you scared to die?"

"Aren't you?"

"When you're dead, you won't even know it, hun. You're final breath's ten times more ecstatic then any breath you've ever made. Why do you think when men die, they have the most rigid erections ever?"

"Have you ever seen someone die?"

"Yes."

"Who?"

"Some breh who tried to rape me—"

"What happened?"

"I made a mistake no girl should make. I jumped into an unlicensed cab coz I was in a hurry. Cabbie pulled up in an alley and made a move. I pushed my knife right through his heart and watched the bastard die."

"How did you feel after dat?"

"Nothin."

"B-but like, you bodied someone?"

"Self-defense, babe. He was obviously reckless as well as dangerous. And who is to say he ain't raped some woman before who tried to make it home. Men like dat don't like women. They screw up their women coz they're insecure. And if they stop them from livin, then they themselves don't deserve to live..." She looked at him vacantly, her elongated eyelashes prettified her fawny eyes. She nuzzled his mushy balls in her wieldy palm. "Let's go back to the bedroom, hun. I'm horny as fuck!"

*   *   *

By the graffitied wall, a bevy of mirth enthusiasts cackled like the crepitations of a bonfire. Lollipop lifted his thumbs aloft as they relayed their brainstormed gambits against their brethren (who occupied similar ground barely a mile away), on how they should be pummeled and shanked. They were aghast to see him but they showered him with synthetic love. These latter-day sinners had danced on the lion's grave too soon, and yet the lion still reigned.

He ran into Mark, spruced in a garbadine *thawb* and wearing an *agal*. He marveled at his groomed beard and the *miswak* in his mouth. Mark looked unimpressed.

"You're head to toe in LV," he said. "But spiritually, you're broke!"

Jardel played on his bike before his father's gate. Lollipop played with him for a while till he saw Laverne, the meddling usurper, walking askew towards him. The locks on her head looked like tamarind fruits. A cervical collar encumbered her throat. He felt inclined to greet her, albeit grudgingly.

"Your dad's not in... That's if you've come to see him—"

"I'm checkin for my bredrin!"

"How you getting on?"

"What do you care?"

"We do care, Trevor. We've been hard on you but not without good reason. You're just wasting away your talents—"

"There you go again. Don't you ever get tired of lecturin? Do you really think dat what you say is gonna make a difference—"

"It's up to you to make that difference—"

"At least we agree there—"

"I don't want another argument, Trevor. I've got a hospital appointment and I'm running late. I'll tell your father that you passed by... to see your bredrins!"

She drove away in a decrepit Saab, presumably one of his father's wretched purchases from Salvage. He wondered what was the cause of her accident.

"She was out ridin wiv your pops the other day and a car nearly knocked dem over," Johnny said. "She swerved, hit a lamppost and landed on tha pavement. Happened right in front of me."

"Jesus! Imagine if she broke her neck!"

"What, you feelin bad for her?"

"Actually, I'm feelin bad for you, Johnny. What's dis tune I hear you dropped? Dashin man in car boots? Whose gonna buy dem records? Spit barz dat's real, man—"

"You sayin I ain't real? If you wanna take the fuckin piss, you can get the fuck out—"

"Calm your skin, cuz. Why you so jumpy?"

"Why shouldn't I be? A couple of fucks on radio wanna fuck up my career, tellin man not to buy my CD—"

"What man?"

"Fuckin Twang and those fuckin mups on Bling—"

"Man like Twang ain't gonna shut up unless you shut him up—"

"Man like Twang's got influence. Two hundred thousand follow him on Twitter..." Lollipop had wondered about his state of mind.

He looked a complete ramshackle. He hadn't bathed nor brushed his teeth, and that was out of character. "... You know what? Fuck dis ting. I've been spittin barz since I was nine an' I ain't gettin nowhere. Every man's rollin wiv dis music ting. It's long!"

"Survival of the fitness, Johnny. Once a breh's got an idea and it makes peez, everyone's on it. Dat's how it's been since dust!"

"Twang's tryin to fuck wiv me. For no reason. Fuckin hater... Breh can't leave me alone. Always gassin bout me on Bling. We ought to fix him—"

"Dunno why you leave it to me to solve your problems, Johnny—"

"He's your problem too. He's got a tune out on you. It's called *Tha Eavesdrop On Lollipop*. It's about what you do on road—"

"What I do on road?"

"Basically it's bout how you're makin peez on road on the back of your young uns. How you had beef wiv Steppy an' covered your arse so you got found not guilty. Basically, he's tryin to bait you up—"

"Why would a man who doesn't know me personally spit barz on how he thinks I roll?"

"Dunno. He says he knows you bodied Steppy an' dat you're gonna get dealt wiv. He said he don't care how long it takes him but he'll find you. He'll leave you where he finds you. He says dis in his tune—"

"Have you got dis tune?"

"He plays it all the time."

Lollipop reclined in his seat. "Boys like Twang are a Fedz wet dream. I know he pushes adverts for Trident on his set. He can try and bait me. I ain't doin nuttin—"

"Can I tell you somethin, Lollipop?" Johnny's brow became askew. "You can't tell no one. No one. Not even your wifey!"

"I swear down—"

"It's Ashy, fam. I think she's ready to duss. I think she's got another man... an' I swear down, yeah... On my kids' lives... If I find out... I think it's Stacey—"

"Stacey yeah?" Lollipop tried to remain impassive. "If dat's what you think, you should take a baseball bat to his head—"

"But Marius says it ain't him coz he's loved up wiv Lydia—"

"So what do you think?"

"I can't afford to be wrong... I gotta be sure... Coz if it's true, I swear down, I'm gonna box him up in tha worst way possible... But I gotta be 100% certain—"

"Put it dis way, Johnny: didn't Stacey and Ashleigh do a ting together at school before she met you? She was a bit of a tomboy back den, but she's fillin out nicely... I know he was pissed when you both got together. I thought man was gonna cry. An' I know he don't like how you treat her—"

"How do you know?"

"Coz he told me. Breh tells me everythin—"

"So why are you tellin me now?"

"We're talkin in confidence, yeah... I can stop right now if you wanna."

"Nah. Carry on... Carry on."

"Dis is him tellin me dis an' so it goes no further. I keep tellin man what goes on between a man and his missus in their own yard is between a man and his missus. But Ashleigh's his dear friend. Why's man lookin to move his breh coz he had a tiff wiv his gal? I've had bare arguments wiv Sophia an' man couldn't care less. But Ashleigh's his dear friend—"

"What bout Lydia? She's peng—"

"She don't connect wiv him the same way Ashleigh does. You can't explain feelings. You can fight feelings but you just give into them... Besides, Lydia's in Manchester. And he sees Ashleigh. Every God damned day—"

"But she won't let him... I know Ashy. She'd never look at another bredda—"

"But he's lookin at her. You gotta remember dat mangina's are the worst thing God created. Worse than Fedz. At least you know where you stand wiv Fedz. A mangina's always lookin to undermine every aspect of a breh's existence. Dey ain't game playas. Breh's get tha hot gals coz they're gully. Mangina's end up in the Friends Zone. Forever, without a look-in. Blaze's a mangina. I banged him up just for lookin at my gal. Stacey's a next one. They live for the pussy, an' they'll die by it... But what I say, like you say, is between us. You don't even tell Ashleigh!"

* * *

Ashleigh and Shakira were unusually taciturn as they rode the Bakerloo Line train to work. The fissile restructuring of departments meant that most clerical positions at Harlesden Brook Hospital were at risk. Even the Dracaena plants brimmed with greater vim than the morose humanoids ploughing for a stipend or less. Only Lincoln, the office anguine, was without anguish. He had thrived through the monotony, having already been assured of his future.

He made Ashleigh a cup of hot coffee. He loitered around her desk making small talk while she hoped he would leave.

"Why don't I buy you lunch on Friday?"

"I've got a day off on Friday—"

"I'd like to have it off with you too."

"You wish!"

"Let me buy you lunch den?"

"No thanks, Lincoln—"

"I hear you're on a mad ting with a porter—"

"Dat's none of your business—"

"How do you manage havin two men in your life?"

"My partner and my son you mean?"

"Your partner black or white den?"

"What the hell does dat matter?"

"I just wanna know if you'd do a black dude—"

"You can't fall in love wiv race, Lincoln. I've fallen in love wiv a man dat can't be replicated in any race—"

"Good answer, good answer. Glad to hear you're doin your bit for race relations!"

Ashleigh laughed mirthlessly.

"Are you white though, Ash? You look like you've had some black in you? Not like dat! Ha ha... I know you had dat... but maybe one of your grandparents? Or great grandparents, if you can go back dat far—"

"Will you just FUCK OFF???"

One or two raised their somber heads from their Dell laptops.

"I like your leg game by the way," he said. He straightened his tie and returned to his desk.

"He's thirty-six years old," Shakira said as they lunched in the cafeteria. "He's got four kids from three baby-moms. They raise the kids while he lives a life of Riley. He's everythin wiv what's wrong in dis country!"

She told Ashleigh that somebody had reported hearing obscene sucking noises coming from the linen room yesterday, where Joleon had hoisted her thighs upon his biceps and his marvelous thrusts plashed with exquisite grit until he curded an ichorous rope of white rivulets between the lips of her cloaca. Only today had he *bonne bouched* her ladyship, moiling her till she wept and brayed and sluiced. Shakira advised she be prudent henceforth. No more fucking during working hours, she said. She had to make do with the *amuse-bouche* he served with his delish mouth in the loading bay, and be content. When she related this to Joleon, he insisted that they defy her.

Nevertheless, the problem of Lincoln remained. He, of the periwinkle shirts and Hermes ties, maintained his impulse to impugn and harass her. His false claim that he screwed her senselessly during a caesura soon reached her aggrieved ear.

"You wish you fucked me," she said, confronting him in the staff restaurant.

He grinned but declined to respond.

"You're pussy deprived, Lincoln. Why don't you go, suck your mother and drink the water!"

She walked away triumphantly. She ate her Greek yoghurt in the quaint courtyard. A South African pediatrician told her she had bewitching eyes and invited her to his cousin's bar called *Lorenzo's*. She turned him down politely. She told Lindsey on FaceTime about the doctor. Lindsey sent a picture of her *Mandingo* in US army fatigues sitting on a pontoon under the hellish sun in Kuwait City. Ashleigh laughed. If only she had possessed her friend's pococurantism. She returned to her desk and switched on her PC. An email from Lincoln awaited her.

> *"Btw Ashley, I kno u're fuckin Jolean the Kojak porter. U go on like a lady but u're really a ratchet. Wat will yr man from Nepenfee say wen he hears dis? C, I kno bout u, u hypocrit lol, but I'll spare u d embarasment if u gimme a lil bit of wat u're givin away 4 3. U gotta a lot 2 lose coz I'll expoze u 4 d sket dat u r."*

She deleted it in disgust. Lincoln observed her from his seat. She raised her middle finger. He chortled quietly. Half an hour later, he slithered to her desk.

"Check your emails?"

"Burn in hell, you muppet—"

"If you lie down with dogs, you get up wiv fleas—"

"I'd never lie down wiv a dog like you, you fuckin hemorrhoid—"

"Doesn't do you any good bein gangsta, Ashleigh. I hear your man's a proper rude boi tho. I wonder what he'll say bout you fuckin some pikey porter... I'm a patient man. I'll give you a week. Then I want your narni on a plate!"

She cried in the restroom. Shakira advised that she report him to her manager. Ashleigh said that would be counter-productive. Joleon suggested that he'd have a quiet word with him, man to man.

"Joleon, I don't want no beef on my doorstep—"

"I'm not gonna beef wiv man at work. What do you take me for?"

"Promise you'll only speak to him? If he provokes you, walk away—"

"No worries, babes—"

"*Walk away*, Joleon. I don't care what he calls me. He's a snake an' he'll blag it!"

Joleon spotted him the following afternoon, slithering along the corridor.

"Yo fella! Stay away from Ashleigh, yeah—"

"So you're Joleon? I was wonderin when you was gonna show up—"

"You don't wanna cross me, mate. So stay fuckin warned—"

"Where's your fuckin cape, Cap'n Save-a-ho?"

Joleon unleashed his vitiating fists into Lincoln. Somebody ululated for security. Ladies loitered on the edge of the ad-hoc scrum. Doctors with stethoscopes tarried with mutual despond. By the time help arrived in the shape of five fending security guards, Lincoln was rended in his own blood and Joleon was the palpable victor. Ashleigh learnt of their priapic duel from the chaffs of her colleagues.

"Maaan, I wish I had two men fighting over my honor—" laughed a dingbat named Daljit.

"In this instance, the correct adjective is *dishonor*," interrupted their officious boss, and summoned Ashleigh to his office.

He permitted her to read the tabulated witness statements. She shook her head woefully at every perceived untruth, every willful misappropriation.

"You're all over this!" he said.

"I- I don't know what you mean—"

"Don't play games with me. Lincoln Rose and that porter went mano a mano over you—"

"Why would anyone go mano a mano over me, Hugh?"

He looked at her with a fatigued glare. "Not that it matters. They've both suspended pending a disciplinary. I overheard the Union rep advising the porter to resign. I hope he doesn't because

I'd like to tell him to his face that he's sacked, after the investigation of course—"

She felt his appraising eye moiling over her as he talked. He was one unsavory, high-browed, malicious technocrat...

"Lincoln started dis... He sent me offensive emails sayin... offensive things—"

"And rather than report those offensive emails to your line manager, you told your porter friend who sought disciplinary action on your behalf in the only way he knew how—"

"I never told anybody to attack anyone—"

He sniggered like a James Bond villain. "There's a misconception that employees at this hospital are only sacked for fighting and thieving. Nobody's expendable, Ashleigh. You're not professionals... I can easily get an arse on your seat to do your job... There are millions of competent people in this country who are unemployed and then you have idiots like Lincoln and Joleon working... As for you, I'm inclined to give you a verbal warning—"

"What for? This ain't my fault—"

"Why don't you let me finish, Ashleigh? As I was saying, I'm inclined to give you a verbal warning for not adhering to Company Policy which, had it been implemented, would not have led to this testosterone bear fest of the most hideous kind... But I won't, mainly because you suffered the gross indignity of being gracelessly propositioned in the foulest sexual harassment email I have ever read. Having said that, I don't think you're entirely innocent—"

"Well, dat's your opinion, Hugh. I was upset. Joleon's like a brother. He warned Lincoln to back off, but Lincoln wasn't havin it. He threw the first punch. Joleon had to defend himself—"

"That's not how nine eyewitnesses saw it. They unanimously agreed that Joleon preempted the incident..." He sniggered again. "... This brotherly relationship you have with Joleon... is riddled with turpitude... so I hear—"

"I'm actually quite offended by dat—"

"Let's leave it at that, shall we?"

"Actually, I'd like to make an official complaint. I've been sexually harassed. I shouldn't have to come into work and made to feel uncomfortable by a stinkin pervert. Dat's not on!"

Hugh crash-landed in his seat. He slid a blank piece of paper and a Bic pen under Ashleigh's nose.

"You go right ahead and make your complaint. By Jove, I will investigate every scintilla of this tragedy. Just you make sure your house is in order in case you open a can of very unsavory worms!"

Ashleigh's pen screeched to an sudden halt. "Fuck it! I ain't gonna bother!"

Hugh collected his pen and paper. "I didn't think you would."

She met Joleon after work at *The Drunken Stupor*. He was eating a lentil curry in a hurry while slurping a glass of limoncello. He rambled on about killing Lincoln.

"You've made things a million times worse, hun—"

"Don't I fuckin know it?"

"I never asked you to fuck him up—"

"Fuck it. It's done now!"

"You fucking Asbo!"

"Why are you talkin to me like dat?"

"Coz you acted like a total cock!"

He seemed impressed by her answer. "Ah well! At least you can go home every night to a man you say you hate an' play happy fuckin families—"

"What's dat supposed to mean?"

"Whose actin like a total cock now?"

"Wheneva you get into a fight, you always, always cut your face," she said after a lengthy pause. Her tone was a tad sympathetic. "Thank God you're not a boxer—"

He pushed her hand away. "If you're not leavin him, I'm leavin you—"

"You're layin dis on me coz you lost your job—"

"Fuck Hugh and his job! I start a job in construction tomorrow. When you get to my status, you come by such opportunities naturally... I'm talkin bout us, Ashleigh... Anyway it's your choice—"

"You're already my choice. Johnny's not even a cunt of a man—"

"Are you still fucking him?"

"I can't believe you're doin dis to me—"

"Dat's a yes den." He pushed his bowl away. "You fuck me. You go home. You fuck him—"

"I'll leave him. I swear on a stack of Bibles—"

"But you still fuck him?"

"You really think I want him touchin me?"

"I don't know your mind, Ashleigh. I'm not even sure you do."

"He's getting worse to live wiv. I've gotta prove to him dat I'm really at work by takin a picture of my work computer wiv the date an time showin an' send it to him when he asks for it—"

"Better the devil you know." Some spittle inadvertently flew from his mouth as he talked. "Tha next time we meet, I'm gonna pour all my love inside of you, an' I'm gonna make sure Johnny Freelander never touches you again!"

13

THE EAVESDROP ON LOLLIPOP

T WANG WAS BLING RADIO'S foremost Music Head. He
constantly worked the graveyard shift for his amorphous
audience. Slow Jamz, or *Baby Makin Music* as he called it, was their
regalement. Tonight was the second anniversary of Steppy's death.
He played *I'll Be Missing You*, by Puff Daddy, Kelly Rowland's *Stole*,
Boys II Men's *It's So Hard To Say Goodbye To Yesterday*, and *I Wish* by R.
Kelly. Then he played his own corollary tribute titled: *Tha Eavesdrop
On Lollipop*.

His lyrics chronicled the final months of Steppy's life: The
cockeyed assertion that Asamoah Nyame was a *gangsta* were false. He
had walked the nonchalant track of a London teenage boy till he
became discommoded into mercantile wares by a life-sapping hellion
named Lollipop. He became entangled in expeditious beefs that
rendered more distress than he bargained for. He was fraught with
naught cohorts. The *mise en scene* became a minefield. The peculiar
fellows, who were in his bedroom as he wrestled with death and
lost, were name-dropped in the chorus. And though the courts had
failed to convict the ringleaders, they were not beyond the holistic
scope of Justitia. Therefore, it was incumbent on anyone who knew
anything to say something. If they feared going to the police, he
would gladly act as a buffer.

"Brap, brap, brap! Big up Lady Stoosh, Lady Valentine, Lil Brazen Raisin, Tumpz in NW9, Lil Fit Megan in White City, Bruiser, Poison, The Willesden East Crew, Santana an' Tha Legless Crew locked in, locked on; DJ Spiderman in NW10, you spit barz like no other... MC Rome, hol it up bredrin... yo kno yo bad ... DJ Smith & DJ Weston, everyone in North Wezzy reppin, locked in locked on... Ladelle and Rebecca, bishes goin on like Cagney and Lacey... My boy, Ratty. Where you been, fam? WhatsApp me, fam. Biggin you up regardless... This is DJ Twang on Bling Radio 90.9 — London's raw convo, uncensored, unscripted, unapologetic... If you're PC, dis ain't for you. We speak the unspoken here..."

After the jingles, he popped open a Coors Light and invited folk to partake in discussions on whatever they wished. Regular people, he had long discovered, were wittier than the excogitated comedy on TV. Conversations ranged from mere japes to sober reflections. Cyril rang to say that the sylph he met in *Shagaluf* last summer was now his fiancé. They planned to marry next spring. Twang remembered the sylph well, how she "licked his balls like a first class stamp" in the club toilets, moments after she met Cyril. But he graciously wished the couple well.

Spin, from the Stonebridge Park Estate, exhibited a serious vibe. "Twang, straight up. I got love for everyone. Don't care what color or religion you are. If I see or do wrong, I'll correct dat action for my conscience. Don't business what the media say coz they stir the ignorant to fight the oppressed an' let the mischief makers go untouched. They legislate to discriminate. Only Middle England's prejudices matter when they write the script... My advice is let's flip it: Don't go on like an automaton. Go rogue on your rulers. Dat should be the focus instead of parring society's problems as the fault of the *boy in tha hood*. The *boy in tha hood's* only a zombie, a blinkin puppet..."

Keegz, a regular from E5, phoned in to speak on the verisimilitudes of snitching. Whoever concealed a murderer was as good as having murdered. Big George from NW9 offered his condolences over Steppy and said those responsible deserved the death penalty. Adiya of the North Kensington Estate disagreed respectfully: The Cosa Nostra were bound by Omerta; the police by the Blue Code. Governments warred fanatically to conciliate their interests. The wisdom of the three wise monkeys was an eternal truth for all those monkeys. Society, therefore, need not be mad at the boy in the hood, who claimed he saw nor heard evil. Governments and big corporations remained evasive when the truth was outed for the sake of national interest and they were innately hostile to whistle-blowers. Mark from the Nepenthe Park Estate claimed that pendulum messages programmed into his cerebrum titillated his anima. The establishment required an enema. They had the temerity of expediting their sanctimony with a straight face. Let them play the men while scratching their balls. Let them blame his pents on hip-hop and consumerism. Let them conflate their solipsism with their Pax Britannica pretensions. Let their beguilement rule Britannia…

Mayada, of Kilburn Park, articulated the ephebiphobia that habitually beleaguered UK society. From the Nepenthe Park Estate, Lindsey launched a bombast against males for not being men. Several males phoned in response to cuss her brimborion trash and gave reasons as to why decent men would never consider a conventional relationship with females of her ilk. Somebody rang constantly from an withheld number. Twang declined to take such calls. A nervy female came on air.

"OK, caller!" Twang said, cracking open a fourth Coors Light. "You're live on Bling Radio. What's your name and where you callin from?"

"I'd rather not give my name."

"OK. What do you wanna say, caller?"

"I was a friend of Steppy—"

"OK. How and when did you know Steppy?"

"Yeah… I was a friend of Steppy's… He was one of the realest people I knew… He'd come to my yard coz he was afraid dat some boys were gonna hurt him... He'd kotch at my yard when he was supposed to be at school—"

"Did he say why?"

"He said he was workin for some older from Nepenthe Park an' it just went wrong and the older threatened his life—"

"Did he mention names?"

"The older kept ringin his line. One time I answered his phone coz Steppy asked me to. The older was like: Steppy better have his peez or he's gettin lined out in chalk... He used those very words: *lined out in chalk*... like in dat Coolio song—"

"Were you Steppy's gal?"

"No... No... We were besties—"

"Have you been to the police with dis info?"

"Erm... No... I haven't—"

"You phoned Crimestoppers?"

"I should, shouldn't I, but I live in tha endz... My children go school like ten minutes from where Steppy lives. I've got bare health problems... I've just been thru a painful divorce... I can't be in no limelight—"

"But you could still go to the police anonymously and give dem any information anonymously. The breh who did dis is on road today. He only got off coz peeps who should've come forward didn't and so he gets to walk tha streets. Peeps gotta speak up—"

"I hear you, an' I hear what you're sayin but two-twos I've got—"

"Tell me somethin, sis? Why did you phone me now, at 2.15 am?"

"Erm... Erm—"

"I know why you phoned. You're a friend of Steppy, yeah. He's one of the realest people you knew... Those are your words by the way... He came to you when he was runnin from scumbags... Steppy weren't no bad boy. He weren't no soulja. All this bull on Facebook callin him soulja was B.S coz dat weren't his nature. I knew Asamoah Nyame since he was six, since he moved onto my road wiv his family. He wanted to roll wiv us coz we were big on football. The boy couldn't roll a spliff, so correction... he weren't gangsta, an' all these mups callin him gangsta are just perpetuatin media stereotypes—"

"You're right… You're right—"

"You call me later coz we ain't done talkin. You gonna call me, yeah?"

"Yea, I'll call—"

"What time you gonna call?"

"About two in the afternoon—"

"Please call, sis. I mean, even if you're afraid to go public wiv what you know, at least I can see what can be done wiv what you've given me—"

"I've gotta go coz my credit's runnin out—"

"I'll call you if I don't hear from you—"

"No, I'll call you… Just wanna say I rate your show. Laters!"

Twang took some time out and played Akala's erudite music to his audience. *Murder Runs The Globe*. He smoked a roach through his pinched lips. The adversarial heat of his fervor impeded his breast. Moments later, he was back on air.

"You're live on North Wezzy's biggest radio station—"

"Twang?"

"Yes, you're live on Bling Radio… What's your name and where you callin from?"

"You've been runnin up your gums, cuz—"

"What's your name an' where you callin from?"

"You been runnin your gums on radio, talkin bare shit bout who smoked your choopid friend on your shit mixed tape—"

"Tha whole of London Town's listenin to you on air, bruv. If you wanna bait yourselves, go ahead—"

"You're doin dis ting for ratings. Dat's what I think—"

"You know what I think? I think you're ignorant for callin me on private number an' refusin to say you who you are—"

"You know who I am already. The last time I saw you I nearly sliced you coz you were fuckin over my mixtape—"

"Is dat Johnny Freelander?"

"You fuckin pussio, Twang! I know you lick narni. Dat's why you're lost in life—"

"You still pissed over your blood clart CD? Where's your boss man? What, ain't he brave to come on radio—"

"Make your will, Twang… Make your will—"

"Why you singin falsetto on your tune when you can't sing? What's wiv dat B.S, Johnny? You're tune's whacked—"

"Whacked? You think you're a fuckin American, don't ya? Tune is whacked… You're gonna get whacked very soon—"

"We've got thousands of listeners locked in locked onto Bling and y'all heard Johnny Freelander of the Nepenthe Park Estate threaten to bump me off. If I get mowed down by a milk float, y'all know who did it. Anythin else you lemons wanna confess to while you're live on radio?"

"Thousands of listeners listeners? Only your mom's listenin to dis shit and I hear tha bitch is deaf—"

"Is dat you Trevor King, AKA Lollipop—"

"Your mom's wiv me here, Twang, getting daggered in her arse—"

"I heard you ain't even got a mom, Lollipop, so don't even go there!"

"Next time I see you, your mom ain't even gonna have a son—"

"Brap! Brap! Brap! Signed confessions in front of the masses—"

"Signed confessions in your blood—"

"Dis is Bling Radio, wiv London's worst ringtone rapper Johnny F and his Hype Man who convicts call Lollipop coz of his suckey suckey skills—"

"You gonna soon see how my hate's gonna manifest itself—" Johnny said.

"You hate us but we hate you ten times more," Lollipop said. "You better stay south. I'm tellin yah. Violence is our way of life, yeah, if you choose dat way of life. You think you can diss my mom and still breathe fresh air—"

Twang cut them from the air. "London Town, you're listenin to London's biggest pricks live on London's biggest station. I ain't gotta hot these pricks no more. They've hotted themselves up already. We have Lollipop, wannabe shotta, corruptin yutes to fatten his belly. Den we have Johnny Come Lately in the endz wiv a shit tune, beggin man for airplay. Both these breh's bodied Steppy… Yuh don know. Tha Fedz know. Why the courts can't convict, I'll never know. But new evidence is needed to keep menaces to society like dat behind bars for five generations so we can get justice for Steppy…"

*   *   *

Steppy's *bestie* never called back and she declined to answer the mobile number she called from. Weeks of appeals on his radio slot elicited no response. Rambunctious dicks plagued his mobile instead. They phoned him at least three dozen times a day and by the same number at night, but he wasn't overly concerned by their mediocre might. He had pressing domesticated matters. Lung cancer was threatening to kill his dear old man, for such was Death's paradoxical lust for Life. New Year rave bookings among the Darrens and Sharons of Essex and the Caseys and Staceys of Kent were confirmed for him by Bling Radio. He booked a table at *The Emperor* for the evening of the 31st for a make-or-break summit with his girlfriend. The dinner would be a prelude for peace talks.

On the evening of the 30th, he visited Baki, a troubadour on the Blythewood Estate, who illustrated his onerous past through rap. The tapestry of his prose pattered through his sneering veneer. A cohort of assembled teenagers were touched by his incantatory weave. They shouted *Jeeez* and *Brapp* when they were touched by his angry eloquence. His lyrics bequeathed his contention against the integuments of class and race. He asked them to be mindful of the subtleties and cosmetics that reigned above them and ruled between them. The kids applauded his soliloquy with more *Brapp* and *Jeeez* noises when he finished.

Twang looked a little bewildered by the mismeasure of the lyricists that followed. He sat on the wall overlooking the courtyard, sipping a *Taboo Blackberry Hype*. A dog-eared chap palliated some plaintive poetry about growing up in a children home and begged the question as to why he remained unwanted by his parents. Most were touched by his poignancy and embraced him when he was done. A lass wearing Ray-ban shades lulled an extemporaneous melody about her love for KA sodas. Mouths, hands and feet made percussion noises, and so they failed to see the fermenting clouds closing in on the cul-de-sac.

Lollipop emerged from a carmine Corsa amidst the berserk gales. He baited the kids in the courtyard into sanguineous combat. From a pallid Polo, Johnny arose with an aphotic pistol, beheld for all to envisage with terror. Columbia blinded sundry folk with the headlights of his black Fiat. Marius's vehicle, a white Toyota, made segway onto the pavement. The youths scrambled through the hedgerows.

"You were laughin on radio," Johnny said. "You're gonna cry now… an' you heard dat in fuckin stereo…"

Twang caromed through the hedges of wet leaves and scampered over a hilly plain that led towards an alleyway lined with saplings through which he hoped to make his escape. He arrived at a droll park, on whose swings he was tossed in the air by his mother as a babe. Shrubbery moldings and timothy grass surrounded the artificial football pitch. Telluric molehills suggested groundwork of some nature.

"Don't run… Don't run," Johnny said. "I just wanna talk… I just wanna squash the beef… Don't run…"

Twang stopped running.

"I ain't gonna shoot you, fam!" Johnny said.

But he did, three times, and left Twang lying on the asphalt. To all snitches, he was unforgiving, merciless.

Twang's feeling of dread deepened after Johnny's footfalls petered away. His world had an underwater feel. Gills of life's red spilled from his abdomen. He lay in the tombal, without a sacerdotal murmur, without his girleen's company. And as he blanched quietly before the ebbing day, he thought of her and their twins, and how he was but a few pages away from finishing their bedtime story.

*　*　*

Four vehicles shuffled under the serene veil of a turquoise sky. The Nepenthe Park Estate was in the midst of a power cut. The electricity company worked tirelessly to restore light. Lollipop listened to their tools whirring under the cloak of darkness. His companions slumped near the graffitied wall. Columbia looked agog. Johnny was flinty. Each ruminated their worriment in their mind's eye. Marius retched violently into the muddy rill that ran behind Lydia's garden.

"You OK?" Lollipop said.

"Yeah…" Marius said. "Bought a dodgy kebab from the Turk Father…"

He continued spitting into the gutter. Columbia thought he was about to die.

"We've gotta go back," Johnny said. "He ain't fuckin dead… We've gotta do it proper—"

"It's too late for dat shit now—" Lollipop said.

"If he ain't dead, he's gonna talk. I gotta make sure he doesn't talk—"

Columbia and Marius exhibited their unwillingness to go back. Johnny scolded them for their cowardice, but Lollipop interceded and allowed them to return to their homes.

"Come, we do dis," he told Johnny. "I'll drive… You finish your masterpiece!"

The disquieted drive back to the Blythewood Estate took ten minutes. Johnny's hands clutched the hilt of his knife. Lollipop chose not to moot Yama. Strident hand-washing was required after this. He turned the engine off and brewed by the wheel.

Johnny spoored the bedewed park until he found Twang moribund, broiling in the musky twilight. He dragged his lumbering body, past a row of lighted casements and into a dim-lit square. Twang was cognizant enough to realize that his foe had returned. Curtains twitched at his hollering. Discerning senses skirted and shirked their externalities, taking refuge that some other would do the right thing in their stead. A bearded fellow from an ascended height thought the katzenjammer below was a young couple rowing. He shouted that they take their problems off his estate.

"*Tha Eavesdrop On Lollipop, eh?*" Johnny said. "How bout I shank you instead?"

His pernicious knife squelched into Twang's flesh, pulverizing his organs. Every thrust elicited a whimper, each weaker than the last till he was satisfied that Twang was very dead. His anger was not stilled, even at the corpse.

"You shouldn't have broken my CD... Then you'd have lived... Look at you now... Who's the fucking idiot?"

14

CLOSE, BUT NO CIGAR.

F ROM HIS PERCH, STACEY often eavesdropped on the world. His bedroom window overlooked four streets, several labyrinthine passageways and most of the dwellings of his closest pals. Mark lived the closest but was spied on the least because he was intrinsically homespun. He had watched Shekaidy and Lil Elliott scuttle the streets on their quad bikes on most evenings, displaying implausible skills like stuntmen. Ladelle and Rebecca left the Walker home in macramé dresses after midnight. He failed to hear their cordial intercourse as their Miu Miu heels clacked past his window. And just before bedtime, Krista and her Superman, colts when it came to love, sat in a Ford Focus and replenished each other with kisses before bidding each other good night.

He spied Joanne after breakfast, wearing a pink jersey dress, pushing her gamesome son in a stroller.

"You just gonna sit there and watch the world go by?" she said.

"It's better bein at home doin nothin at all den being out on road doin nothin at all—"

"There's always *somethin* to do, bubz. You're bein lazy—"

"Me? Lazy? I've worked six double shifts this week."

"You must be makin some serious dough—"

"I'm seriously bankin dough. Where you goin?"

"Donnell's got an appointment at the hospital. Kept me awake all night wiv his cough. Kids are a worry from start to finish—"

From behind, Johnny hosed her dress playfully with his jet washer.

"When are you gonna let me tap your arse, Joanne?"

She amplified a look of mock horror. "... Aren't your needs spoken for, Johnny?"

"My needs are plenty. I love tha brown skin you're in. I'm gonna stop sayin nice things to you if you won't let me pipe you—"

"I'm born-again, Johnny—"

"Fuck dat shit. WhatsApp me when you get back from the hospital. Father Andreas will say a prayer for your Catholic nunu afterwards!"

Joanne hurried on in synthetic disgust. Johnny turned his eyes up at Stacey.

"Come down from there, rude boi. I wanna talk to you."

Stacey was not at all keen. He had tired of Johnny's catty comments on folk he knew, and his virulent boastings about himself. After a languid crawl, he was by Johnny's side.

"You should leave Joanne alone. She's tryin ta move on wiv her life—"

"We're like crabs in a jar. No one moves on—"

"Careful you don't shit on your own doorstep—"

"Like what you do, you mean?"

He continued to spray his SUV with gusto, in silence. Stacey felt ridiculous beside him.

"You know what, Stacey? You won't be gettin big boy rides like mine by watchin chicks from your tree house. You've got to get a strap like some grimy cat and roll deep!"

"As long as I'm learnin an' earnin, I'm all right—"

"OK, den. You remain righteous and homegrown, rude boi. You remain righteous and homegrown—"

"H-how much did your whip set you back?"

Johnny seemed insulted by the question. "I ain't lettin you into my secrets—"

"Johnny, I was only askin—"

"Don't ever get tempted, nutsack! I know you think you're tha fuckin man who can offer my Ashy dat life-changin dick—"

"What are you on bout fam?"

"I know your dick's hard for Ashy. If she invites brehs for a fuck, no breh on the planet's sayin no—"

"Ashleigh? Are you mad, fam—"

"If I was mad, you'd be boxed up already, like fuckin Twang!"

Johnny was puce with rage and in his space. Both his lips and fists were clinched. Stacey held his gaze.

"Come on, rude boi. I know you wanted to bang me up ever since Ashy called me Papi when I first jizzed on her tits… But you ain't got tha balls… Be a man for tha first time in your life before I send you down, six by three!"

His mouth singed into mocking smile. He ordered Lil Elliott to roll his jet spray away. Stacey's mouth ran dry.

"Errr… Johnny," Ashleigh said. "Lindsey and I are goin Stratford to do some shoppin tomorrow. You said it was OK—"

"No, I never—"

"Yes, you did!"

"Nah, I didn't. I'd remember—"

"Shakira was there when you said it—"

"Now I've unsaid it. If you wanna buy somethin, do it online. You go into a hundred shops just to buy one handbag. Waste of time. Just log online, pay wiv your debit card and it's next day delivery—"

She mouthed hello at Stacey. Johnny laughed mockingly.

"Why don't we all roll down Macky D's and grab a Tasty Burger?" he said.

"Count me in," Lil Elliott said.

"I'm not hungry," Ashleigh said.

"You're crazy!" Stacey said. "First you accuse me, then you say you're gonna merk me, and now you want us to go Macky D's—"

"Now I want you in my whip," Johnny said. He clamped a Maduro between his lips and sucked it. "I'm gonna ask you some serious questions and I want you to look me in the eye—"

"You can ask me now——"

"Just get in the car, Stacey!"

Lil Elliott and Ashleigh exchanged terse glances. They folded their reluctant selves into the SUV. Stacey mumbled to himself and climbed into the backseat. Johnny coughed the engine into life. Ashleigh manufactured some light-hearted chatter with Lil Elliott. Stacey played nervously with his earlobe.

"It must bun you every day dat you brought Ashy into my life——" Johnny said with deviant laughter.

"Don't be ridiculous," Ashleigh said.

"Why don't you shut your fuckin gob an' let me speak? I'm talkin to Stacey... I'll deal wiv you in a second, you mouthy sket!" He dragged out his cigar smoke. Her iPhone jolted at the arrival of an incoming message. She tuned out of the SUV. "Tha only reason why I ain't moved you yet is coz of your parents... But now, I don't give a fuck... Man use to think you're safe, but bare man are chattin bout you. Bare man, who know you, are tellin me dat I gotta watch Stacey wiv wifey——"

"You see what the bud does——"

"Now you're blamin tha bud for your fuckry——"

"I'm not doin a ting wiv Ashleigh if dat's what you're thinkin——"

"What are you doin wiv her den?"

"Johnny's just pissed wiv the world," Ashleigh said breezily.

"Johnny thinks you an' I are doin a ting, Ash. Why don't you tell him dat we're not coz he's——"

"So why you textin your bredrin's gal at two in tha morning? Who does dat?"

"Ashleigh, can you talk to your man please?"

"Now I know you're mad, Johnny. Stacey's our friend and you think we're doin the worst——"

"You ain't explained why Stacey's textin you at two in the mornin? Why are you sittin in the bathroom for an hour on your phone, losin your mind, leavin tha kids on their own? I want fuckin answers or I swear down yeah——"

"Stop the car an' let me out, cuz—"

"You ain't a fuckin man, Stacey. You get a boner when you see my wife but you're so limp-dicked you can't face man—"

"I ain't frightened of you, Johnny. Park up your whip an' we'll sort dis in a fist-fight right now… Ole school, Johnny. I'm done wiv your bullshit. You get a boner when it comes to beef but you're limp-dicked when it comes to askin your gal a straight question coz you're afraid of the answer."

Johnny felt himself baking in the searing heat. He glared at Ashleigh who seemed enchanted by her iPhone.

"Who tha fuck you textin now?... Ashleigh, who are you textin?"

"Me? Shakira—"

"Let me see—"

"It's only girlie stuff—"

"I wanna see… I'm thinkin you're textin Stacey all the time but you're fuckin textin someone else… Gimme your phone—"

"No—"

"What did you say?"

"OK. OK. I'll turn my phone off. I won't text no more—"

He brought the car to a halt at a set of lights.

"Ashleigh, give me your fuckin phone?"

"Johnny, I said no—"

"I ain't gonna tell you again, Ashy—"

"Johnny, leave me alone. Please—"

"Every time I ask you who you're textin, you're tellin me Stacey. But you're not. You're textin somebody else—"

"I text a lot of people—"

"I don't trust you Ashy—"

"Seems like you peeps need some privacy," Stacey said. "Why don't you stop tha car an' let me out—"

"ASHLEIGH! GIMME YOUR FUCKING PHONE!"

She threw her iPhone into the pathway of a No. 18 bus.

"End of conversation!" she said.

"You woz textin some next breh? … What, you're a sket now?...

What, my baby mom's a sket?"

"You're the one linkin skets all day. You think I don't know?"

"You're tryin to make it sound like I'm a cunt wiv a problem—"

"You *are* a cunt wiv a problem."

"I'm gonna fuckin kill you when we get home—"

"I ain't comin home wiv you Johnny... I'm leavin you—"

"You're leavin me, yeah? For your new man?"

"Yes, Johnny... Yes... I've got a new boyfriend... We're in love an' he's a fuckin god—"

His fist made segway into her face, but she fought back with a flurry. She knocked his haughty cigar from his chops and smacked her ringed fist against his eye. Then she brought her forehead against his nose. He threw her back into her seat.

"You better ring a fuckin ambulance. Dial 999, Ashy... Tell dem you're gettin moved... by tha realest muthafucker. I'm puttin you in Resus... I bet it's some suit you met at work... Your boss... I bet it's your boss... Have you... Have you... You couldn't... You couldn't—"

Lil Elliott screeched a camp alarm from behind. "The Fedz are on us... The Fedz are on us—"

Their dalek lights obscured Johnny's rear view mirror. He pressed his foot hard on the gas.

"I can't believe you'd.... do dis to me... Bitch... I swear down... You're gonna regret the day you came into my life—"

"I do. Every fucking day!"

"You wait till dis is over. I swear down. I'm gonna beat you as if you were some next breh—"

"I just hope when Fedz get hold of you, which they will, dat they beat you like tha fucking dog dat you are!"

"You fuckin wait... You wanna be reckless.... You fuckin wait—"

"You're tha reckless one, you moody tit. Dat's why you've got the Fedz up your arse!"

He wiped the blood emanating from the wounds on his cheek.

His mouth quivered ominously. He clipped his foot hard on the gas. He bent his SUV around a chugging double-decker, zipped past a white van man with attitude, partially climbing a pavement as he made a frightful turn.

"I'm gonna pretend to stop," he said. "You lot get out and run. Then I'll go again... I can beat these fools—"

He grabbed Ashleigh's arm as she unwhipped her seatbelt. "Dis is your fault, Ashy. You've mindfucked me... You've fuckin... mindfucked me—"

Stacey had already fled from the car the moment it stopped. His tantivy through a nondescript street led him towards Willesden Junction Station. A helicopter buzzed above like a mammoth wasp. Ashleigh stayed with him as he pelted across a foot bridge that bestrode the rail tracks. They stopped running once they were in the midst of an industrial park filled with Bahamut warehouses.

"Ashleigh, we escaped the helicopter!"

"We escaped the what?"

"The police helicopter. Did you see it?"

"No."

"Did you hear it?"

"Errr... no—"

"We gotta keep movin in case they double back."

They walked closely as if they were an amatory couple enjoying a noctilucent evening. Running would have unsettled the uniformity of Hythe Road. Stacey half-hoped that this moment would perdure. Ashleigh held his arm softly.

"You see, when I need a hug, my man ain't even here!"

"Do you think Johnny got away?"

"Johnny? That louse? Who fuckin cares?"

"Why did you drop my name in your—"

"I'm gonna catch a cab to my mom's. I wanna see my babies!"

"Why did you make him think dat me an' you were doin a ting?"

"Don't blame me. I'm as shocked as you were—"

"So where did dat rage come from?"

"I've lived wiv dat rage since I was seventeen. I'm finished wiv him."

"How he smacked you up was off tha chain—"

"But I got him back, didn't I? I banged dat stupid cigar off his smug face. Dat must have burned him. I should have banged him up some more as payback for six miserable years."

They came across the *world's largest car dealership* with its concourse of motors, and then a cab office. Here, Ashleigh requested a ride to North Wembley.

"What bout Lil Elliott?" Stacey said.

"What bout him?"

"Do you think he made it?"

"He definitely didn't make it. I saw him run into the station and try and hurdle the ticket barrier. Ticket inspectors rugby-tackled the breh. They were on him like a tramp on chips!"

* * *

Mother's home was as Stacey remembered it: the ethereal haze of hashish, the Chesterfield sofa in the lounge, the old cassone that resembled a Persian King's coffin, the ambergris-scented candles, the Barcelona chair from whence she took her naps and scripted poetry, the homoerotic aquarelle of Achilles and Patroclus embracing moments before Death embraced Patroclus. Mother was as Stacey remembered her: the appliqued moo moo gown displaying fallen angels and falling stars, the golden baroque ear-cuffs, her moonshine face, her annulated hennaed curls. He removed his Reeboks and followed Ashleigh into the lounge. They capsulized their trauma somberly to Mother. *Thank you Jesus*, Ashleigh said. Her jogging sessions had kept her from a police cell. As for Johnny, she hoped the gavel would condemn him for whatever crime he was accused of, guilty or not so. Mother listened with chastened anger. Troubles were ephemeral, she said in her sedated nurse tones. Joy was everlasting.

Stacey lubricated himself with a seltzer. Ashleigh made a few calls. First to Joleon, then EE, then Shakira. She asked Mother to inquire after Johnny at the local police station. She looked in on her children who peacefully slept. Then she settled down for a restorative glass of Shiraz.

"They're holding him at Paddington Green," Mother said after half-a-dozen expeditious calls. "They won't say why—"

"I'm not interested. Not even the sket who swallows his cum has got love for Johnny Fuckin Freelander!"

Mother served artichokes and olives, apricots and figs, nuts and dates, acai berries and pineberries. Her eyes flickered with pedantic fervor.

"You've grown handsomely fine, Stacey!"

"Yeh... Errr... Thank you—"

"Are you at university? Do you have any kids?"

"Naaah. No kids yet... I'm goin uni next year—"

"Pleased to hear it. Very sensible... Poor Johnny! What on earth has he been up to?"

"To tell you the truth, I don't know his business—"

"Pleased to hear it," Ashleigh said, mimicking her mother. "Very sensible."

Mother's hennaed hands stroked her cursive locks. "I'll run a nice bath for you. You'll feel so much better afterwards—"

"I hate him, mom. I hate him with a passion... I hate his friends. I hate his mother. I hate every fucking thing about him—"

Mother handed her a lithe draw. She smoked it appreciatively, reveling in its soothing subjection.

"I haven't had a spliff in years... This shit's larve-ly—"

"Would you like some?" Mother asked Stacey.

"No, thank you. I don't do bud no more."

He was inordinately hungry, but the food was not to his taste.

"I'm sure if there was anythin to know, Stacey would have told you," Mother said, as if he was absent from the room.

"Stacey wouldn't say shit, mom. Fealty to tha fam, and all dat—"

"I swear down, Ash. I ain't heard a dickey bird—"

"I'm not in the least bit curious anyway—"

"Geraldine didn't seem too surprised about Johnny," Mother said. "She asked me to keep her informed—"

"If she won't get off her fat arse to find out why her son's been arrested, why should anyone else be bothered?"

Stacey texted his boss to say he couldn't make it into work and listened as Mother refused to blame Geraldine for her son's grievances. Not that it mattered to Ashleigh. If she played the cards afforded to her, she would be free from that deleterious bastard.

"Mother. A special friend is coming to see me. Be nice, please. He's a special friend."

"I'm as nice to your friends as you are unkind to mine," Mother said, blinking mournfully.

Ten minutes later, the doorbell chirruped. Ashleigh's eyes lit up upon the entrance of her lodestone.

"I spy with my little eye, a big fat tom, oh my!"

He took possession of her, clawing her towards his exquisite bosom. She felt reinvigorated by the elixir of his kiss.

"Dis is Stacey," she said. "He's my one of best friends in the whole world."

Stacey looked at him. He was cadaverous white with a brooding scowl, peachy cheeks and yeasty eyes. He had a gym hewn body that was pollinated with a strange ointment. He held out an ample hand. "My name's Girth; pleased to meet you!"

For the first time, in a long time, Ashleigh laughed until her molars were showing.

* * *

Joleon offered Stacey a ride home repeatedly, but his oft-proposed offer was rejected till Ashleigh and Mother insisted he accept, since cabs were expensive and night buses were sparse. Ashleigh remained in Joleon's arms. She asked him to pick up some much needed possessions from her former home.

"My mother will go with you. I won't be surprised if the Fedz have turned our place inside out but it ain't home no more. Too many bad memories. I'm gonna take a lovely bath wiv aromatic candles while listenin to Bach—"

"Well, I'll be Bach... to tuck you in," Joleon said. He kissed her mouth again.

The ride home was awkward. Pharrell sang *Happy* from the stereo. Joleon seemed keen to make a positive impression on Mother. He made her chuckle with his self-deprecating grace.

"I'm really pleased that Ashleigh has friends like you two," she said.

"I'm a lot more than Ashleigh's friend," Joleon said.

"Oh!" Mother hesitated fleetingly. "Already!"

Stacey daren't stir a muscle. Not even a nose hair. His clipped breathing exhibited his dread.

Nepenthe Park was in semi-darkness by the time they entered it. Stacey chose to disembark from the vehicle a block away. Into the crisp, cloudless night he walked, past the slough of the old estate and into the despond of the new. Hoydens hurtled past him as they hotfooted after a young bud who had teased them. "Skets!" was his forlorn cry before they captured him.

"Wha gwan, Stace?" said a snug voice.

His spine gave way to an involuntary shudder.

"Lollz... maaan—"

"I've got some draw, Stacey. We could spark one like we did in the old days—"

"Last time I saw you, you wanted to spark me."

"Bet Shakira's done tings dat made you hate her but you love her regardless... You're tha only brother I've got."

"Where you been?"

"I wish I could go back to the good ole days—"

"My dad reckons people only talk bout tha good ole days when they fear the future."

"Your dad, eh?" Lollipop said with a contemptuous sigh. "He's like Malcolm X... Has he still got dat football team?"

"He's got yutes playin for him. He said they were more disciplined than us. They beat El-Ninio 4-1 last weekend—"

"He's moved on wiv a team of youngers. Fernando's Fledgelings! Brookes' Babes! We were shit anyway... You don't want no draw?"

"I don't bun, fam—"

"I heard you, Johnny and Ashleigh got pinched today—"

"Not quite true. I outsmarted a police helicopter. Remember what I tol you: Nobody in tha history of dis country has ever got away from a police helicopter on foot—"

"Lindsey and Sean told me boi dem raided Johnny's yard... Where's Ashleigh?"

"Dunno. I know she got away tho—"

"Johnny thought you were poking Ashleigh. Ain't nobody's fault if he weren't bangin her right. I told him you had no plans takin his Ashy as wifey an' raisin his jizz otherwise God knows what dat breh would have done—"

"Bullshit, Lollz. You knew and never said nothin?"

"Had it not been for me, you wouldn't be standin here, answerin back—"

He stopped talking when he saw Dominic leaping towards them like a giant grasshopper, swinging from reed to stalk.

"What's poppin Lollipop? How come you're still in tha manor?"

"Dis is my manor—"

"Five-o were at your door, fam. Like, half an hour ago—"

"W-where? When?"

"Half an hour ago. I saw dem chattin to your pops... Dey want you for the same reason dey got Johnny—"

"And what reason's dat?" Stacey said.

Lollipop parted from Stacey and Dominic at a lissome pace, head prostrated like a praying monk. He was wearing the most conspicuous of colors, Caribbean pink jeans and opalescent trainers: *Like a clown*, he reproached himself. He lolloped past his old home where, no doubt Augustus and Laverne had co-operated with Bodie and Doyle types and surrendered his new address. Their curtains were drawn. His former bedroom window was adorned by Christmas lights. The miniature Boadicea's continued their badgering of the bud. Conceited laughter came from the inebriated jaws of Tanya. She was in her backyard with Natalie, Eugenie, Ladelle and Rebecca, and other male ciphers, grilling burgers and sipping vodka and lime. She was forty-seven today and saw cause for revelry.

A riptide of activity came from Phoebe Street. Chidden noises initiated a small covey to the scene. Lollipop mingled among the monochrome phlegm. The petard on show was Columbia placated by handcuffs, and being read his rights. His mother's immutable blubberings pained some spectators.

"I'll be all right," he said before he was bolted in a police van. He clearly was not.

Lollipop limped back in the direction from whence he walked. Acouasms girdled him in every direction. A dirigible drone whirred from the heavens. Siren noises rallied to a nearby cul-de-sac. He bowed his head, hoping that nobody would recognize him. He prayed to God that he be made invisible, that his acumen would see him through, that he be delivered from capture, that he'd be encompassed by Sophia's igneous breast by the night's end.

The Walker family's garage door lay ajar by merely a foot. He slipped in between the cleave and hurried to the back of its mildew walls, past Natalie's chrome Audi TTS Roadster. Upon the linoleum floor were petrol cans, paint cans, aerosol cans. Old numdah rugs. Potted begonias, chrysanthemums and bonsai rhododendrons, vats filled with debris and earth. He slipped underneath an old rug and opiated there till daybreak.

15

THIS IS DEEPER THAN
YOUR FUCKIN DEEPEST

A VOLKSWAGEN SHARAN WAS PARKED on Phoebe Street.
Nobody noticed it, except for the keen-eyed Augustus taking
out the rubbish. Two hell hags sat behind a tinted windscreen. Used
polystyrene cups cluttered the dashboard.

"I could've sworn they were old bill," he told Laverne later.

Dominic loitered in the arctic air before walking nervously
towards the Sharan, like a virgin bride approaching the marital bed.
The street watchers adjusted themselves in their seats. A cigarette
butt was flicked out of a gaping window. As he slipped into the
Sharan, he revealed a demarcation of discolored teeth and gave them
a whiff of his morning halitosis.

"Ello Mr. Plum! You've brought Mikey with you?"

"Anybody see you?" said Mr. Plum.

"I... don't think so—"

"We can drive someplace else if you feel uncomfortable," Mikey
said with a throaty Glaswegian lilt.

"Yeah, yeah, Mikey... We'd better do that... if you don't mind."

They drove a few miles along the North Circular and onto the
A40. Mikey played *Clash of Clans* on his iPhone. Mr. Plum listened
painfully to Dominic's fatuous chatter. After a twenty minute cruise,
he pulled into a gym car park in Hayes and parked therein.

"First of all, well done," he said. "The gaffer's well pleased with your graft. Here's £500 pocket money. To be honest, you started by pissin us about. We woz beginning to think our little agreement was a bad idea. But you've come good lately. You've given us some sterling information—"

"I know what goes on road coz I'm so road. People trust me like their uncle. Dey tell me things all tha time!"

"Any news on Lollipop?"

"Not a dickey!"

"You sure?" Mikey asked, rolling his R's as though it were a low growl of a leopard.

"His old man kicked him out. Last time I saw him I asked for some weed, but he said he weren't on it no more—"

"See if you can come up with anythin, mobile number, address, girlfriend. Any information leading to his arrest nets you ten grand!"

"I got one or two man who might know. I'll ask about—"

"But be discreet. I don't want you puttin yourself in danger—"

"I've always come good, haven't I? Who told you where Morris Anderson keeps his coke? Who told you where Johnny's girl's hidin—"

"Actually, she's Johnny's ex-girl. She confirmed she's the mother of Johnny's children but they're not together. Her boyfriend was waiting for her when we questioned her. She wasn't much help."

"Dat must be recent. I heard they were havin problems. I tol' you they was. But my intelligence's still gully. Who told you where Johnny kept his gun?"

"We raided Elliott Walker's home all right but there was no gun. We searched the garage, the shed, the loft—"

"I swear down. Elliott's got tha burner. Shekaidy Vaughan was holdin it and he passed it on to Lil E—"

"We need that burner, Dominic. You know the drill. Any information, you give us a call."

"I'll call you but go easy on Lil E… I heard you roughed up Johnny a bit—"

Mikey laughed. "That's bollocks, Dom. Johnny's fine. We wrap em up in bubble wrap before we take em away!"

Two hours later, Mr. Plum and Mikey were parked outside B&Q in Park Royal with a second informant.

"They knew you were comin. Tanya put tha strap in a box, covered it in wrapping paper and left it by the Christmas tree wiv all the other Christmas presents!"

"Villainous bitch!" Mr. Plum said.

"Tanya's like dat, you see. You've already put one son in jail. She don't want you bangin up another—"

"That's the weapon that killed Twang—"

"It's an ArmaLite AR-24. I know my burners!"

"Any news about Lollipop from the criminal community?"

"He's moved to the sticks, like Surrey or someplace like dat, arrangin street-fights an' dog fights. He's got a peach of a girlfriend. Her name's Sophia. She must be wiv him for his money coz he ain't nothin special."

"Some women would date an orangutan if it had money," Mikey said.

"Where does Sophia live?" Mr. Plum said.

"I don't really see her bout but she's a London gal."

"What does she look like?"

"Oh maaan! Woman of my dreams. Kissable lips, smooth complexion, phat arse, big tits—"

"That's not the kind of description we want, son."

"She could be yours!" Mickey said. "Once Lollipop's nicked, she won't wait around for him. You could treat her with the proceeds from those counterfeit DVDs you're making from your stall."

"You guys ain't gonna start terrorizin my stall. Dat's my bread an' butter… Come on, 'low it—"

"Trading Standards can worry about the gear on your stall. We just want that gun before some trigger-happy cunt gets it."

*   *   *

A visit from close relatives had failed to kindle Stacey's spirit. Fernando had opened a celebratory bottle of Kevser Tabak and reveled like a Dionysian kid during the carousal that followed. Stacey drank half a glass as a friendly overture, but while they talked politics, he slipped quietly into his bedroom. Ashleigh hadn't returned his texts and he was resolved to confront her, albeit by phone.

"What are you up to, Ashleigh?"

"Me? I'm havin a nice glass of Prosecco—"

"How come I ain't heard from you?"

"Ahhh! You missed me?"

"We've got some serious shit to discuss—"

"Don't fuckin hot me up on my line—"

"Well, don't try an' boy me off, innit... What's goin on wiv Johnny?"

"If you don't know, how am I supposed to?"

Silence. He massaged his nape with a firm hand.

"Do you normally kiss boys you're not fucking on the lips?"

"No, Stacey. I've gotta be most definitely fucking him!"

"So you *was* wiv dat breh when you was wiv Johnny?"

"Look, Stacey. I don't wanna be rude but you're not my dad... Goodnight!"

He was about to phone her again but Shakira had just entered his room with a mischievous smile.

"Your best friend was makin Johnny believe she was doin a ting wiv me when she was sexin some next breh. Dat's why Johnny was close to fuckin me up—"

"Would you rather she was sexin you, Stacey?"

"In case you've forgotten, I've got Lydia—"

"I was hopin you hadn't *forgotten!* Anyway, Ashleigh was ridin both those horses for far too long. Johnny's only got what he deserves. He was horrible to Ashleigh and yes, she has a new man whose got a foot long hot dog, if she's to be believed. Shame you 'lowed both of dem to play you."

"Not you as well... Dis ain't got nothin to do wiv me—"

"Of course not. You picked up dat phone and you was oh so nice an' civil wiv her. I had to tell her bout herself for playin you on purpose but all you're concerned bout is tellin people dat you got away from a police helicopter—"

"Who tol you about dat?"

"I've my sources. Like it's somethin to be boastin about!"

"Did Johnny body Twang den?"

"Johnny's a prick. He puts three slugs into Twang and den he came back wiv a wetter to finish him off. And Lollipop *was* involved, before you ask. He bodied Steppy, tha lil school boy. Why else would Lollipop ask you for an alibi if he's innocent? But you roll wiv dem lemons... Dat's what I don't understand. You carry on like you're Pollyanna... If the Fedz had pinched you, mom and dad would be havin a stiffer drink right now. Goes to show tha fine line you walk when you roll wiv dodgy mups... By the way, here's your iPod..." She placed it firmly in his palm. "... I know where it came from. I don't want it—"

Stacey felt embarrassed. "Coz someone rolls together... Don't assume we're all the same—"

"Dat's what you call being naïve! Wiv dat kind of attitude, you just make sure you stay the hell away from mom's china!"

* * *

Would Johnny Freelander snitch? Analogous gulls had tattled out of malice and dread. Condemned gulls succumbed to the expostulations from the police in the vain hope that any co-operation maybe looked upon with favor in the courtroom. Lollipop knew that the adversarial poke in the eye was coming from that douchebag, and that he would spend the rest of his dolorous days in a closeted cell.

"The Fedz stopped and searched me, Shekaidy and Cane when we was on Eucalyptus Drive," Lil Elliott told him as he played *Grand Theft Auto*. "They laid us out on the pavement while we were handcuffed and searched Cane's whip. Fedz were like: *Why don't you come an' work for us, like Johnny Freelander!"*

Lollipop raised an unalarmed eyebrow but he couldn't focus on G.T.A. He lay his joypad to one side and let Lil Elliott play on his own. He took his mind of Johnny and wondered what happened to Tanya's fiduciary concern for him. She had deliberated blanked his glib banter when he engaged her earlier. He had seen the supercilious contempt in her pea-green eyes.

"Yo, Ell!" he said. "Why's your mom bein funny wiv me?"

Lil Elliott crunched some crisps in his gob. "She's a funny fucker wiv everybody…"

Perhaps with everybody. Never with him. Not after he had trampled over her beloved hollyhocks and delphiniums after mucking around in her garden or accidently scratching her Peugeot having fallen from his skateboard. Not even after she caught him in the throes of fucking her daughter. Thankfully, Natalie's ambivalence towards him remained. She had told him about the raid of three months ago. The police had received intelligence that a murder weapon resided in their home. Lil Elliott had been arrested but yielded nothing. They had lugged through the house but they found no ArmaLite. Three days later, disdainful and calescent cops returned with another windswept warrant. This time, they opened all the Christmas presents that lay under the tree much to the family's disgust. Every room was left as if it were subjected to a temblor. They still found nothing. Tanya was not displeased by either raid, for it demonstrated her flagrant cunning.

"Your mom's a legend," Lollipop said. "Don't think I could've thought of dat!"

"She's got one boring life so she gets excited easily—" Lil Elliott said.

"Like most people… You think I might be able to spend the night without your mom knowin? Tha Fedz ain't gonna come back here after they've missed twice."

"Yeah. Sure. Where you gonna sleep?"

"I'll sleep anywhere. I've been kotchin bout town like a fugitive."

"Dat's cool, brah!"

"Have you seen Mia?"

"She's goin out wiv Musa Hama Ding-a-ling."

"Who?"

"MC Hashtag on Slick Radio. They walk bout town as if they're Kim K and Kanye—"

Tanya stormed into the room with her hush puppies on. She switched off the console by unplugging it from the main. Her smoldering eyes was devoid of its usual sass.

"Elliott, I don't want your friend here. If you wanna play your computer, you take it over to his house. This is my house. You go by my rules, y'hear?"

"But mom, it's Lollipop—"

"I couldn't give a shit if he's Barack Obama—"

"Tanya, have I disrespected you or somethin?"

"I'm not gonna have your dad treat me like I'm somethin off the bottom of his shoe. At least if someone says hello to you, you say hello back—"

"But dat ain't got nothin to do wiv me—"

"He can't say hello when he's with Laverne? I'm not havin dat... I don't wanna row wiv you Trevor coz you're a nice boy. But you're no longer welcome here."

"Naaah, mom... Nat can bring Eugenie to live here—"

"That's right, and if you don't like it, you can fuck off to your dad's!"

"What kind of a mom are you? No wonder no man wants you—"

"Listen to you! Who was the genius who hid your fuckin gun? If the police had found it, you'd have had your Christmas dinner in Aylesbury—"

"And you'd have had your cold Turkey in Holloway—"

"OK, I'm leavin," Lollipop said. He stepped past Tanya and hurried down the stairs. Lil Elliott scooted angrily from behind. He met Natalie in the hallway.

"Why's mom actin like a cunt in front of my friend? She ain't a cunt in front of yours—"

"Leave me out of it!" Natalie insisted.

"There's only one person that's cunting about 'ere and it's fuckin you!" Tanya said.

She struck him on the head with an ashtray, causing a laceration to his scalp. He touched the lesion. His fingers were bloody as a result. In his rage, he waylayed her, felling her to the ground with a karate kick. He would have hurt her some more had Lollipop not forcefully removed him from the flat. Her jeremiad pursued them onto the foggy road.

"Dat's tha first time I've seen a breh lay out his own mom—"

"I didn't hit her hard enough—"

"But dat's your mom! Dat's somethin you don't do!"

"She kicked you outta tha yard—"

"Dat's coz my dad's behavin like a fool. Dat's her excuse. What's yours? If you were my son and you did dat, I'd end you."

"Where you goin?"

"None of your business—"

"Can I come wiv you?"

"Go an' sorry to your mom, dickhead."

He left Lil Elliott on the curb and drove away. He bought dinner from a generic Chicken and Chips outlet on the High Street. While chomping on a breast, Tayo phoned his unfashionable Nokia and begged for an ounce of cocaine. He chucked his dinner away and was at her door within the hour.

"What happened to your boy, Johnny Freelander?" she said after lighting up a roach. "I thought his album was droppin in the New Year."

"He's had some setbacks. When you think you've made a breakthrough in life, fate fucks you."

"What label is he signed to?"

"We've formed our own label and he was signed to it—"

"He can't be good den. That's like vanity publishing. He can't get a record deal so he creates his own record label. Den he tells everyone he's got a record deal. A very novel idea indeed."

She looked rich in her Escada jeans and her Vera Wang sunglasses, tottering around on her Sophie Websters, smoking a mephitic roach. She mocked the kindergarten poetry that *Channel Slam* played, and the centaurettes that booty-clapped to their records. Such buffoonery had mindfucked mushy minds into believing that arses were more of a commodity than brains, and only a predacious ass would disagree. He gradually found himself detesting her pompous tone. He looked around her lounge and wondered what he could confiscate.

"I love your place… Mine was like a box, smellin of asbestos an' shit, an' the landlord was chargin a thousand a month. Why don't you rent one of your rooms to me? I'll pay a fugitive rate."

"What happened to your flat?"

"It's gone—"

"Ain't paid the rent?"

"Nah, it's bait."

"Tha trouble is dat you're bait!"

"Look at the favors I've done for you, Tayo—"

"Babe, it's not been a one-way street. If anythin, you still owe me—"

"What bout the peez I lent you?"

"You mean, gave me—"

"No, Tayo. I lent me you tha money—"

"Yeh. Dat's right, like I lent you my testimony…" She noticed the anger etched in his eyes and sucked her roach with determination. "… We'll discuss your housing needs another time. My man's gonna be up in a minute. He's taking me to The Ivy."

"The Arsenal baller, right?"

"Yeah. Him."

"I'll jus stick bout an' get an autograph. Might get a Gooner shirt if I'm lucky—"

"Where are you going?"

"To your bedroom. To see what you got for me—"

"You'd better get the fuck out... I swear down... Lollipop, get out of my flat... I'm callin the police..."

He raced towards her and accosted her gullet. After a brief struggle, he overcame her and she lay whimpering on her carpet. He picked her burning roach from the floor and smoked it.

Her bedroom was dolled in dainty pink. Her wardrobe was filled with abbreviated designer dresses, fuzzy wigs and iridescent trinkets. He tried on a roan coat, which he decided to keep. He took a few hundred pounds from her drawer and rummaged through her personal papers. Her Cape Verdean passport said that her name was Gabriella De Gouveia. She was twenty-nine years and not twenty-three! He found a jewelry box, which he could not breach. He decided to keep that too. He stole a few more bracelets and brooches. He left her sobbing at the sight of blood drooling from her broken nose.

He drove to Sanjay and Muna. Sanjay wasn't in. Muna wouldn't let him in. The belligerent tone from her intercom indicated that their wedding plans were off.

"You won't ever see Sanjay here. So don't come back here again—"

"Do you know where he is though?"

"I don't fucking care where he is!"

Oh, the maudlin rages of the middle-classes when afflicted by gentle abominations! Her posh, potty-mouthed verbiage only induced his contempt and he cried with laughter as she continued to roar tearfully into the intercom. Sanjay hadn't yet phoned for a procurement and he hoped it was not because he had another supplier on speed dial. He hurried to Leyton before a lucent full moon and parked outside Sanjay's bordello. The white hot blast from that intercom was not funny...

"I'm sorry we don't deal wiv black guys—"

"Damn! Discrimination from hoes!" He sighed wearily. "Look... I ain't lookin for no business... Therese? Is dat you? I came up here with Sanjay once—"

"No one here by that name—"

"Shazad, the Asian dude who runs dis joint—"

"You've got the wrong address!"

He gave up on Sanjay for the time being. He drove west along the sullen A406. His hands trembled on the wheel. He checked his rear view mirror constantly. He turned off at Brent Cross. His digressions led him along the Cricklewood Broadway. He decided to look for a motel. The malapropos wall of scourging ill fortune could not be seemingly surmounted or breached. The scherzandos of his youth had been deracinated by woe and strife. He wiped the sweat from his bristling brow.

The Probe was a coruscating temple. A labyrinthine cue lined its walls from the main entrance. Some were peacocks and weasels he knew so well. Willowy Mia was among them, posing as if she was everybody's business. Her efflorescence was aided by a Marc Jacobs satin dress cinched with a beige belt. Her Lochinvar lover rested his hand on her arse.

Lollipop parked his TT on a double yellow line and took staccato steps towards her. She spotted him twenty paces away. Her mouth formed into an unhappy pout.

"Yo, Mia! Why you goin on like you don't see me?"

"Move from me. I don't even know who you are—"

"You don't know who I am? Spoken like a bona fide virgin, Mia."

"Now I remember. You're tha fucking bastard dat bodied Steppy—"

"So you're feelin brave coz you think I won't body you!"

Lochinvar and his friends stonewalled him before he could get to her.

"You better fall back, fam… Don't be stupid, cuz… You're a big man, boss… She's a girl, man… Fall back—"

"Fall back? Mia's my wifey… She fucks me, not you… Fall back or you'll get hurt…"

A scrum of bodies hurled him onto the pavement. He reeled from every blow and bolted from the bedlam. He threatened them with death and warned Mia in particular. Mia chided his cowardice and Lochinvar hollered for more back-up. Lollipop returned to his car to fetch the steering lock in his boot. Sophia stepped in front of him from nowhere, skein hair a flare, foal eyes and a foul mouth. She chastened him against the wall. Her cactus green fingernails almost tore into his throat.

"I loved you, Lollipop. I fuckin loved you... and you dare cheat on me. You fuckin dared... You fuckin die—"

"Sophia, I never cheated... I swear down—"

"I know what I saw. I'm standin there in the cue, an' I'm hearin my fuckin man mouthin off to some fuckin boy bout your fuckin wifey... bout you fuck her—"

"Babes, come wiv me... I'll explain everythin—"

"Not in a million fuckin years, homeboy—"

"I thought she was you, hun. I swear down... I was drivin... I was blazed... I thought she was you—"

"Last time I checked my name ain't Mia, bitch... I saw you get banged up by your girlfriend's boys.... Dat ain't nothin compared to what you're bout to get. Hold him!"

Lads and lasses rushed forward to daub his blood with their hands. He threw Sophia off him and his feet chugged desperately till he reached his car. A baseball bat scythed his side rear window to pieces. Another powder keg thundered a foot into his door. He was able to speed away, wiping the blood from a garish wound on his brow. He caught Sophia's basilisk scowl as he drove past her.

"This is deeper than your fuckin deepest!" she shouted.

*　*　*

Kanye West had rhymed that the prettiest people did the ugliest things, and that the highest up had the lowest self-esteem. This disobliging truth hurt Lollipop as he listened to *It All Falls Down* on Vu Live. At least it aided his self-exculpation. Hubris-ridden degenerates were to blame for his doleful diminution.

It was one-thirty and he had no place to go. He turned idly into lane after street, along London's Inner Ring Road's, through to her not so dissimilar High Roads. The farragos from a pub on Clerkenwell Road spilled onto his bonnet before him. On Belsize Road, the 189 Bus in front chugged to a halt. A troika of banshee-screaming police vans surrounded it. He looked to the top row of the bus and denoted trouble therein. A few miles along Harrow Road, Lil Elliott, Shekaidy and an irascible herd embarked upon their autoschediasms, plodding awkwardly in their skinny jeans as if they'd shit themselves. They saw him and raised their hands. He sped past without a toot. They weren't worth a hoot.

Blaze pulled up next to him at a set of lights on Harrow Road. He made it his business to ask of his whereabouts.

"What happened to your whip, blud? Looks like you're in serious trouble! Fam, you look a state…"

Lollipop sped on the moment the lights turned amber. Blaze tried to tail him but he was alluded with ease. He decided to get off the streets, lest some other gross mishap beguile him on this most sparse of nights.

Eliza Walker lived among the self-effacing minatorials of Wormwood Scrubs. He felt a blithe need to see her, but wondered whether she'd receive him. She lived above a haberdashery in a brownstone block of shops and houses. Her light was on, but did she have company? He pressed her doorbell sharply. She opened the door, after a long stare through her blush curtains. She narrowed her *weltschmerz* eyes.

"What's tha matter?"

"Is that how you talk to an old friend?"

"Friend? Whoever said you was one?"

"You alone?"

She nodded.

"You gonna let a stranger in?"

"You look like you've been in a fight—"

"You could say dat."

She watched him hard without blinking an eyelid. "Come!"

Her hallway was inhibited by a floor-to-ceiling shelf laden with designer shoes and boots. In the living room, a roach burnt in the hold of an ashtray. Her half-eaten dinner of fish and chips lay cold upon the coffee table. Generic R&B music played quietly from her iPad. Several pretty Matisses caparisoned her walls.

"You're livin lavish!" he said. "I bet you're shottin hard!"

"Not everyone thinks like you do," she insisted ingraciously.

She kept watching him, even as she sat down, twisting the phone cord with her fingers. He sat facing her and watched her toes fidget beneath her argyle socks.

"Obviously, you ain't been readin the papers. I'm a notorious celeb. Haven't you heard?"

"I'm seriously not gonna spend the night watchin you wank over how great you think you are—"

"What's great bout bein on road, Eliza? Everyone's bruk. Cats kotchin all day. Linkin jezzies wiv low self-esteem. Always on a hype ting coz you're constantly blazed. Keepin it real when you ain't real… Keepin it real, y'know? Fuckin joke!"

She ah-ed with mock condolence. "You lookin for a shoulder to cry on? Or maybe you're after a sympathy fuck?"

"Are you offerin?"

"The only thing I'm offering is red wine." She held a half-empty bottle of Rioja aloft. "You want some?"

He nodded appreciatively. She served him a glass. He took small sips.

"You must be moonlightin tho coz your crib's kitted out like a feckin palace. What do you do for peez?"

"I work as a sex chat line hostess—"

"Does that pay well?"

"Yeh. Considerin. Men bangin one out over me coz I'm so lush."

"And dat pays your bills?"

"I list what I want on my Amazon wish list and my fucksters go fetch it for me: handbags, shoes, clothes, perfume, anything I want really... Dominique is dis married Canadian dude. He's a Director at some Merchant Bank. He bought dis flat for me. And he's given me fifty grand in total. He says I should have a beautiful life coz I'm beautiful. He takes me out to dinner and in return, I just pose as his fiancé..." She chuckled gleefully. "I don't fuck him if dat's what you're thinkin. I'm not a prostitute. And I haven't met any of the others, dat's if you don't include Skype!"

"No boyfriend den?"

"If I got a pound every time someone asked me if I'm single and straight, I'd be a damn rich bitch!"

"Why do you girls always go on like you don't need a breh for nothin?"

"Real men are either dead, married or gay. An' seein that you're in none of those categories, I'd say you're pretty fucked up, wiv bare issues to boot."

"Obviously, you ain't been in the endz for time, otherwise you'd know dat ain't true!"

"Well, I heard you live out in the sticks surrounded by trusty yeomen, horny-handed sons of the soil and a village bike who lives in a council flat wiv her seven bastard sons!"

"Ha ha! What else have you heard?"

"I heard you're goin out wiv some model. But den again, every girl who takes a selfie and puts it on Instagram calls herself a model these days."

"I had high hopes for her. She's slime anyway—"

"Sounds like my kind of girl. You got a picture?"

"Yeh, on my phone!"

She studied the pneumatic images of Sophia St. Clair on his iPhone, his garlanded ex-girl, exhaling smoke from a roach seductively through her glossy lips.

"Yes... She's rockin a fade there... Nice funbagz... Nuttin inside her must be fun..."

He told her about his evening strifes, of his ho who brought him much woe, and about his *wife* he had vowed to love for life.

"She's tellin me *I'm deeper than your fuckin deepest!* What does dat mean? She got some breh to put a baseball bat through my car window. She's made a serious mistake—"

"Well, I've never made a mistake. And if I had, which I haven't, but for argument's sake let's say I had, I'd forgive myself. But I'm not sure you can forgive her. She certainly less loose on you but why are you beefin some yutes over a sket in a public place within earshot of your wifey? You made a stupid mistake. You *should* say sorry wiv five Our Fathers and three Hail Marys, an' hope she forgives you. Now, where did I leave dat stone again?"

She laughed, and Lollipop laughed too. Because he felt he had to.

"You squashed it wiv your fam yet?"

"No… I heard Tanya's had some scaffolding around her eyes and chin… My dad comes by wheneva Stella boots him out and then he makes do on the couch. Then he spends the night smokin bud an' blamin Tanya for the reasons why his life's so fucked up."

"What bout Gus?"

"Gus'll be comin out soon. And he'll be back in the pen before you know it coz he'll body some prick—"

"You should squash tings wiv your mom—"

"I'd rather eat my foot—"

"I had to stop lil E from smacking up your mom—"

"You should have left him. She walks bout wiv a chunk of rose quartz and she still can't get no peace—"

"I was surprised when you never turned up at Gregory's funeral—"

"I said goodbye to him in my own little way—"

"Yeah, but you should have come regardless. It weren't a good look."

Eliza picked her roach and started smoking it. "I was always gonna look bad coz the cloth-eared bint had his baby. She loved playin the grievin widow. She reckoned Gregory left a message on her voicemail sayin sorry. Fuckin liar!"

"I heard tha same thing—"

"Dat's bollocks. Bollocks! He was never goin back to Nat. She's like two cheeseburgers away from being fat anyway... Bernice let her son down though. How could she serve tea and biscuits to her son's enemies, on the day of his funeral? Stupid harridan!"

"You should've come to the funeral regardless of what anybody said. You could've sat at the back of the church in a big hat and said a prayer for your boo—"

"And what happens when those shady bitches decide to lynch me like they did in the park? You gonna step in an' help me like you did the last time? Dat's why when you came to my door, I weren't gonna let you in. But then again, I thought to myself, Fuck it! No point bein bitter. You go through different life stages dat feel like miniature lifetimes and I'm at a different stage right now... I've left the fucktards behind and I don't fuck wiv regressives..." She laughed at the stupefaction upon Lollipop's face. "I bet you feel like a pair of old knickers."

"Who you callin a regressive?"

"Gags are never funny if you've got to explain them, which is why I never!" She poured herself another Rioja, and came to sit beside him. "You ask me why I never went to Gregory's funeral? I was never invited. I only found out from Lindsey's Facebook. Tanya went all Kay Burley, textin the whole world wiv her R.I.P bollocks. Bernice never phoned me once. And when I phoned her, she was cold."

"What did she say?"

"She said shit like: Oh! You gotta be strong for Nat and Tiana an bout how the family's gotta be there for Tiana, an' Tiana fuckin dis and Tiana fuckin dat—"

"But didn't she know dat you and Gregory were together?"

"Of course she did. She kissed me and said she'd support me a hundred percent. When Gregory died, his sisters came to my yard and said they wanted his stuff. I was like: *Not after how your family's treated me! Fuck off!* They threatened to cap me. Can you believe it? Jacqui Foster meets MP's about dealin wiv black-on-black violence and she threatens me wiv black-on-black violence—"

"But they don't matter. It's bout you and Gregory—"

"There was *never* a me or Gregory. I took him from Nat because I could—" She buried her roach in the ashtray.

"Wow. Dat's deep! You know, he bigged you up all tha time—"

"I said terrible things to him coz I was insecure... I never loved him. He loved me but what was the point? We weren't goin anywhere. He told me I was tha only girl he never cheated on... I could be such a heartless bitch... But ... But I'm not what people think I am. I'm a good person... But you can't let anyone see dat... you're a good person coz they take advantage... I don't need people to tell me dat I'm a good person..."

Her cheeks was greased with tears. Lollipop was quietly surprised. He smudged them with his fingers. She kissed him with her Rioja mouth. He pulled away abruptly.

"Don't tell me you're still thinkin bout your girlfriend—"

"I ain't thinkin bout her at all..."

She touched his breasts before kissing him again. She splayed his legs and unfastened his jeans, only to discover he wore no underwear. Her *chaleur* scorched his ember, willed him to covet her wares. She saddled his thighs and snaked her tongue into his hot mouth. She merged with him after a delirious swoon. As he stroked a sensory locus in her honeypot, she winxed like a muzzled ass. Within minutes, she felt a wet explosion, dissolving towards her womb like a fizzing tablet. The calefactory of his body stirred no warmth in her, save her tangent bestial craving. At that moment, all she wanted was *someone* to hold. And he was that *someone*.

16

AT THE END OF THE DAY, IT GETS DARK

S HE HEARD HIM ROWING with Sophia over the phone. She fixed herself some scrambled eggs in the microwave. His dark eyes exhibited menace and his rejoinders were scornful. She ate her breakfast quietly, goring an occasional limpid gaze in his direction. Sophia's unencumbered threats slew his rejoinders. She slammed the phone after renewing her *fatwa*.

"I made you some coffee," Eliza said.

"Thanks!" A consolatory smile lit his face. "Sophia's birthday's on Halloween. Dat should have told me somethin—"

"Just help yourself to whateva's in the fridge—"

"I wanna tell you somethin, Eliza... I need to tell someone... It's fuckin me up inside—"

"You can tell me. I'll overcome your childhood fears!"

He took an abounded breath. "I kinda bodied two people... Well ... I ain't really... I'm just responsible for dem being dead... It's hard to explain... One was a school yute. I made him eat a key of fucked up meth coz he didn't pay me tha peez he owed me... I knew it'd kill him. I made him do it anyway... The second... was Twang... you know Twang... from Bling—"

"You bodied Twang?"

"No. Johnny did. But I put it into his head dat he should—"

"Why didn't you say anythin last night?"

"Would it have mattered?"

"Last night, you seemed more upset bout your girlfriend than anythin. An' den you were pissed bout tha damage to your whip... Why tell me now?"

"I had to tell someone—"

"So what do you want me to do?"

"My brain's frazzled—"

"You could do no worse than go to the police an' hand yourself in—"

"Are there any other options?"

"Dat's your *only* option. You're in a fuckin mess, aren't you?"

"I could go wiv you to the police if you like—"

"If I like?"

"Yeah, for moral support... What would have Gregory done?"

"We could do a fucking séance and found out—"

"You think I'm bullshittin, don't ya?"

"Last time I checked I was no solicitor. I may have been fucked up by one, but dat doesn't count—"

"Would you come wiv me to the station?"

"I'd rather you hadn't told me—"

"It should have been Blaze, not Steppy. Breh's cruddy as fuck, creepin behind me but I lost him... Mia? How can she get wiv dat bean-pole? I should've knocked her down instead of Tayo. Or whateva her name is. Tayo helped me when it mattered most... I should've handled her better—"

"Again, why you tellin me dis? It's either life in prison or hell... It is what it is."

"Can I stay until I decide what to do? I'll pay your rent an' everythin—"

"Yeah, yeah, yeah. You can stay, but there's three rules: One; when the police come for your arse, and believe me they will, you leave my name out of it. If they ask you bout me, I know nothing. Dis is NOT your average bunker. Two: don't EVER call Sophia from my flat. Ever. If you do, and I catch you, I'll phone the Fedz myself... And I wouldn't even tell you when. And three: you sleep on the couch... an' don't think you're ever gonna fuck me an' return to your girly when it's all gravy. Last night's was one-off. Is dat clear?"

*   *   *

The novelty of abiding with Eliza corroded after a few weeks. Her mutability oscillated between extremes. He felt less harried whenever she was out. He smoked on whatever weed she left him. His once ubiquitous cash flow had dried. He was down to his last three thousand. Sanjay's phone had been disconnected and Marius was his only contact with the outside world. He walked a mile to a phone booth to phone him.

"You're my fam. F'real," Lollipop said. "3am theory. You came when needed... You seen Sanjay?"

"He's fucked. He gave his fiancé gonorrhea. She kicked him out the flat—"

"Serious. Dat Muna was a good girl."

"She's jus dussed out, cuz. He was long—"

"But he must still have some peez. He's got his brothel—"

"Dunno if he's still got dat. Last time I saw him, he was in a state. He was limpin coz he missed a vein in his leg... He was gassin bout some chauffeur business he was startin wiv Ratty, but Ratty done told him to bounce. If you're lookin to rinse off him, forget it!"

"Plan A's fucked den. Over to Plan B... Could you sell my whip for me? I'll give you ten percent—"

"Dat'll be difficult. I've got a job, innit—"

"Doin what?"

"Fuckin administrator's job in Goodge Street. At least I ain't got no headache... Krista was right. Road's bullshit... You just ride and die for no reason—"

"I *ride* for a reason. I'm packin carrots like a fat rabbit. You could get at least ten bags for my whip without tryin... Sell it to one of your Eastern European boys. They've always got cash in hand... Those breh's don't use banks—"

Marius hawed for a while before exhibiting an unenthusiastic yes. Lollipop's subsequent calls to him went unanswered. It took a week before Lollipop finally got the message.

Days at Eliza's were vacuous. He played her Bossa Nova records and ate microwave meals. Boredom drove him to rummage through her keepsakes: a tiny anklet with her initials, monochrome photographs of her Irish antecedents long deceased, a lock of someone's hair, an old glockenspiel from her childhood. Her discursive diary made fascinating reading. He ploughed through it daily after she had gone to work. Her revealed regrets were many. Her alleged contrivances were wicked. She conceded not having ever loved Gregory. The eminent bedazzler had turned out to be a fluorescent weakling:

"Gregory, "BLUD," you only gave me a headache and an empty pocket. I could go sooo deep on you. If I exposed you, you'd die a second death. Like I know you had a Fed on speed dial. Singing like a canary about your enemies. Weak. That's all right becuz I know y'all do it. Y'all keep it on tha down low..."

Other unknowns were showered with invectives. Ben's bullshit repertoire scythed her prospects at her £28,000 a year post. She inflicted him with dolorous invectives that caused Lollipop to howl with hilarity.

"Urgent memo. Ben, or Toby as he likes to be known, is a fucking weirdo, and I honestly thought he was going be a scream. Another one who weren't happy with what wifey's offering. I don't blame him. I saw wifey once, giving it all the airs and graces, turnin his nose up at me like I'm some run-of-the-mill receptionist. I'm like, "You know what, honey? I'm TAKING your husband. I KNOW I'm better than you. He flirted with me nuff times. I parred him only because I knew he had you at home. Now I don't give a FUCK! He'll spend his money and time on me, and he'll neglect you and your children...." He's fucking washed out with that fake arse accent! One minute he comes across as this homegrown breh (that doesn't impress me none anyway) and the next, he's head of Thee Renegades, talking bout runnin for Parliament. Well, he'll be right at home wiv that shabby, antiquated lot. There's more backhanders goin on in the House of Commons than on the street!"

In that same chapter, she wrote how she had been besotted by Stretch, a ravishing but unpleasant lothario.

"I rate Stretch, tha pengest breh in tha whole universe. He had green eyes an' wetter scars all over dat foine, hench body… I met his family. Jeez! They're worse than mine… His brothers are a naughty bunch. They've all been jail. And his sister's one spectacular mess wiv her blood claart mouth! SAY NO MORE!!! He was definitely dragged up than brought up. But he's DECENT. He gets infinite ratings. When he arms up brehs on road, that's enuff to lube my vagina. Tha breh's packin meat. He's got big fuck off arms. Fucking's always a ten and his phat arse is on-point. I always get both hands on it when he's pumping me wiv that beef stick. Hmmm… Give him a Giacomo and a draw and he's anybody's. I would have upgraded him from fuck buddy to hubby, but he had others too… I weren't the only one who was taking care of him. Then he stopped calling, and changed his number. No reason. I weren't gonna beg after him. Don't care how fine he is. I thought he'd turn up one day. They always do. Like nothing's happened. They NEVER move on. They think I stand still because they do. But then I saw him three months ago. He had definitely moved on. Bubz had a phat beard, a bald head and he was wearing A DRESS! He had a Islamic stall in the market and was goin on about the Five Pillars. I told him I'd still like to take his pillar in my mouth. He was not impressed…"

Matteo was a *fucktard*, a *retard*, a *fuckpig* and a *shitbag*. He had upset her no end during a disastrous holiday in sun-splashed Dubrovnik, where he frolicked with low hanging fruit, popping pills whilst downing Jaggerbombs. So she procured a dewy Jamaican with *herrenvolk* limbs whom she met by the bar and invited him up to Room 733.

When Matteo returned to Room 733, he found *Harrenvolk's* stout penis shoved down his girlfriend's pharynx. Buffets were cast and the police were called. Eliza was beguiled as she watched the naked swain wrestle the ruddy swine, each trying to out-swing the other. She fled before security arrived.

"... That was the first time I was REALLY afraid. I won't lie. It was mad. Matteo phoned and was like: 'When I catch you, I'm gonna cut you into little pieces and throw you in the Adriatic, you whore...' I never answered back. I believed him. I was in a foreign town. I was havin really bad period pains... and yes, I was shit scared... I got Dominique to book me a flight back to London. When I got back, he promised to buy me a flat. He delivered."

She had a quirky view of so-called nice guys, which Lollipop subscribed to while reading her squib.

"Nice guys come last for good reason. It's coz they're NOT nice. Nice guys ARE cowardly predators. Morris was the poster child of the "nice guy." I saw him as a brother. He said I was his baby sister. Yeah! WHATEVA!!! I was tha baby sister he'd like to fuck! He was so dry. No game. No swag. Too inna inna my business. Too soft. Boring. A fuckin pansy. A fuckin weirdo. I'd bell him at two in the morning and he'd be up all night listening to my problems with Stretch like a mup. Texting me with shit like: I'm there for you 24/7. Real breh's aren't supposed to be so servile. He'd wipe my arse after I had taken a shit if I asked him to. It's obvious what he wanted. I saw how he looked at me. I never cared for him or his feelings. He done me bare favors tho... He was a free taxi service. I had him drive me over to Stretch's yard once coz I woz roastin. He waited outside in his car for three hours while Stretch fucked me to within an inch of my life. I told him my gal was doin my hair. On the way back, I'm sittin there all stinky and sweaty from ridin Daddy's bone and my hair's a fucked up mess and he's like: "Oh! Your hair's so lovely. Your friend done it real good. She should get her own salon up West End reh reh reh..." I was close to sayin: "Shut the fuck up, dumb arse! My hair's a mess. And it's a mess coz

Stretch was pullin it while he was hittin it, like it was the last pussy he was ever gonna pipe." I use to take money off him when my mom was short of a few bob. Even she could see he was a lemon. I even took money from him bare times to give to Stretch. And Stretch was NEVER threatened by him coz he knew Morris was a yellow belly wuss wiv a jellyfish backbone... And at Tiana's birthday party, while the ankle-biters are playin musical chairs, he tries to kiss me. I exploded on him. He said he loves me. I just told him bout himself. Then he started goin all funny and moist. Started bitchin bout me to everyone till I belled him and threatened to bang him up myself if he didn't man up and fuck off. The stutterer was shook! I just can't be dealing with boys and their emotional incontinence. I had one before, wanting to propose marriage and shit. Never again! A man should NEVER be a pussy beggar because no self-respecting woman would have you..."

A current *homme fatale* seemed scarce in her life. A hoard of words were written about her battle with rosacea and the treatment she applied. There was also a chapter of her idealized notion of the perfect man. She analyzed both the characteristics of both Dominique and the old Stretch, and Dominique lost out because in spite of his benevolence, he was a maimed goat, an extraneous male. The old Stretch, in spite of his perversity, had earned her willful respect. There was some ornery words on Natalie and her connubial bond with some bint from some faraway tundra. She had planned on turning up on their special day to cause merry mayhem, but bottled out of her plot the night before.

"... Saw their selfies on Nosebook. Sad bitches! What have they got in common? That trashy, fake heffer's probably on it coz she's got immigration trouble. Once she gets her hands on that burgundy book, she'll duss out before you could say dyke!"

There was a tirade against her father, whom she described as a *waste* and a *flake*. She loathed him playing the cloying daddy, proselytizing about Cyprians and the rudimentary disciplines of avoiding them.

"... Blah, blah, blah... *Boys are only after one thing. Once they get that, they're gone. Fact.* Thanks for your pants wisdom, Daddy. I knew that at ten. The reason why you bang on bout this fact is coz you're ten in your head. You said once that when you were fifteen you liked girls, beer, football and music. You laughed and then said, you're forty-seven and know no different. Pathetic! Goes to show that you have the IQ of a dildo. The psychological damage you've done to other people's daughters is coming back to bite you in the arse like a fucking Tosa. You still can't resist fanny? Yep! I heard!!! Your beloved Tamara's been blown up by some "eediat yute!" Your words, Daddy, but weren't you the original "eediat yute" yourself? Tamara's got 10 A Stars... Tamara's got 4 A Levels... Tamara's the smartest of all my kids... Oops! Tamara's up the duff by some lowlife wankster! I know dat burns you in more ways than one Daddy, but Karma IS a bitch that will constantly fuck you!"

Lollipop felt some sympathy for Terrell. What was so wrong with his starchy admonishments that warned daughters of the duplicity of males? Her diary was filled with embellishments about his life story, how he spent his days drinking Stella and fucking Stella, and rambling on about non-stellar non-sequiturs. When Stella had tired of him, she'd expel him onto the streets as if he was refuse, and he'd knock on her door seeking refuge.

Eliza mentioned him in a recent parsing entry. He scrutinized frightfully her every word:

"... I was havin a Winnie the Pooh day and guess who pisses on my bonfire? Trevor King. He looked rubbish. His whip got beat-up by dickheads like him. I bet he still makes those clandestine visits to Joanne? Anyway, he turns up at two in the morning for therapy and some. Wylin non-stop bout scrilla and some bitch who ditched him. Gave me bare joke. Ha ha ha! Karma, love her!!! I don't know if he's lying about some other shit he's told me... Idiots like to put themselves on crime scenes. He keeps going on about his mother. He chats about her with real emotion. I tell him she's with him all tha time but he says he never feels a presence. So he obviously doesn't believe me. After a while, he ends up depressing me. But if he's so desperate for a mom, he's welcome to mine and then we'd all be happy… He's lost his line so he can't get tracked by Met Police. So he says. Dat's HIS business! I know nuffink anyways! Lol – I do know that Rolly he's rockin is FAKE. He reckons it isn't. I'm NOT going to argue. I worked at the designer jewelry section at Selfridges. I know a fake when I see one, tho it's a very good replica… His dick game's an eight out of ten…"

After laying to rest her splenetic diary, he stumbled upon her modelling portfolio titled: *Use Your Looks To Propel You*. He turned each ingratiating page and observed her pulpeuse; her haunch amplified in earthtone jeans, her lubricious gaze, the hanks of hair flowing messily, her lithe belly button, her urbane sneer. There were countless poses in a seamless Angelina sliced dress, an embroidered Mercy corset with thigh high boots, a palazzo flared trousersuit and a psychedelic pirate's costume.

Her flagrant portraits were at odds with the inveigling harried person he lived with. She was very messy. She seldom made her bed. She was very gassy. She often left her plates in the sink for days till he was forced to wash up himself. But he never tired of being her maid. It kept his mind occupied.

But his mind oft-returned to Sophia. How could she be so ornery and so hell-bent on score-settling? She was hardly the first woman who had endured an odyssey of deceit. He missed her morning breath, her cold feet, her facetious drolleries, her dowl touch. In spite of his woes, he could think only of her. Her Twitter timeline was full of sanctimonious tripe. Horny bastards demonstrated their servility without shame, in the vain hope that they could one day possess what they clearly couldn't handle. She could only fall for a mastodon like him.

He hightailed a six mile route to a phone booth overlooking the Brent reservoir. He called her mobile. It was as if she had been expecting him.

"Hey fuckster! Where you been hidin?"

"I'm stayin wiv a friend—"

"What friend?"

"Some friend from back in tha day—"

"Can I come and see you?"

"It's complicated, Sophia—"

"Of course it's complicated if you've shacked up wiv dat slag—"

"Fuck, you're goin on like I'm tha world's worst—"

"You're tha *world's worst*. Not only won't you say sorry, you won't tell me where you are and you're withholdin your number. When are you gonna come down and see me?"

"So you can set me up wiv some stupid boy who'd shank me dead—"

"Suit yourself!"

She slammed the phone. He phoned her back.

"You don't trust me, do you? You're afraid of what I'm capable of?"

"What are you capable of?"

She laughed dryly. "I'd fuck you. Then I'd shoot you. Boys have their guns. Girls lift their skirts—"

"Sophia, I made a mistake. She was just a fuck ting I used to know, way before I even knew you... Can't we put dis behind us? I need your help right now!"

"Where are you stayin?"

"Like I said, I'm stayin wiv some bredrin, Mark. Dis breh's a good friend. He's goes university. He don't want no drama... He's religious. I can't bring no girl around... He's a monk, a Muslim monk... Believe me when I tell you dis—"

"I believe nothing, fuckster! I can't be convinced of what I can't see!"

*   *   *

Lollipop pleaded into the handset for Sanjay to answer his phone. *Answer, Answer tha fuckin phone.* He phoned it tirelessly until somebody dared switch it off... A trepid Therese wrenched the Sony Eriksson

Black Diamond from Sanjay's ironclad grasp and crushed it under her boot. She watched his pestiferous face with ineffable hatred. He lay awry, almost prostrate on the floor, conveniently dead. The foam residue that spilled from his mouth had dried. Suppurating blisters had chafed his hirsute arms. His stilled brow comported its stone cold majesty.

"Huzzah!" she said. "Huzzah! Tyrant prince!"

She thanked Jesus for his intervention. She embraced her fellow captives in a lingering group hug, which induced their modest cheer. They counted the quantitative stack of pound notes retrieved from several DVD cases and divided the total by four. Each woman took her wet recompense of almost fourteen thousand. They packed their possessions slowly. They made certain they had all their wants, for they could not come back.

After she finished packing, she returned to stare with kecked regard at the unshrouded but spurious spawn of Asmodeus, whose jackboot had been against her throat for years, who had sodomized her with scamp regard, who had employed a quack doctor to abort the twinned homunculus he had impregnated her with, who had permitted hundreds of repulsive sprites to depredate her daily. Surely, his soul was now being scorched in superlative hell-fire. They departed the ailing house on tiptoes, and in silence. They coalesced into the teeth of the abounding, autumnal night and mingled with the peregrine and the native.

* * *

Eliza barely said a word to him that evening. She communed on WhatsApp while drinking Absolute Vodka with Cranberry Juice. He tried to make conversation. Her answers were terse. The doorbell broke the ice. Terrell, sprinkled with hailstones and rainwater, goose-stepped into the lounge wearing a designer stone-colored raincoat. He froze when he saw Lollipop, jeans unzipped and smoking weed.

"Can we talk in private, Eliza?"

"Just say what you wanna say, dad—"

"But it's private—"

"So it's obviously not important?"

"Eliza please—"

"Dad, say it or shut the door behind you on your way out!"

"I… I… need somewhere to stay for a bit… I had a fight with Stella—"

"You must think I'm some sort of motel—"

"Where else can I stay?"

"Premier Inn's cheap and cheerful. Ask Lenny Henry."

"Hi," he finally said to Lollipop.

Lollipop waved without saying hello. Eliza poured herself another glass of vodka and garbled the lyrics of *Papa Was A Rolling Stone*.

"I wouldn't come here if I had some place else to go—"

"You sleep on the sofa, dad. Lollipop sleeps in my bed, and all you boys are happy!"

She had sex with Lollipop just after midnight. She amplified her mewlings and called him Daddy. After humming her way cheerfully through breakfast, she ambled off to M&S. Lollipop sat by the dining table in a state of undress, sipping Cîroc out of a coffee cup. Terrell crept into the room reluctantly, and after a while he summoned up his courage.

"Hey, young blood! You know it's disrespectful having sex with my daughter when her old man's in the next room?"

"Shouldn't you be havin dis conversation wiv Eliza?"

"Blouse beat, man! What's it with you people? Your old man was always sniffing around Tanya. I know he's been there coz she's loose. Now you wanna sniff around my baby gal. Have you lot got some fetish wiv my family?"

"Look, I don't mean no disrespect, but I ain't got nothin to say to you—"

"I beg you, bredrin. Man to man. Why are you here? You can stay at your dad's. You don't have to be here. Just do dis favor for me—"

"Dis ain't nuttin to do wiv me, fella." Lollipop rose to his feet in an abhorrent fury. "You wanna put dis on me coz you think you can... but I ain't gonna let ya... I ain't movin out. You're the last one in. You move out. I'm still gonna batter Eliza's punani when I feel like it... And if my dad was really fucking your wife, fool for you for only bitchin bout it."

Terrell had noticed that Lollipop's stern hand had lifted the vodka bottle from the breakfast table. He smirked disdainfully and retreated from the dining room. Later, Lollipop told Eliza of their encounter.

"Of course, he ain't gonna have it," she said. "You're a man. You have a penis an' you're fuckin his daughter—"

"Dis is the last thing I need."

"You should have just faded him—"

"I was ten seconds away from glassin him—"

"Don't even give him ten seconds next time."

"He reckons my dad and your mom were doin a ting—"

Eliza almost spilled her cappuccino. "That would make us brother and sister den, wouldn't it?"

They had sex again that night. They were deliberately raucous and intense, and they chortled their way through it.

"So?" Terrell said in the morning. "You wanna be a slut?"

"I've got dis fever, dad. I can't resist him—"

"He's using you to get me, Eliza—"

"No, dad. I'm using *him* to get at *you!*"

"You hurting me, Eliza... How... how can you hurt me?"

"How can I hurt you??? It's always been about you, you selfish pig. You only cared on your own terms. You fuck up my perception, my innocence an' you're the one dats hurt—"

"Blood's thicker than water, Eliza. Dat's how it supposed to run—"

"But it's never run like dat an' it ain't gonna. At your age, you're still thinkin wiv your bloody cock. If Terell Walker could get laid, then he'd definitely keep that appointment. I needed a father years

ago. I don't need one swingin by, tryin to play the wise old fool. At
the end of the day, it gets dark—"

"Look! You don't understand these thugs. When they need you,
they swallow you. And when they're done, they spit you out—"

"No, that's what I do, big man. I'm the slut. Remember?"

That evening, she consorted playfully with Lollipop in full view
of Terrell, whose grief was palpable. She sat on his loins while he
played with her hair. Their conversation was laced with innuendo,
and Lollipop flashed his Seal knife occasionally at the light. That
night, their kinetic congress resonated throughout the flat. Terell
packed his bag with egregious melancholy. He slammed the door
behind him and wandered teary-eyed into the caliginous streets.

17

THE WAGES OF SIN
IS DEATH.

B LAZE HAD AN INSATIABLE appetite for computer games. Every
night, he knelt before his TV screen like a supplicant at an
altar and played on his X-Box till his eyeballs burnt sore. Soccer
and Racing Cars games were his forte. His crude boasts upon
victory deterred further challengers, who prided their ego above
all else. Shekaidy was the latest to get a hammering: 6–0 on a Pro-
Evolution Soccer.

"Fucked you up again, didn't I?"

"You play dis game day and night—"

"Come, let me beat your arse again—"

"Naaah, I'm goin to my yard—"

"Come we go again, Shekaidy. We'll play for dough—"

"My baby mom's 'lowin me time wiv my girl tomorrow an' I
gotta be up early… I'll take your peez some other time, fam!"

After Shekaidy had left, Blaze logged online and challenged
other gamers around the globe. He defeated Zeebo from Hyderabad
in a series of nail-biting contests. Adnan from Alexandria was
annihilated easily. Seaker from Cincinnati was victorious in their
first encounter but he won the next two unconvincingly. He was
midway through their fourth game when his mobile raged.

"Blaze, it's me—"

"Who's me?"

"Your wet dream."

"Who?"

"The girl you were wanking to in an open field sometime back—"

"Waw! Sophia babes! 'Low dat... Waw! It's you... I'm surprised you're phonin me—"

"Well, I'm surprised dat your surprised."

"Dis is a set up—"

"Don't be fuckin ridiculous—"

"Who's there wiv you?"

"Nobody. What bout you?"

"I'm... I'm by myself—"

"Let me come over den—"

"Look, Mami. If you were gonna bell me, you would have done so, like yongs ago... I know Lollipop's wiv you... Put dat dickhead on tha line—"

"Lollipop and I are so over. He was fuckin some ratchet on tha side. The next time I see him, his life won't be worth livin. He fucked wiv tha wrong woman—"

"I heard about dat. But I weren't sure it's true—"

"It's true!"

"Wowzers—"

"Can I have your address please? I wanna come an' see you."

He shilly-shallied on the phone. What was *really* driving her into his arms? Revenge? He sensed her restlessness. His indecisiveness surely exhibited weakness. He reluctantly surrendered his address. He listened as she repeated it back.

"Your boy done knows my address from before. I whooped his arse nuff times on FIFA... Make sure you come alone though... Come in somethin sexy... I don't want no surprises. If you bring your boy, I got Plan B and C intact. As much as I'd like to pipe you raw, I ain't fallin for no honey trap..."

Seaker from Cincinnati had trumped him at FIFA 7-1. That barely mattered. He told Seaker that he was poised to pollinate

London's sexiest female in an hour and he'd tell him all about it this time tomorrow. He tidied his room and straightened his bed. He brushed his teeth and counted his condoms. He drenched his armpits with Lynx and his jowls with Joop. He slipped on a white Versace Polo shirt and bought a kitchen knife in with him for company. Then he hovered impatiently by the window sill. After fifteen minutes, she emerged gracefully from a black Mercedes Vito. She wore a fuchsia bodycon dress, gridded and seamless. She held a Michael Kors travel bag loose in her hand. He met her on his doormat. She kissed his cheek with her lapis lazuli lipstick.

"Wow!" said he. "You're hawwwwt, Mami!"

Her dress barely contained her bronzed orbs. She roped her thick braided extensions together while watching him with her compelling eyes. His eyes gored at her supple concave, and at her comely fundament.

"Do you live alone, Blaze?"

"Mom's gone Tunisia wiv my sisters. I would da gone but I got a business to run..."

She scanned his room and gave little indication that she was listening.

"... I only work weekends. I cut more peez in the market in dem two days than Lollipop does in a whole week... Then I'm on my X-Box, merking breh's all over the world—"

"You just do what you can wiv what you got—"

"If you want any CD or DVDs, let me know. I'm way ahead of everyone else—"

"Have you got Ruthless P's new CD?"

"Dat's my biggest cash cow right now." He planted the CD in her hands. "You can keep dat, babe. I've been breakin necks, cashin cheques... an' mixin decks wiv my Rolex—"

"No bullshit lies please, Blaze." She picked up another CD cover. "What you playin? Call of Duty: Ghosts? How ironic?"

"You're a gamer too?"

"I couldn't work a controller to save my life... But since you asked, I like a different kind of controller."

"When you said you were comin, I was thinkin, you're either not really comin or you're settin me up..."

Those compelling eyes fell upon him intently for the first time. She pretended to laugh. "You know I don't hold back, Blaze!"

"What about Lollipop?"

"I went off dat dickhead a long time ago, like the twelfth of never."

"What did you ever see in dat fucker?"

"Dat's an existential problem for us girls. We just go from one idiot to tha next."

"So you wanna get wiv me to get Lollipop back?"

"It's a superficial world, Blaze. You only want me for my looks—"

"Naaah, Mami! You're more than just the sum of your parts. I love your brain too."

"Really? You're sapio-sexual? You get a boner when I start goin on about quantum mechanics?"

She removed a bottle from her handbag.

"Vodka?" he said.

"Indeed," she said.

He wilted like warm lettuce as she reclined on his bed.

"I need some milk to go wiv these cakes, Blaze!"

She was serious. She rolled up her dress purposefully to reveal her gams. "When I look at you, I'm turned on!" he confessed.

"When I look at myself, *I'm* turned on." She crocked her finger, inviting him towards her. "Why don't you take your clothes off, hun?"

"You first?"

"I might scare you—"

"If I take my jeans off, I might scare *you*—"

"I *want* to be scared!"

They laughed. His anxiety slowly acquiesced. He removed his shirt, unbuckled his jeans.

"You're serious, aren't ya? But what bout your man? He's gonna go maaad—"

"Fuck dat," she said. "And come an' fuck dis!"

She rolled down her rhinestone G-string. He rolled his eyes with wonderment, and she rolled him onto the bed as if he were a Persian rug. He tried to grope her with his piqued paws. She thwarted him by holding down his wrists. She sat on his face and submerged his mouth into her crack, and exhorted him as to how she wanted it. She soughed as he worked her with marauding determination, delighting in the final salvo and surge of her nectar onto his palate. When she was relieved, she slipped up her rhinestone G-string. He looked discombobulated by that thrill. She looked at him with a tincture of warmth.

"You're a horny bastard, aren't you? Looks like tha cavalry came without tha trumpeteer!"

He looked at his pants and chuckled uneasily. "Gimme… like half-an-hour, an' we'll go again. Dat's tha first time dat's happened… Dat's coz you're choong—"

"You're lucky I planned to spend the night."

"Lollipop could never do tha things I can—"

"I'm gonna let you do things to me dat fuckster weren't allowed to… I bet you're thirsty, Chicken! Let me give you a splash of my drink!"

She exerted herself forward and splashed the contents of the bottle onto his face. He felt his eyesight expunging. His skin seared from his flesh. He lunged at where he thought she might be, but he crash-landed into a mountain of his CDs. He cursed her till there was no spit in his mouth. She cursed him tenfold and spat on his burning face. The room already swarmed with a legion of larrikins. They were pitiless as they watched him writhe with agony.

"This was a whole lot easier than I thought," she said.

"Ruthless P CDs should only make peez for Ruthless P," Marvin said. "Not for fat cats like you, Blaze… Tonight's your last night, fam! You better say your prayers!"

She reveled in his caterwauling, and his cruel cruciation that followed. She said she would bedight him, and she told him no lies. They gagged his mouth with twisted rope and she mocked that he was about to die. She sang a mournful dirge to the guttural cadence of his stifled wailings:

> *"Cry your every breath,*
> *Death is very scary.*
> *There is nothin left;*
> *No Eden garden prairie…"*

Bloody giblets were surgically removed from his body with a Deba bocho. She slipped a souvenir morsel into a matchbox as it dripped with congealed blood. They saturated and fed him with kerosene, and he passed out from the corporeal affliction he could no longer bear. Then she ignited him with a Swan Vesta matchstick, and then lighted a contemptuous cigarette for her rapt content. By the time she was driven away through a coverlet of several stilled streets, he was crepitating like a fagot inside an infernal house.

* * *

Lollipop was delighted that Sophia had agreed to meet him and winnow away their differences. Her tone had been conciliatory. There was none of the maelstrom bullshit he was served last time round…

The temperature was twenty-three degrees, the year's hottest day thus far. He slipped on a pair of drainpipe jeans and a D&G shirt. A Seal knife was his concealed accoutrement. Misbegotten thoughts plagued his mind as he splashed Cool Water upon his unshaven jowls. If she could genuinely forgive him, hope would not have died. They could make fetal plans for their future. They could disappear to some *Last Of The Summer Wine* territory. They could elope to an islet in the English Channel before escaping to

Rotterdam on a rented yacht and start an anonymous life on the continent. But as he stepped onto the street, he remembered his own rules on the *spontaneous grind*:

> *"Rule one, when you link someone business or pleasure, make sure you're met by a face you can vouch for. It reduces the risk of a set-up. Rule two, never agree to carry out somebody else's plan exactly. If the plan's to go north, then you say let's go north-east and don't compromise. And finally, never sleep wiv a girl who's got more problems than you!"*

He phoned Sophia again from an old telephone booth that stunk of piss. Rather than meet her outside Footlocker on Kilburn High Road as prearranged, he insisted that they meet in the McDonalds in Neasden, three miles away. She was to meet him at five as opposed to three. She was snarky. She threw specious reasons on how he'd messed up her day. If he wanted this resolved, he would not relegate her like some floozy, having already displayed his tender disregard towards her fragmentary emotions.

"Sophia! Just be there!"

She hawed some more before she said yes.

He wore a dark jacket and turned his collar Cantona-like to adumbrate his features. He arrived at the McDonald's just before 4pm and ordered a collation of goodies. He sat by the window overlooking the car park. The restaurant speakers played blue-eyed soul. People radiated their usual suppleness. Babes chewed their fries and sucked on straws. The blithe constabulary ordered Big Mac Meals. A pair of blatteroons cracked lavatorial jokes at an adjacent table. Lollipop kept watching the road.

Sophia leapt out of a black Mercedes Vito some thirty minutes later. He tried to catch the face of the man who had driven her. The shadows masked him well. His fries became unpalatable. The slow-burning nausea threatened to loosen his bowels. He rubbed his vermillion cheeks as he made for the toilet.

When he returned, Sophia was seated alone, typing into her iPhone. She wore a pair of quilted denim Balmaine jeans, and Balmaine leather boots. She rose to greet him, pecking him with her rufous lips. Her metallic eyes seemed lifeless. She was without perfume.

"Hello, Chicken!" she said.

He analyzed her from head to foot. "You're as tick as a deluxe milkshake. Maybe dat milkshake needs a straw in it—"

"I don't know why you bussin joke. I haven't forgiven you and I don't intend to unless you can persuade me to change my mind."

"Do you want me to order you some food, drink—"

"I could do wiv an LPR but McDonald's don't do those!"

"I don't know where to start—"

"Start at the ending."

"The endin?"

"Start where it *ends*. Why did you fuck dat ho which effectively *ended* our relationship. Why you moved on Twang and *ended* his life? Why did you *end* any future you might have had? Start at the *ending*."

"Don't you love me no more?"

"Sorry?"

"Don't you love me?"

"I can't give you what I ain't got—"

"Sophia, you dun know tha trouble I'm in... I just need to know whether you're wiv me or not?"

"Well, you saw to dat by messin wiv some waste bitch—"

"She ain't important. You mean everythin to me—"

"Dear me! No wonder girls get stressed in dis fucked up rigmarole—"

"You're tha only reason why I've come out my hideout—"

"Where are you livin right now?"

"Wiv some elder from back in tha day... You remember Sanjay... tha Asia bredda wiv me tha day dat I chirpsed you. Him? We're livin in a flat in Leyton—"

"Really?"

"Yeh, really—"

"Where's your line in the sand?"

"Sorry?"

"You lie every time you open your fuckin mouth—"

"I ain't fuckin lyin, Sophia…"

He placed his hand over hers but she flinched unintended. She knew she had given the game away. Not that it mattered.

"My, my! Haven't we all been naughty? You did your shit and you're lyin low. I did mine an' I'm ridin high… Dat's tha difference between you and I—"

"What did you do?"

"Well, my dear Munchkin. I went to see Blaze—"

"No, fuckin tell me you didn't!"

"Well, you wanted me to get to know your friends better—"

"So you'd screw a fugly mup?"

"No, Skank Ho Breath! You fuck skanks. I don't. He's got a face like a ballsack. My brother's pissed coz he was shottin his CD an' gettin rich. So I set him up. I let him eat my arse as a treat. Then I set the cunt on fire—"

"Naah, Sophia. You're gassin—"

"I knew you'd say dat. So I brought a souvenir."

She plucked a matchbox from her cute pink purse and handed it to him.

"Open it, Lollipop, ex-love of my life…"

He recoiled at what he found, a rotting index finger. He leapt away from her, as if she was a pariah.

"Oh! And check dis vid wiv me and your friend Gregory…" She swung her legs from under her almost child-like, as she played a short clip on her iPhone: Gregory lifeless in his coffin, and Leon fretting inaudibly, tooth grinding tooth, and from behind, she kissed the videophone screen with her tulip lipstick. "… He wanted to smile but rigor mortis had already set in—"

"You. Sick. Fuck!"

"I know. Dat's why you love me… Gregory loved his daughter.

Shame he'll never know whether she'll end up wiv a fucker like him—"

"What kind of evil fuckry are you on?"

"The worst kind, babe. Of course you helped, Trevor. You're just a glorified bullshitter. I'm smarter than you can possibly imagine. I told you dat I'm deeper than your fuckin deepest—"

"You've snaked me, yeah?"

"I'm not dat predictable—"

"I saw you come here in a van—"

"Dat's my brother, Marvin Crowe AKA Ruthless P—"

"And what does he want wiv me?"

"It's not him who wants to turn you into worm food, baby. Say hello to Gregory an' Blaze when you meet dem in say, ten minutes—"

"Sophia, go fuck yourself. Coz you're so fuckin vain, you probably do anyway!"

He walked stridently through the exit. A pair of spaniel-eyed clodhoppers were at his heels. She kept calling him *fuckster* in a mocking tone. He skedaddled along the road. A vehicle snarled in front of him. Louts sprung from every door and grabbled him towards a gaping door.

"Get him in the van," she said.

The stramash that ensued constricted his flight. The jaws of the transit van seemed poised to swallow him. He could taste the metallic rubber that resided therein. He fought back with every sinew and through every tidal swing. He wriggled adroitly from his jacket till they were left holding it. He drew his knife from an undergarment and crunched it into somebody's breast. The wounded fellow slumped to the ground, aghast at the expeditious flow of his own blood, terrified that his sentiency was being sucked from his flesh, and that there was nothing he could do. That caused a stour among his cohorts who attempted to cajole him. He could not be cajoled. From the clamorous herd, Lollipop galloped pell mell like a steed, in spite of Sophia's pterodactyl keenings.

* * *

Death, death, dearth was all around. What cove would hide him? What carapace would protect him? What comforter would hold him? How the cat calls tormented him! He sat in the hot tub and washed the grime and blood from his body. His wounds stung as he cleaned them. Newsbots on *Sky News, London Tonight* and the BBC each ran segments on the murder of Marvin Crowe, slain by suspect *Trevor King*. Trevor King was wanted over a slew of crimes. Trevor King was one of Europe's most prominent *gangstas*, and should not be challenged. A passport photo of Trevor King in better times was shown for the benefit of Londoners.

"Please, please dial 999," insisted a New Scotland Yard PR merchant.

A suspicious fire had claimed the life of Alpha Koroma. His body had been ustulated. The index finger from his left hand had been severed. They suspected a ritualistic killing. The senior investigating officer described the scene as the most horrific she'd ever seen in her twenty years of policing. Lollipop submerged his head and wept under the bath water.

London Tonight featured regional rapper Ratty. He had reached No. 1 in the Singles Chart with his creation: *Suckin Eggz* featuring Tora Bora and Robin Cruz. He sat on the couch and moved his head around like an old tortoise. The presenter was schoolmarmish. He repeated her questions to himself before answering them. Three minutes into the interview, he appeared more relaxed, and what followed was his rudimentary hype.

"Dis weren't no overnight Cinderella story... Dis was years of grindin an' hard work... I never compromised my integrity... I just gotta thank God I made it... No. 1 in the UK, No. 1 in Sweden, No. 1 in Holland, No. 1 in Germany... I just wanna dedicate my success to my mom, love ya. My manager Muna... an' to my boy Twang R.I.P... Justice for Twang. I love ya bro!"

Suckin Eggz! Befitting title, Lollipop thought.

Eliza looked as lugubrious as he when she walked into the bathroom. She wrestled her prairie skirt to her waist and urinated into the toilet bowl.

"You piss like a horse!"

She ignored him till she finished. She wiped herself clean.

"Sophia's evil," he said. "She is... so madly evil—"

"You been to see her?"

"I won't be seein her again. She's got Gregory's blood on her hands—"

"Gregory? Gregory Foster?" She whistled her amazement. "You're one helluva conspiracy theorist. Don't tell me she smoked Tupac an' Biggie as well?"

"I don't know what planet you're on, Eliza... She... Marvin... I'll be gone soon anyway. What does anythin matter?"

"Where you gonna go?"

"Everywhere I go, I always seem to take a shovel wiv me and dig myself a hole—"

"I'm pregnant, Lollipop."

He reached for a towel and climbed out of the bath. "Oh. Fuck!"

"What do you mean, oh fuck?"

"I can tell, innit... You got dat pregnant glow—"

"In case you're NOT wonderin, YOU'RE tha father... You should at least know dat... I've always wanted a baby, but you don't have to be involved... I mean, it ain't as if we've got a future... So let's just keep dis nice and simple—"

"How... how many weeks are you?"

"Eight weeks."

"It's gonna be a boy... We should call him Maxwell—"

"You're usin dat shovel again—"

"I wanna help in any way I can—"

"We're ain't ridin dirty like the good, the bad and the pregnant—"

"You know what you could do? You could snitch on me an' claim a reward. It ain't like—"

"Very dishonorable and no thank you!" she interjected.

He made a muddled exit. She bolted the door after him, removed her clothes and showered in near seething water.

* * *

The journey to Bristol Prison had been an exhaustive one. How Ashleigh rued the necessity of making it! She wondered if a Dear John letter would have sufficed Johnny Freelander. Mother, having damned him with distinct aspersions, suggested that she face down his belligerence and throw off the barnacles. The cur could do her no further harm. His impulses were ashes. They had always been. The days of geisha-like subservience were long over.

After some banter with a female screw during the customary search, she was directed to Table Nine. The chief overseer maintained a vigil over them from an oaken chair. She watched the incarcerated greet their affiliated. A paunchy lad with bearded whiskers took his bashful son to the play area. The child appeared reluctant to play with anything, in spite of his father's cool attempts.

She spied the prisoners. Woe, the fleshpots of prison. Cor, the fleshpots of prison. Many were from London's badlands. Some were of rib eye steak quality. Wanton and callow. Sinewy and untallowed. Some reeked of hircine deprivation. Some were wasted in here. One in particular looked Homeric as he sat patiently, his arms folded over his bletting bosom. He aired his groin by splaying his legs as far apart as possible. Chestnut brown, broad-nosed, strong-mouthed; caked beautifully on top with an uncluttered cornrow dome. *Peng-a-leng*. He caught her staring and winked suggestively. She settled her gaze elsewhere.

Johnny shuffled towards her in a pensive adagio, wearing an orange bib that reminded her of football sessions at school. He bore an enameled snarl.

"I thought you weren't gonna come, Ashy!"

She pecked him with a paltry kiss. "What makes you say dat?"

"You say you're gonna come but you never do..." He probed

her with an observing eye. "Your hair looks different... Yea, it suits you... You're lookin peaaak, Ashy—"

"Let's sit down Johnny, shall we?"

His chin quivered involuntarily. Hers stiffened. He had groomed a haystack of hair and a faint moustache.

"We just heard on tha radio, bout Nero Sandz—"

"What bout him?"

"He got smoked in his crib—"

"When?"

"Just heard, innit. Breaking news on TMZ... He got bodied in his shower... Three breh's emptied bare magazines into him in L.A... It's mad! Why you cryin, Ashy?"

She dampened her eyes with her sleeve. "Dat's all I hear bout. Young people dyin all tha time—"

"You danced for him sometime back—"

"I'm not here to talk about Nero Sandz—"

"Aight. Aight..." He seemed heartened by her obvious distress. He watched her fidget with her Pandora bracelet. "How is Jardel and Caydee-Lee?"

"We're good."

"Thanks for tha pictures—"

"Dat's OK—"

"When are they're gonna come up and see me?"

"Wheneva your mom brings dem up—"

"What, can't you bring dem?"

"I'd rather your mom brought dem, Johnny—"

"My mom ain't come to see me. She ain't belled me. She's more interested in her new life. Shekaidy says she's gone on some Caribbean cruise wiv her new man. She's heartless—"

"You're no different—"

"Run dat by me again Ashy, coz I ain't got a sense of humour—"

"Carry on Johnny an' I leave... an' dat won't be funny—"

He elicited a wry smile. "OK, Ashy. I understand. You want your coffee black. You got a new look and a new attitude. I get it.

I done some serious thinkin an' I know I weren't nice. I was sick in tha brain when I poured dat kettle over you—"

"Dat's the past now, Johnny. But den again, we can't exactly look to the future—"

"I have a future, Ashy... My lawyer Ben Brown's one bad bwoy brief tho. His plan's cold. He's sayin I should plead guilty an' co-operate... Lollipop's tha one they're after. Old Bill's already been in to see me bout him. They're on him hard. I jus tagged wiv Twang. It was his idea. And you know wiv Lollipop, no one can say no to him coz man are scared of him. He's on my line every day, chattin shit in my ear. Well, he can ram dat up his mother's box.... I said I'd make a full confession on Steppy... I might be out in ten, twenty years—"

"You lot can make a cat giggle—"

"You know I ain't forgiven you when you goin on all bait-like. You weren't your normal self dat day. Normally I say, Ashy, let me check your phone. And den you say, Here Johnny! Bom. Phone checked. All over. So why you sayin I ain't got no right? What's yours is mine—"

"No. What's mine is mine—"

"I was thinkin: Has my Ashy got some next breh? Dat was my first thought in the police cell. Has my Ashy, my wifey, been doin nastiness behind my back? I went mad in here, I'm tellin you... Got into fights wiv screws an' shit... But I know you... I just know you wouldn't do shit like dat... I know you..."

She wanted to tell him about Joleon, her fellow terpsichorean; how they had auditioned for the world famous Norea Agency. Caydee-Lee had asked to call him daddy, but she thought it was too soon. He had taught Jardel to ride a bike and play pool, and Lukas was already an attentive big brother. Only yesterday, Joleon surprised them to a day out at the Old Truman Brewery. They took a stroll along the South Bank with Caydee-Lee upon his shoulders. He was a useful tool when it came to home repairs, and equally adept with her concupiscent needs. His reptile tongue frequently made insatiable segways into her, stirring whirlpools and unsteering tides.

His bi-colored penis was like a rounders bat and its preponderance ensured that she slept soundly. He was impulsive and attentive. He was respectful and demonstrative. They were flying to Sharm El Sheikh next Thursday. The children had never been abroad. And, even better! She was going to propose to Joleon. She had already purchased the ring, a Solitare engagement ring. And she was going to marry him. There was little Johnny could do about these revelations, perhaps holler like a lunatic, but the prison guards would swat him like the blood-sucking mosquito that he was and his *debellatio* would be complete. These howitzers lay on the spit of her tongue. She couldn't quite dare herself. He was still yowling away…

"…Dat's tha one good thing he did. He bodied Marvin. But I gotta look after myself, still. It's business. Everyone fucks wiv Fedz if it means savin your arse… I'll get my boys to check on you, innit. In case you need anythin—"

"Why would you do dat, Johnny? I could end up fucking any one of dem, remember? I'd have Stacey any day of the week and twice on Sundays—"

"You want me to do man an injury?"

"Too wrongs don't make a right Johnny, but it makes us equal—"

"So you *did* fuck Stacey?"

"Johnny, there's three things I've known about you for a long time. First, you're practically stupid. Second, consider yourself lucky you're not lyin in a cemetery. And third… I never thought I'd be saying dis but you do have amazing karma—"

"You're doin your best to fuck wiv my head—"

"You're misleadin yourself again, Johnny—"

"How do I know you ain't set me up—"

"I set you up? You did dat all by yourself. You wouldn't see a bus comin until it was right on top of you—"

"Instead of supportin man, you wanna laugh at man coz he's down an' out—"

"I think we've reached the point where I really must say goodbye—"

He clutched her hand, beseeching her tender nature. "... All right, all right... Can't we stop arguin? Please? Dis is crazy... You're lookin for any excuse just to walk out on me... I... I need you more than ever, Ashy... My mom's turned her back on me... I ain't got no friend... My people don't visit me... I only got you... an' the kids... I know I fucked up... God, I fucked up... but don't leave, Ashy... I only got you—"

"You left us a long time ago, Johnny. You told me you'd be different coz you never had a dad. But you insisted on bein a wreckin ball. You couldn't fix up. Or man up. You never knew if you were gonna make it home to your kids or if you're spendin the night in prison. Or if you're comin home in a body bag. Dat's some outlook, even for a dumb arse..." She wiped the tears that fell without prompting. "... I'll always love you coz of our children, but you'll never ever see me again. You've been an albatross around my neck for so long, and I'm finally glad to be rid of you. I have moved on. I'm a woman an' I have needs. I can go ravin. I can do my dancin. I'll do whateva the fuck I want without askin General Zod. I really hated you at one point... Doesn't matter now... I mean, look at you in dis shit pit. There's nothin left to hate."

Johnny kept sniffing while she spoke. Sometimes he tipped his head and scratched his beard. "... Fuck off den, Ashleigh... Fuckin waste bitch! I don't bizniz no more. Bout you wanna show me fuckry. Have a good life without me den, yeah—"

"Don't you worry bout dat, you fucking Asbo. I intend to!"

She rushed from the room. Her ears echoed with his desperate plea for Ashy, his Ashy to come back. For old time's sake. She never looked back. For her sake.

18

THE GUILELESSNESS
OF GUS.

A S GUS WALKER TOOK his first free steps from the prison
gate, the sanctum of his bosom still broiled with vengeance.
His dumpy social worker stood with him among the willow trees
that looked like Weeping Angels in the penumbral twilight. The
pavement was cluttered with merry folk embracing some of the
slowpokes he had maliciously terrorized. They funked under his
icy glare in spite of being smothered by their mothers, in spite of
their uncles, fathers and brothers keeping watch. But Luke George
was not perturbed. His vinous mouth had kept him in good stead.

"So you're gonna come good for me, Luke?" Gus said.

"I'll make a few calls... I'll see what happens—"

"It's gotta happen, Luke. Lives depend on it... I got your
number, brah—"

"Bell it in an hour!"

"We can give you a lift home if you like..." said Luke's sister.
She had high eburnean cheekbones and was Olive Oyl thin.

"We're waiting for his mother—" said his social worker.

"Do you mind?" Gus said.

"Your mom said we should—"

"*I said, do you mind?* I'm talkin to my people dem and you keep
buttin in—"

"Once I handover to your mom, you can do whatever you like."

He kissed his teeth. She sought shelter under a Weeping Angel from the crafty rain that began to spray her. Even the elements mocked her.

"Much love for dat, still!" he said to Olive.

As Luke was led away by his family, Gus' thoughts turned to his own, and then to his enemies that were prevalent. He had vowed retribution on those that had appropriated him to partake in woefully conceived connivances that had reaped no reward and emboldened nobody. Like the one that had been proposed to him, that had led him into prison in the first place.

Lollipop's hortatory skills had unveiled Gus' guilelessness. He was told to be ready at three in the morning, and to wear black. He waited outside his home, pulling facial expressions that would have funked Dracula. He cupped his moist genitals and muttered bitter thoughts. At three minutes past eleven, Marius pulled up in front of him in a Toyota Yaris, pumiced and prim in powder blue Versace. Lollipop, wearing a tomato red Polo T-shirt, sat in the backseat. Gus climbed into the front passenger seat disinclined. Marius' sturdy limbs steered the Yaris away.

Gus wiped his beady orbs. The veil of sleep floated over them. He cradled his ropey gut and read scraps of text speak on his Blackberry from his mother. She wanted to know his whereabouts. He deleted her messages without replying. Having exited the A406, the roads metamorphosed from the surfeits of old shops to the clusters of new penthouses. He saw signs that said Crouch End and Finchley; then Tottenham and Walthamstow.

"I can see you, Gus, in five years," Lollipop said. "Wristwatch the size of Leeds, drivin big boy rides wiv phat wheels, peng gal givin you the suckey suckey till you skeet... I ain't talkin bout no Fool's Paradise... Dis could happen Gus, once you spark dis prick."

"Fam, I could go jail for dis—"

"Don't be stupid. You gotta do moves or get moved. How can you be on dis an' be thinkin bout jail? Dat don't make sense—"

"But *you* could do dis—"

"I could do anythin, Gus. I could remove your appendix wiv a rusty spoon."

Both Lollipop and Marius laughed loftily. The engine of the Yaris cackled in tandem.

"Gus, if you're goin jail, you may as well make it worthwhile," Marius said after a long pause.

He parked in a cul-de-sac compressed with sleeping cars and loitering cats. Lollipop made a brief phone call and mumbled some imperceptible words. Gus turned his body halfway round to watch him. After he finished his call, he leaned forward to instruct Gus.

"Dat's him…" He pointed to a spindly automaton with elfin hair unbolting a garage. "Fuckin waste him!"

Gus scampered across the road on bended knees. Spindly never saw him coming. His face was pummeled repeatedly by fist and foot. He held out a trembling hand once the assailing stopped.

"If it's money you want, just take it," he said. "But please… please don't kill me…"

Gus licked his lips with verve as he spotted to the corner of his eye, a plank of soiled wood. Spindly rose shakily to his feet but he was on the concrete again. Gus drove the weapon against him till it splintered in his hand.

He hurried back to the cul-de-sac. The Yaris had vanished. He phoned Lollipop's Pay As You Go line.

"Where are you cuz?"

"I had to move, fam… Flames—"

"Where are you?"

"Did you do it?"

"Yeh, I did it. Breh ain't movin… Where are you?"

"Greenpond Close—"

"Where's dat?"

"Walk back up the main road, turn right an' walk till you reach the lights… Turn right again an' then it's fourth… Nah, third… Nah, definitely third road on your right… You'll see a church…

Greenpond Close... We're there... Hurry up, blud."

Gus peeled onto the main road. Morning had broken. The burghers of Walthamstow were nowhere to be seen. Rain spewed frigidly from the sky. He searched wearily for the traffic lights at the right turn. Each road duplicated its counterpart. He stumbled upon undesignated lights, police lights riotously wailing, charioteering towards him. He charged for broke towards the back streets. Sweat and rainwater coalesced his brow. He hurdled across garden fences and saltated through a decrepit graveyard. He found himself closeted in another cul-de-sac, scurrying among the dustbins like a chastened rat. The police demanded his surrender. He held his hands in the air.

The police besieged him with questions. Why was he in Walthamstow during those small hours, with neither money or motor? Why assail a respected middle-aged businessman to a pulp? Why decline his wallet stuffed with credit cards and cash? Why not remove his diamond-encrusted Rolex that landed idly on the pavement? And what was his motive? He answered *no comment* to every question. They charged him with *causing GBH with intent* and remanded him into custody. He pleaded not guilty but the court found him otherwise and he was sentenced to four years in prison.

He spent much of those perfunctory days pondering the glib ideology of the mountebanks from the hood. Their duplicity gyrated a discordant rattle in his heart. How dare Lollipop and Marius, Gregory and Johnny breast-beat their zestless drollery, and goose-step around the locality like Caligulas, and get away with it? Upon sleeping, he endured the same nightmare: digging ditches with a pickaxe in a hundred degree weather with his naked body cauterized by a white sun. He'd wake up hollering, and a doctor would induce a pill to help him sleep again.

Natalie had sent missives about her brother's health but they were dismissive of her concerns. Doctors, psychiatrists and social workers tried to tinker with his untethered centring. They hoped he would integrate with kindred spirits that shared his prison, and that they could prop up the existential lows exhibited by the loss of liberty. He finally opened up to a young social worker named Elif. He told her what bugged him: Limp-dicked fools that were *gangstas*-by-proxy; Nominal *gangstas* casting aspersions upon his status in their putative pauperized mindsets. He had been hoodwinked by their fawning praise. He had wanted their respect yet they had been pernicious with him in every respect. He told Elif of their tangential nature.

"You ain't gonna know a liar till he lies to you. Breh's left me stung. I just wanted dem to show me love but they're tha biggest bitches wiv tha biggest issues. Bunnin weed, fuckin skets, kotchin, reppin their dry endz, beefin for no reason. Nobody's graftin peez no more. Those bitches owe me, and I'm collectin like a bailiff."

Then there were the visceral idiocies of his mother and sisters in their dealings with so many tardy men. How so many waste men reclined in the main armchair watching *Sky Sports*, sending him to the fridge to fetch a beer and forcing him to relinquish the remote control. Francis liked to compress his mother's tits with his beastly mitts and rub his crotch against her derriere while she cooked his favorite Shepherd's Pie. For that reason, he'd refuse to sup. Dinner was contaminated. Tony liked to invite his friends round, and they often engaged in bawdry banter at his mother's expense. Habib was impertinent and would slap him around. Gus finally snapped back on Guy Fawkes night while his family watched the fireworks somersault in the garden. He came off worse. Habib sucked the air from his gut by fisting him full square in his belly. He crawled into bed and cried the night out. Habib was soon dumped in favor of Marco who left his mother in a mound of debt after taking unsecured loans out in her name. Gregory had orgiastically fucked both his sisters and would have fucked his mother had he not walked in.

"I forgot my dinner money. I come home at lunchtime an' they're both starkus bollocus in the shower, messin bout like... like... I slam tha front door an' they're shittin demselves. Dat evening, everybody's moist. Gregory's handin out peez an' all those porno hoes are lappin it up..."

He ached for sex since he had been proactive at thirteen and he compensated by wanking religiously. Onanisms kept him sane. Joanne kept writing to him out of loneliness and he coveted her for his erogenous pleasures. Later, she complained how men used her dispassionately. The only man she loved was Lollipop, and he alone possessed her heart. This revelation bequeathed his apoplectic rage.

"Joanne's got a good heart an' a buff body but she ain't got no brain... I told her when I come out, no one's gonna lay a finger on her. Not even Lollipop. He don't care bout her skin!"

Elif was seconded elsewhere, and Gus never saw her again. Her replacement was a technocrat proclaiming the same monolithic mantras he had heard so often from jobsworths. Hence he kept his feelings to himself, but he complied with his anger management therapy and demonstrated progress. Then the letters from Joanne ceased without reason.

Stricken by her loss, he punched the wall and broke several bones in his hand. And before he closed his eyes at night, he could see Lollipop before him, lying as always. This unscrupulous pedlar of lies, this squalid distiller of truths, this prevaricating palm-nut vulture. Lying, lying, lying. Lying about his adumbral status, lying low whilst he played hi-jinks with people's lives, lying between Joanne's legs for his ephemeral pleasure... soon to be lying in his own excrement.

* * *

Tanya, of the teal eye shadow and aubergine jumpsuit, watched him weltering in the catharsis of the declining day. He was as rough-hewn and unrefined as his latent father in the dew of youth. He possessed that elegant menace she apotheosized in a jaguarondi, her favorite animal. Somewhere inside, there was a good boy fighting to get out.

"You're like a spare part just standing there," she said somberly.

Gus took an age to turn his head towards her. He made her cross the street to meet him. He was underwhelmed by the emotional tidal wave that followed. She spoke tersely with the social worker who looked inordinately pissed. She hugged him again.

"You're my little grizzly bear, you—"

"OK, mom. Dat's enough… It ain't as if we're meetin for the first time—"

"Do you want a kebab? I know you love kebabs—"

"I had a fat boy's breakfast. I eat once a day—"

"Once a day? A growing boy like you needs proper sustenance—"

"I'm drinkin bare water, boxing, weights, bare cardio exercises—"

"Elliott's been pushin weights. I don't know why coz it hasn't made a blind bit of difference. He only started because you had. Anyway, if he's not using them, I'll see to it that you do."

Gus squinted at the moondogs in the sky. He remembered hating being hemmed in a bunk-bed with his big brother and being kept awake by Tiana's bawlings. He was already missing his tranquil cell.

His social worker left in a dudgeon after Tanya took issue with her boilerplate drivel about Gus' *needs*. What did these apple-red harlequins and Third World hayseeds know of Gus' *needs*? What did the ayah know? The liberty! No wonder her boy was finicky. For a moment, she wanted to tear the paperwork the cumbersome crone had given her and stuff it down her querulous throat. Gus was only ferly because he was special. He was not fulminating like they supposed.

"Don't you like my new car?"

"Naaah!" He barely looked at it. "You're always buyin off Augustus. He's always fuckin you over wiv second-hand whips… I hope you ain't organized some stupid drink-up for me—"

"I only invited a few friends; Shekaidy, Cem, Abdul, Kayden, Moussa. Nana's there too… I've invited some pretty girlies… Roanna… Jennifer… Juliet…" She winked mischievously. "… You might wanna let ease your frustrations—"

Gus' small mouth noodle-sucked his sadist pleasure. "I already got someone lined up for dat—"

"I've got you condoms… I've got you some draw. They're in the glove compartment."

As he smoked the draw, he became less bereft. His mother was not as inquisitorial as he had anticipated, and that suited him fine. The car reeked of cannabis. She daren't wind the window down in case he complained of the cold. As the old hatchback sped down the pipe of the MI, clouds of sheep grazed the agrarian amidst the lacustrine cavities. Moribund towns vegetated along the motorway. Haulers and their cargo choked along a bisected track with their bulging headlights and virulent engines. It was close to nine o'clock when he read signs that said Luton and Watford, Wembley and Neasden. He glowered at a group of faunlets on segway boards. They were but small cogs, hag-ridden by domestic woes. He had scorned and slighted them in the playground, and they honked like wild geese at a bevy of women embellished in bandage dresses and platform heels. The propulsion to chastise them again was irresistible.

"Mom, Look at dem idiots… Dey go on like they sooo bad—"

"Yes, let them… You've got Eliza's room now. I've put in new floorboards and changed the furniture. I bought you a new double bed. And tomorrow, you and I are shopping for new clothes in Westfield's… You'll have a girlfriend in no time—"

"Why you makin plans for me?"

"I'm not making plans for you, darling?"

"Yes, you are. You're like, I'm puttin you in Eliza's room… I've arranged a drink-up… You're comin shoppin… Mom, I don't roll like dat no more. I've got plans as soon as I reach home—"

"What are your plans?"

"I ain't tellin no one my plans—"

"OK, babe. We'll go shoppin whenever you're ready—"

"I need money, mom. You got any money?"

"I've got as much as you need, darling—"

"Certain donuts are gonna get prang when they hear I'm back on road—"

"How bout if we go on holiday, spend two weeks in Cyprus—"

"I'm gonna have my day in the sun on road—"

"Your dad's coming down to see you. Maybe you can tell him your plans—"

"I don't want you lot embarrassin me, fightin again—"

"No one's gonna fight. We promised—"

"'K den. Since you lot made the effort!"

"We're makin an effort. So before you go off on one of your plans, make sure you think of us too."

"I always think of my family. No one's thinkin bout family. Don't think I don't know what's been goin on… like I know how Lil Elliott gets boyed up on road… like how Nat an' Eliza got played by Gregory—"

"I thought you liked Gregory—"

"Gregory's a fucking chief. I should go an' piss on his tombstone!"

"When Gregory died, I wanted to go to his grave and drive a stake where his chest cavity would have been. But where would that have got me? After all, he's Tiana's father. For her sake, we've gotta forgive him—"

"Dat's bullocks!"

"Ask your dad if you don't believe me—"

"You want me to ask the man you hate?"

"I don't hate your dad. We made you, didn't we? Everyone was made through an act of love—"

"Who showed me love while I'm inside? Only you, nan, Elliott and dad on a regular basis. Joanne kept writin an den stopped… Nat, wheneva she could. Eliza, never—"

"Eliza's too busy seein Lollipop. They've shacked up together. The last time I saw her was in Stonebridge Market. The bitch just walked past me—"

She noticed the ill-concealed dislike on his face and stopped.

"You say we're one happy family," he said mournfully. "But the world keeps fucking our family…"

* * *

Tiana Walker was the unlikely star of her uncle's home-coming. She sang a spellbinding confection of Ariana Grande songs. Her great-grandmother, Tanya's mother, cadaverous of face because of the ravages of cancer, had crooned to her concord. The striplings helped themselves to the rum punch and raved to Devlin and Giggs. Terrell stood in the foreground and debated *politricks* with Ladelle and Rebecca, Natalie and Eugenie. He took earnest sips of Angostura Rum from a glass.

"You're not dat deep Terrell!" Tanya said. "You know nothin bout nothin, you pretentious shit!"

"You're tryin muzzle me coz you're brain-dead—"

"You don't need to muzzle a fuckin sheep—"

"My God, you're bitter. I understand though. When I go deep, you can't comprehend. That's why you don't believe in nothin—"

"Meh—"

"Isn't dat supposed to be *Moo*?"

"Speakin of cows, how is Stella? You still yammin tha dung she feeds you on?"

"How's Augustus? He's been run out of town coz regressives like his no good son pumped bullets into his front room. He ain't comin back to sell you his jumble sale crap for a looong while—"

"He's supported this family in more ways than you can ever dream of, tosser!"

"There's nothin between your ears, except cloth—"

Gus sunk his teeth into a heavily buttered scone. Then he dropped it and watched it roll across the sisal carpet onto the parquet floor. He consumed several crisps and a few more sausage rolls. Then he slathered his chips with mayonnaise before slotting them into his mouth, moaning his pleasure as he did so.

"Mom said you weren't goin to eat cuz of your exercise regime," Natalie said.

"She believes anythin I tell her. She's been a joke of late—"

"Go easy on her—"

"Go easy on her? She lied to me. She said she ain't gonna fight dad coz of me. Lasted two seconds. So sad."

"Sad's a fuckin understatement—"

"I could save the world if I cared—"

"Whose world?"

"Mine. Yours. Everyone's—"

"You've always wanted to be a superhero. Here's your moment. I could do with bein saved."

"So you and Eugenie got married?"

"I'm so in love wiv her it's unreal—"

"Serious?"

"I know it's a cliché, but Eugenie's the best shit dats ever happened to me. I wifed her for dat reason... Who would've thought I'd end up as the pink sheep in the family?"

He had watched Eugenie in the garden earlier, by the wrought-iron table under the muse of the full moon, armed amiably with a bottle of Evil Monk and a Sovereign Blue cigarette. Her tiger print dress was toffee-wrapper tight. Her vamp-red hair swept over her foundation-caked forehead. He had watched Terrell giving her diaphaneity the cursory eye many times already. They clearly felt the same ferocity towards their recently subscribed in-law.

"She's humble and human," Gus said. "I'll keep myself out of the pen to make sure I'm there for Tiana's Confirmation."

"Just make sure you keep yourself out of the pen full stop!"

"Life better treat me good den."

"We've all gotta take a few knocks in life. Sometimes you're a hammer in life. Another time, you're a nail..." She raced past Gus, barged past a pair of dancing queens. "...MOM... MOM! WHAT DO YOU THINK YA DOIN?"

She dived on Tiana and snatched her from Tanya's bind.

"I was only givin her a sip, Nat—"

"Mom, she's only seven—"

"I remember giving you a drop at her age—"

"Yes, and look how I turned out! Don't you dare do dat again? Cheeky bitch!"

Terrell, the diabolical patriarch, drip-fed wily words into Rebecca's ear but she moved away and said nothing. He desired some static in the house.

"Don't let Tiana anywhere that woman," he said. "Otherwise she'll be an alky by the time she's twelve—"

"Oh shut up, Terrell!" Tanya said. "If you wanna give me lip, you'll be out my front door wiv my toe up your arse—"

"How can you feed alcohol to a likkle girl, teh raas? If social services were here, they'd take the girl into care—"

"Why don't you just back off and discontinue mekkin an arse out of yourself?"

"Now you're tryin to be wrong an' strong, wrong an' strong—"

"Who you think you are and who you really are ain't the same—"

"Mom, don't say another word," Natalie said. "He's just a wind-up merchant—"

"You lot haven't got a scooby doo," Terrell said. The room came to a halt as he angrily buckled his coat, chafed by the apparent disrespect. "You are a fuckin genius, Tanya. You've brainwashed all my children against me, you and dis fucking country… No hellcat's gonna put heat on me… I'm only here coz of Gus, you know. I ain't here to be disrespected like fucking Coco the Clown… And don't ever beg me to deal wiv tha next family crisis… I should have kept my mouth shut and let Tiana od'ed on the sauce!"

"Oh shut up dad!" Natalie said. "And fuck you for saying dat."

* * *

Gus had snuck out during the row. He took a circuitous route around the Nepenthe Park Estate with a cockeyed limp. He kicked bins onto the pavement and left the fetid litter in his wake. A Sedan broke suddenly as he vaulted into the road. His currish eyes leered at the driver who deemed it prudent to drive on without cussing.

He headed for The Sidings that ran adjacent to the North Circular, that overlapped the estate like a fortress, and took shelter under its red-bricked railway bridge. Spiteful rain, accompanied by spleenful gusts, sprinkled him. He rolled himself a spliff and pulled heartily from it. He blew cute small rings into the air. That strumpet Eugenie could *never* be his sister. She was a smooth talking devil, charming that half-witted mottled drove with wit, music and alcohol. "She's tha best shit dats ever happened to me," Natalie had boasted. "She'll be the making of Nat," his credulous mother had declared. Nothing had changed. No lessons learnt. They still salivated over strangers.

Eugenie had filled him with peppy passions, yet left him feeling plaintive and pathetic. He shut his eyes and imagined her Junoesque sinuosity elegantly arrayed before him; her *khamri* lips craving for him, her honeycombed face saturated with his jism. The hubris of the obscenely gorgeous was such that they could mutate from houri to whore, preserving their virtue while vitiating his vice. She called him *darling* without meaning it, or believing it, nor was she yearning for the day when he would really be her darling. He spun his spliff into a drain and traipsed towards the estate again.

As he crept onto the front porch of a partitioned house, his breath became labored. Looking through the downstairs window, he spied a figurine with a pompadour of black curly hair watching television. He tapped the window repeatedly. When Joanne unbolted the door, he squealed with rustic delight.

She took a fatigued intake of breath. "Gus!"

"Yeh, it's me… Gus Walker! Lovin you but still not lovin police… Ha ha…"

She wore an abbreviated Lady of the Lake nightgown that fell around her dumpy thighs. Her charcoaled nipples were like cylindrical bullets pressed against her gown. She folded her arms to conceal them from his eyes.

"Everyone knows you got the best head game ever!"

"Are you faded?"

"I've just come out tha slammer… You don't know dat coz you stopped writin but we'll get to dat later… It's all bout ya prettiness now, not ya pettiness! You gonna give Papi a kiss?"

She gave him a quick conciliatory one on his cheek, albeit reluctantly. He clacked his tongue mischievously.

"Aren't you pleased to see me, AKA super fly, gully, bad man, tha illest—"

"Course, babes. Shhh! My man's upstairs—"

"I'm your man, Jo—"

"Why don't you come by tomorrow? My son's upstairs—"

"Is he asleep?"

"Yes—"

"Then he won't hear a thing!"

He scented her tensile dread. He ached for her phantasmality that she hideously masked, not the cant of her deprecated religion. He tasted the argan-oiled tang on her body.

"We're gonna play a pretend game… Your name's Eugenie… an' you're my girlfriend…"

He threw her into her doorway and her feet gave way. He slammed the door behind him and divested himself from his clothes. The eerie surfeit of his strength constricted her struggle. Her gown was savagely torn.

She wept. "But Gus… You're *supposed* to be my friend…"

* * *

"Tha Baretta Cougar," Luke said as he presented to Gus the small ordnance.

Gus snorted like a vexed mustang as he explored its rigid black edifice. Accidently-on-purpose, he took aim at Luke and they laughed; Luke laughing because he felt compelled to. The wind slammed itself repeatedly against the front door.

"A Cougar, you know? Why's it called a Cougar?"

"Cougar's a breed of lion… You're thinkin… I know what you're thinkin—"

"You'd better go, Luke… You ain't been here and you ain't seen me."

Luke collected the pound notes that were scattered before him. He dropped several projectiles on the dining table without uttering a syllable and left without saying goodbye, though in his mind's eye, it most certainly was.

Gus planted the projectiles in the Cougar. He listened to the patter of feet upstairs, and to a desolate voice that cried "Mommy!" The child exhibited anxieties he recognized so well from his own reveries. He had allowed Joanne to cradle him on the condition that they both stopped sobbing.

"You're tha best mom ever," he had told her, and he smiled as the child was soothed.

There was barely any edibles in Joanne's cupboards. He hurried from the flat into the driving wind to the nearest café where he ordered a full English. After an hour, he rode a cab to Kensal Rise. Throughout the journey, he clasped the Cougar in his pocket lest it would somehow escape him. He held it tighter as he rang the doorbell of his destination. Nobody answered. So he shouted Lollipop's name at the top of his voice.

"Gus!" Lollipop exclaimed. He was topless. The blue tracksuit bottom he wore belonged to Eliza. "Why you ringin the doorbell like dat?"

"I've been ringin for like, ten minutes—"

"Manz on a phone call—"

"Manz out here shiverin in the cold!"

Lollipop took quick glances to his left and right. "Yeh, yeh... come in, Gus. Don't bait me up, cuz!"

He followed Lollipop into the flat. He was instructed to take off his shoes before entering the lounge. He refused point blank.

"Eliza's gonna be pissed if she sees you wiv your shoes on."

"Eliza's always pissed. Is she in?"

"She's got a hospital appointment... She'll be well happy to see you though—"

"Why do you say dat?"

"She's your sister—"

"She never came to see me when I was in the pen."

"Didn't she?"

"Neither did you."

Lollipop sat down and sighed heavily. "I couldn't come. I'm a wanted man... You got me at a bad time, fam. I just heard bout my bredrin, Sanjay. He's dead. They found him dead in his flat after two fuckin months—"

"Wowzers, fam!"

"When did you get out?"

"Yesterday... I got out yesterday—"

"Cool, fam. Maybe we might ave a likkle drink-up to celebrate... I'm not in tha mood tho... World's come on top!"

He poured some Cîroc into a mug for Gus, who took suspicious sips.

"So what, you're wiv Eliza now?"

"Nah, nah blud. Come on! Me wiv Eliza? Naaah! Dat's like... incest!"

"My mom reckons you're together—"

"She thinks dat coz your pops was down here for a few days sayin dat same shit. But he got tha wrong end of the stick."

"What gwan on road?"

Lollipop scrambled to the window and searched the world outside. "You haven't brought the Fedz wiv you—"

"Why would I do dat?"

"They're lookin for me hard. I thought dey might have offered you a deal—"

"I went jail for you and not said a word. Why would you—"

"Aight, Gus. Calm down..." Satisfied, he returned to his seat and drank from his chalice. "... You seen your mom?"

"My mom? Yeh, she's good."

"You seen anyone since you come out?"

"I see Joanne."

"Joanne?"

"Yep. She was tha shit back den. Apparently, you used to bone her."

"Dat Joanne… I ain't seen her for time. How is she?"

"She told me I was impure… I don't know what she meant."

Lollipop felt like he needed another drink but he was loathed to leave his seat to seek out the last Cîroc bottle upstairs. His mind had drifted from Sanjay's decomposed cadaver to Joanne's disembodied grace. She was the most humane of all the people he knew, and the most loving. She was only sixty-four inches tall, and lying down, with large fleshy hands, larger than his own. Her gelatinous lips had prized him with the supplest of kisses. Her teeming rondures were a curse, for she had been besmirched by the satyrs of the streets who treated her as a dishrag with which they wiped their dripping, dank penises. But she loved him purely and had told him so innumerably but he had refuted her love because so many had partaken of her. Converting to Christianity brought no redemption in his eyes, for she always seemed susceptible to cock. But he realized her worth now, and she was worth a thousand Elizas and ten thousand Sophias. Had circumstances been different, he would have assailed Gus. But who was he to judge on what was amoral and depraved?

"So where are all the big man?" Gus said. "I heard big man were livin in Marylebone wiv tha bright city lights—"

"The big man?"

"Yeh, Johnny… Marius… Ratty—"

"There ain't no big man in police cells. Johnny's on remand, singing like a canary."

"Was it coz you made him promises?"

"Johnny's a pussy. Pennz's too raw for dat prick. Ashleigh was gettin piped by some breh while he was rollin on road. Tha penny never dropped—"

"Boo fuckin hoo—"

"Yuh dun kno."

"After three years, man should be showin me bare love—"

"Don't worry, lil G. I'm gonna look after you—"

"So who are we fixin?"

"We're fixin no one—"

"We're gonna make waves like we use to, fam—"

"We ain't makin waves on nuttin. I shouldn't have sent you on dat mad mission, Gus. Road's bullshit… Tha way we live is bullshit, Gus—"

"You goin on religious now?"

"Religion ain't got nothing to do wiv dis. Give tha road ting a bly… Go do somethin decent. There's fuckin nothin for man on road, only madness. Goin on road shouldn't even be an option—"

"I'm the end product you worked so hard to create—"

"I'm uncreatin you now, brah. What peez I've left is yours. I'm gonna wait till your sister returns an' den I'm cabbin it to the nickin shop— "

"Too late for dat now." Gus downed his drink and smudged his mouth with his sleeve. He would not partake in this crow-eating fest. "Where's Marius?"

"Dunno. Man duss out on me when I asked him to sell my whip—"

"I need to find him—"

"Why?"

"He fucked me over. May as well make it worthwhile, he said… I'll spit my beef to his face before I fuck him up—"

"Are you seriously talkin bout my boy Marius? He's sik! Are you seriously pissed coz he sold you dat line?"

"Why? You backin him over me?"

"I ain't backin him over you—"

"You remember when we drove East? He was like the fuckin mockingbird dat won't shut up. Goin on like he's some macro big man! I heard what he said bout my mom too, dat he'd like to fuck her. Said she was a cock monkey—"

Lollipop realized that Gus was clasping onto something in his pocket. He stood up slowly. "Let's have some breakfast first, lil G; then we go find him. You hungry?"

"Nah, I ain't—"

"I got some Pepperoni Pizza in the microwave... You just warm dat up and I'll go put some clothes on upstairs.... Den we blow..."

Gus lolloped from his seat and fired apace with his gun. Lollipop hit the ground with a mighty thud. A bullet had torn through his throat. The second, third and fourth bullets punctured his breast. He took two high-pitched wheezy breaths and fell silent.

Gus washed his hands under a running tap and dried them with a clean rag. He inadvertently stepped into a lake of claret as he searched Lollipop's pockets and counted a hundred and thirty pounds. *The spontaneous grind!* As he made for the front door, Eliza had already opened it, laden with a few shopping bags. She froze at the sight of his implacable visage, sluiced with clot and tissue matter. She smelt the burning flesh, the coruscating metal. She placed a nerving hand against her womb.

"Gus, what the hell have you done?"

He strode past her in a cumbersome brood. She let him leave, fearful of what he might do if she tried to stop him. She fell upon the unconscionable in her kitchen. Sputum had fouled every visible orifice. Smoke was still rising from his bosom. His sardine eyes stared without flinching. The Cîroc bottle lay on the floor unbroken. She called his name repeatedly, but he was never going to answer. She hurried onto the street and raised the alarm but she was nobody's business. Finally, a kindly bawcock made himself available and followed her to the kitchen. He searched for signs of life but was doorstepped by death. His hands quivered as he dialed 999.

* * *

"I know that cat," said the bawcock. "He was brought into the police station the day I got arrested for re-tweeting some shit. I didn't think the next time I'd see him again he'd be dead."

Eliza looked blankly at him. The surrealistic happenstance had yielded an emotional void.

"You got any family you can call?"

"No."

"Can I get you a drink... Some tea—"

"If I drink somethin, it'll make me sick!"

He was willing to put her up in his spare room at no charge but she declined his offer, though she couldn't return home. It was cordoned off by Forensics.

"My name is Femi, by the way... Who was the guy to you?"

"He was my... man."

"I'm really, really sorry—"

"I should be used to it by now. My ex was also killed. Now this one. You don't really wanna get too close to me... I've been hexed since the day I was born."

Femi seemed lost for words. She was glad that he looked so discombobulated.

"Well, I'd better go and find my mother and tell her what my brother's just did—"

"Your brother?"

"You can't even begin to understand where someone like me comes from. I'm not your problem and I'm not a charity case, and we always go back to what we're used to!"

Her drive towards the Nepenthe Park Estate had been almost fuliginous. The sunlight seemed spellbinding. Her mouth was arid. Her palms were clammy. Small herds of curious folk were dotted in and around her old neighborhood. Laverne was speaking to Fernando and Sondra. Krista pirouetted on her toes as she drove by. Ladelle observed her with cod hatred. Police vehicles parked outside her mother's home. A policewoman tried to prevent her from entering.

"I live here," she insisted. "... And I'm pregnant!"

Lil Elliott sat alone in the lounge with a New York Bulls cap covering his face to shield his abjection. He said nothing in spite of her repeated questions. She met Tanya in the dining room. She was already moist with hysteria.

"Oh look!" she said. "It's our very own Belle Wattling!"

Eliza felt wretched as Tanya moved forward slowly.

"His body's not even cold and you're already on the prowl—"

"Is Gus here?"

"Why? Because he killed your boyfriend?"

Eliza shrugged and felt her eyes welling. "I just wanna know if he's OK—"

"You wanna know if he's OK?" Tanya removed a Nike Dual Fusion from her right foot. "You wanna know if he's OK? What did you tell him? What did you tell him dat made him shoot his brother?"

"What?"

"What did you tell Gus that made him kill his brother?"

"I ... I.... I didn't say anythin, mom. Why would I—"

"You, bastard spawn of Satan. I should have wrapped dat umbilical chord round your fucking neck on the day you were born... To think I almost died bringing you into this world... How can I ever face Augustus again? You've destroyed my family... You're the one who should be wearin a concrete overcoat... Selfish scum..."

The Nike Dial Fusion flew towards Eliza and clipped the top of her head.

"Mom... I'm pregnant... Don't..."

Hands held Tanya back before she could make segway. A policeman berated her for attacking a pregnant woman in spite of her grief. She said she didn't give a fuck. If Eliza Lorraine Walker ever set foot at 213 Nepenthe Park Road, she would be extirpated without warning. Her bullocky followed Eliza onto the streets. Her tears muddied her make-up. The maggots and misfits of the neighborhood had cued outside the Walker family's front gate.

"She said she'd be back in a Balboni," Lindsey said. "But she's come back to hell in a handcart."

"It's all gone Pete Tong for tha bitch!" Ladelle said.

Sondra pitied her despair and invited her to her home but she waved the invitation away. She stumbled sullenly on her Perspex heels in spite of a doleful voice calling after her. She walked on, mindful of the scolds whose gripes remained unwashed. As she reached her BMW , Natalie swept her into a tight entwine and Eliza sobbed into her bosomy valley.

"I'm so, so sorry, Nat—" she said.

"You silly little moo!" Natalie said.

19

BLESS THE BEASTS AND THE CHILDREN

S TACEY HAD AN EPIPHANY, though it only aided his anxiety. It came to him in that luminary hall during the fifth verse of "Abide With Me." Augustus kept glaring through him. His umber brow was furrowed. His vast eyes amplified his blighted aspect. What could placate them? They left him on occasion when he whispered into the ear of an Ursuline nun. His unconsoled daughter Kasia sat several rows behind them, garlanded in licorice black. He saw her last when he was eleven. She told him he'd changed. She hadn't changed a bit.

Lydia put his hand on his lap and blanketed it with her pair. He felt anathematized by her touch. Mark, or Abu Daoud as he was now known, was seated next to them; a *mishaba* of plastic beads was wrapped around his right wrist. He sung no hymns nor said amen to the Psalms. Dominic, the schlemiel, was dressed in a shabby safari jacket. Tafari, of the granite face and Gandalf beard, sloped forward in his seat like a decrepit falcon. Fernando, of the parched cough, covered his mouth with a handkerchief. Sean sat next to Lindsey and her jaunty iPhone. Marius thought the hymnody was bland and willed it to end. The carrot-haired vicar spoke in a reedy voice about the afterlife.

After Lollipop was put into the ground and the mourners had waddled away to their worldly repiners, Stacey asked Fernando for his car keys, and Lydia asked to accompany him. They sallied along the street in the Subaru. He ballooned his cheeks with a wistful puff.

"Dis ting's fucked up! You don't get a bly from nobody, not even from God!" he said.

"Why did Kasia come back after all this time?" she said.

"She told em she was livin the American Dream when she weren't. She divorced her hubby after a year an' her luck went south. Lost her yard, her job. She even lost her mind at one point. She was too proud to ask for help. Laverne got her cousin to track her down. She was workin at Wendy's in Queens. She got put on a plane back to Heathrow."

"America ain't better than here. I don't care what anybody says—"

"Well, here ain't exactly Shangri-La—"

"No, but it's Nepenthe Park. A lot of good people live here. You never hear their stories an' their lives but they breath hope and life."

"I can't get my head my round Blaze though. Marius said Lollipop threatened to set Blaze on fire... I know Lollz lost his head in tha end but I don't think it's something he would do—"

"You didn't think he would turn on you though, his one-time best friend. He messed up so many lives just to keep his head above water. He was never goin to get any peace in return."

"I use to think of doin a detour along dat route, jus to get a lil somethin for somethin an' duss, but everybody does dat. You can't jump off road when you feel like it—"

"I'm glad you never. You would have lost me if you had."

"Really?"

"As much as I love you Stacey, I would have let you go. I couldn't live wiv dat poison."

Her voice hinted a soupçon of sorrow. He was grateful that she came home when she did. She arrived last night from Manchester and had stayed with him the night. The tumult of his mind abated a little. Their organic cravings caused them to coalesce into an apt entwine. He drank his fill from her savory mouth. The pillow talk that followed underscored their *weltanschauung*. As she laid her head against his bosom, she asked about Ashleigh and whether she was simply his vicarious lover, since his Snow Bunting has fallen seamlessly for a Martial Eagle. He said that Ashleigh had been both gamine and graceful when they were both fifteen. Such exhibitions lured his affection. He had a thing for delicate flowers. But she was no daisy and she never considered him as anything but a potted plant that she watered on occasion. Lydia Atoussi was his love encapsulated.

He parked outside the *Salameh and Salem* store and made her wait in the Subaru. A young woman clad in *hijaab* was perched on the stool behind the cash register like some exotic bird of prey. He instantly recognized her in spite of her metamorphosis. Her lips curdled when she realized who he was. They called out to somebody from behind the curtain. Then she bent her head over a lifestyle magazine.

Mr. Salameh emerged from behind the curtain and greeted him with an affecting smile. "What can I do for you, young man? Can I tempt you with the latest iPad?"

"I don't know if you remember me... I came to your shop three years ago wiv my friend... I stole four iPods. And I'm so, very sorry... It weren't as if I needed it... We were just bored and bothered... and stupid... I've come to pay for dem an' say sorry... If you still ain't happy, I'll wait while you call the police... I'll just take any punishment dat comes—"

Mr. Salameh's face had undertaken several contortions while he listened. "Yes... Yes... How can I forget? You was the one who escaped me?"

"Yes, I was."

"And you say you are here because?"

"I... I... just wanna put things right... I want my conscience back. I don't wanna be a hypocrite dat hides well."

"A hypocrite that hides well?" The tepid indignation in his voice was palpable. "I always believed that people would rise from their graves again. But this? ... What's your name?"

"Stacey Brookes."

"Stacey Brookes. When the police arrested your friend, he wouldn't give you up—"

"My friend's dead. His funeral was today. We came here dat day and caused you trouble... I even remember disrespectin the lady behind the counter—"

"Who? Mahreen?"

"Err... Yea... We sort of like tricked her into—"

"She's my youngest son's wife!"

Stacey was beginning to think that coming back was a woeful idea. Who would seriously be interested in his bootless piety? A tuft-haired Jackboot with bloodhound cheeks sternly guarded the exit.

"I'm sorry to you, your daughter-in-law, and your employees for the trouble. Dat's why I'm back to apologize, to compensate you... I'm gonna pay cost and damage. If you're not satisfied, you call the police. I ain't runnin nowhere—"

"How did your friend die?"

"His brother killed him... but... they didn't know... they were brothers—"

Salameh scratched the cluttered hairs on his chin. He gestured for the Jackboot to return to work.

"I respect you for coming here... But I must ask: Why did you steal? Nothing worse than a common thief—"

"We were just bored and outta pocket—"

"Bored? You live in an inexhaustible world and you're bored? No, not bored. Lazy. Youth with energy but idle. And lazy. Are you still bored?"

"I'll doing a BSc degree in Architecture at UCL dis summer—"

"And what do you want to do after that?"

"I want to be an architect."

"You want to build and construct, yes?"

"I wanna do dat, and more. Dat's my focus. No slip-ups. I get a real buzz out of it."

"Do as you say, brother." Mr. Salameh put an affecting hand on Stacey's shoulder. "The lesson you learnt from here was payment enough. I see it's been paid in full."

The boreal clouds slowly churned its fodder, and by the time Stacey had left *Salameh and Salem*, Cricklewood Lane was matted with rain. He stared at that very pavestone where that deceased tempest Lollipop, and that *charmante* serpent Sophia first met, that hot sober July, and countenanced for a while the lachrymose wane of the dead, and the lifer who was as good as dead. He sniffed away the maudlin tear and inhaled the air's sapidity. The rote was patent, though the route was not.

Lydia, his appurtenant love, was now established in the driver's seat, and she hooted the horn at him.